'The spirit of a new age is beautifully captured'
Choice Magazine on *Ribbon of Moonlight*

Also by Margaret Kaine
from Hodder & Stoughton

Ring of Clay
Rosemary
A Girl Of Her Time
Friends and Families
Roses for Rebecca
Ribbon of Moonlight

About the author

Born and educated in Stoke-on-Trent, Margaret Kaine now lives in Eastbourne. Her first novel, Ring of Clay, won the 2002 Romantic Novelists' Association/Reader's Digest Of Love and Life New Writer's Award and the 2003 Society of Authors' Sagittarius Prize.

Find out more at www.margaretkaine.com.

Margaret Kaine

Roses for Rebecca

HODDER

First published in Great Britain in 2007 by Hodder & Stoughton
An Hachette UK company

This paperback edition published in 2018

1

A CIP catalogue record for this title is available from the British Library

Paperback ISBN 978 1 473 67865 1

Typeset in Plantin Light by Palimpsest Book Production Limited,
Falkirk, Stirlingshire
Printed and bound by CPI Group (UK) Ltd, Croydon CR0 4YY

Hodder & Stoughton policy is to use papers that are natural,
renewable and recyclable products and made from wood grown
in sustainable forests. The logging and manufacturing processes
are expected to conform to the environmental regulations
of the country of origin.

Hodder & Stoughton Ltd
Carmelite House
50 Victoria Embankment
London EC4Y 0DZ

www.hodder.co.uk

For my husband

ACKNOWLEDGEMENTS

I would like to express my appreciation to all
members of the writers' workshop at the
Leicester Adult Education College, with an extra
note of thanks to Biddy Nelson, who is
so generous with her time.

My gratitude to Emily Humpage for her memories
of the Marks & Spencer store in Hanley, and to
my brother, Graham Inskip, and my sister-in-law,
Philippa Kaine, for their patience in answering
my queries. To Audrey Willsher for sharing her
knowledge of London.

To Isobel Siddons, archivist at the National
Gallery, to Christine Hallett and Jane Brooks of
the University of Manchester, to Andy Edwards,
Cemetery Management, Stoke-on-Trent,
and especially to John Abberley,
Potteries journalist and broadcaster.

"Paths come into being
as we walk on them."

Franz Kafka

I

"I'm a saggar-maker's bottom knocker!"

Hearing the words, Rebecca glanced along the bar. She grinned – just as if! She wished the stranger had been her customer instead of Sal's. He sounded far more interesting than "Beery Bill", as he was known locally. The brawny docker leaned forward to tell her yet another of his tasteless jokes. "Oh, give it a rest, Bill," she said with impatience. "Two of your tales in one day are enough for anyone!"

She knew he wouldn't take offence. He was one of their regulars, as were most of the customers in the corner pub. But now, yet again, Rebecca's gaze was drawn to the other end of the bar. The dark young man was tall, well built, and definitely good-looking. Intrigued, she sidled along on the pretence of needing a couple of tonics and bent to pick them up from a low shelf.

"Oh, yeah," Sal was saying. "And what's that when it's at 'ome? I wasn't born yesterday, yer know!"

"It's a real job," he began to protest, then paused as Rebecca straightened up. "Well, if it isn't Aphrodite rising from the sea – or should I say from behind the bar!" Startled, she gazed directly into a pair of admiring grey eyes.

1

"Aw, Rebecca, you serve 'im," Sal complained, turning away. "This bloke's an absolute nutcase! He doesn't even speak the King's English!"

"Are you?" Rebecca challenged, taking his half-pint glass from him.

"Mild, please," he said, and she pulled down the decorative handle of the beer pump.

"Well," she repeated. "Are you a nutcase?"

He laughed. "No, but you can't deny it's a good chat-up line."

"What? The saggar-maker's bottom knocker, or the bit about Aphrodite?"

"The first. The second was just for you – I couldn't resist it."

"I take it Aphrodite had red hair, then?"

"It's not red!" His gaze swept over Rebecca's shoulder-length waves. "It's burnished gold, and don't you let anyone tell you different."

"My, you're a bossy type!"

"Comes of being a teacher." He smiled. "My name's Ian by the way, Ian Beresford."

Rebecca hesitated, then said, "I'm Rebecca Lawson."

"The full version! You don't answer to Becky, then?"

"No, I don't!" Her tone was sharp, final, and Ian raised his eyebrows – she had a temper to match then!

Rebecca began to move away. "Come back – please?" he said softly, then frowned as he watched a couple of men ogle the girl who seemed unsuited both to the area and to the work she was doing. And

2

she certainly didn't have the Cockney accent he was hearing all around him.

He glanced around the shabby pub, liking its old mahogany bar, the row of pewter tankards and Toby jugs above, the small intimate alcoves with their stained-glass windows. What history there was between these walls, and he wondered grimly how many men in the past had left its warmth and comfort to face the horror of fighting a war.

"Penny for 'em?" Sal had returned to use the optics.

Ian smiled. "I was just admiring your pub and your barmaid. She's not what you'd expect, is she?" he said. He grinned at her, his implication clear as his gaze swept over Sal's ample cleavage and her bottle-blonde hair.

Sal bristled. "And I am, I suppose! I don't just work here, you know! Ron Bowler – that's my husband – he's the landlord. And Rebecca, who you can't take your eyes off, is my niece. So watch your step!" She moved away, and Ian gave a grimace. He hadn't meant to offend her. He saw Rebecca glance across in his direction and smiled at her. She was an absolute stunner. He didn't think he'd ever seen such a beautiful girl. And to think he'd only come in on the off-chance of meeting Johnny Fletcher!

The pub was beginning to fill up; Saturday lunchtimes were always busy, and covertly, Rebecca watched him, noticing how he always turned to look over his shoulder when newcomers came in. A few minutes later, having served the man next to him, she said curiously, "Are you expecting someone?"

3

Ian glanced up. "Yes, I am actually," he said. "A bloke called Johnny Fletcher. He said I'd always find him in the Unicorn on Saturday lunchtimes, so I thought I'd surprise him."

"Johnny Fletcher? Oh, I know him, I've served him lots of times. He used to live a few doors away. But he's moved. It was his mum – she couldn't stand living among all the bomb damage any more. They've gone to live with her sister, I think. Sal told me she keeps a boarding house in Southend."

Ian frowned. "Damn!" he said. "I should have written first. I wanted to look him up so we could have our own VE day – we were demobbed a bit too late for the original one."

"Tough luck!" As Rebecca moved away, Ian gazed despondently into his mug of beer. Not that he'd blame anyone for wanting to get away from all the destruction. He'd known, of course, that London had suffered greatly in the war. But not even the newsreels had prepared him for the scale of devastation he'd seen in the city that morning. How anyone could remain cheerful in such surroundings was beyond him, and yet there was an air of determination everywhere. It was as though people thought that if they could survive the last six years, they could survive anything.

"Fancy him, do you?" Sal said tartly, as she waited for Rebecca to finish using the till.

"What if I do?"

Sal shrugged. "No accounting for taste!" But Sal was notorious for her sharp tongue, and Rebecca ignored her.

"He's come looking for Johnny Fletcher."

A man standing nearby, with the apt nickname of "Dewdrop", turned round. "Who did yer say was looking for 'im?"

"The bloke at the other end of the bar," Rebecca said, wishing the man would invest in a handkerchief. She watched him saunter in Ian's direction, and then began to serve a sudden rush of customers. But when a lull eventually came, Sal asked her to fetch another crate of brown ales.

"I know Ron usually does it," she said, "but . . ."

"How is he?" Rebecca jerked her head in the direction of the ceiling.

"Still coughing his guts out. But never mind – I'll sweat it out of him. Can't have him laid up for Christmas, we'd never cope!"

With reluctance, Rebecca opened the cellar door, switched on the light, and began to make her way carefully down the steep, stone steps. She hated going into the cellar, even though her uncle kept it well. Her gaze darted around fearfully. Rats were a real menace since the bombing. Hiding among the rubble, disturbed and terrified, they were finding their way into everyone's homes. She'd seen one down here once, a hideous black thing – its pink beady eyes glinting in the sudden electric light as she switched it on. She'd screamed, watching in horror as it scuttled away. The sound of the rat's scrabbling feet had haunted her for days. Mice she could just about cope with, but rats? Never!

Rebecca shuddered, picked up the heavy crate and struggled back to the welcome noise and smoky atmosphere of the bar. Her gaze went immediately to where Ian had been standing. He'd gone! Desperately, she looked among the group around the dartboard, at the table where a couple of men were playing shove-halfpenny, at the skittles corner. But there was no sign of him. She might have known, she thought dismally, that nothing exciting would happen for her. Wasn't it always the same? You're unlucky, she reminded herself. Surely life's taught you that?

Her disappointment must have shown, because Sal came along and nudged her. "Don't worry, he hasn't done a runner. He's in the Gents!"

"Oh!" Rebecca felt her cheeks redden.

"A pint of bitter, beautiful, and have one for yourself." A portly middle-aged man fished in his pocket and offered a ten-shilling note.

"That's very kind of you." The money for her free drink would go into a small pot she kept at the side of the till. In any case, she only ever had lemonade. Most women coming into the pub, unless they drank stout, preferred a short to beer. Gin and orange, or port and lemon were the most popular, but she didn't like either. On her birthday, Ron and Sal had treated her to a couple of liqueurs, but they'd only given her a headache. In any case, Rebecca had her own reasons for not wanting to acquire a taste for alcohol.

"Penny for 'em?" The customer obviously expected a chat for his money, and Rebecca made an effort to be friendly. "Are you all ready for Christmas? It should be a good one, being the first since the war ended."

He looked glum and scratched his liver-spotted bald scalp. "Can't think what to buy the wife! I know she wants a new frock, but she's used up all the clothing coupons."

Rebecca's gaze slid away as she saw Ian pass behind him. He looked over the man's head and gave what was, for Rebecca, a heart-stopping smile. When he walked slowly to the other end of the bar and glanced along at her, she said hurriedly, "Buy her something romantic, like scent."

"That wouldn't do for my Gertie," he told her. "She'd just think I'd been up ter summat."

Flashing him a sympathetic smile, Rebecca walked slowly along to where Ian was obviously waiting to talk to her. "I only missed Johnny by a couple of weeks," he said, "his next-door neighbour came over and told me."

"Same again?" Rebecca stretched her hand to take his glass. He shook his head. "Not for me. I must be off soon. I'm only down here for a couple of days."

"Rebecca!" Sal was struggling to meet the impatient demands of a group of football supporters.

"Sorry! The local team are playing at home!"

"Football!" he said with a shrug, as she began to move away. "Not for me – give me tennis any day."

Frustratingly, it was fifteen minutes before she was able to speak to him again. He was quietly smoking a cigarette, and she knew he'd been watching her. "Hello," he said.

"Hello." She suddenly felt shy – after all, he'd already told her he didn't want another drink.

"I was wondering," Ian said, his eyes holding hers, "believe it or not, this is my first time in London. You wouldn't fancy coming sightseeing with me, would you?"

Rebecca's nerve-ends tingled. She didn't need to think about it – of course she would go! But it wouldn't do to seem too eager. "Okay," she agreed after a suitable pause. "I can't get any time off today – but I could meet you tomorrow."

"Where?" Ian spoke hurriedly. The pub was beginning to fill up again, and as two men crowded behind him, he stood up and leaned across the bar. "Trafalgar Square, by the lions, ten o'clock!" she whispered. He nodded, and began to push his way out through the crowd.

Rebecca saw him wave as he left, then said to her next customer, "Your usual, Charlie?" She was flustered as she served him, her mind racing. Maybe this was her lucky day after all! What was the title of that song – "Life is just a bowl of cherries?" Not in her case it wasn't – at least not so far, and her throat tightened as the dark, haunting memories threatened to surface. But she pushed them resolutely away and forced her mind to think of the more immediate problem of what to wear. Maybe Sal would let her borrow her new hat, the one with the jaunty feather. Yes, that was it. It would go well with her warm check coat. And court shoes of course. Everyone knew that high heels flattered a girl's legs. It would be not only her first proper date; she was exhilarated at the thought of wider horizons, new experiences. She'd become almost like a hermit since her return six months ago – living and working with Ron and Sal, never straying from the East End.

Later, however, to her dismay, Sal was scornful. "You must've been born yesterday, girl, to believe anything a bloke tells you in a pub!" she said. "Meet you in Trafalgar Square? It'd be a fool's errand, you mark my words." She glanced sharply at her niece. The girl was such an innocent in some ways. Well, it wasn't surprising when you considered where she'd been living for the past few years! "If you'll take my advice you'll forget it."

2

But the following morning found Rebecca standing on the outskirts of the imposing square. Would he be there? And then suddenly she saw him. Although it was December, he wasn't wearing a hat, his only concession to the chill being a camel scarf. Ian stood tall and straight – his dark hair, free from the constraints of Brylcreem, lifting gently in the breeze.

When Ian saw her threading her way through a small cluster of sightseers, his immediate thought was – how Titian would have loved to paint her! He moved forward to meet her. "You came."

"I did." For a few seconds they stood in awkward silence.

"I thought we'd go to the National Gallery," he suggested, "seeing that it's so near."

"I've never been."

He glanced at her in surprise. "Would you like to?" When she nodded, he explained, "Art is one of the subjects I trained to teach, so while I'm down here, I want to see as many paintings as I can. And," he grinned, "I promised my dad I'd try to see the *The Fighting Temeraire*." Rebecca bit her lip. She didn't know anything about art. Nor had she ever heard of *The Fighting Temeraire*. The only painting she had heard of was the *Mona Lisa*, although in the small sitting-room behind the pub there was a gloomy-looking print called *The Stag at Bay*. She decided to remain silent, and within seconds they were climbing the steps up to the imposing building, only to be met by a notice: "*Due to extensive bomb damage, only nine of our 36 rooms are in use.*"

"The remainder of our collection is still in store," a helpful curator told them, "but we hope to have more rooms open, and a lot more paintings on display by the end of January."

Curiously, Rebecca followed Ian as he walked into a large, airy room, with framed paintings lining the walls. They both glanced up at the corrugated iron roof. "It's going to be a massive job renovating this place," Ian said grimly, "the Nazis have a hell of a lot to answer for!"

Rebecca looked around, amazed by the sheer size of some of the paintings, but her first impression was one of an almost reverent silence. There were a few other people there, but they rarely spoke, and then only in hushed voices. When Ian paused before a still life, Rebecca began to wander round, studying what she knew must be well-known works of art.

"What do you think?" Ian joined her after several minutes. She hesitated. "I know they must all be famous, but I'm not keen on some of them – that one over there for instance."

Ian smiled down at her. "Of course you're not. Art is all a matter of individual taste."

"But this one," she said, "I think this is absolutely wonderful. The scene is so peaceful, you almost feel you're there."

"You obviously like landscapes. Now I'm more of a portrait man, myself." As they walked slowly through the nine rooms, Rebecca became more and more absorbed. All this, only a few miles away, and yet she'd never been, not even before the war. Briefly, she wondered how many people lived all their lives in the capital without ever visiting one of the famous art galleries.

"Right," Ian said later, "now for Buckingham Palace." He took a map out of his pocket and concentrated. "Perfect! We can go down the Mall to Admiralty Arch, and then stroll through St James's Park."

"You sound like a guide book," Rebecca laughed.

"Sorry! Is that okay with you?" He looked doubtfully at her high-heeled shoes. "You did quite a bit of walking and standing in the gallery."

"I'm fine," she said, hoping that the pinching around her toes wouldn't get any worse.

"I suppose you've seen the Palace before," he said, as they made their way along the wide road.

She nodded. "I came as a child."

He glanced at her, but Rebecca didn't elaborate. St James's Park was a peaceful oasis after the busy London thoroughfare, and at first they walked beside the water in companionable silence. Then Ian took out his cigarette case, opened it and offered it to her, but she shook her head.

"I was just thinking," he said, "that Charles I

walked through here on his way to be beheaded in Whitehall in 1649."

"You know, you're a mine of information!"

Ian affected an American accent. "Stick with me, kid, and you'll go places!"

She laughed. "Yes, I know – to Buckingham Palace!"

They stood outside the gates, and Rebecca smiled at one of the impassive guards in his smart red uniform and bearskin. Expressionless, he stared ahead. "Do you think the King and Queen are in there?" Rebecca peered up at the blank windows of the Palace, hoping for a glimpse of the two princesses.

Ian glanced up at the masthead. "No, the flag isn't flying. I expect they've gone to Sandringham or Balmoral." Seeing her disappointment, he teased, "Never mind, you've still got me."

She smiled up at him, liking the warmth in his eyes. "Where next?"

"I thought we'd get some lunch. I don't know about you, but I'm famished."

"Me too." Rebecca hesitated. The best place would be a Lyons Corner House, and the nearest was at Charing Cross – the one she'd been taken to on her eleventh birthday. She brushed aside the memory, trying desperately to block it out. "Good idea," she said. "I know just where to go."

He held out the crook of his arm, and she tucked her gloved hand in to link him. It was chilly and their pace was brisk, but despite that, Ian was anxious to learn more about the girl at his side. "What do you like to do, Rebecca? When you're not working, I mean."

"I don't get much time for hobbies," she told him. "Running a pub's a seven-day-a-week job, so as I live there, I try and help Sal as much as I can. I do get days off, of course, but I have to catch up on things then." Seeing his enquiring look, she laughed, "You know, washing my hair, laundering and mending. All the things women have to do and men don't."

"I have to wash my hair, as well, you know!"

"Oh yes?" She glanced at his "short back and sides" haircut, and then lifted a tress of her own hair. "No comparison!"

He laughed. "Accepted." But Ian felt curious. Rebecca didn't talk like a Londoner. There was the hint of a lilt there. "Have you always lived in London?"

She shook her head. "No. I was evacuated to Wales when the war broke out."

"Ah, that explains it. The way you talk, I mean."

"What's wrong with the way I talk?" Rebecca's voice was sharp, indignant, and Ian hurriedly said, "Nothing at all. It's lovely. Different, that's all."

"Different from what?"

Gosh, she's spiky, he thought. "How everyone else down here talks, that's all." He glanced at her, as they went into the café. "Hey, I'm not criticising, I was actually paying you a compliment."

Rebecca reddened. There she went again! Her temper rose far too quickly. But she hated people commenting on the way she spoke. She got it all the time in the pub. "Sorry," she said briefly.

14

Ian asked for a table for two, and to her delight they were shown to one by the window. Rebecca, studying the menu, was savouring the moment. To be sitting here, opposite an attractive young man, was certainly an improvement on how she normally spent her Sundays!

"Let's have the full three courses," Ian suggested. "I certainly won't get much at the place I'm staying at! At least it'll be 'off ration', here."

Rebecca pulled a face. "I know food is restricted, even in the big hotels, but don't tell me that people who can afford to eat out don't do better than the rest of us, even if the restaurants can't charge more than five shillings. After all, they can save their coupons and then use them at home!"

He laughed. "I can see you're a bit of a rebel!"

"Of course I am! I warn you, people with hair my colour can't be passive about things!"

"I'd better watch my step." But his eyes were smiling at her, and it was with reluctance that she looked down again at the menu.

"I'm going for the oxtail soup," she declared. "Followed by roast lamb."

"Snap!" Ian said promptly. "How about pudding?"

"Definitely treacle sponge."

"I'll join you. But I bet it'll be light on the treacle and only a spoonful of custard."

"What a feast!" She laughed, and Ian studied her face, liking her wide smile. He hadn't been able to get her out of his mind the previous night, had counted the hours until he saw her again. Watch it, my lad, he thought – you're in danger of getting in deep with this one. But as he watched Rebecca's shining eyes gazing around the room, he could only think that he didn't care. With that rich hair and pale, almost translucent, skin, she was absolutely gorgeous.

Eventually, a waitress in a white cap and frilly apron came to take their order, and afterwards Rebecca told Ian that they were called "Nippies".

"I can see why," he grinned. "They certainly seem to be quick on their feet!" He relaxed back in his chair then, as he gazed at the girl sitting opposite he suddenly realised that he knew hardly anything about her. "Tell me about yourself," he said impulsively.

She looked at him, and he saw a shadow pass over her face, and when she smiled, it was forced. "Age before beauty! You go first."

"Well," he paused, "I live in Stoke-on-Trent. And you already know I'm a teacher. At least I would have been if Hitler hadn't got in the way. Would you believe that war broke out just as I was about to start my first job? Luckily the same school took me on when I got back. As you know, there's a huge shortage of us at the moment." He paused as the waitress brought their soup and rolls, then added, "I've been really lucky. I was in at the beginning, and came right through without a scratch."

"Where were you?" Seeing his eyes cloud, Rebecca half wished she hadn't asked the question. Everyone knew that servicemen didn't like to talk about "their war". As one weary soldier had told her

16

when, hot and dishevelled in his uniform, he'd called in the pub on his way home, "We just want to put it behind us and get on with ordinary life. I've dreamed of this pint for months, girl. Don't spoil it!"

So now, when Ian said tersely, "I was in a prisoner-of-war camp for a couple of years," Rebecca didn't pursue the subject.

"I wonder how long it will be before rationing finishes," Ian mused. "I bet it will be longer than people think."

"I can hardly remember life without it."

"No, you'd have been – how old? When war broke out, I mean?"

"You're fishing?" she grinned. "I'm eighteen, if that's what you're trying to find out."

He smiled, took a bite of his roll, and after a few seconds, said, "I'm quite a bit older than you, then."

"What? Fifty?" she teased.

He laughed. "Twenty-seven."

She looked at him, liking what she saw. Ian's brow was broad, his dark eyebrows expressive, and then there were those unusual grey eyes. Definitely handsome, she decided, and said, "Twenty-seven's not old. Anyway, you look younger."

And you, Ian thought, look older than eighteen, but he managed not to say so. Maybe, at last, he was learning to be more tactful! He studied Rebecca's face, trying to assess what made her seem older than her years. It was something in her eyes, he decided, and wondered just what she'd experienced during the past few years. These days one never knew.

17

The waitress came to remove their plates. "All right, ducks?"

"Very nice," they both said in unison, and laughed.

"And how do you like being a barmaid?" It was obvious that Rebecca was reluctant to talk about the past, so Ian decided to keep the conversation light.

She smiled. "It's okay. You meet some real characters, I can tell you. But they all treat me with respect. Ron would soon sort them out otherwise."

Ian frowned. "That's your uncle, isn't it? I didn't see him."

"No, he's got the flu." She laughed. "You couldn't miss him! He used to be a heavyweight boxer – he's even got the cauliflower ear to show for it."

"Sounds scary!"

"Oh, he can be tough all right. But he's been good to me."

They both looked up expectantly as the roast lamb arrived, and almost with reverence, Rebecca began to eat. Surreptitiously, Ian watched her, noticing how carefully she cut the small slice of meat. Then, hungry, he ate too, and for a few moments there was silence between them. The rest of the meal passed in a similar manner; light conversation, enjoyment of their pudding, and yet, when their eyes met, the magnetism between them brought colour to Rebecca's cheeks. She gazed at his hands as they lay on the table. Most of the men she knew had rough calloused hands. Ian, with his well-cared-for nails, seemed to belong to a different world.

"You're so lovely, Rebecca," Ian said quietly, and as she looked up at him, he caught his breath at the shy, soft look in her eyes. Suddenly, he felt a desperate urge to leave. He wanted to be away from other people, to have her to himself.

"Come on," he said, fishing in his pocket for money to pay the bill. "Let's get out of here. I thought we'd go and see the Houses of Parliament. What do you think?"

"Could we catch a bus? To be honest, my feet are killing me."

He grinned. "I'm not surprised in those shoes." He noticed her wince as they stood up. "Change of plan. How do you fancy the pictures, instead? Although we won't have time to see the full programme." Ian laughed at the relief on her face, and Rebecca couldn't believe it when the thriller they saw, starring Googie Withers in *Pink String and Sealing Wax*, portrayed the murdering wife of a pub landlord.

"I'd better warn Ron to be on his guard," she joked as they came out into the early evening.

Ian glanced at his watch. "Time's getting on, sweetheart. I'll have to think about collecting my things from the YMCA, and catching my train."

Although Rebecca felt a glow of pleasure at the endearment, the thought of his leaving London deflated her. Ian hadn't said anything about seeing her again! And suddenly she knew that she couldn't bear the thought of this being just a single date!

Ian, meeting her gaze, could hardly drag his own away, but time was running out. After studying his map again, and one of the Underground, he said quickly, "We could walk down one of those streets

19

to the Victoria Embankment, and then later take the Tube. What do you think?" Then he grinned. "Hang on, just listen to me, telling you about your own city!"

She smiled. "It's not, really. I wasn't quite twelve when I was evacuated. And I've only been back about six months."

Then, minutes later, they were strolling hand-in-hand to look at the ships on the Thames, but in reality both immersed in their own thoughts and emotions. Rebecca, acutely aware of the magnetism between them, and of how attractive she found him; Ian, relieved that as he had hoped, here in the dusk, there was a chance of some privacy. Gently, he led her into one of the gardens, and at last was able to draw her into his arms. For a moment he just held her close, and then looking down into her vivid green eyes, lowered his lips to her willing ones. Their first kiss was gentle, questioning, but when their lips met a second time, it was with swift and unexpected passion. Shaken, Rebecca leaned her head on his shoulder for a few moments and when they eventually drew apart, Ian gazed down at her, his face taut, his eyes searching her own. "Rebecca, you do know what's happened, don't you?" She shook her head.

"I think I've fallen in love with you!" He touched her hair in bewilderment. "I just can't believe it's happened so quickly!"

He kissed her again, then said with desperation, "I've got to go!" They turned to retrace their steps and glancing across the river, Ian warned, "Look at the mist coming over, you're in for some fog."

20

"Yes, we get real pea-soupers down here," Rebecca said, but she wasn't worried about the fog, she was still reeling from the storm of emotions that Ian's kiss had aroused.

They made their way to Charing Cross Underground Station so that Ian could take the Northern Line to Euston, and Rebecca the District Line to Stepney. When eventually they faced each other among the milling crowds, Ian said quickly, "I'll write, I promise!"

He kissed her again, a brief farewell kiss, and Rebecca stood watching until his tall figure disappeared from sight. When she turned away, she fervently hoped he had meant what he said. That he would write – after all, she realised with panic, how else could she get in touch with him?

"Well, what do you expect when he never gave you his address!" Sal's tone was almost complacent. "And you know what I think about that!"

"I've told you – he said he'd write, and what's more I believe him," Rebecca snapped, her shoulders rigid with resentment. Furiously, she scoured the frying pan, rinsed it and put it to drain.

Sal picked up a tea towel. "Your cousin Bert said he was going out for a bottle of milk, and that was ten years ago!"

"Give it a rest, Sal," Ron complained, still feeling weak after his dose of flu. "Haven't I got enough to do, without you rabbiting on!"

"It's only Friday," Rebecca pointed out, although she was sick with disappointment. It had been foolish to expect that Ian would write the minute he got back. And Sal's "I told you so" glances, once the postman had left, were beginning to get on her nerves.

Gloria, too, was scathing. When Rebecca came to live at the pub, Gloria, a discontented brunette, lived two doors away, and was the only girl nearby of a similar age. The two of them had drifted into an uneasy friendship.

"You know I come round on a Sunday," she complained, lighting a cigarette.

"That doesn't stop me from going on a date!" Rebecca wafted away the smoke that Gloria was blowing in her direction.

"Well, you never considered me! Mind you, I couldn't do that meself. Let some stranger pick me up like that!" Gloria's small brown eyes flickered disdainfully over the other girl.

"He didn't 'pick me up', as you call it. You make me sound like a streetwalker! Sal met him, didn't you?"

But Sal refused to be drawn. "I served him a drink, that's all."

Gloria raised her finely plucked eyebrows and Rebecca snapped, "I'll prove you both wrong, you'll see!"

The waiting was agonising. Twice during the week Rebecca heard the song "Give Me a Kiss to Build a Dream On" played on the wireless, making her think wistfully of those romantic moments on the Embankment. And then on Saturday morning, an unfamiliar envelope plopped on to the mat at last. And the postmark was Stoke-on-Trent! Seizing it eagerly, Rebecca ran quickly upstairs to the privacy of her bedroom, sat on the bed, and tore it open.

My darling Rebecca,

I've had several goes at writing this letter. None expressed what I really want to say. Meeting you has been the most wonderful experience of my life, and our day together on Sunday will be one that

23

*I'll always remember. I meant every word I said.
I've fallen in love with you, and can hardly believe
that you feel the same about me.*

*I'll try and come down again before Christmas
and will write and let you know when, as soon as
I can. Until then sweetheart, please take care of
yourself, and think of me sometimes,*

> *With all my love,*
> *Ian*

Rebecca read the letter again, and again, lingering over the magical words, *I've fallen in love with you.*

She almost danced down the stairs, and waved the envelope in front of Sal. "There you are, you doubting Thomas! *And* his address is on the top! That proves he's not married!"

Sal, who'd been convinced her suspicions were right, softened slightly as she saw Rebecca's shining expression, but then she shrugged. "Can we expect a decent day's work out of you now?"

But nothing could dampen Rebecca's mood, and she hummed softly as she helped to prepare for opening time. Down again before Christmas, he'd said!

And Ian was true to his word. This time he was travelling down on Saturday morning, staying just the one night – again at the YMCA near Euston. Rebecca pleaded to have the night off. Ron and Sal, after a few grumbles, gave in. But there was a condition.

"I want a shuftie at him," Ron told her. "You know what time we eat – in the afternoon after the pub closes. Bring him tomorrow!" And when Ron spoke in that tone, even the toughest of their customers obeyed.

"She's a funny one, that," Ron said, after Rebecca had gone upstairs. "I suppose she still hasn't said anything, you know – about . . ."

Sal shook her head. "Not a dickie-bird. Like I told you – when she first arrived and I took her along, she just stood there like a frozen statue. I sometimes wonder if I should've let her settle in first!"

"Nah," Ron said. "It was best to get it over with."

"I wish she would, though. Talk about things, I mean. But if I try and draw her out, she just clams up!"

He shrugged. "You'll just have ter be patient and give 'er time."

Ian had suggested they meet in Oxford Street. *"I won't get there until lunchtime,"* he wrote, *"so we can get something to eat, and then maybe you could help me with a bit of Christmas shopping."*

This time, Rebecca chose her shoes more carefully. A lower heel was a must, if she didn't want to hobble again, but she still wanted a pair that showed off her trim ankles. She decided to ignore convention and not wear a hat. It would only hide her hair, and it was that which had first attracted him to her. She'd hated it when at school they called her "carrot head". But the colour had deepened as she got older, and although she tried not to be vain, she couldn't help being proud of it, allowing the russet waves to cascade to her shoulders. She'd had enough of concealing it in a hairnet or headscarf during the war!

Fortunately, the weather was dry, and Rebecca waited in Marks & Spencer's doorway. As she anxiously scanned the crowds, she began to worry if it would have been better to meet him at Euston, then at least she would have known whether his train was on time.

But suddenly he was there, hovering behind a large woman holding the hands of two squabbling children. They were blocking the pavement, and above the family, Ian's eyes met hers and he gave a helpless shrug. Then seconds later, she was in his arms, and he was hugging her as if it had been months instead of weeks since they'd last met.

He held her away from him, his gaze searching her eyes, her face, her hair, and then, despite people passing, bent and kissed her. "You're even more beautiful than I remember." She blushed, and he laughed. "Come on, let's go and get a cup of tea or something."

Once inside a small café, Rebecca slipped off her winter coat, revealing a green spotted frock with a crossover bodice that clung to the soft swell of her breasts. Ian felt that he could just sit and gaze at her for hours, but soon they were pondering what to order, and eventually decided on Spam, chips and peas.

"Do you think anyone would stare if I made a chip butty?" he grinned, when the food arrived.

"A what?"

"You Londoners know nothing," he said. "Watch." Ian took a piece of bread and butter, placed five succulent chips doused in salt and vinegar on top, doubled it over and bit into it.

Rebecca copied him. "Mmn," she murmured with her mouth half full. "Is this what they eat in Stoke-on-Trent, then?"

"Stoke," he told her. "No one at home uses the full name. Yes, they sure do. But our speciality is oatcakes. Just wait until you've had a couple of those with your bacon and egg!"

Rebecca felt a warm glow. Surely that meant he intended to take her home to meet his parents? One in the eye for Sal, she thought with satisfaction.

Ian wanted to go to Liberty's, so later they walked to Regent Street and went into the distinctive black-and-white store, where he bought his mother some lace-edged handkerchiefs. "She'll keep them just for best," he grinned, "you know what mothers are like."

Rebecca didn't answer, and Ian was thoughtful as they browsed around the ground floor of the shop. He still didn't know anything about Rebecca's personal history. Sometimes, in an unguarded moment, he could see sadness in her eyes, but he prided himself that he had enough sensitivity not to probe. She was obviously enjoying the unique atmosphere, and he smiled as he saw her pick up merchandise, look at the price-tickets and, with a horrified expression, quickly replace them.

"Not quite in our income bracket," he whispered. "Still, I got what I came for. Shall we go back to Oxford Street?"

She nodded, and within the next hour, Ian bought a warm paisley scarf for his father, and a pair of lined gloves for his mother.

Rebecca glanced at him. "You're very close to your parents, aren't you?"

"Yes, I am. They made a lot of sacrifices for me. I'm not only the first one in our street to go to university – I'm the only one!"

"What does your father do?"

"The same as most people in the Potteries. He works on a potbank." At Rebecca's enquiring look, he explained, "That's the local name for a pottery factory."

Ian suddenly stood aside to let a woman pass. She was pushing a wheelchair, seated in which was the huddled figure of a young man. "Poor devil," Ian murmured afterwards. "Did you see the burns on his face?"

Rebecca, who had tried not to stare, nodded. "Ex-RAF, probably."

"God, I was lucky," he said grimly. "Sometimes, you know, it makes you feel guilty."

"That won't help anyone," she told him.

But Ian didn't reply, and seeing the closed expression on his face, Rebecca wondered if she had said the wrong thing. They walked along in silence, then he said suddenly, "Look, I don't know about you, but I've had enough of shops."

"How about Hyde Park?" Rebecca pointed at a passing bus, and they sprinted to catch it, clambering up on to the high platform. Breathless, Rebecca led the way to a seat near the front.

"Going in for the Olympics, are we?" bantered the conductor, as coming along, he gave them a ticket from his rack. With an admiring glance at Rebecca, he winked at Ian, and then turned to an old lady. "Hello, darlin'. Off to meet your boyfriend, then?"

"Cheeky devil!" But she was smiling.

"They raise everyone's spirits, don't they?" Rebecca whispered.

"Who?"

"Cheerful conductors."

"Yes, it all helps." But Ian was looking out of the window, still appalled at the sheer extent of the bomb damage. Wars? They were so blasted futile! What did they ever achieve except misery and grief? Yet the whole of England had known that this time there was no alternative. And it was only now that the truth about the horror that had been taking place in German concentration camps was becoming widely known. Ian remembered his mother weeping when she'd first seen the Pathé News. The scenes showing the emaciated figures of survivors had upset her so much that they'd left the cinema without seeing the next film.

Rebecca glanced at him with unease, realising he was lost in his thoughts. Somehow, their encounter with the man in the wheelchair had changed the easy camaraderie between them. But a few minutes later walking beside the Serpentine, Ian's mood lifted, and seeing him smile down at her, Rebecca said, "You were going to tell me what your father did."

"I was indeed. He's a thrower, which means he

29

shapes pottery on a potter's wheel – a very skilled job. When I was a kid though, he used to tease me that he was a saggar-maker's bottom knocker, and the name always made me laugh. There is such a thing, but it's not common. It's what they call someone – usually a young lad – who beats out a wad of grogged fireclay to form a bottom for a saggar."

"What's a saggar?"

"A clay box in which ceramics are fired."

"As I've said before," she grinned, "you're a mine of information."

"And as I've said . . ."

"I know," she laughed. "Stick with you, and I'll go places!"

Ian grinned when Rebecca told him of Ron's ultimatum. "He wants to give me the once-over, is that it?"

"Something like that! You don't mind, do you?"

"Of course not."

Rebecca smiled up at him, and he thought with a pang of her youth. She seemed so innocent, so unspoilt, so trusting. He stopped and suddenly took her into his arms, wanting to hold her, and, both relieved the weather was mild for the time of year, this was how they spent the rest of the afternoon. Strolling, pausing, cuddling and kissing. Rebecca only knew she had never been so happy.

But once evening approached, the weather began to turn colder. Ian looked down at her. "Are you getting chilled?"

She nodded. "A bit."

"Hungry too, I'll bet," he said, then added, "Look – isn't that Speaker's Corner?" He pointed to where a thin middle-aged man, with a trailing striped scarf, stood on a soapbox, haranguing the small cluster of people around him.

"What's he on about?" As they grew nearer, Rebecca strained to listen to the rasping voice.

Ian grinned. "The evils of drink! Being a barmaid, I don't think you'd better listen."

"He's right though," she said later, as hand-in-hand they left the park, "alcohol does have a lot to answer for."

There was something in her tone that made Ian glance sharply at her, but Rebecca was busy watching the traffic as they waited on the kerb to cross the road. They walked until they found a Lyons Corner House, and both settled for a pot of tea and toasted teacakes.

"That's better," Rebecca said, putting down her cup.

"Now what shall we do?" Ian asked.

"Could we go and see *I Know Where I'm Going*?"

"Who's in it?"

"Wendy Hiller and Roger Livesey. Sal says it's set in the Isle of Mull and the scenery's lovely."

"We could certainly do with a change from all this," he said grimly as, after they'd left the café to find a cinema, they passed a gaping hole where a building had once stood. "Don't you find it depressing, living amongst all this destruction?"

"You could say that," she said quietly. Ian looked down at the slim girl by his side. She had still never

31

mentioned her parents; and, not for the first time, he wondered whether they'd been killed in the Blitz. But if that was the case, he couldn't understand why she hadn't told him. I may have fallen heavily for her, he thought, but she's still a mystery to me in some ways.

The film was romantic and uplifting, and yes, the scenery was beautiful. But this time, an empty double seat on the back row proved irresistible, and at last in the semi-privacy of the dark cinema, Ian was able to kiss Rebecca as he'd longed to. Deeply, and passionately, and when she removed her coat, and he felt her soft body pressing against his, he kissed the soft hollow of her throat. "I love you," he whispered, and they sat entwined, lost in each other as the story unfolded on the screen.

"It was good, wasn't it?" Rebecca said later, as they came out before the second showing. She glanced up at him impishly, "What I saw of it, that is!"

He grinned, and squeezed her hand. "We did see bits! Did you notice who was in it? Valentine Dyall – you know," he deepened his voice, "'The Man in Black.'"

"Oh, on the wireless! I thought I recognised that voice. He used to scare me stiff."

Ian laughed. "I always used to listen to him when I came home on leave – still do." He glanced at his watch. "Come on, it's time you were getting home – I'll see you to the Tube."

But later, before Rebecca went to bed, Sal once again tried to "talk some sense" into her niece. "It

32

won't last," she warned. "No," she held up a hand, "you don't need to tell me – one look at yer face is enough. You've gone and fallen for him, haven't you?" Her face, creased and tired, after a busy evening, suddenly sagged. "Don't you think you've had enough heartache in your life, without going looking for it?"

"How do you mean?" Rebecca, angry at having her happy mood spoilt, glared at her aunt.

"Well, stands to reason, don't it? He won't be able to keep it up, yer know – all this coming and going! Train fares cost money, my girl, and so does staying in London – even if it is at the YMCA."

"He could stay here! There's the box-room, and we could easily borrow a camp-bed," Rebecca said defiantly.

Sal stared at her. "You're not slow in coming forward, are you? Well, that'd be up to your Uncle Ron. *And* it'll depend on whether he takes to him. There's something else," she called with a worried expression, as Rebecca went up to bed. "Don't forget – he's twenty-seven, and you're only eighteen!"

And a young eighteen at that, Sal thought grimly, switching off the lights.

4

O ver six feet tall, bullet-headed and heavy-jowled, Rebecca's uncle was the most menacing-looking man Ian had ever seen. With a mottled misshapen nose and a thick neck bulging out of his collarless shirt, he got up from his chair to shake Ian's hand, revealing a thick leather belt which supported not only his trousers, but also a gigantic "beer belly".

"Pleased to meet you, Ron," Ian managed to say.

"Likewise!"

Sal bustled forward, hot and perspiring from the kitchen. She was feeling flustered. Although she'd tried to take extra care with the dinner, it was always pot luck, with having to be in and out of the bar all the time.

Ian held out his hand, and she wiped her own on her apron before taking it. "Dinner's ready so you can sit yourself down next to Ron. The joint's a bit small, but it should stretch to four. Now would you like a beer?"

"I would, thank you."

"Get him one, will you, Rebecca."

Obediently, Ian took his place at the table, and glanced around. The room was crammed with furniture, with the square table taking up most of the floor space. There was a heavy ornate sideboard displaying china dogs and ornaments on lace doilies, and against the back wall stood a moquette three-piece suite in a faded shade of green. Above it was an old print of *The Stag at Bay*, while on the wall opposite, a bevelled circular mirror hung on a chrome chain.

"So, you're a teacher, then?" Ron said, settling back in his chair at the head of the table, and hooking his thumbs in his belt. He surveyed the young man before him with suspicion. Ron didn't hold with what he called namby-pamby men who never got their hands dirty. But maybe teaching wasn't such a bad job. After all, someone had to educate the little blighters!

"Yes, that's right," Ian said, trying to think of what to say to a man he knew instinctively he would have nothing in common with.

"Hated it meself – school, I mean. Mind you, I played truant most of the time!"

"Yer always were a tearaway," Sal said, as she put a steaming plate before him. "Get stuck into that, there'll be plenty of time for rabbiting later!"

Rebecca brought in a half a pint of mild, and sat opposite Ian. He looked down at his plate. Whatever her other qualities, cooking was obviously not one of Sal's strong points. Not only did the thin slices of beef look dry and the mashed potatoes lumpy, the pale, watery liquid over the carrots and cabbage was an insult to the word "gravy". Ian thought wistfully of the crisp roast potatoes and fluffy Yorkshire pudding his mother usually served, and manfully began to eat.

After a meal eaten in total silence, Ron replaced his knife and fork. "Lovely grub, Sal! I see you've polished yours off, Ian."

Ian nodded, still chewing on his last piece of beef, and said, "Yes, thank you, Sal. I was hungry."

She began to collect up the dirty dishes. "I'm not surprised. I bet our Rebecca's been trailing you round all over the place!"

Rebecca just smiled, and got up to help. Like everyone else, she hadn't spoken once during the meal. Was it considered bad manners here, Ian wondered, to talk while you were eating? But then common sense told him it was more likely that after a busy few hours in the bar, Ron and Sal would have had enough of chat. Food would be their priority. And to his relief, pudding was much better – a traditional rice pudding, nice and creamy with a good brown nutmeg skin on top.

"I can just leave this on the bottom of the oven to take care of itself," Sal told him. "Do you like skin?"

"Yes, please."

"Cat got your tongue, Rebecca?" Ron said suddenly, and Rebecca reddened. Ever since they'd got here, she'd felt awkward. Ian looked so out of place in that familiar shabby little room. She also felt embarrassed. Whereas Ian looked smart in a white shirt and tie, with a Fair Isle pullover, Ron sat at the table in his braces. Why he needed both a belt *and* braces was a mystery to her. The room was unbearably hot. There was a good coal fire in the grate, as they never had any difficulty with their coal ration.

36

Ron had a barter arrangement with one of their customers. "I'd rather be wet and happy on the inside," Stan, a widower who lived alone, declared, "than miserable and warm on the outside!" So, in return for free beer, a sack of best nuts would regularly appear on the back doorstep.

Rebecca felt ashamed of her embarrassment. And, not for the first time, she felt bitter that fate had taken her away from her own background and sent her to live in a totally different one, hundreds of miles away. Our formative years, she thought wryly, all we evacuees, and then we're supposed to be able to come back and slot in as if nothing had happened! But she was also on edge. She desperately wanted Ron and Sal to like Ian, wanted them to invite him to stay at the pub, but even the minimal conversation was stilted.

Ron, after making an effort, was wondering what sort of a bloke wasn't interested in football! I mean, he thought, it doesn't make sense! Not if he's normal, that is! He liked a man to be a man, one who liked a drink, and a joke. Sal said Ian only drank halves! That said it all, as far as Ron was concerned. "I mean," he complained to Sal that evening when they went up to bed, "he just ain't one of us, is he? Why on earth does she want to take up with a Northerner?"

"He ain't a Northerner, you daft bat," Sal told him. "He's from the Midlands. And she doesn't like anyone round 'ere."

"More fool her," he grumbled.

"He's not so bad. He's got nice manners – I'll say

that for him. Unlike some I could mention!" Sal looked meaningfully at her husband, but he was busy hanging up his trousers by the braces on a partly open wardrobe door.

She yawned. "Let's face it, Ron, she could do worse. Well, can he stay in the box-room next time he comes? She'll be wanting to know!"

"I suppose so," Ron said, but his attention was on Sal's ample cleavage that was brimming over the neckline of her low-cut nightgown. Even though it was winter, she still liked her bit of glamour, and he certainly wasn't complaining. "Shove over, Sal. You're enough to drive a bloke barmy!"

She obediently wriggled along the bed to give him more room. You could say what you liked about Ron, and she knew more than most he was no film star, but there were worse husbands. In all the years they'd been married, he'd never once knocked her about. Now this Ian might be good-looking, but he was a bit too quiet for Sal's liking. Her old mum had warned her that they were the ones to watch out for. "Yer never know what's going on in their heads," she'd always said. And Sal had never forgotten Harry Potts, the man who'd lived next door. Kept himself to himself, he did, hardly spoke to a soul. And then the police had arrested him for doing unmentionable things to a little boy. Sal had never trusted quiet men since. Maybe, she thought, that was what had attracted her to Ron. He might be loud and blustering but he was all "up front". As for reading books, as Ian had asked him – she didn't think he'd ever opened one in his life. No, he was a simple bloke was Ron, and not too difficult to live with – as long as you didn't cross him. She had a lot to be thankful for, she reminded herself, and with resignation turned to face him when his heavy hand crept round to fondle her.

The following day, Rebecca cleared out the box-room, washed the doors, window-frames and lino, and polished the single chest of drawers. Two hooks behind the door would have to serve as a wardrobe. The room was sparse, and the borrowed camp-bed well used, but she made it up with warm flannelette sheets and a threadbare grey blanket. They didn't have a spare eiderdown, but Sal asked around the customers, and one offered a shabby cerise taffeta one. Rebecca decided that if she put the off-cut of carpet that served as her own bedside mat by his bed, then Ian should be comfortable enough.

Christmas came and went, and then to her delight there was a trunk call by Ian from a call box to say that he was coming to London for New Year's Eve. The pub's telephone was situated on a wall behind the bar, offering so little privacy that when he ended by saying, "I love you," Rebecca felt too self-conscious to respond.

But it was a different matter when he arrived, and within minutes she was in his arms. But she had to work, of course, so until closing time he simply sat in a corner of the bar, although Ron noticed with disgust that he made two halves of beer last all night. But Rebecca, exchanging affectionate smiles as she busily served behind the bar, knew Ian was enjoying himself. He was a people watcher, she decided, as she saw his gaze roam around the smoke-filled room, and saw him turn with interest when the wizened old man everyone called 'toothless Billy' came in.

"Now we're talking," one man shouted. "Get the lid up, Ron!" and, "Give us a tune on the old Joanna, Billy," called another.

Billy grinned and waved, then went to sit at the piano. He waited expectantly until Ron put a frothing pint on the top, and then struck up "Knees up Mother Brown". The room erupted with a raucous chorus, and two women got up and began to dance, while people drew back to give them room as they lifted their skirts above their ample knees. Rebecca glanced over to Ian, who was singing and joining in with the others, and she laughed. It was wonderful to have him here. This was going to be the best New Year's Eve ever!

Ron had grudgingly allowed Rebecca to leave early; and later, full of anticipation, she and Ian went to Trafalgar Square, to join hundreds of other people in the euphoria of knowing that 1946 would herald a new way of life, one that offered the hope of lasting peace. Rebecca clung to Ian among the throng, thrilled by the high spirits of those around her, joining in as everyone counted aloud the dramatic strikes of Big Ben. And then 1946 was in, and Ian seized her in his arms, his face cold against hers, and squeezed her so tight she squealed, before they became just two of a mass of people kissing everyone around them. A middle-aged woman in a fox-fur stole flung her arms around Ian, and Rebecca found herself in the scrawny embrace of a Scot, who teased, "Happy Hogmanay. Now do ye want to know what's under my kilt, darlin'?"

"No thanks," she laughed, and as he grasped her hand, she stretched out to catch Ian's, and then others joined them to form a row of people singing "Auld Lang Syne".

"Look!" Ian grinned afterwards, and pointed to the lions' fountain, where several young people were splashing about, shrieking with glee. "Gosh, isn't this great? Just sense the atmosphere, it's like wine. You could almost get drunk on it!"

"I know," Rebecca laughed up at him. She was so happy, so much in love! "I'll always remember tonight," she said, as they made their way back to Stepney. "It was wonderful when that woman sang 'When the Lights Go Up in London'. Her voice just soared above the crowds – I had tears in my eyes, and I wasn't the only one."

"Her name's Zoe Gail," Ian told her. "She's married to Hubert Gregg, who wrote the song."

"How do you know all these things?"

Ian grinned. "I've told you . . ."

Rebecca laughed. "I know, stick with you and I'll go places!" We've got our own special joke already, she thought with pleasure.

But when they got back to the pub, it was to find a bad-tempered Sal waiting for them. She was dog-tired. Not only had it been an exhausting night in the bar, she'd just begun the "change", and a dratted nuisance it was. She never knew when her periods were coming, and her hormones were all over the

41

place. She could, she'd been thinking with resentment as she huddled in an armchair in her dressing gown and with a scarf over her curlers, do without having to wait up for young people! But there had been no way she was going to go to bed until they came back. Even then, Sal intended to keep her ears open, although fortunately, there was a creaking floorboard on the landing. And when they burst in, Rebecca rosy and glowing, Sal felt such a sharp pang of envy for her youth and energy, that her voice was like a razor as she snapped, "Do you know what time it is?"

"Sorry, Sal," Ian came forward, and kissed her on the cheek. "Happy New Year."

"Yes, well it is for some! The rest of us need our sleep." Sal bustled forward, and pointedly held open the door to the stairs. "Who came in first?"

"I made Ian do it," Rebecca said.

"Right, so we'll blame him then if we have any bad luck!"

But lying in bed, with only a thin wall separating her from Ian, bad luck was the last thing on Rebecca's mind.

5

Sal didn't really understand what she'd got against Ian. He'd been down once a fortnight during January, was always polite, smartly dressed, and obviously thought the world of her niece. But Sal didn't feel easy with him. And, she knew that Ron certainly didn't. But then, she reasoned, it could be a class thing. Not that Ian was any different from them: after all, Rebecca had told her his father worked on a potbank, which was what they called a factory up there. But you couldn't get away from the fact that he'd been to university and was a teacher. That was bound to change someone, and it must be that, Sal decided, which made him seem sort of stand-offish.

Then one Monday morning, the postman brought not only Ian's weekly letter, but another envelope postmarked "Birmingham": and, as Sal told them later, she knew as soon as she picked it up, it was bad news. "This shiver went up me spine," she said, as she sat in tears at the table. "Two years since I've seen her, and now she's gone! Pleurisy, that's what the doctor said."

"You grew up together, didn't you?" Rebecca busied herself making a fresh pot of tea.

"Gert was only the same age as me," Sal sobbed.

"First cousins we were, and she was round our house as often as she was in her own."

"I remember her," Rebecca said quietly. "She was lovely, she used to give me pear drops."

"Never had any kids of her own – just like me," Sal said. "But she'd got a kind heart, had Gert. Took in stray cats she did – remember, Ron?"

"I remember the pong," he said. "Don't know how Arthur stuck it."

"There are more important things in life to complain about!" Sal snapped. Suddenly her shoulders slumped, and she looked years older. Anxiously, Rebecca hurried forward to pour out the tea, and put an extra spoonful of sugar in her aunt's cup. Sal raised tearful eyes to Ron. "The funeral's on Friday, at three o'clock in the afternoon. We'll have to go! Arthur says we can stay the night with him."

Ron nodded. "No problem," he reassured her. "I'll ask Flossie to come in and help Rebecca."

"Isn't it this weekend that Ian's coming?" Sal dabbed at her eyes, and blew her nose.

Rebecca nodded. "That won't make any difference – he doesn't usually get here 'til Saturday lunchtime. And don't worry about getting back, I'll cover for you."

"You're a good kid," Ron said gruffly. "Will you be all right staying on your own?"

Rebecca smiled. "I'm eighteen now – remember?"

"I suppose I still think of you in pigtails!"

"That was a long time ago, Uncle Ron," she said quietly. "In a different world."

He looked at her for a moment, then turned away.

44

"Aye, well, I'll go and sort the cellar out. You sit there a bit, Sal. Me and Rebecca can manage the lunchtime trade."

And over the next few days, Rebecca did what she could to help by pressing Sal's one black dress, and sponging her black velour hat. She paused, wondering just how many funerals in the past few years these clothes had witnessed. Too many by far, she thought grimly, her eyes clouding. But she pushed the thoughts away. Ian was coming this weekend! She still couldn't believe so much had happened in such a short time. I've been swept off my feet she thought, and it's absolutely wonderful.

Train times were checked, and on the appointed day, Ron and Sal, sombre in their funeral attire, prepared to leave. Rebecca listened to Ron's last-minute instructions, and assured him she could cope. "Don't worry about a thing," she said. "Flossie will be here soon, and I promise I'll call last orders promptly at ten!"

With backward glances, they were gone, and within half an hour Flossie arrived. Past retirement age and stiffly corseted, she'd been a barmaid all her life. Now, she just helped out in local pubs when needed. "Suits me fine," she told Rebecca. "I don't want a steady job, not at my age. But it's nice to earn an extra bob or two, and it gives me a chance ter get me glad rags on!" Rebecca glanced at her carefully structured silver hair, which was piled on top of her head, and held in place with small fancy combs.

Flossie believed in what she called "gilding the

45

lily", and wore a full mask of make-up, drop earrings, and a triple row of pearls resting on her wrinkled cleavage. Her squat fingers she adorned with chunky rings. "Just because a woman's no longer in her prime, it doesn't mean she can't be decorative," was her motto, and she was a great favourite with the regulars. Rebecca liked Flossie, who had generously brought with her a block of Cadbury's milk chocolate to share.

The rest of the day passed uneventfully, but it was still with relief that Rebecca locked the door behind the last customer. Some nights weren't nearly so quiet. Tempers could quickly rise, arguments provoked, and Ron often had to intervene. But it only took one word, one veiled threat, and the sheer force of his personality and bulk was enough to sort out any trouble. Now that Flossie had left, Rebecca yawned and went into the kitchen to make a cup of cocoa. The living quarters felt eerily empty, and she shivered, feeling suddenly nervous. Don't be silly, she told herself, but nevertheless turned and went quickly to check that the bolts were secure on the back door. But before she reached it, there came a sharp knock.

Rebecca jumped in fear. Who on earth could that be? Should she ignore it? Could it be Flossie who'd forgotten something? Now don't panic, she told herself. You're in control; you don't *have* to open the door. Then suddenly she heard Ian's voice. "Hello? It's Ian."

Heady relief flooded through her, and she hurriedly unlocked the door to see him standing before her, his face wreathed in smiles. "Surprise! On an impulse, I decided to come down tonight. I intended to phone from Euston Station, but there was a queue outside the telephone box." Ian came in, carrying his small cardboard case and with one arm behind his back. With a flourish he presented her with one perfect red rose.

She stared at it in astonishment. "How on earth? It's the middle of winter!"

Ian smiled. "My secret," he said, and pulled her into his arms. "God, I've missed you." They clung together for several minutes, before Ian asked, "Where's Ron and Sal? I hope they won't mind my coming early."

"They're not here." Rebecca told him about the funeral. "They won't be back until tomorrow." She clasped a hand to her mouth in consternation. "Oh . . . they'll go spare when they know you were here!"

Ian could only stare at her. "You mean we're on our own? Look, perhaps I'd better go."

"Did anyone see you come in?"

"No, I didn't see a soul."

"Then don't be silly, of course you must stay." She looked up at him impishly. "It's not as if you have evil designs on me, is it?"

Ian laughed, and followed her into the kitchen. "Don't you be so sure," he teased, putting his arms around her waist. "What are you making?"

"Cocoa. Do you want some?"

He hesitated. "I wouldn't mind a drop of brandy if that's all right. I feel a bit chilled – it's freezing out there."

Rebecca went to the sideboard, where Ron kept a few bottles. Spirits were still in short supply, but as he said, tapping his nose, he had his contacts. She poured out a generous measure and handed it to Ian, who had gone to sit on the settee, and then put on a reading lamp before switching off the bright overhead light. "That's a bit cosier," she said, placing the rose, so elegant in its glass vase, on a small coffee table. A few minutes later, she returned with her cocoa, and went to sit beside him.

"This is the first time we've ever had the place to ourselves." Ian smiled at her and put his arm around her shoulders. And so they sat entwined, Rebecca drowsy after a hard day's work, Ian feeling tired after teaching all day and travelling. He glanced at the Westminster chime clock on the mantelpiece. It was eleven-thirty and late enough to go to bed, but he was reluctant. These moments of privacy were too precious. Always, when they were out together, there were people about. Here at the pub, it was only snatched minutes when Ron and Sal were out of the room. The prospect of spending time alone with Rebecca, just the two of them, was much too enticing to sacrifice.

"Are you very tired?" he said gently.

"Only a bit." Within the circle of Ian's arm, with her head resting on his chest, she wanted to stay there forever.

"Then let's make the most of it. The fire's gone down – shall I make it up?"

She nodded, and he put on a few more pieces of coal, and picking up the poker, stirred the embers.

Together, they watched the fire begin to glow, and Ian offered her a sip of his brandy.

Rebecca shook her head. "I'm not keen on alcohol."

There was a flat tone to her voice, and he said, "That's a strange comment from a barmaid."

"I'm not one, really. I just work here because it's the best way I can pay back what I owe to Ron and Sal."

"And that is?"

"Giving me a roof over my head, a home."

Ian put down his glass. "You know you never have told me about your life before you came here." He looked searchingly into her eyes, seeing the shadows there, the uncertainty. "When people love each other, there shouldn't be any secrets between them."

"It's not that I'm keeping anything secret," Rebecca said in distress, "it's just that some things I find difficult to talk about."

Ian kissed her, a long, tender kiss. "Not with me, sweetheart. You can tell me anything."

Rebecca looked down. She'd locked these memories away for so long. But she knew that Ian was right, and he'd been so good all these weeks, never probing, never asking.

"I grew up a few streets away from here," she began haltingly. "My father was a docker, and Mum took in ironing. There was never much money, although we were happy enough." She paused, and Ian could see her lips twist with pain. "When Dad wasn't in drink, that is." She looked up at him. "I used to dread Fridays when he got his wages. It was

49

straight into the pub, and we never knew what mood he'd come home in." She looked up at him in bewilderment. "I still can't understand how Mum could go on loving him after the way he treated her. Even after he gave her a black eye or split lip, she'd be laughing and joking with him a few days later. It's only the drink," she used to say. "That's not your real dad!"

"Did he hit *you*?" Ian's voice was tense.

"No, never. Mum always used to make sure I was in bed when he got home. But I could hear it all going on, even from upstairs."

Ian looked down at the lovely head resting on his shoulder, trying to imagine that same head, smaller, frightened, burying itself in a pillow, trying to shut out the violence in the room below. "Does this bother you?" He raised his glass.

She shook her head. "No, don't be silly."

"There's nothing wrong with it in moderation, you know."

"I'm beginning to learn that. But it wasn't just Dad. Where I was evacuated, the people were Welsh, and very strong chapel. They despised anyone who drank alcohol, talked of it as the 'demon drink'. I suppose some of that rubbed off on me." She gave a wry smile. "Sod's law, isn't it, that I should end up living in a pub!"

"How long were you there?"

"I was just almost twelve when I went. I was one of the oldest, so I looked after some of the little ones on the train journey. We had no idea where we were going." She hesitated. "Mr and Mrs Parry were okay,

I suppose – but very strict. I always had to call them that, never Auntie or Uncle. They weren't used to children, and must have been horrified when two kids were billeted on them. The other was an eight-year-old boy. He hated it and came back to London. Many did, you know. People called it the 'phoney war' at first. Anyway, Mum wouldn't let me come home, she made me stay, said I'd be safer there." Tears began to course slowly down her cheeks, but she didn't care. Now that she'd allowed the painful memories to surface, the words began to pour out. "And she was proved right. There was a huge warehouse near Tilbury Arches, people used to flood there to use it as a shelter. It took a direct hit during the Blitz, and Mum was killed. I remember Dad coming to Wales to tell me. It was the only time I ever saw him break down and cry. Then a year later the Germans killed him as well. He was an ARP warden by then, and had just come off shift. They got him and the house. Sal took me to see what was left of it as soon as I came back." She looked up at him, heartbreak in her eyes.

"That was my home, Ian, where I'd grown up, and there was hardly anything left. And then I saw part of a wall, still with some of the wallpaper on. It was such lovely paper. Mum and I chose it together. She said the pink cabbage roses would make us feel we had a garden." Her voice broke, and Ian gazed helplessly down at her. Eighteen years old, and yet so much heartbreak. He could only hold her close as at last she wept; her tears painful and choking, ones she'd held back for far too long.

51

"I'm sorry," she whispered. "You haven't come all the way down here to have someone cry over you."

"Oh, sweetheart, don't apologise. I think you're marvellous. It takes real strength and courage to come through all that." As Rebecca straightened up and dabbed at her eyes, he said, "Why not have a drop of brandy? It will help, honestly, and one small drink won't hurt."

After a second's hesitation, Rebecca nodded, and Ian went over to the sideboard. She watched him, her heart full of love. It hardly seemed possible that only a few weeks ago he hadn't been in her life.

"Here you are." He handed her a glass. "Just sip it slowly." Rebecca obeyed, and felt the fire of the brandy warm her. She took another sip, and leaned back against him. They sat for several long moments in silence, Ian full of compassion for the tragic girl beside him, Rebecca shaken with emotion, but also with a sense of release. She'd been unable for so long to talk about what had happened, but with Ian beside her, his strength had given her the courage she needed. Slowly she sipped the rest of her brandy, and looked up at him. "I do love you, so very much."

Ian's voice thickened. "I love you too, my darling."

The fire crackled into a blaze, the flames throwing a soft glow over the small sitting-room, and gradually, Rebecca began to feel the golden liquid of the brandy relaxing her taut nerves. When Ian drew her close to him, their kisses, tender at first, became deeper, more passionate, their mouths searching, exploring. Rebecca felt as if fire was coursing through her veins, and when Ian began to fumble with the buttons on her bodice, she helped him, easing the dress off her creamy shoulders and down to her waist. Her slip followed, and then after a shy hesitation, her brassiere, and Ian drew back slightly, tracing with one finger the outline of her breasts.

"You're so beautiful," he whispered. And then he was stroking, kissing, until the confines of the narrow settee became too restrictive, and they slid down to the floor to lie together, to undress each other, while the urgent need to express their love grew ever more desperate. Then, as skin lay against skin, there was no other moment, no other world but this, and caution was forgotten . . .

Afterwards, quiet and shaken, Ian got up and went to his jacket hanging on a chair by the table. He took a cigarette from his case, flicked his lighter, and inhaled deeply, gazing down at Rebecca, who was still curled up drowsily in the firelight. She had pulled from the settee her silk slip to partly cover herself, but still the beauty of her naked limbs stirred him yet again. Ian groaned inwardly. He blamed himself for this. He was the older, the more responsible one. And yet their coming together had been so natural, so right, that he turned savagely. The devil with convention, or even religion, that said fulfilling a love like theirs outside marriage was wrong. What bewildered him was that they had come so far, so soon. He saw her stir and look up at him, saw her eyes suddenly widen at the realisation of what had just taken place, and stubbing out his cigarette, he went to hold her close, to murmur words of love and reassurance. "Marry me, darling," he whispered. "We love each other, we know we do. Why wait?"

Rebecca reached out her arms to cling to him, her head buried in his shoulder. Never in her life had she felt so warm, so loved, so secure. And their lovemaking had been a revelation. Her lips curved in a half-embarrassed smile at the memory, and then suddenly she was raising her lips to his, and once again time meant nothing.

6

The clock was chiming three when eventually they went upstairs to sleep together in Rebecca's narrow single bed. As she pointed out to Ian, this way his own bed wouldn't look rumpled. At six a.m., as they'd agreed, he reluctantly got up, collected his suitcase, and quietly let himself out of the back door. It was still dark, bitterly cold with a slight frost, and the streets were deserted. Ian looked searchingly up at curtained windows as he walked swiftly along the pavement; not one showed a chink of light. Maybe he'd be lucky, and no one would ever know that he'd arrived the night before.

Rebecca heard the back door close behind him and turned over, stretching her legs into the warm space where Ian had lain. The room was icy, and burrowing down beneath the eiderdown, she yawned and tried to go back to sleep. But it was no use. Not only did she have a headache from the brandy, but also, over and over again, scenes from the night before kept playing through her mind. As she lay there, Rebecca suddenly realised that her life had changed. She was no longer a girl, a virgin. She was a woman now. She knew she should be feeling guilt, shame at betraying her working-class roots. After all, no decent girl was supposed to do what she had done – not before she was married! But how could she think of their spontaneous, wonderful lovemaking as something ugly? Rebecca refused to let anything spoil the cherished memory. For that was how she felt – cherished, precious and loved. And sudden tears pricked her eyes, as she realised just how many years it was since she'd felt like that. There had been no affection while she'd lived in Wales, not even a touch or a hug. There had been too much sorrow in her life, too much horror. Now at last there was hope, excitement, and she lingered over Ian's whispered words, *"Marry me, darling."* Today, she thought happily, today, we'll make plans.

Ron and Sal arrived back just after opening time. They both looked strained, and said the funeral had been harrowing. "Arthur was in a terrible state," Sal said. "And he's threatening to get rid of the cats. Gert wouldn't have liked that, wouldn't have liked it at all!"

"Well, as I said on the train, don't get any ideas about them coming 'ere," Ron told her. "I can't stand the wretched things, never could!"

Rebecca busied herself making her aunt a cup of tea, knowing that Flossie could cope with the first customers. She kept her face averted, afraid Sal would see something different in her; that the heat would rise to her cheeks, her eyes betray what had happened. But Sal didn't seem to notice anything, and by the time Ian got there an hour later, Rebecca had at last begun to relax. Suitcase in hand, he came in through the bar, and one of the customers called,

"Rebecca, the bad penny's turned up!" She laughed and lifted the flap on the bar for him to go through to the back.

Ian gave her a quick kiss on the cheek, then their eyes met and a message flashed between them, anxiety on his part, reassurance on hers. "Ron and Sal have just got back from Birmingham," she said for the benefit of customers. "Sal's cousin died, and it was the funeral yesterday."

"Oh, I'm sorry to hear that!" Ian went through into the sitting-room.

"Sorry to hear your bad news," he said, meeting Ron in the doorway. Ron nodded and jerked his head in Sal's direction.

"She's taken it badly."

Sal was sitting in an armchair, her feet resting on a leather pouffe, a cigarette in her hand. There were dark circles under her eyes, and she looked utterly weary.

"Rebecca's just told me," Ian said awkwardly, "about your cousin. I'm very sorry."

"We was like sisters when we were kids," Sal said, "but I suppose it comes to us all." Her hand shook slightly as she took a sip of her drink, and she carefully replaced the cup on its saucer.

Ian glanced around the room, which looked so different from the previous night. Then, it had seemed cosy and seductive, the surroundings shadowed in the warm firelight. Now, with Ron and Sal's suitcases dumped in the middle, and the fire low, it was again just a poky back room behind a pub. "Is there anything I can do to help?"

"You could make that fire up," Sal said. "And after closing time, could you go and fetch some fish and chips in? I don't feel up to cooking anything."

"Of course, I'll be glad to." By now Ian was feeling distinctly ill at ease. Ron and Sal had been good to him, and how had he repaid them? His only consolation was that he and Rebecca planned to get married – and as far as he was concerned, as soon as possible.

But, as Rebecca said, when that night they went to the pictures, "It's hardly the right time though, is it? For you to ask them, I mean – not with the funeral and everything. Sal's really upset about it. And she and Ron had a row on the way back. She thinks they should take a couple of Gert's cats."

"How many did she have?"

"About fifteen, I think – all strays." Rebecca was all for it, thinking two cats would scare off any mice or rats down in the cellar.

"And Ron doesn't want to?"

"He flatly refuses!" She glanced sideways at Ian. "You know you'll have to ask his permission? After all, I'm under twenty-one!"

"Don't remind me," he grimaced, fishing in his pocket to find money for their tickets as they neared the cinema paybox. The prospect of approaching the truculent Ron with a request to marry his niece, and quickly, was not one he relished. Ian was well aware of the gulf between them. He was uncomfortable with Ron. Ron was uncomfortable with him. It was just a fact of life. Not only that, but Ian had known Rebecca for only three months, was much older, and wasn't even a Londoner.

"So you think," he said, as they strolled home after the film, "that I'd be better leaving it until next time I come?"

Rebecca said, "Definitely." She looked up at him and grinned. "I'll praise you up a bit in the meantime. And I'll be extra nice to Ron, so he'll find it difficult to refuse. He's a big softie at heart, you know."

"You could have fooled me," Ian said with feeling. He anticipated trouble. Still, he thought wryly – I've survived fighting a war, surely I can handle an ex-pugilist landlord?

On Sunday afternoon, Gloria was irritating Rebecca even more than usual. All she could do was moan on and on about not being able to go dancing. "That cow at work let me down – again! So, there I was, stuck in the house on a Saturday night!"

Rebecca winced. She hated the word "cow" when applied to women. Probably comes from working with the real ones so much, she thought, recalling her initial fear of the huge beasts when she'd worked as a Land Girl during the last couple of years of the war. But as time went on, her experience on the farm near the Welsh village where she'd been evacuated had taught her that, like humans, animals had their own personalities.

"Daft, I call it," Gloria complained, "Mum not letting me go on my own!"

"You're the daft one," Sal snapped, who was sitting

with her feet up reading the *News of the World*, "wanting to go dancing on yer own! You'll get yourself a reputation, my girl! And then there's the getting home – at God knows what hour!"

"I might have found someone to bring me! Tall, dark and handsome," Gloria claimed, stubbing out her cigarette in an ashtray.

Like Ian, Rebecca thought, with a touch of smugness. Dancing had long been a bone of contention between herself and Gloria. Rebecca couldn't explain, even to herself, why she'd always been reluctant to go. I suppose I needed a period of adjustment, she thought. Seeing the bombed-out site of our house affected me so much. All I wanted was to stay here, in the pub with Ron and Sal. The irony was that the very weekend Ian had come into the bar, she'd decided it was time to shake herself out of her apathy. She'd only ever been to a couple of village dances in Wales, and due to the war, there had been a distinct shortage of male partners. Rebecca, feeling she would have to include Gloria, had never suggested going dancing to Ian. They had too few hours together as it was, to want to share them with anyone else.

"I still don't see why you couldn't have come last night," Gloria shrugged her narrow shoulders, flicking listlessly through an old copy of *Picturegoer*. "Ian wasn't coming down."

"It wouldn't seem right," Rebecca said. "Going dancing without him. After all, he is my boyfriend."

Sal looked at both girls thoughtfully. They were so different. Gloria sat there, as always with a fag between her scarlet lips, her attitude brittle and rest-less. Rebecca, Sal suddenly noticed, looked serenely happy. It was only geography that had brought the two girls together, Sal was well aware of that. Gloria wasn't a bad girl, but she wouldn't have been her first choice as a friend for her niece.

"So you keep telling me, Rebecca," Gloria said with sarcasm. "Of course, I've not been privileged to meet him." She glanced archly at her friend. "Afraid of the competition, are you?"

"You flatter yourself!" Rebecca knew that if Gloria hadn't had a weekend job on a stall at the market, she would have met Ian long ago. Maybe, she thought, I'm being selfish. It wouldn't hurt just for once to have someone else along, and the prospect of dancing with Ian, of being held in his arms in a waltz or a slow foxtrot, was an enticing one. "I tell you what," she said. "I'll write and ask Ian if he'd like to go to the Palais. And I'm sure he won't mind you coming with us." After all, she thought, we'll have the rest of the time on our own.

"Fantastic!" Gloria's whole face lit up, and Sal thought how much prettier she looked when she wasn't scowling. If life doesn't treat her right, that girl will grow up into a right misery guts, she thought grimly. Funny that, 'cos her mother's just the same. She'd split a farthing, would Bessie Brady.

The young couple had fallen into a routine where each wrote once a week, so Rebecca was surprised to receive an extra letter a couple of days before he was due to visit.

My darling,

I'm devastated, but I won't be able to come down on Saturday after all. My grandmother's ill, and I'm afraid I'm needed up here. She lives a couple of miles away, and we're all going over to take it in turns to stay up with her during the night. She's always been a wonderful nan, and I'm sure you'll understand that I have no choice. I'm missing you terribly, and hate letting you down, particularly after our wonderful night together. Remember, sweetheart that I love you, and hopefully it won't be long before you're wearing my ring,

All my love,

Ian

PS. I'll write again soon. Maybe I can make it next weekend, instead.

Bitterly disappointed, Rebecca put the letter into the top drawer of the chest that doubled as a dressing table. But she understood, of course she did, there was no question about that.

Sal, however, was not so charitable. "He says he can't come because his grandmother's ill?" she said, raising disbelieving eyebrows. "Well, we've all heard that one. It'll be her funeral next, you mark my words."

Incensed, Rebecca flashed, "What is it that you've got against him? Why do you always look for the worst?"

Sal felt a bit ashamed. She had no business going

62

on at the girl like that. "Oh, take no notice of me," she said defensively. "You know how I feel about men! Even your dad, and he was my own brother . . ." she broke off.

Incredulous, Rebecca stared at her. "Do you think I didn't see what went on when I was a kid? And hear it all?"

"Maybe," Sal said with bitterness, "but at least Duggie was only evil in drink. My dad was a rotter through and through!"

Rebecca was shocked. She knew none of this, even though Sal was talking about her grandfather – the one who'd died when she was little. "You know, Dad never used to talk about him," she said slowly. "When I asked him once, he just said he was one of the old school – you know, when children were seen and not heard."

"Not even fed, half the time," Sal told her.

"Did *he* drink as well?"

Sal nodded. "And gambled and knocked my mum about. He led her a terrible life. Oh, he was good-looking all right, but handsome is as handsome does in my opinion. He certainly wasn't much of an example to our Duggie, I can tell you that!"

Then suddenly she realised that Rebecca was at last talking openly about her parents. Thank God for that, Sal thought! It was unnatural, the way the girl had gone inside herself. Maybe now they would be able to share memories, remember together the good times. Because there had been some, and it was far better she dwelt on those, rather than just the bad ones.

Rebecca looked at her aunt, wondering whether it was her unhappy childhood that had etched the hard lines around her mouth, and given her a sharp tongue. How little we know of other people, she thought with surprise, even those closely related to us. "You must have thought you'd struck gold when you met Ron," she said.

"Well, he's no oil painting, but at rock bottom he's sound as a bell. And that's what counts in the long run." Sal glanced at the young girl facing her. "Just remember that. Look beneath the surface, that's all I'm saying."

"But you don't know Ian like I do. Or you wouldn't be so suspicious," Rebecca protested.

"That's true. And it's nothing against him personally, love. But I've known two handsome men in my time, my father and our Duggie, and it was all skin deep. But then, as I said, I've got a jaundiced view of most blokes! Come on," she dabbed a powder puff over her face, "it's time we went to dazzle the punters!"

Thoughtfully, Rebecca followed her aunt into the bar and went to unlock the pub's double doors. It's a good job the women in our family were a bit better, she mused. Her mother had been gentle and loving, someone who liked to read, and to listen to music on the wireless. Her parents, too, were like herself, decent and hardworking. So at least she didn't come from all bad stock. Ian's family sounded very close and supportive. Well, she'd soon find out, because she was hoping that once they were engaged, she would be going up to the Potteries to meet them.

"Won't they mind?" she'd worried. "That they haven't met me first?" But Ian had shaken his head. "No, sweetheart, I don't want to delay things. The sooner we're engaged, the sooner we can plan the wedding."

But now, as Rebecca turned to greet the first customers, all she could think about was seeing him again. Never mind, she consoled herself, as she handed over a frothing mug of best bitter – if Ian comes next weekend, I won't have too long to wait.

7

But on Wednesday morning, Rebecca began to develop a sore throat. By the evening, she was running a temperature, and on Thursday morning, with a head cold and aching joints, it was obvious that she was in for a nasty bout of influenza. Miserably, she managed to write a few lines to Ian, telling him not to come. The following week was spent huddled in bed, hot and sweating beneath the eiderdown, with Sal bringing up aspirins, barley water, and honey and lemon. To her bitter disappointment, she didn't hear anything from Ian. There was neither a letter nor a phone call, and in her weakened state, Rebecca began to feel fretful with worry.

Sal's disapproval was in her compressed lips, but she managed not to say anything, at least to Rebecca. "I mean," she said to Ron, as they washed glasses after closing time. "You'd have thought he'd have sent her a card, or at least bothered to go out to a call box!"

Ron frowned. "Maybe he's got the flu as well."

"He could still write a few lines. He must have got her letter, because he never came."

By the weekend, Rebecca, still a bit weak and with

the remnants of a cough, was downstairs again. On Sunday afternoon when Gloria came round, she was full of curiosity. "So you haven't heard from him since when?"

"A week last Wednesday," Rebecca admitted. She was worried sick – Ian had never missed before. Was it possible that he'd also had the flu?

Rebecca's cheeks flamed at the memory of their lovemaking. Perhaps his flu might have turned to pneumonia, he could even be in hospital. But then, she thought miserably, surely he'd have sent a message through his parents or something.

Gloria almost seemed to be relishing the situation. "Maybe he's just got fed up of all the travelling – train fares aren't cheap, you know!"

"I do know," Rebecca flashed. "That's why he didn't come every week!"

"Well, it doesn't look as if he's coming at all!" Gloria spread out both her hands and surveyed the nail varnish. "Do you think this red is a bit too bright?"

Irritably, Rebecca shook her head. As if such things mattered when her whole life was in crisis! "He probably did write, and his letter got lost in the post," she said stubbornly.

"But he hasn't phoned either, has he? It's a bit odd, if you ask me."

"I wasn't asking you!"

Gloria ignored her. "So, have you written again?"

Rebecca nodded. "Yes, I wrote on Friday."

"Well," Gloria said, relenting. "You'll probably hear from him in the next few days."

But Rebecca didn't. Every morning she rushed to the hall as soon as she heard the post arrive. But there was nothing. And there was still no phone call. Day followed day, and she wrote again, but when there was still no reply by the following Monday, she became frantic.

"I don't understand it!" Almost in tears, she returned yet again empty-handed from the hall. "What's happened to him?"

Sal looked searchingly at her. "Are you sure you didn't have a tiff?"

Vehemently, Rebecca shook her head. "He asked me to marry him," she said, and saw Sal's eyes widen with astonishment. "If it hadn't been for Gert's funeral, he was going to ask Ron if we could get engaged."

Sal stared at her open-mouthed. "Engaged?" Shocked, Sal sat heavily in an armchair. "Flaming Nora! Well, this puts a different slant on things."

"So now you'll see why I can't understand what's happened. It isn't as if it was just a fling or something."

"I don't know what to say, girl. It's a bleedin' mystery!"

Rebecca gazed miserably at her. No matter how she tried to shut it out, there was one appalling, treacherous possibility. Yet she felt disloyal even allowing the thought to enter her mind. But it was insidious, lurking, filling her with fear. Had that night of lovemaking made Ian lose all respect for her? After all, they hadn't known each other very long, and yet she'd willingly, gloriously, lost her virginity to him at the very first opportunity. It had been as though all she'd been taught, all she'd believed about her morals, had counted for nothing. There had been such a vulnerable longing within her, a need to be held close in his arms, to feel his skin against hers. She had wanted to give, to love, and to be loved in return. Passion had swept both of them away, she realised that now, and in the eyes of the world, her world, she had done a shameful thing.

Yet every nerve in her body cried out against even the thought that there had been anything cheap or tacky about that night. And Ian had felt the same, she knew he had. He wasn't like that! He *wasn't* one of those men who was just "out for what he could get", as people called it! Hadn't they talked about spending the rest of their lives together? Night after night she tossed and turned, getting up early, peering out of the window for the postman to turn the corner, only to turn away in despair. Ian's red rose lay pressed inside a book, its romance now blurred with misery.

And then over the next few days, her anxiety ballooned to nightmare proportions. Ashen-faced, she emerged from the bathroom again and again. It just couldn't be happening, it couldn't! But the fact was that she was normally as regular as clockwork, and her period was late! She pored over her diary with desperation, hoping she'd made a mistake. Then as the hours turned into days and the days into weeks, Rebecca tried to convince herself that she'd missed her period because of her bout of flu. And all through her despair, one thread was constant. There was still no word from him.

At the weekends, Rebecca was permanently on edge, looking up each time the pub door opened, anxious and distracted in her work, short-tempered with the customers.

"What's up with misery guts?" one man complained. "Smiles don't cost much!"

"She's still not too good after the flu," Sal muttered, but cast an angry glance at her niece. Problems were one thing – everyone got those. But you didn't let them affect your work. "Your face would turn the milk sour," she said sharply, as she passed by Rebecca behind the bar. "Make an effort, for Gawd's sake!"

Rebecca bit her lip. She was out of her mind with worry. Her second period was already three days late. She couldn't be pregnant, she couldn't! Surely it wouldn't happen the very first time? It would be just typical of me, she thought bitterly. After all, I'm unlucky; I've always known that! What has life thrown at me so far? A father who was a drunkard; sent away from home at twelve, and then orphaned at fourteen! She turned away, as desperate tears welled up in her eyes. What on earth was she going to do?

"Why don't you write to his mother?" Gloria had challenged the previous weekend. "Ask her if her precious son is poorly."

"Don't be daft!" Rebecca had snapped, not wanting to admit that she'd had the same thought. But embarrassment held her back. How could she write to the mother of a twenty-seven-year-old man, complaining that he hadn't been in touch? How humiliating was that?

70

"I told you from the beginning it wouldn't work," Sal said, "not with him living up there! And as for this marriage talk, well a man will tell you anything to keep you sweet. You'll find that out!" She cast an anxious glance at her niece. Rebecca's skin was very fair, as was the case with most redheads, but lately she was looking positively pasty. Lovesick, I suppose, Sal thought. Thinks her heart is broken. Well, maybe it is, but she'll have to get over it.

Ron didn't say much at all, but from his glowering expression it was obvious that if Ian did turn up, he'd better have a good explanation.

But on Wednesday, Rebecca finally came to a decision. She had to do something or she'd go mad! Again and again, she reassured herself that if something had happened to him, then his parents would have let her know. So, the obvious answer seemed to be that he'd simply dumped her. Rebecca knew that was what everyone else thought. But she still clung stubbornly to her conviction that he wouldn't let her down so badly. Not the Ian she knew and loved. No matter that he'd ignored all her letters, that he hadn't come to see her. She was going to swallow her pride and go to find *him*.

On Saturday morning, Euston Station was crowded with people. The smoke from the engines made Rebecca feel nauseous, but then so did a lot of things lately. She popped a barley sugar into her mouth, and when her train was announced, followed others along the platform. There seemed to be a lot of people going to Stoke-on-Trent, and then she realised that the train went all the way to Crewe. "*Oh, Mr Porter!*" The refrain of the old music-hall song came into her mind, the one about someone ending up at Crewe by mistake. She'd better make sure she didn't doze off and do the same; she felt so tired lately.

Eventually she spotted an empty carriage and climbing in claimed a seat by the window. But it wasn't long before it filled up, and she was slightly discomforted when a priest took the seat opposite. Rebecca didn't go to church; she'd had more than enough religion when she was an evacuee. Mr Parry had been not only a well-respected solicitor, but also a lay preacher, and he and his wife had considered it their Christian duty to take Rebecca with them to chapel. She'd lost count of the number of sermons she'd sat through, although most of them she'd spent daydreaming of what life would be like when the war ended.

The journey seemed endless, not helped by the fact that twice she had to face the cramped WC along the corridor, struggling to keep her balance as the train swayed along. And that was despite having "gone" when she was at the station. The urge to "spend a penny" was becoming more and more frequent, and sitting in her corner seat, gazing list-lessly out of the window, Rebecca knew it was no use trying to deny it any more – she was definitely pregnant! All the signs that she'd read about at the library were there. She often felt nauseous first thing in the morning, there was tingling and tenderness in her breasts, and now she sometimes had to run to get to the lavatory in time. I even look pinched and unwell, she thought, but then that could be down to the worry of it all. She could only peck at the sandwich she'd brought, but did manage to drink the bottle of water. Sal had made her a flask of tea, but Rebecca had discreetly poured it down the sink and replaced it with water. She hadn't been able to face tea for days.

Despondent, she tried to take an interest in the passing scenery or to read *Woman's Own*, but it was hopeless. She was too restless, too much on edge, too apprehensive to settle to anything. She just longed to see Ian, was desperate to be drawn close in his strong arms, for him to kiss her, to smile at her, to tell her that everything was going to be fine. Because if he didn't – then Rebecca didn't know what she was going to do. How could she face this pregnancy on her own? She'd be an outcast, she would have brought shame on Ron and Sal, have let them down, have . . .

"Are you all right, my child?" Rebecca stirred out of her reverie to find the white-haired rotund priest staring at her with concern. Suddenly she realised that her cheeks were wet with tears, and fished hurriedly into her handbag for a hanky. Embarrassed, she glanced around the carriage and then realised that the other passengers must have got off at stations along the way. She'd been too immersed in her despairing thoughts to notice. She glanced at the black rosary beads on his lap. Rebecca didn't know much about Catholics, apart from the fact that they didn't eat meat on Fridays. And that Ron scoffed that they walked straight out of eleven-o-clock mass into the nearest pub for a pint! And of course, everyone knew they didn't believe in birth control. Or sex outside marriage, Rebecca thought with acute embarrassment. She felt guilty even meeting the priest's eyes. But he was waiting for an answer, and so she said, "Thank you, I'm fine."

The priest hesitated, then said, "I don't want you to think I'm prying, not at all, now, but you've been looking very troubled. Is there anything I can do to help?"

His soft Irish brogue was warm and persuasive, and for one fleeting moment, Rebecca was tempted to share her worries, her fears. But instead she just shook her head. "Not really," adding awkwardly, "thank you."

Ten minutes later, the train drew into Stoke-on-Trent station, and as they both stood to reach for their luggage, the priest turned to her again. "Just remember now, me name's Father Flynn, and you can find me at St Mary's, any time." He didn't wait for an answer, and a few seconds later, he was gone.

Rebecca stepped down from the train, and let the throng of people pass by her as she tried to get her bearings. Then picking up her small brown case, she began to walk towards the entrance. Ian had told her he lived close enough to the railway station to be able to walk to it, so at least his address would be easy to find. After asking a porter for directions, Rebecca went outside into the chill air, glancing up at the grey April sky, and glad she'd brought an umbrella. Opposite the station there was a large statue of Josiah Wedgwood, and behind it an imposing building called the North Stafford Hotel. Otherwise the road seemed reasonably quiet. A ten-minute walk the porter had said, and as she crossed over to find the right turning, Rebecca's heart began to hammer painfully. At last she was going to find out why Ian had disappeared out of her life.

She would never believe that he'd stopped loving her, not until she heard the words from his own lips. Rebecca still clung desperately to her belief that Ian had meant all that he'd said about their getting married. Well, she told herself unhappily, he did so at the time, she was positive about that. So what had changed? I'm just so bewildered by it all, she thought with misery, as she paused to check that the seams were straight on her stockings. She tucked a stray strand of hair beneath her jaunty hat, and squared her shoulders. She may be feeling queasy, she may be full of nervous apprehension, but anything was better than remaining in ignorance.

She saw College Road on the right, and turning into it began to walk with renewed determination. The only sound was the tapping of her court-shoe heels on the pavement, and Rebecca was certain of one thing only. Whatever the outcome, Ian had a right to know that she was carrying his child.

8

Redwood Avenue was a row of neat, semi-detached houses, each with its own tiny patch of front garden and wooden gate. Rebecca walked slowly along, her gaze searching out the numbers, and when she realised she was approaching Ian's home, her step faltered. Nervously, she shifted the small case to her other hand, halting before number fifteen, and opening the gate closed it with a loud click. The bay window was screened with net curtains, and there was a thick film of dust coating the frame of the dark green door. So Ian hadn't been teasing when he told her that the smoke from the pottery kilns hung like a pall over the Potteries. "It's really hard work for the women," he'd said, "particularly if the wind's in the wrong direction. I've known Mum have to take her washing in and do it again."

The memory of his words brought with it an image of Ian's sensitive, attractive face, of his loving expression as he smiled down at her, and it gave her courage. Hardly able to believe that within minutes she would actually see him again, Rebecca lifted the iron knocker and tapped gently. But although she stepped back in anticipation, her stomach churning with nerves, there was no sound of movement. After another minute, she lifted the heavy knocker and this time rapped more sharply. She could hear the sound echoing through the house, but again there was nothing – just an empty silence. There *had* to be somebody in! After all her hopes, her fears, her long and tiring journey, to find the house empty was so bitterly disappointing she felt dangerously close to tears. She rapped again, even louder – but there was no response. Rebecca picked up her case and casting a last despairing glance at the blank windows, closed the gate behind her.

She stood in confusion on the pavement; then, realising it was already past lunchtime she glanced up at the grey sky and, deciding the rain would probably keep off a bit longer, crossed over to the park entrance opposite the house. Going in, she walked past the children's playground and found a bench on which to sit, just within the tree-lined boundary. It was turning a little chilly, and glad that she was wearing her warm check coat, Rebecca took out a small greaseproof-paper package from her bag and opened it. But the sandwich looked limp, and its corned beef filling didn't appeal at all. She suddenly craved something sweet, perhaps a currant bun or a cake. Surely she could get something like that at the railway station? It wasn't far and she would be warmer there – it was depressing sitting here alone.

At the station, glad of the noise and bustle that greeted her, she pushed open the heavy door to the café, and saw displayed in the glass case on the counter, not only currant buns, but iced ones too.

The bored-looking woman behind the counter glanced up. "Yes, duck?"

"Do you have anything to drink besides tea?"

"Bovril do yer?"

Rebecca nodded, and a minute later was sitting at a corner table, biting into a currant bun. It was slightly stale, but the candied peel gave it flavour, and with the sparse scattering of sugar on top, it revived her spirits. She even managed to eat an iced bun as well. The next hour and a half passed with agonising slowness, as she sat and fretted, constantly checking her watch. Maybe they'd all gone to visit Ian's grandmother – after all, she might still be ill. And as it was Saturday afternoon, his parents might have gone shopping. And maybe Ian was at the library or something. Rebecca's thoughts whirled in ever increasing circles.

Restlessly, she glanced down at her small card-board case. At least she'd brought a few things with her, which meant that if there was no answer again, she could try that evening, or even tomorrow. She wondered whether she should go and find some-where to stay overnight. After all, she couldn't be sure what the situation would be with Ian, or even whether his mother would offer to put her up. Yes, she decided. There's bound to be somewhere fairly near to the station.

But not, she thought wryly, as she walked back out into the fresh air, the hotel opposite! She couldn't imagine what it would cost to stay there! Rebecca walked past College Road this time, and continued down to what seemed to be a main road. She hovered

78

on the pavement, uncertain which way to turn, then decided that right looked the best bet and began to walk up a slight incline. Apart from a couple of buses, there was little traffic, and she glanced around curiously. On the other side of the road, there was a large, grimy-looking building. A notice on the outside told her that it was an earthenware factory, and she remembered Ian telling her that the local name was a potbank. It looked blank and forbidding, and putting down her case to change over hands, she wondered what it would be like to work there. There was a cemetery just past it, and nearing the top of the hill, she came to a bridge over a canal and paused to rest for a moment, looking down at the grey water. So, this was the Potteries, she thought, recalling reading Arnold Bennett's novels. There were no barges on the canal, but could it be the one used for bringing china clay from Cornwall? When she lived in Wales, the local library had been Rebecca's refuge. Going there had been an excuse to get away from the stiff, formal atmosphere of the Parrys' home, and reading had meant that she could sit quietly and not impose on their ordered way of life. She saw a board telling her that the park's name was Hanley Park, then came to a roundabout, passed a large Masonic Hall, and to her relief saw a substantial Victorian terraced house with a sign, The Commercial Hotel, on the opposite side of the road. Crossing over, she went into the small vestibule, waited a moment, then shook a small brass bell on the reception desk. Eventually, a middle-aged man came through from the back, scratching his head, his braces hanging down over his trousers. He yawned, and Rebecca guessed that he'd been having an afternoon nap.

"Yes, duck?"

"Do you have any vacancies for tonight?" He nodded, and pulled a register towards him.

"Oh, I don't want to book in now, I just wanted to be sure I could later – if you know what I mean." Rebecca smiled at him, and he grinned, his gaze sweeping over her admiringly.

"Don't worry, luv, we've got plenty of room."

"How much would it be?"

He told her, and said, "We do an evening meal at seven, if you're interested. That would be extra, of course."

"Thank you. I might see you later, then." She turned and left, retracing her steps back to the road leading to the station, and again turned into College Road. A few minutes later, she was in Redwood Avenue.

There was no reply! Rebecca stood back and stared at the house, noticing that dust and smuts not only lay on the panels of the front door, but also on the wide windowledges. She left her case and going back into the street, scrutinised the neighbouring houses. All had doorsteps that were either whitened, or polished with red Cardinal, and gleaming wood-work. Even as she stood there, she saw a woman come out of her house further along, wipe down her paintwork, and then go back in. This was a road of high standards then, and from what Ian had told her about his parents, how they'd worked hard to send him to university, Rebecca guessed that his mother would have been no exception. Yet the Beresfords' doorstep was scruffy. Could she be ill? After all, everyone knew men were hopeless at housework. Or was his grandmother worse and they were spending all their spare time at her house? But whatever the reason, nothing explained why Ian hadn't been in touch.

In desperation, Rebecca wondered if she should go and slam the knocker really hard in the hope that someone in one of the neighbouring houses might hear. Or she could go and knock at *their* door. But then, they might ask questions – neighbours could be nosy. Mr and Mrs Beresford might be the sort of people who kept themselves to themselves; she didn't want to cause any embarrassment. Also, although Rebecca was determined to try and find Ian, it didn't mean that she didn't feel humiliated by it. Suppose the neighbours had heard about Ian's girlfriend in London? They would guess who she was, would realise she'd come chasing after him. No, she thought, retrieving her case and closing the gate behind her. There had to be a better way.

She decided to walk further along the short road and around a bend she could see at the end. A local shop, that was what she needed. Maybe someone there would know something.

It was the right decision, because within minutes she saw a shop on the corner of two roads. She pushed open the door with its advertisements for Bisto and Colman's Mustard, and as the bell tinkled, two women in the queue looked around to stare curiously at her, before carrying on with their conversation. The woman behind the counter, in a green crossover overall, was busy weighing and filling blue bags with dried fruit.

"Looks as if Mrs Bott's baking termorrer," one of the women murmured. "I'll 'ave to as well. Ern goes mad if there's no cake in the 'ouse. I'd like to see 'im try and eke out the rations!"

"Shouldn't be long though, before it all eases up. It's gerring better already in some ways."

Rebecca stared at them, fascinated by their accent. One was a thin, wiry woman, with hennaed hair; the other, her curlers partly covered by a turban, was younger and plumper. Both wore unbuttoned coats beneath which Rebecca could glimpse pinafores. As they carried on chatting about their cleaning routines, she turned and looked around the shop. On the wall next to her hung various cards displaying hair slides in tortoiseshell and pink and blue bows, pocket combs, fine hairnets, sleeping hairnets, pencils, erasers and babies' dummies. Rebecca averted her gaze from the latter, and saw in a narrow passage behind the counter, a small sack of potatoes, flanked by another of carrots, and a smaller one of onions. There was a bacon-slicing machine at one end of the counter, and a glass display case beneath it containing a few meat pies, a block of yellow cheese, a wedge of corned beef and a small tray of eggs. The shop smelt vaguely of fresh bread mixed with polish.

The thin woman moved to take her turn to be served. "Just a packet of Oxydol, please, Maggie."

Rebecca waited impatiently while the other woman

handed over her ration book. "I'll 'ave two slices of bacon while yer've got it on." Then there were six ounces of cheese and half a pound of mixed biscuits to be weighed out, but at last she turned and left.

With the shop now empty, Rebecca moved forward to ask her questions, hoping desperately for answers. Because her logic told her that this shop, within a few minutes' walking distance from her home, would be somewhere Mrs Beresford would regularly use. Ian and possibly his father would buy their cigarettes here. This small woman behind the counter, with her iron-grey perm and tired face could hold the key to the whole mystery. What was her name again? Oh yes, Maggie.

Rebecca put down her case, forced a friendly smile and asked for a quarter of Mint Imperials. As the shopkeeper reached up to a shelf behind her, Rebecca opened the clasp on her purse, found money and sweet coupons and placed them on the counter. She watched as Maggie tipped the tall jar on to the scales, weighed out the correct amount of Mint Imperials, put them in a small white paper bag, flipped it over and expertly twisted the ends. Then, just as Rebecca was wondering how to begin, Maggie gave a curious glance at the suitcase and said, "You're not from round 'ere, are you?"

Relieved at the opening, Rebecca said, "No, I'm from London." She hesitated. "Actually, I've come to visit the Beresfords in Redwood Avenue, but there's no reply. You don't know if they're away or anything, do you? Only I was wondering if it's worth my coming back tomorrow."

Maggie stared in stunned silence at the flame-haired girl standing before her. Then she said slowly, "You mean Mr and Mrs Beresford, and Ian?"

"That's right," Rebecca said. "They live at number fifteen."

Maggie swallowed hard. She could only think – oh my God! She remembered now that Grace Beresford had told her that Ian had got himself a girl in London. This must be her! But surely . . . As Rebecca waited for her to answer, Maggie came out from behind the counter, and swiftly moving to the shop door, did something she'd never done before in her entire working life. Despite the early hour, she turned over the open sign to read "closed", and temporarily shot the bolt.

Rebecca watched in bewilderment, which turned to apprehension as she saw the serious expression on the shopkeeper's face.

Maggie said quietly, "It would be no use you coming back termorrer, duck, there'd still be nobody in." She shook her head in disbelief. "You don't know, do you?"

"Know what?" Rebecca stared at her in confusion. Then, as she saw the concern in the small woman's eyes, she felt her first flicker of fear.

"It was the football match," Maggie said, her voice heavy. "When Stoke City played away at Bolton about three weeks ago. I thought everyone knew about it – it was in all the newspapers. A wall collapsed on the supporters. Dreadful it was, thirty-three people lost their lives." Even now Maggie could hardly believe it had happened.

Rebecca thought frantically. She could recall something about it. But three weeks ago she'd been ill with the flu. She hadn't felt up to taking much interest in anything, let alone reading the newspapers. Then suddenly she remembered that Ian's father had been a huge football fan. "Are you trying to tell me," she said, her hand going to her throat, "that Mr Beresford . . ."

Maggie nodded. "He was killed outright."

She saw the girl's eyes widen with shock, and could only think – you poor kid! Because that was only part of it and Maggie knew she had no choice but to tell her the rest – and it was better to get it over with.

"I'm sorry, love," she said, and now her voice wavered. "I'm afraid Ian was killed as well."

The terrible words hung in the silence between them. Maggie saw the blood drain from the lovely face opposite, saw the girl struggle to speak, and when she did, it was to whisper, "There must be some mistake. Ian didn't like football."

"That's right," Maggie said, "he never bothered with it. Apparently he'd been planning to go down to London for the weekend, but it fell through at the last minute. Only his dad's brother, Colin, lived in Bolton, and as they'd all been under a lot of strain with the old lady being so ill, Jim thought it would be a good idea to meet up with him and watch the game together. A bit of a break, like." Maggie's mouth twisted. "Ian only went with him as a favour, knowing his dad didn't like travelling on his own. The cruel thing is that if they hadn't stood with his brother

85

among the Bolton supporters at the end where it happened, they'd have been all right." Maggie gave a heavy sigh, adding, "Colin was badly injured, he died later in hospital."

But Rebecca was leaning against the counter for support. Ian couldn't be dead! He was young, he was full of life. They were going to be married, were going to spend the rest of their lives together! How could he be dead? Wildly, desperately, she stared at the careworn face before her, then seeing the depth of sorrow and sympathy in Maggie's eyes, knew it was true.

Maggie, however, hadn't yet finished. "I'm ever so sorry, love. And nobody knows when Mrs Beresford will be home. That poor woman – she was so strong, so brave. How she got through that double funeral, I'll never know. But what made her crack was her mother dying the very next day. It was one burial too much. Had a nervous breakdown, she did, and it's not surprising. She's out at St Edwards, at Cheddleton – that's the mental hospital. No one can tell how long she'll be in there – or if she'll ever come out."

As the reality of the heartrending words began to register, Rebecca couldn't speak as her throat closed with horror and despair. She was in a nightmare – this couldn't be happening! Then, with trembling legs she turned to go, and somehow managed to mutter, "Thank you for telling me."

"Hang on a minute," Maggie said. "I think I might have something for you." She went to the small passage where the vegetables were kept, bent

86

down and a few seconds later returned with a news-paper. "Yes, I thought there'd be one there. People save their old papers for me – they're useful for wrapping the firelighters. Here, take it with you." Then she withdrew the bolt, opened the door and stood aside. "I'm so sorry, love," she said again. She stood and watched as Rebecca, the newspaper tucked under her arm, made her way unsteadily along the narrow pavement. She saw her stop and fumble in her pocket for a handkerchief, and then with slumped shoulders, seconds later disappear round the bend.

It was the saddest sight Maggie had ever seen in her life.

9

Maggie repeated the sentiment later that evening. "The saddest sight I ever saw in my life," she told her sister, as they sat in their comfy chairs each side of the fireplace. "White as a ghost she was. Crushed, that's the only word for it. She was such a nice-looking girl too, with lovely red hair."

"You might have brought her through for a cup of tea, at least," Enid's narrow face was flushed with indignation. "A shock like that! How do you know she was all right? I'm surprised at you, our Maggie."

"I probably would have done, if you'd been in." Maggie looked shamefaced; she'd thought the same thing herself, only too late. "But to be honest, I felt that wrung out after I'd told her, I wasn't thinking straight. And she just seemed as if she wanted to get away, be on her own, like."

"I wonder why Mrs Beresford didn't let her know?"

Maggie shrugged. "Who knows? Maybe she was in such a state, she never thought about it. Or perhaps she didn't know how to get in touch."

Enid sat with her knitting idle on her lap. A devout Methodist, it was rare that she swore, but now she said, "It's a bloody catastrophe, that's what it is, the whole thing. And they were such a well-respected family, as well. As for poor Mrs Beresford, well if this is her reward for working hard all her life, it makes you think, Maggie, it really does."

Maggie sat in silence for a few minutes, watching the flames of the coal fire in the grate, then said, "I wonder whether she's gone back to London. One thing's for sure, there's nothing round here for her, not any more."

After leaving the shop, Rebecca had managed to walk back along Redwood Avenue, but by the time she reached the Beresfords' empty house, her legs were trembling so much that she stopped to lean weakly against the gate. The simple wooden gate she knew Ian must have opened so many times, both as a small boy, and as a young man with all his life before him. Hot, hopeless tears began to rain down her face, and as she felt the sobs rising in her throat, desperation to find somewhere private, gave her the strength to move away, to walk more quickly. There was only one place she could go, because there was no way she could face the prospect of a public train journey. Retracing her steps yet again, almost stumbling in shock, she managed, oblivious of the curious stares of passers-by, to reach the hotel.

The same man came to the reception desk, and looked with alarm at the distraught ashen-faced girl, as she said in a strangled voice, "A single room please, just for tonight."

Silently, he pushed the hotel register towards her,

and with a shaking hand, she wrote, "*R. Lawson, The Unicorn, Stepney, London.*"

"Are you all right, love?" Dennis Salt didn't often have a young lady to stay, and certainly not a looker like this one. But something had happened since she came in before, and as sure as hell there'd be tears on the pillow that night – he'd put money on it.

When Rebecca nodded, he said, "And will you be wanting dinner?"

Rebecca didn't feel as if she could ever eat again, but knew she'd feel even worse if she didn't have something. "Could I possibly just have a bowl of soup in my room?"

He hesitated. "Well, we don't usually do room service . . ." but Dennis recognised trouble when he saw it, and this girl looked as if she'd had a basinful. "All right, then. I'll bring it up meself."

"Could you just leave it outside the door?"

"Of course." As she picked up the key, he came round to the front of the desk. "Here, give me your case."

Wearily, Rebecca followed him up a narrow staircase and along a small corridor to a room at the end. "Bathroom's opposite," he said, and unlocking the door, went into the bedroom, and put down the case. Then Dennis surprised himself by saying, "How would you like a nice cuppa?"

"Thank you. Could I just have a glass of water, and . . ."

"Leave it outside? Of course." He must be getting soft, he thought wryly, as he padded back down the stairs.

In the small cheerless room, Rebecca unwound her scarf and with shaking fingers began to fumble awkwardly with the buttons on her coat. Once it was undone, she let it fall limply to the floor. Next came her shoes, and then she collapsed on to the single bed, to curl up in a tight ball, able at last to cry as she'd never cried before, with deep racking sobs, and whimpers of pain. Ian was dead! She'd never see him again, never hear his voice, his laughter; never be held in his arms. The life she'd hoped for, the life that had promised so much love, so much happiness – had been torn away. And she wept too for Ian, who had been too young to die. He'd had so much to offer. He'd have been a wonderful teacher, she knew he would. Just as he would have been a wonderful husband and father.

And with that last word, the realisation hit her like a sledgehammer. Ian's death didn't change the fact that she was pregnant – the only difference was that her baby would be a bastard, would always bear the stigma of being illegitimate. Dimly she heard a tap at the door, and after a few minutes, her eyes swollen with tears, she went over to open it. A tray was on the floor, and on it was a glass of water, and two malted milk biscuits. Rebecca picked it up and put it by the side of the bed, then wearily bent down to retrieve her crumpled coat and hung it in the shabby wardrobe. She turned, and seeing the folded newspaper on the linoleum, took it back to the bed, propped a pillow against the wooden headboard, and, feeling unutterably tired, managed to eat the biscuits and sipped at the water. Then she forced herself to look at the front page. The heading was stark: THE BOLTON CROWD DISASTER.

Her eyes blurring with tears, Rebecca struggled to read it. Minutes later, she knew that on the ninth of March, 1946, at Bolton Wanderers' ground at Burnden Park, an estimated 85,000 spectators poured into the ground, although the official attendance number was given as 65,419. Many were drawn by the presence of Stoke City star, Stanley Matthews, with fans even climbing over the walls once the turnstiles were closed. Crush barriers had collapsed and people were smothered, with 33 killed and 520 injured. Surprisingly, although the game was delayed for a time, it was allowed to resume, and it wasn't until the players reached the dressing-room after the final whistle that they were told of the extent of the tragedy. Some of them, the article reported, broke down in tears.

And so again did Rebecca. She tried in vain to close her mind to the appalling images of fear and chaos. Ian must have been terrified, must have realised the danger he was in. And within her was the sour knowledge that if she hadn't had the flu, hadn't stopped Ian from coming to London, then on that fateful Saturday he would have been safe with her. His father would still be alive, his mother well and living in her own home, and they would all be making wedding plans. Just that one small decision – could people's lives really be so insignificant that they hung on such a slender thread?

She remembered the priest on the train, recalled his words, "You will always find me at St Mary's."

Not me – she shook her head slowly, grimly. I won't find you anywhere, Father. Her faith, never very strong, had been badly shaken when her parents were killed and her home destroyed. But now, Rebecca finally came to a decision. She didn't believe in God – not any more.

The following morning, frozen in misery, Rebecca sat huddled in the corner of a crowded railway carriage. Emotionally exhausted, she stared listlessly out of the rain-spotted window. She was beyond thinking; she was hollowed-out, her mind blurred after hours of tossing and turning with grief and anxiety. She also felt bitterly hurt that she hadn't been told of Ian's death. It was as though she, the girl he planned to marry, was of no importance. Or had his mother been in such a state of shock that she hadn't thought of it? Oh well, she thought miserably, I don't suppose I'll ever know. But eventually the rhythm of the wheels lulled her into an uneasy doze, and she stirred only when the train reached Euston. Once the other passengers had collected their belongings and left, she reached up for her suitcase, and stepped down on to the platform. Feeling weak and with a dull headache – she'd only managed one slice of toast for breakfast – she wondered whether to go into the station café, but was too desperate to get home. The crowded Underground, and the jolting of the Tube journey drained her even more, but then at last she was on familiar ground, with the welcome sign of the Unicorn only yards away. On legs that suddenly began to tremble, she went through the gate, past the stacked crates of empties, and pushed open the back door.

Sal, sitting with her feet up on the leather pouffe, reading the *People*, glanced up quickly as she heard the back gate close. "Ron, I think she's back!"

Rebecca came slowly through the small passage that led to the sitting-room. While Ron exclaimed, "Flaming Nora!" Sal jumped up, and shocked by the wretched appearance of her niece, put a protective arm around her shoulders, ushering her to an armchair. "Sit down, girl. Whatever's wrong?"

"He's dead, Sal!" Rebecca whispered. "Ian's dead."

Stunned, they could only stare at her in bewildered silence, until struggling against tears, she whispered, "There's a newspaper in my case." With a perplexed glance at Sal, Ron got up and a few minutes later came back already scanning the article. Silently, his face grim, he passed the newspaper into Sal's anxiously outstretched hand. Seconds later, she looked up in horror to stare first at her husband, and then at the white-faced girl before her. "You mean . . .?" Rebecca nodded.

Ron said heavily, "I read about this at the time, but never connected it with Ian. He always told me he wasn't interested in football!"

"He went with his dad – as a favour. They were *both killed*." Rebecca's voice rose with hysteria.

Sal drew a sharp intake of breath. With increasing concern she looked at the drooping figure in the chair before her. "Get her a drop of brandy, Ron."

"No," Rebecca shook her head. "I don't want any brandy." Her voice broke – the very word conjured memories of Ian, of his tenderness, of their passion on that Friday night.

"I'll make you a cup of tea, then." And Sal had gone to the kitchen before Rebecca could protest. Ron stood about awkwardly for a moment, then followed his wife. "This is a bugger, and no mistake!"

"I can't believe it. Out of the blue, like that!" Sal willed the kettle to boil more quickly, as she spooned tea into the pot. "Do you want a cup?"

"I think we'd both better 'ave one." Ron leaned against the sink, his beefy arms folded across his chest. "Bloody hell, Sal! She hasn't had much luck, has she?"

"That's an understatement! She looks like a corpse, herself," Sal said. "Here, go and ask if she's had something to eat."

Ron returned promptly. "Not since a piece of toast this morning." Sal left the tea to brew and went into the sitting-room. "What do you fancy, darlin'? I fetched the cheese ration yesterday – I could grill you some on toast – it won't take long."

"Thanks, Sal." And a few minutes later, when Ron handed Rebecca a cup of tea, to her relief she discovered that her aversion had disappeared. Sustained by two slices of toasted cheese, she haltingly began to try and describe what had happened during the past twenty-four hours.

Ron and Sal listened to the whole sorry tale, and Sal, who prided herself on being non-emotional, felt tears prick at her eyelids at the image of Rebecca knocking in vain on the door of Ian's home, and then discovering from a stranger such terrible news. "You should have come back here straight away," she said, indignant at the thought of Rebecca being alone with her grief in a strange hotel room.

"I couldn't face the journey."

Looking at Rebecca's wan face, Sal could well believe it. She glanced at Ron, who was now reading the newspaper article in depth. She didn't know what to say to the girl, but it was no use relying on her husband to say anything helpful, he was useless at talking about emotions. And then she thought of Mrs Beresford and her heart went out to her. No woman deserved to lose her husband, son and mother in a matter of days. And what would they do to her in this mental hospital? That's what they were calling them these days, but they were still the old asylums – and everyone knew what dreadful places they were. I dunno, Sal thought sadly, you can build up your whole life and have it knocked down – just like that.

Rebecca sat staring down at her hands. Would this terrible day never end? Now she had another mountain to face – because she was going to have to tell her aunt and uncle about her pregnancy. And she may as well get it over with. She was terrified of their reaction, was dreading seeing the look of horror on Sal's face, and fearful of Ron's anger. She looked up at them in despair and gathered up her courage.

"Sal—"

But Sal interrupted her, getting up briskly and saying, "No more talking! I'm going to fill a hot-water bottle, and then it's off to bed with you, girl." Rebecca hadn't the strength to argue. She felt so weak that she thought she would only just make it up the stairs. It was a huge effort even to get undressed, but eventually she was able to climb into her familiar bed, and at last, with the heavy stone water bottle warming her feet, she drifted into the welcome oblivion of sleep.

It was three days before Rebecca felt up to facing the public bar, but then, knowing that her absence placed an extra burden on Ron and Sal, she forced herself to make the effort. At first there were sympathetic glances, embarrassed eyes that avoided her gaze, and a few awkward mutterings of condolence. Although she hadn't been aware of it, the manner of Ian's death had been much debated since Ron had told them the news. "Yer just go out of the 'ouse to go to a flaming football match, and that 'appens," one man, an ardent supporter of West Ham, said soulfully. "It just shows, yer never know when yer turn will come."

"You can't believe it can yer, that they'd play on after something like that?" Ron said. "But from what I read, it was the police who wanted the game to go on. Said it was safer than trying to tell the crowd that people had been crushed to death."

"Yeah, that could have made people panic, I suppose." The West Ham supporter stared bleakly into his beer. "It don't 'arf make you think."

"Did Stoke win?" another man asked.

"Nah. It was a goal-less draw. Mind you, Bolton had won the first leg of the tie, so they were the ones who went through."

"As if it flamin' matters!" Ruby, the pub cleaner, had just finished her morning stint and was indulging in her regular glass of stout before going home. She glared at them, her round face crimson with indignation. "If that isn't typical of you bloody blokes. There's poor Rebecca mourning her young man, and you stand there blathering on about football! Yer make me sick!"

"Aw, shut it, Ruby," the West Ham supporter snapped. He turned to Ron.

"Wimmin shouldn't be allowed in the public bar!"

"And we all know where you can stick *your* opinion!" Ruby snapped, flouncing off into a corner.

Ron just shrugged. "It's a free country, Ted."

"Yeah, well some of us come in 'ere to get away from 'em."

But within a week talk had drifted to other topics. Battered by air raids, over the last six years the East Enders had become hardened to the tragic and needless deaths of young and old. Life had to go on – it was the only way to cope. And so Rebecca quietly did her job, and if her smiles were rare, then that was understood and not commented on. Somehow she managed to portray a semblance of normality during the long days, but only she knew how different it was in the dark hours of the night. And, as each day passed, she constantly struggled to find the courage to tell her aunt of her condition. Not only was she dreading her shameful confession; she was also fearful. Sal was uncompromising in her moral views. She was disdainful of religion – "bleeding hypocrites, the lot of 'em" – and despised what she called "cheap sluts". Despite her slightly brassy appearance, the customers knew they could only go so far with their jokes in the bar.

But Rebecca agonised that the longer she remained silent, the more likely it was that Sal would find out for herself. Luckily, although she often felt nauseous she hadn't suffered from morning sickness. But what if she began to "show" early? What if someone guessed? Some of the older women boasted they could tell if a girl was pregnant before she knew herself. "It's in the face," they'd say knowingly, "a sort of pinched look around the nostrils." Anxiously, Rebecca would study her own face in the mirror, but as she looked pale and drawn from grief and lack of sleep, it was impossible to see any change. The only certainty in her life was that she'd already missed two periods, and her third was two days late.

When, on the first Sunday after Rebecca's return from Stoke, Gloria came round for her usual visit, it was obvious that she'd already heard of Rebecca's tragedy.

"Bad news travels fast," Sal said with sarcasm, noting the girl's black cardigan, which was much too big for her. "That's Bessie's isn't it?"

Gloria nodded solemnly. "Mum said I ought to wear black as a mark of respect. I'm ever so sorry," she said, settling down on the settee and gazing with sympathy at Rebecca. "It must have been awful for you."

"It was," Rebecca said shortly. "Do you want a cuppa?"

"Don't mind if I do."

Rebecca escaped into the small kitchen. She just wasn't in the mood for socialising. Her mind was too unsettled, too full of trepidation – because just minutes before, Ron had announced that he planned to have Tuesday night off to go to Walthamstow dog track. "I'll stop at Sid's overnight, Sal. It'll give us a chance for a good natter."

"More like a good binge!" Sal almost snapped, but wisely held her tongue. She'd rather he got drunk somewhere else than at home. He never became nasty-tempered or anything – just sloppy and romantic – or so he thought! But he nearly always got "brewer's droop", as he would sheepishly call it, and that caused a right palaver!

So now, as Rebecca moved automatically around the kitchen, her brain was feverish with the certainty that on Tuesday night she and Sal would be alone. Once the pub was securely locked up, and they had their usual cocoa, then that *had* to be the moment. Already she felt sick with nerves at the prospect. But she knew that she had no choice. Her aunt was going to have to be told that her unmarried, eighteen-year-old niece was three months pregnant.

"It's a good job Ron doesn't do this often," Sal grumbled on Tuesday night. "I don't know about you, but I could do with putting my feet up."

"So could I." Rebecca, who had spent all night dreading this moment, hung the tea towels over the beer pumps. "I'll go and make the cocoa, shall I?"

"That's a good girl."

Once in the kitchen, Rebecca took two beakers out of the cupboard, and with unsteady hands mixed cocoa, sugar and milk into a paste. Minutes later, her stomach churning, she took the steaming drinks into the sitting-room. Sal was resting her head on the back of an armchair, and Rebecca waited until her aunt had nearly finished her cocoa. Then knowing she could no longer put off the moment, she felt sick with nerves.

Quietly, she said, "Sal . . ."

"Mmm . . ." Sal was gazing into the embers of the dying fire.

"I've got something to tell you."

"What's that, then?" But Rebecca was floundering, the words sticking in her throat. "Spit it out, girl."

"I'm pregnant."

The two fateful words hung in the air between them. Sal slowly raised her head and stared speechlessly at her niece.

Rebecca said in a shaky voice, "It was when you and Ron were away at the funeral. Ian turned up early on the Friday night. And once he was here, it seemed daft to send him away." Her voice broke. "It was purely by accident, Sal. None of it was planned. I know we should have told you, but—"

"From the bombshell you've just dropped, it's quite obvious why you didn't!" Sal's tone was harsh. She leaned forward. "How far gone are you?"

"Three months."

"I want to know, *exactly!*" Sal's voice was so sharp that Rebecca flinched.

"I've missed two periods, and now I'm overdue with my third."

Sal's lips tightened. "Right! Come on, upstairs!" Already on her feet, Sal was going to the sideboard where she opened a cupboard and took out a full bottle of gin.

"What—?"

"Don't argue, just do as you're told!" Roughly, Sal grabbed Rebecca's arm, and began to hustle her out of the room and up the steep stairs. "Now's our only chance – while Ron's out of the way!" She pushed Rebecca into the small, draughty bathroom, drew the curtain over the frosted window, and turned the hot-water tap full on.

"Sal? What are you doing?" Rebecca, who, for the past week had lived in fear of recriminations, shouting, even tears, was hovering, totally bewildered.

Sal turned to face her. "A hot bath and a good dose of gin can sometimes shift something that shouldn't be there, if you know what I mean. That's why they call it 'Mother's Ruin'. My word, you've led a sheltered life in that Welsh valley, my girl, if you didn't know that!"

Rebecca, horrified, backed away. "I'm not sure . . ."

"Look, it's nature's way. It'll only work if it's meant to." Sal's expression hardened. "I bet we're too bleedin' late! You should have told me before!"

"But—"

"You're in no position to argue! Go on, get your clothes off." Sal began to unscrew the top off the gin bottle. "No need to bother with a glass. And tip it down, do you hear? Never mind how you'll feel termorrer, that's nothing to what your life will be like if it doesn't work!"

Almost in a daze, Rebecca undid her suspenders and took off her shoes and stockings, kicking them to a corner of the room. "It brings on a late period, is that it?"

"Something like that." Sal was now running the cold tap, and testing the temperature of the water.

"I'm sorry, Sal," Rebecca said, almost in tears. "I didn't mean to let you down—"

"Yer should have thought of that at the time!" Sal snapped. She turned off the cold-water tap. "There, that should do it! Just get yerself in and keep the water as hot as you can bear. And try and drink yourself stupid. No messing about, mind! When I come back, I'll expect to see that bottle at least half-empty." She turned at the door. "Get on

103

with it, girl, time's running out. That's if it hasn't already!"

By now the small room was filling with steam, and as condensation began to trickle down the cream painted walls, Rebecca took off the rest of her clothes and put them outside on the landing. Then she closed the door and gingerly tested the water's temperature. It was hot, very hot, but she forced herself to climb in, lifting first one foot and then the other, before eventually managing to sit in the almost unbearable heat. The bottle of gin was on the floor, and leaning over she hesitantly reached down for it. If drinking this stuff could really "bring her on", then why not? Raising the bottle to her lips Rebecca took a large mouthful, only to gag and splutter as the dry sour spirit hit the back of her throat. She shuddered with distaste, and it was several minutes before she could face trying again. Recalling Sal's order, "*don't mess about*", she gritted her teeth and tipped up the bottle, almost choking as she forced down the neat gin. Lifting up her hair, she leaned back against the hard enamel bath, and sank further into the hot water, clutching the bottle between her breasts, and gazing with despair at her reddening body. It was this body, with its longings, its needs, that was the cause of all her heartbreak.

And yet, Rebecca was glad, yes she was, she thought fiercely, glad that she and Ian had loved each other so completely on that Saturday night. Nobody could ever take that wonderful experience away from her. Not like they'd taken Ian away. She missed him so much. Tears of grief and self-pity began to trickle down her cheeks – she still couldn't believe she'd never see him again. Wallowing in misery, Rebecca stared up at the ceiling through blurring eyes, and it was several minutes later before she took another swig from the bottle; grimacing and shuddering she forced the spirit down her throat. Ian, she thought with despair, was the third person she'd loved who'd been taken away from her. And that was before she was nineteen. Perhaps she was jinxed. Perhaps she'd been the one to bring bad luck to Ian. Perhaps if he'd never met her, he'd still be here.

The future, bleak and uncertain, stretched before her, one where she knew she could end up not only without a job, but homeless. She wouldn't be the first unmarried pregnant girl to be disowned by her family. And the desperate hope of a solution to her nightmare gave her the courage to tip the bottle again, and somehow swallowing the gin seemed easier this time. Miserably, she topped up the hot water until the heat was almost unbearable once more, then lifted the bottle and drank again. And now rivulets of perspiration were running down her face, mixing with her salty tears, and she lifted the bottle again, and later once more, now spilling some of the gin, not caring that it slopped down her chin and into the water. She tried to focus on the level in the bottle, and with desperation she took one last slurp, and leaning over, shakily tried to stand the bottle upright on the floor. And then the dizziness hit her, and Rebecca could only collapse back into the bath, while water slopped on to the floor, and above her, the ceiling dipped and swayed.

Sal was sitting hunched before the dying fire, a cigarette in one hand, and a cherry brandy in the other. She couldn't bear to think what would happen if tonight's shenanigans didn't work. Their lives would be a bloody nightmare! And she certainly couldn't predict how Ron would react! Still reeling from Rebecca's announcement, Sal was furious. She'd never have thought the girl would let them down like this. And the deceit! Look at the way those two had covered up the following day! After all she and Ron had done for her, as well. It would bring shame on them, this would, and it wouldn't reflect well on the Unicorn, either!

Anxiously, Sal stubbed out her cigarette, drained her glass, and banked down the fire. As the Westminster clock on the mantelpiece chimed twelve, she went upstairs to hammer on the bathroom door. "Rebecca? Can you manage on yer own? Do you want me to come in?"

Vaguely hearing the noise, Rebecca, half-comatose, stretched out her hand to clutch the side of the bath. She tried to haul herself out, but slipped and fell back. Feebly, she tried again, and then Sal was there, putting her hands underneath Rebecca's armpits, lifting her up and dragging her limp body out of the water. Rebecca tried to stand but the floor wouldn't keep still, and as her legs buckled, Sal struggled to hold her upright and began to dry her roughly with a towel. "I've put a bottle in your bed," she muttered, "and I've brought your night-dress. Come on, hold up your arms."

Weakly, Rebecca did as she was told, and then

with Sal's arm supporting her, leaned against her aunt as they staggered out on to the landing and into the small single bedroom. Sal had put a bucket at the side of the bed, and was thankful she had, as already Rebecca was bending and retching, and then the bile and vomit was coming up, again and again. When Rebecca at last straightened up to crumple on to the bed, Sal, now fighting her own nausea, hurriedly picked up the bucket and shoved it outside the door. She tucked the bedclothes around her niece, opened a window slightly against the fetid smell, and pushed the glass of water she'd previously brought up nearer to the bed. Looking at the wan girl lying on the pillows, Sal said, "There's nothing more I can do for you. It'll be a rough night, but you'll just have to get through it!"

Rebecca moaned, her eyes closed, and with one last glance Sal left the room, leaving the door slightly ajar. After emptying the revolting mess, she rinsed the bucket, mopped the bathroom floor, and then crossed the landing to her own bedroom. Tired and fraught, almost shivering with fatigue, she got into the double bed, but it was a long time before she could get to sleep. Ever since the news of Ian's death, Sal had been feeling uncomfortable, even guilty about the way she'd criticised him. Well, now she knew the truth. Ian Beresford, for all his education, had been no better than the rest of 'em. He'd abused their hospitality – that's what he'd done – and taken advantage of that naïve kid. Nothing changed, Sal thought with bitterness, as she punched the flock pillow to find a soft place. It's us women who pay the price; always was and always will be.

The following morning, Rebecca opened her eyes, only to shut them in agony against the daylight streaming through the thin unlined curtains. Her tongue felt coated, her mouth tasted foul, and as she lifted her head from the pillow, the movement brought with it intolerable pain. At least she was alive! There had been times during the night when she'd felt so dreadful, she'd thought she was dying. Suddenly desperate for the lavatory, Rebecca forced herself to sit up, and wincing at the pain in her head struggled to sit on the side of the bed. Then she made her way shakily along the landing.

Sal, who had checked on her niece earlier, heard the cistern flush and hurried upstairs to Rebecca's room, to find her back in bed and huddled beneath the bedclothes. "Gawd, you look terrible!"

"I feel it." Rebecca whispered.

Sal glanced at the empty glass. "Water first, then dry toast," she said. "And stay where you are. I don't suppose . . . ?" She jerked her head in the direction of the lavatory.

Rebecca feebly shook her head then clutched it, wishing she hadn't. And for the next few hours, she just existed in a vacuum, feeling utterly wretched, until Sal came up with a bowl of soup. "Try and get this down yer. Then after that, I want you up and moving about. You needn't come into the bar, but you're to keep going up and down these stairs. All right?"

"I'll try. Is Ron back?"

"He is, and he's got a hell of a hangover!" Sal's lips tightened. "Anyway, I told him you'd got a gyppy tummy."

"Thanks." Rebecca felt ghastly; she had never felt so ill in her entire life. And that was how she remained throughout the rest of the long miserable day. Still too ill to sleep properly, she woke up the next morning with a pasty face and dark circles under her eyes, and only she knew the effort it took to resume her work in the bar. It was not until the following morning that she fully recovered. And as the long, anxious hours and days passed, she came to dread the searching question in Sal's eyes, the strain in her face.

Rebecca could only woefully shake her head. The ordeal, the pain, the sickness, had achieved nothing.

"You should have done it weeks ago! It was too bleedin' late, like I said." Sal hissed, taking her opportunity while Ron was out of the way.

"I was expecting to get married, remember?" Rebecca turned her head, not wanting Sal to see how easily tears still sprung to her eyes.

But Sal was in no mood for sympathy. "There's only one thing for it!" She leaned forward and lowered her voice. "Old Ma Burton in Victoria Street. She's done the trick for one or two around 'ere, especially during the war."

Rebecca froze. Sal couldn't mean one of those sordid back-street abortions? Rebecca might not have known about the gin, but even she had heard of women nearly dying through such things. Of infected instruments and clumsy bungling that often meant they could never have children again! In any case, it was against the law! Filled with horror, she tried to imagine some strange old crone doing unspeakable things to her body. It was barbaric! And suddenly, for the very first time, Rebecca felt a surge of protectiveness towards her unborn baby. This wasn't just about herself; she was carrying Ian's child within her. And now it was with overwhelming shame that she realised that even before Ian's death, all she'd thought about was her own predicament. How could she have been so blind, so selfish?

"Oh no!" She stood up and backed away, holding up her hands as though to ward off evil. "No way!"

But Sal was adamant. "At least you could try. Although I think you might be too 'far gone' anyway. And I've heard she's clean, at least!"

"Never!" Rebecca's face was flushed with anger and determination.

"Never, never, never! I am *not* going to get rid of my baby! I'm not going to have some strange woman killing Ian's child!"

Sal stared at her in stupefaction. "But the other night, with the gin—"

"That was different! Don't ask me why, but it was. I was just trying to bring on my period then, at least that's how it seemed. But this . . . oh, no, Sal. This is *wrong*." Rebecca might have tried to solve her problem with a hot bath and gin, but it wasn't the same as having her baby ripped out of her womb. Ian's child didn't deserve that.

Sal opened her mouth to retort, but just then,

Ron came in from seeing to the draymen. "Cripes, it's nippy out there. Talk about spring! I could murder a cuppa char, Sal."

"I'll get it," Rebecca said hurriedly, glad to escape into the kitchen, away from the disbelief and agitation in her aunt's eyes. Her mind was spinning with the emotions of the past few moments, but when she found her hands beginning to tremble as she filled the kettle, Rebecca knew it was because she had to face another trauma. Staring in desperation at the flaking whitewash on the wall, she knew there was now no alternative. Someone was going to have to tell Ron, and Rebecca was praying that she wouldn't have to be the one to do it.

After Ron's interruption, Sal went upstairs, pleading a headache. She desperately needed privacy – to be away from Rebecca's strained, anxious face, and eyes that were accusing yet defensive. Already Sal was bitterly ashamed that she'd ever suggested a risky abortion. She'd panicked, that's what she'd done. She could be a stupid mare, at times! And yet, as she lay in dejection on top of the cerise eiderdown, Sal could only wonder whether Rebecca knew how cruel people could be where bastards were concerned. Had she realised that her kid would carry that stigma all its life? But, uncomfortably, Sal knew that her main reaction had been a purely selfish one. All she'd thought about was the shame of it all! How it would reflect on her and Ron. How the whispering would start, the nudges, the knowing looks. And as for Rebecca, she couldn't have any idea of how this would affect the rest of her life.

Although Sal had to admit that the girl had guts. Even a fairly hardened drinker like herself would cringe at half a bottle of neat gin. And she knew how to stand up for herself, as well. The way she'd stood there, green eyes blazing, defending her baby! She'd got her temper from Duggie, of course, and

Sal thought wistfully of her brother. He might have been bad-tempered in drink, but she'd never forget how he'd been her champion when they were kids. Nobody could bully Sal when her brother was around. And then there was Milly. A gentler soul never lived. She'd been far too good for their Duggie – why she even read books! But like so many others, she'd fallen for his handsome face. And Milly had loved him despite it all, and had been devoted to Rebecca. This baby would be their grandchild. Sal hated herself for what she'd said to her niece, what she'd suggested. Rebecca was right – the gin thing *was* different. Sal's lips twisted. That's another thing you've got to live with, she thought, crossing her arms over her ample breasts. And hope Rebecca forgives you.

But did she forgive Rebecca? It was too soon to know. The girl had let them both down and herself. But nobody could deny that she'd had the roughest of deals. For Ian to be killed like that . . . if there *was* a God up there, he had a bloomin' strange way of going about things!

But now, she had to decide how to tell Ron. Would it be better when he was on his own, or when Rebecca was in the room? With Ron, there was no way of knowing. Sal might have been married to him for donkey's years, but even she couldn't predict how he'd react to this! Nor what he'd decide to do. Because Sal knew that her husband would be the one making the final decision. After all, it was his name above the door of the pub, and Ron had always been a strong believer in a man being the head of his household. Sal had never gone against him before – at least not openly – but if he decided to disown that girl downstairs . . .

It was with trepidation that Sal glanced at her watch. After closing, she decided, that'll be the best time.

That evening, the atmosphere between Sal and Rebecca was tense as they worked together in the bar. Even Ron, not the most sensitive of men, noticed. "What's up?" he muttered to Sal.

"Tell you later!" She turned away, flashing a brittle smile as she took an order for a round of drinks.

Rebecca, too, was busy. There was a darts match on, with a visiting team, and one or two were more than interested in flirting. "Hello, beautiful," bantered one man with a cheeky grin, "what time do you get off then?"

"Too late for you!" Automatically, she bandied repartee, while beneath her bright voice, her stomach churned with nerves. After closing time, she thought, that's when it'll happen. I can tell from Ron's face that he's guessed something's wrong. He'll never let it rest until tomorrow.

"Never mind him, sweetheart!" Another darts player leaned over the bar, wiping the beer off his moustache. "How about the pictures? Rebecca, isn't it?" He turned to the others and winked. "I wonder if what they say about redheads is right? If yer know what I mean?"

"Shut yer mouth, and 'ave a bit of respect!" Ron stood belligerently behind Rebecca, and once she'd moved out of the way, muttered, "The girl's still mourning her boyfriend, for heaven's sake!"

"Sorry, mate, I didn't know." Shamefaced, the drinker moved away back to his team at the darts board, and Rebecca heard one whisper, "*He was one of them killed at that football match up in Bolton.*"

Meanwhile, Sal played the part she always did, lending a sympathetic ear to maudlin customers, quipping with others, while all the time her eyes kept flicking to the clock on the wall.

"The takings are up tonight!" Ron went to the sideboard to fetch his nightcap. Cocoa was all right for the women; he liked a tot of whisky before going to bed. Tired, he slumped into an armchair.

"Good," Sal said, but her tone was flat and he glanced sharply first at her, and then at Rebecca, who was sitting white-faced on the sofa, mug in hand.

"All right, you two. What's going on?"

Sal, her face set in hard lines, glanced at Rebecca. "Shall I tell him, or will you?"

Ron's eyes narrowed. There was a short silence, then Rebecca said, "I'm pregnant, Uncle Ron."

Ron's heavy jaw dropped open. He swung round to face Sal. "She's what?"

"Pregnant! Up the duff, whatever you want to call it!"

Ron could only stare in stupefaction at his niece. "But when—"

"I'm three and a half months." Rebecca's hands twisted nervously around her empty mug.

"Remember when we went to Gert's funeral?"

Sal said. "Apparently Ian turned up late on the Friday night and stayed over!"

"It wasn't planned, it just happened," Rebecca told him, her voice beginning to tremble. "He'd decided to come down early to give us more time together. I didn't know – honestly I didn't. And he had no idea you would both be away. I said to Sal, it seemed daft not to let him stay."

"Staying isn't all he did, is it?" Rage swept over Ron. This bloke had sat at their table, taken their friendship, and then he'd gone and . . . "He never said a bleedin' word when we got back! And now we know why! The dirty devil!"

"It wasn't like that," Rebecca protested, shocked and horrified by the slur. "We were in love, we were going to get married!"

"Then you should have waited until he'd put the ring on yer finger!" Ron was now shouting, the veins bulging in his thick neck. "You stupid little cow! I thought you'd got more self-respect!"

Deeply humiliated, Rebecca stammered, "There was nothing wrong with what we did. If Ian hadn't died . . ."

"Nothing wrong? Nothing bleedin' wrong?" Ron turned in fury to Sal. "Flamin' Nora, where did she get such daft ideas?" But Sal decided it was wiser to remain silent, and just shrugged.

"I didn't mean it like that," protested Rebecca. "I don't mean in a general way . . ."

"Oh, it was different for you and him, was it?"

The angry sarcasm cut into her, but Rebecca was defiant. "Yes, it was!"

"And what makes you think he'd have married you?" Ron's voice was scornful.

"Because I know him!" Rebecca turned her head away, "Or rather, knew him!"

Silence fell in the room, and with a curse, Ron turned away, went to the sideboard and poured another whisky. Then, glass in hand, he stood and glared down at his niece. "All right," he said. "So where do you go from here? Perhaps you'd be kind enough to tell us!"

"I'm not having any back-street abortion!"

"Nobody's suggested that!" Ron gazed at the flame-haired girl, her face full of distress. This was a blinder, and no mistake. He shot a sharp glance at Sal, suddenly aware of her uncharacteristic silence. "And how long have *you* known?"

"She told me that night you stayed over at Sid's. We tried the gin and bath thing, waiting to see if that worked, but no luck – she's too far gone."

Ron sat heavily in an armchair. He just couldn't believe that Rebecca had been so stupid. She'd fallen into the oldest trap there was. That bloody Northerner, he thought grimly. If I'd had the chance to get my hands on him, I'd have half killed him meself! He looked across at Rebecca. "Yer've let us down, girl, and yerself as well."

Rebecca felt a sob rise in her throat. Ian should have been here with her, she shouldn't have had to face this on her own. By now, she would probably have been with him, living up in the Potteries. They would have started a new life together, have been looking forward to the baby coming. She turned her head away, trying to control threatening tears. Ron drained the rest of his whisky, and stared morosely into the glowing coals of the fire. His shoulders slumped as he thought of the next few months. An eighteen-year-old girl, living under her uncle's roof, and pregnant? He wasn't even a blood relation! A few nasty tongues would try and make something of that!

"What about those people in Wales?" he said abruptly. "Would they take you in?"

Sal made to interrupt, but Rebecca, thinking of the cold formal household, of the endless services in the local chapel, was already shaking her head. No, it would be no use looking for support there. And after all, she thought, how could I expect it? I was only an evacuee forced on them.

"Not a chance!" She looked down in misery. It was hateful, being dependent on other people like this. If only her mother had still been alive, she would have stood by her, Rebecca just knew she would. Then suddenly horrified, she realised the significance of her uncle's question. Could it mean that Ron wasn't prepared to let her stay on at the Unicorn?

For one long minute, Ron, his expression unreadable, gazed into Rebecca's anxious eyes. He wasn't daft; he knew what she wanted to know, what was on her mind. But he was in no mood to make any decisions tonight. The girl would have to sweat for a bit. It had been a bloody shock this had, and coming after a hard day, he'd need some time to deal with it. "I'm off ter bed," he muttered. "Are yer coming, Sal?"

At his tone Sal got up, put the fireguard in place

and with one despairing glance at her niece, she followed him.

Shaken, Rebecca collected the two mugs and Ron's glass, and taking them into the kitchen, washed and dried them, then she switched off the lights and, unutterably tired, went to bed. But sleep was impossible. Tossing and turning in anxiety, Rebecca eventually curled up into a ball, remembering the night she and Ian had slept in that same bed, drowsily content, wrapped in each other's arms, full of plans for the future. Now that future had been cruelly snatched away from them, and she was only too aware that her fate, and that of her unborn baby, was dependent on one man. And what he would decide, she found it impossible to guess.

In the adjacent bedroom, Sal lay quietly beside her already snoring husband. Any hopes she'd had of talking about Rebecca's future once they were on their own, had evaporated as soon as she saw Ron's clenched jaw, and the rigid set of his shoulders. But Sal was finding it impossible to sleep; her mind was racing too much. God alone knew what would become of Rebecca, if Ron refused to let her stay. There were homes for unmarried mothers of course, but many were not much better than workhouses, from what she'd heard. And didn't they take the babies away after six weeks and farm them out for adoption? Somehow, Sal couldn't see Rebecca agreeing to that, not from the way she'd flared up over the abortion. She turned over restlessly to stare in the dim light at the thickset hunched shoulders of the man lying next to her. No matter how Ron felt about it, there was no getting away from the fact that this baby was family. And what was more, she was determined to remind him of it!

The following morning, Rebecca and Sal, both tired and heavy-eyed, sat at the breakfast table in an atmosphere almost unbearable with tension. Ron, with his daily paper propped up before him, ate his toast and dripping in silence. Rebecca toyed with her Shredded Wheat, while Sal, who only ever had a fag and a mug of strong tea in the mornings, sat and watched them both, her eyes inscrutable.

Then, minutes later, Ron folded his paper, and heaved himself up from his chair. "Right, I'm going fer a walk." Without a backward glance, he went out of the room. Seconds later they heard the back door close behind him, and then the click of the gate as he left.

The two women looked at each other in consternation, and then Sal shook her head. "It's no use asking me," she said, seeing the plea in Rebecca's eyes. "He's never uttered a word about it since last night. Just let him alone, that's the best plan."

Rebecca bit her lip. She felt awful; it was all her fault, she was the one who'd caused all this trouble. "I really am sorry, Sal. I keep saying it, I know, but I am."

"Yes, well maybe you are." And Sal's expression, for the first time since Rebecca had broken the news, softened slightly. "Well girl, we'll just have to wait, won't we? It's no use trying to hurry Ron when he's got a decision to make!"

"Do you think . . . ?"

Sal shrugged. Then impulsively she turned on her way to the kitchen. "If it was left to me, well . . . and I'll say this once, Rebecca, and then we won't mention it again. I owe you an apology, girl. I should never have mentioned old Ma Burton. I just don't know what came over me. I feel ashamed of meself."

Rebecca managed a weak smile. "That's all right, Sal. I know you meant well at the time. But you do understand, don't you, why I couldn't go through with it?"

"I've told you, I regret I ever suggested it. I panicked, I suppose."

"Well," Rebecca said. "I'm in Ron's hands now. We'll just have to wait and see." But although her voice was steady, the fear in her eyes was obvious.

"That's what women are supposed to be good at – waiting," Sal said wryly.

But they didn't have to wait long, because within half an hour Ron came back. He flung his cap on its hook behind the door, and stood in front of the fireplace, thumbs hooked inside his thick leather belt, legs astride. Both women, on hearing him return, had taken up apprehensive positions in the small sitting-room, Sal in her usual armchair, while Rebecca sat uneasily on the edge of the settee. But Ron looked at his niece and jerked his head towards the bar. "Yer can go and refill the optics. I want a private word with Sal."

At the sharpness of his tone, Rebecca flinched, then did as she was told. Sal got up and went to lean with her back against the edge of the table. "Well?" she said quietly.

Ron faced his wife. "We both know what we've got to decide. I suppose *you* want me to let her stay?"

Sal nodded, but remained silent.

"Have yer thought this through? If she does stay, I mean?"

"Not completely. Have *you* thought of the consequences if we don't stand by her?" she challenged,
and saw Ron's eyes shift uneasily. "She's family,
Ron, and so is that baby."

"I know that, Sal." Ron moved away from the
fireplace and sat heavily in his chair. "It'll disrupt
all our lives, though! I mean, what about when she
has it? I take it she wants to keep the kid?"

"She hasn't said, and I haven't asked her," Sal
told him. "But I'd put money on it!"

"It's a bugger, and no mistake," Ron said, scratching
his balding head. He looked across at her. "But where's
the money coming from? Because I can tell you now
that if she does stay, I'm not having her serving
behind the bar in one of them maternity smocks.
Blokes come in here to get away from all that!"

Ron was right about the expense, Sal realised.
The Unicorn was a popular pub, but they only just
broke even. Money was scarce, what with the war
just finishing. And then sadly, so many men, some
of them regulars, hadn't come back.

"Maybe she could do the cleaning," she suggested.
"Yer know Ruby's been on about retiring." She
sighed. "In any case, Ron, I don't think I could live
with meself if we disowned her. After all, we're all
she's got."

Ron hesitated. That was true. Not that the pittance
Rebecca earned would support a kid as well. But,
dammit, he'd grown fond of the girl, it had been
good to have a bit of young company in the house,
and she was a hard worker, he'd give her that. And
Sal was right – Rebecca *was* family.

Ron glanced at his wife, seeing in her eyes not only anxiety for her niece, but also a shadow he hadn't seen for some time. "It's brought it all back to you, hasn't it?" he said gruffly. "Yer know what I mean . . ."

Sal nodded. She knew that to the outside world she was the typical pub landlady, brassy, buxom and cheerful, and so she was most of the time. But long ago, Sal had desperately wanted a family, children of her own. Ron had been in the ring then, often coming home battered and bruised, but most of the time with money in his pocket from a good purse. However, as the months and years passed, they'd had to accept that it wasn't to be, although only Ron knew how deeply the disappointment had affected her.

She looked up at him. "Maybe we've been given a second chance." Her voice was low, but her words made it impossible for Ron to refuse.

"All right," he said. "Go and tell her, she can stay, and the kid as well." As Sal's face lit up with relief, he warned, "But not a word to anyone mind? There'll be plenty of time to face up to that when we have to. And that includes Gloria. She'd be bound to tell her mother. That woman's got a gob on her like an open coffin!"

As Sal nodded in agreement, Ron asked, "When do you think she'll start to show?"

Sal considered. "Well, she's slim, and all that work as a Land Girl will have given her firm muscles. I reckon not until after five months, not so anyone would notice." She looked at him. "You're a good bloke, Ron. I reckon they broke the mould when you were born."

"Yer mean my ugly mug broke it," he joked, but Sal went over to him and kissed the top of his head. "You'll do fer me," she said. Gratified, Ron watched her go into the bar to tell Rebecca. He was still unsure whether he'd made the right decision. If there'd been any alternative . . .

Rebecca, waiting in the bar, had found her hands were trembling too much to do as Ron asked; instead she stood leaning against the beer pumps and, for the first time since Ian was killed, she decided to say a prayer. After all, what had she been taught during those long years in Wales? God was always there; you had only to ask for his help. Maybe He is, and maybe He isn't, she thought, but I'll do it just in case.

When Sal eventually came in to find her, Rebecca, sick with anxiety, turned immediately. She searched Sal's face in desperation, then hardly dared to believe what she saw in her eyes. "He said I can stay?"

"Yes – don't worry – we'll stand by you. But," Sal warned, "Ron doesn't want anyone else to know you're pregnant, not even Gloria. I agree with him – it's best to wait until we have to."

Rebecca nodded, so overwhelmed with relief that she could hardly speak. Seeing the young girl's eyes fill with tears, Sal held out her arms. "Come here," she said awkwardly, and drew her niece to her. "Yer not alone, girl. Me and Ron will see you right."

Ron, standing in the doorway, could only think that if Ian hadn't gone to that blasted football match, what a different story it would have been. A shotgun wedding maybe, but inside the safety of marriage, soon forgotten. But now, through a cruel twist of fate, the young teacher had lost his life, and Rebecca and her child were left without support. And suddenly, as he watched the emotional scene before him, his doubts disappeared. Ron prided himself on his strength; after all, hadn't he been one of the toughest fighters on the boxing circuit? Well, he could use that strength now in a different way.

The following three months passed quietly, at least on the surface. Life went on as usual, with trade picking up over the summer months. Both Sal and Rebecca were knitting furiously, although careful to keep their needles and wool safely out of sight when Ruby was around. Sal concentrated on bootees and mittens. "Stands to reason you'll need these," she said, "what with a November baby. Mind you, I'm not tackling a bonnet."

Rebecca laughed. And she did laugh more lately. The sadness was there, of course, but the raw edge of her pain was becoming blunted as the months passed. It helped that she now seemed to be concentrating totally on the growing life within her. It was a source of wonder to feel the fluttering movements, a constant reminder of the life she and Ian had created. And as for the knitting, she'd discovered that she had a talent for it. She'd learned at school, of course, but that had been boring stuff, beginning with dishcloths, and then progressing to a scarf. But now, as her fingers moved nimbly, her brain concentrating on a pattern, Rebecca found the occupation therapeutic. And then there was the sense of achievement at the resulting tiny lacy matinee jackets.

"It says here," she said to Sal, poring over *Woman's Weekly*, "that you need four little jackets, and then some larger-sized ones."

"Well, you'd better do those complicated things," Sal grumbled. "You're twice as fast as me. You don't seem to drop stitches, either."

Ron glanced at them both from behind his newspaper. The constant clicking of knitting needles got on his nerves, but he never said anything. In any case, it was cosy in a way, seeing Sal and Rebecca working together, full of plans for when the kid arrived. But this peaceful time wouldn't last much longer, because Rebecca's body was thickening, and despite those baggy cardigans she'd begun to wear, people would soon begin to notice.

"Have yer sorted it with Ruby?" he said abruptly. "About her retiring, I mean?"

Sal looked up. "Yes, I was meaning to say. She's going at the end of next week." Ron nodded. "Not a moment too soon."

Rebecca pulled her cardigan across the mound of her stomach. Each day seemed to make her condition more noticeable, and she'd already decided to be in bed with a supposed cold or something when Gloria came round on Sunday.

"So," she said quietly, "are you going to be asking Flossie?"

"Well," Sal said, "I thought we'd ask her to fill in for a bit, until we get someone more permanently.

Of course, once you're over having the baby, we'll have to re-think things, see how they work out. But it's no use making plans too far in the future, not at this stage."

Rebecca nodded. That all made sense. And it was only right that she should pull her weight by doing the cleaning, both in the pub and in the living quarters. And she was determined to pay the same amount towards her keep from the smaller wage she'd get. But although she was willing to tackle most jobs, there *was* one . . .

Sal, seeing the troubled expression in Rebecca's eyes said, "Come on, out with it, girl. What's bothering you?"

Rebecca hesitated, glancing uneasily at Ron. Then the words burst out. "Would I have to clean the Gents?"

Both public lavatories were out in the back yard, the Gents situated just around the corner from the Ladies. But although Ruby cleaned both regularly, Rebecca always had to hurry past the door of the Gents to avoid the stench. "They're nothing but pigs, some of 'em," Ruby would say as she came out grumbling, and Rebecca was already recoiling at the thought of having to do it.

Sal remained silent. This was Ron's department. He was the one who would be paying Rebecca's wages. And her husband was frowning. He said sharply, "Okay, it's not a job many'd choose! What is it you're saying – that you think you're too good for it? Better than Ruby, are yer?"

Rebecca flushed. "No, of course not. It's just

that . . ." She cast a desperate glance at her aunt, but Sal, although she could sympathise with how Rebecca felt, remained silent.

"Cleaning the bogs is part of the deal, Rebecca," Ron said shortly. "Either you do the whole job, or I'll have to get somebody else."

Rebecca stared at him in dismay. But then, she thought miserably, what had she expected him to say? He wouldn't let Sal do it, and he certainly wouldn't do it himself, not when he was paying good money for a cleaner. "All right," she said with some reluctance. "I'll do it."

"Good girl." Ron heaved up his bulk. "I'll go and open up."

Later, lying in bed, Rebecca couldn't help wondering just what else fate had in store for her. Eighteen and cleaning men's lavatories! Not a very glamorous life! But then, she comforted herself before she went to sleep, at least I have my baby to look forward to.

13

"**S**he's never!"

"It's right, I'm afraid, Ruby. She's nearly six months gone."

Ruby stared round-eyed at her employer. "Yer know I thought she'd put a bit of weight on lately, but I never imagined for one minute . . . I suppose it was that Ian?"

Sal nodded. "According to Rebecca, they were going to get married."

"Oh, the poor kid!" The two women were sitting on opposite sides of the dining table, toasting Ruby's long-awaited retirement. "Must've bin an awful shock, though. Not just for 'er, but for you and Ron as well!"

"You can say that again!" Sal drained her glass and poured another sherry for both of them. "I never would have thought it – not our Rebecca."

Both women were silent for a moment, then Ruby, a buxom, red-faced woman, said slyly, "Go on though, Sal, admit it – we've all been tempted in our time."

"Not me," Sal said sharply. "I had more bleedin' sense. I told Ron straight off, that he could forget any o' that malarky until I had a ring on me finger."

"Ah, well you were lucky. Now my Bert, between you and me, wouldn't take 'no' for an answer," Ruby shrugged. "He married me though, once I found out our Dolly was on the way. Rebecca won't find me looking down me nose at 'er – it'd be a case of the pot calling the kettle!" Ruby turned as Rebecca came into the room. "Don't you worry, ducks. It's not the end of the world."

"It seems like it, at times!" Rebecca managed a smile, thankful that Sal had already told the cleaner the news. She liked Ruby.

"You'll miss the tips though," Ruby said. "My job won't pay as well as working in the bar. Are you all fixed up with everything you'll need?"

"I've got all the matinee jackets, mittens and bootees, but nothing else yet."

"Money a bit scarce, is it?"

Rebecca nodded, and Ruby leaned forward. "Only me sister's got a stall on Watney Market, selling kids' clothes. It's all good quality, mind – she doesn't stock any rubbish! I could vouch for you."

"How do you mean?"

"She'll let you have the stuff when you need it, and then you pay for it on a weekly card. I see her every week, so I could take the money for you."

"That's good of you, Rube," Sal said. "Because she's insisting on being independent."

"Right, let's see what you'll need. I've had four of me own, so I know what I'm talking about." Ruby counted off the items on her podgy fingers. "You'll need four woollen envelope vests, four flannelette nightgowns, at least two dozen terry nappies, three rubber pants and a rubber sheet, three cot sheets, two baby blankets . . ."

"Glory," Sal said. "Sounds like a shipping order." She picked up the bottle of sherry and refilled Ruby's glass and her own. They'd be pickled at this rate, she thought, but for once she didn't care.

"If it had been a summer baby," Ruby said, "she might have got away with a bit less. But with drying indoors . . . I suppose you'll be using a drawer for it to sleep in at first?"

"Most people do round 'ere," Sal said. "And as for a cot – when it's needed, I'm sure someone'll lend us one. Same goes for a pram."

Ruby took a sip of her sherry and snorted in derision. "They might, they might not! You'd think they were all saints, to listen to 'em at times!" She glanced at Rebecca. "It won't be all plain sailing, you know. You'll 'ave to grow a thick skin. And for Gawd's sake don't you go out in public without a ring on your finger!"

"She's right," Sal said. "You'd better get a brass curtain ring from Woolworth's."

Rebecca flushed. "I suppose I'll have to wear one of those awful maternity smocks as well!"

Ruby cackled. "Better that than parading your swollen belly for all to gawp at. And at least you'll be in fashion – maternity smocks are one thing that'll never go out!"

Rebecca laughed. She was a proper tonic, was Ruby. "I'll miss you," she said suddenly.

"Oh, I'll be turning up – only on the other side of the bar! Is Flossie coming in to take over?"

"I hope so. And," Sal warned, "remember, Ruby, not a word to anyone until after Ron's had his say."

"Me lips are sealed, promise!"

On Sunday morning, Rebecca silently handed Sal a note she'd written to Gloria. The plan was that just before lunchtime, Sal would push it through the letterbox of Gloria's front door.

"Folk love a bit of scandal," Sal had warned. "Once some of 'em leave the pub, the news will be round 'ere like a dose of salts."

And so Rebecca had written, "*Dear Gloria, Just a note to let you know that I'm expecting a baby in November. I didn't want you to hear it from someone else. If Ian hadn't been killed, we would have been married by now, but it wasn't to be. Hoping to see you later, Rebecca.*"

Ron waited to make his announcement until most of his regulars were in. It was a widespread custom for the men to come out for a pint or two while their wives cooked the Sunday dinner, and trade was brisk. Ron waited until there was a lull and then nodded to Sal. She went out into the sitting-room to join Rebecca, whose days of serving in the bar were now officially over. "At least," Ron told her, "until next year."

Alone in the bar, Ron ignored a couple of men waiting to order, and reaching up, jangled the brass bell which hung above the bar. There was surprise and not a little annoyance. "'Old yer 'orses," one bellicose man bellowed. "It ain't last orders yet!"

"I know that, Sam. Now listen up, you lot, I've

got something ter say!" His resonant voice reached every corner, even the snug on the opposite side of the bar, where the customers, mainly old women, stopped gossiping, and turned to peer up at him, consumed with curiosity.

"Now yer all know our Rebecca. Well, you might have noticed she's not behind the bar any more."

"Aw, don't say she's left. She's a lot easier on the eye than you, mate," one man quipped.

"No, she hasn't, Fred, but she won't be serving in 'ere for a while. You all know 'er bloke was killed in that football disaster up in Bolton?" There was a murmur of assent. "He was a Stoke supporter," someone muttered.

"That's right. Anyway, they were going ter get married. But," and here Ron drew a deep breath, "they sort of jumped the gun a bit. The truth is, he left 'er with a bun in the oven. She's due in November." As the murmurs of shock resounded around the room, Ron held up his hand. "Me and Sal are standing by the girl, and I'm telling you all now, that I want 'er treated with respect. You all know me, and I'm not a man to cross. So, I'm warning yer – mark what I say." Towering above the bar, he stared challengingly at the sea of faces before him, noting the ones with shifty looks and sly grins, glad to see a few with expressions of concern, and nodding in agreement. "All right – so now yer know." Ron turned away. "Right, Joe, a pint of your usual, is it?"

Sal waited for a full ten minutes before she rejoined her husband, where the atmosphere in the bar was distinctly more subdued than when she'd left. Some customers avoided her eyes, one or two muttered that it was bad luck, but Ron had timed it well. Within half an hour last orders were in and shortly afterwards they were able to close.

Rebecca hadn't been idle. When her aunt and uncle went into the sitting-room, the table was set, and their Sunday roast ready. Despite her inexperience, Rebecca had managed to cook a better meal than Sal, a fact that Sal shamefacedly admitted. "Cooking was never me strong point, was it, Ron?"

"Yer don't do so bad," he said loyally.

"Well, I can take over a lot of it now," Rebecca offered. "To be honest, I quite enjoy it."

"Yer welcome," Sal said with relief. "And that'll be a big help. It's always a bind, having to run in and out, keeping an eye on things."

Ron looked on approvingly. If the girl pulled her weight, then maybe things might turn out all right after all. "So," he said, turning to Sal, "when are yer goin' round ter see Flossie?"

"After Gloria gets 'ere," Sal said, lighting up a fag.

It was half an hour later, when Ron had gone upstairs for his usual Sunday afternoon nap, and Sal was getting ready to go and visit Flossie, that the loud knock came at the back door. "That'll be Gloria now," she called. "I'll let 'er in."

But when she opened the door it was to see Gloria's mother confronting her. She moved forward as if to come in, but Sal blocked her way. She was fussy who came into her private living quarters, and Bessie Brady was definitely not on her list!

135

"Is it true, then? What's in that note?" Bessie demanded.

Sal stared with distaste at the small thin-faced woman before her. Ron always said Bessie had a face like a ferret on her, and as she stood there, her small eyes glittering with indignation, Sal could see what he meant. "Rebecca would hardly have written such a thing if it wasn't," she snapped.

Bessie straightened her narrow shoulders and her head came up like a fighting cock. "Well, yer 'ave me sympathy, Sal. But I've just come ter say that our Gloria won't be coming round on a Sunday no more. And I'm sure yer'll understand why."

For a moment, Sal didn't speak, and when she did, her voice was like a splinter of ice. "It's not catching, you know."

"Maybe. But you know what they say. Birds of a feather an' all that! I've got me daughter's reputation to think of."

"She's not old enough to come round and tell us 'erself, then?"

But Sal's sarcasm was wasted on Bessie. "She wanted to, but we decided it was best this way. Just as long as yer know where we stand."

"I think you've made that very clear!" Sal closed the door quite deliberately in her neighbour's face, and seething, went back to the sitting-room, where Rebecca, who had heard every word, was sitting white-faced on the sofa.

"Don't let it upset yer," Sal snapped. "She's no loss! Not that I'm surprised – Gloria never did have a mind of her own."

"She's still the only friend I had. I don't know any other girls of my own age." Rebecca didn't think Sal understood how much she missed young company.

"Yeah, well there are better fish in the sea, believe me!" Sal slumped down in an armchair, and frowned. "You know it is strange how there aren't many young girls around 'ere. It must be something in the water."

But by that evening they had a new problem – because Flossie, although not unsympathetic, said she didn't feel up to working on a regular basis.

"It's me varicose veins," she told Sal. "Agony they are if I stand on me legs too long. So, I'm sorry, luv, but you'll 'ave to find someone else."

Now, as Sal tried to think of where to find her new barmaid, she looked at the girl sitting opposite. There was no doubt about it – the punters had liked having an attractive young girl behind the bar. And even in pregnancy, Rebecca was a looker. There'll be a few blokes sniffing around once that baby's born, Sal thought suddenly. And if one of them was prepared to marry her and to take on the kid, that might be the best thing all round. Not that Rebecca had ever shown any interest in any of the local young men. Ron always said the girl thought herself too good for them. Well, after this lot, Sal thought grimly, she might have to lower her sights.

14

When her brother came home and told her about the vacancy at the Unicorn, Katie O'Brien looked up from her magazine and stared at him with suspicion. "And just what sort of pub is it, may I ask?"

"Perfectly respectable – even for the likes of you!" Conor ducked as Katie threw a cushion at him. "Aren't I telling you the truth, now? Mind you," he grinned, "the previous barmaid did get herself into trouble!"

"Oh, did it herself, did she? Now isn't that just typical? It's always the girl's fault – the man's never to blame."

Conor grinned. "Not if he can get away with it."

"I heard that! And such a thing for a married man to say!" But the young woman who came into the room was smiling.

"Anyway, twerp," Conor said, "you'll be needing the money to pay us rent. So go on – take yourself along there!" Katie glared at him, then burst out laughing. "I don't know how you put up with him, Maura."

"Oh, he has his good points."

"So you think I should go for it?"

"It can't do any harm," Maura pointed out. "The pub's only a couple of streets away."

Katie frowned. The reason she'd come over to England earlier than she'd planned was because she longed for a change. It was also in response to an appeal from Conor for help, as Maura was just recovering from rheumatic fever. *"Just for the first few months,"* he'd written, *"I worry about her getting overtired, and I'd feel happier if you were here."*

But Katie still wasn't sure. She'd been so thrilled to come to London – to work in an East End pub hardly fitted in with her dreams. But Conor was right. She did need to earn a wage to help out with expenses. She'd already been here for two weeks and didn't she eat like a horse?

"Don't let the look of the landlord put you off," Conor warned. "He might be an ugly devil, but he's civil enough."

Maura winked at Katie. "You seem to know this pub very well! And here have I been thinking you were out at work."

"It was only the second time I'd been in! Sure and can't a man have a drink without the women carping at him?" But his eyes were soft as he looked at his wife, and not for the first time Katie thought how lucky they were to have found each other.

At the Unicorn, Sal was rapidly getting bad-tempered. It wasn't that she minded working every shift, but still struggling with hot flushes and the vagaries of the "change", she desperately needed time off. The only applicant so far for the job had been someone Ron described as "an old scrubber", so when the fresh-faced Irish girl approached the bar, and asked to speak to the landlord, Sal went to fetch Ron with alacrity.

Katie, although warned, blanched slightly as the burly man with a face on him, as she told Maura later, "that would frighten the horses" approached.

"I've heard you're looking for a barmaid," she said, giving him what she hoped was a winning smile.

"S'right." Ron looked at the young girl before him, and couldn't believe his luck. "How old are you?"

"I'm nineteen. And haven't I grown up in a pub, and been serving in me father's bar in Dublin for the last twelve months?" Katie had hoped to do something different, but after all she didn't want her wages eaten up with travelling costs.

Already Sal was moving up behind Ron. "And why would you be looking for a job in a pub like this?" She felt suspicious – a girl like this could do better for herself.

"Because it's near where I'm living. But," Katie hesitated, then decided to tell the truth, "it would only be for a few months, though. It's me intention to train for a nurse."

Sal exchanged glances with Ron. This couldn't be better, and she could see that he was impressed. Then, looking at Katie again, seeing the humour and intelligence in her eyes, Sal suddenly thought of Rebecca. Impatiently she waited until hours and wages had been agreed, and then said, "Come on through to the back for a minute. There's someone I'd like you to meet."

When the sitting-room door opened, Rebecca was on her knees polishing the brass fender. Pushing back a tendril of hair from her forehead, she turned round, saw the stranger, and scrambled awkwardly up.

"This is my niece, Rebecca," Sal said. "It's her job you'll be taking on. And this is . . ." Suddenly embarrassed, Sal realised she didn't know the girl's name.

"Katie. Katie O'Brien."

"Hello." Rebecca smiled, holding out her hand, only to withdraw it hurriedly on seeing the smudges of Brasso on her fingers. "Sorry, I'm in a bit of a mess."

"Don't worry," Katie grinned, "when's the baby due?"

"November."

"And are you hoping for a boy or a girl?"

"I don't mind, as long as everything's all right." Rebecca felt a sense of relief that the other girl was acting "normally". Most people tended to evade the situation, as if her pregnancy didn't exist. She smiled back at the other girl. "I hope you'll like it here."

"Of course she will," Sal said briskly, and turned to leave. Katie followed her, mouthing "Bye" over her shoulder, and as she walked home was not only excited about getting the job but also slightly envious. She didn't think she'd ever seen such wonderful hair. And that face! "Talk about Maureen O'Hara," she

141

told Maura later. "And that's when she's pregnant, for heaven's sake."

But her sister-in-law was frowning. "Maybe, but what do you know about her? We don't want you getting into bad company."

"She looked more like a saint than a devil! *And* she was wearing a ring on her finger!"

"Conor said she wasn't married," Maura said stubbornly. "So just be careful, Katie."

And at first Katie was wary. But then eventually she heard the full story of Rebecca's tragic romance. "Sure, and there but for the grace of God . . ." she said. "Wasn't there this divine man who used to come into our pub in Dublin? Now if ever his eye had fallen on me, I'm not sure I'd have had the strength to resist." She grinned. "Mind you, one thought of the priest and me mother would have put the damper on it. And then there'd be the Catholic guilt! *All pleasure is sin,*" she whispered.

Rebecca collapsed with laughter, and Sal, coming down the stairs, was glad to hear it. As she'd hoped, the two young girls were becoming firm friends, with Katie's easygoing nature and merry sense of humour lightening the day for them all. It's working out very well, Sal thought with satisfaction, very well indeed.

And Rebecca was feeling better than she had for months. With the Irish girl, there was none of the irritation she'd felt with Gloria. Katie didn't play games, she had a direct way of talking which Rebecca found refreshing.

"Lord above," Katie said, coming in early for her lunchtime shift and finding Rebecca pasty-faced in the kitchen. "What in heaven's name is up with you?"

"I've just finished in the Gents," Rebecca said, pulling a face. "What a flaming job."

Katie shuddered. "Rather you than me. I hope you wrapped a scarf or something tight around your mouth and nose."

Rebecca stared at her. "Now why didn't I think of that?"

"Because you're not going to be a nurse, and I am. I rather fancy meself in a mask, looking all mysterious and gazing up at a handsome doctor." She struck a pose, fluttering her long dark eyelashes. "What do you think?"

Rebecca laughed, then felt a sudden pang of envy. "You're so lucky, being able to have a career."

"Now what sort of talk is that? Once the little one arrives, there's no knowing what the future will hold." Katie glanced curiously at the other girl. "What were your ambitions, by the way?"

Rebecca shrugged. "I'm not sure. I'd intended to work in the pub for Ron and Sal for at least twelve months. You know, get settled back in London. And then I met Ian."

"But there must be some job you fancied doing. What did you want to do when you left school?"

"Come back home to London," Rebecca said wryly. "I couldn't think any further than that. The war was still on, and I knew I'd have to work as a Land Girl until it finished."

"You must have had some ideas," Katie persisted.

Rebecca hesitated. "I've always liked clothes and fashion." She looked down disparagingly at the blue maternity smock she was wearing. "Don't judge me by this, for heaven's sake. Whoever designs these things? Look at me, I'm like a house-end to start with, and then they cover me with spots! A plain colour would make me look slimmer – although I think it would take a miracle for that to happen."

"Or the baby popping out!"

Ron, coming in, thought yet again how good it was to hear the sound of laughter. With each day that passed, Rebecca was becoming more like her old self. Quieter maybe, but it was a relief to see a smile on her face again. "She's young," Sal kept telling him. "Give her time, she'll come through it, you'll see."

And so the weeks passed uneventfully, with Rebecca settling into a domestic routine. She cleaned the pub and the living quarters, cooked most of the meals, and listened to the wireless. She did that a lot these days, enjoying "Workers' Playtime" at lunchtime, and doing her chores to the Light Programme in the afternoons. It was also company when she rested, although her fingers were always busy. Word had got round about her skill with the needles, and she was beginning to earn a little extra money by knitting for other people. Some still shunned her, but occasionally someone would bring skeins of wool and a pattern, hand them to Sal, and Rebecca would charge them an hourly rate. Katie was perfectly willing to give up ten minutes to sit with outstretched arms, the skeins looped over her hands, while Rebecca wound the wool into balls. "It's not just the extra cash," Sal told Ron. "It's something to occupy her mind."

And so Rebecca was reasonably content as she waited for the last weeks of her pregnancy to pass. But in the night, disturbed by the baby kicking, and uncomfortable because of her bulk, sleep often evaded her. And it was at those times that her thoughts would turn to Ian. She thought of him in the daytime of course, but it was only in those silent, sleepless hours that she allowed her underlying grief to surface. Its raw, painful edge was beginning at last to soften, and her thoughts often turned to that first day in the pub, when Ian had called her Aphrodite. Drowsily retracing their days out sight-seeing in London, she would dwell on the first time they had kissed on the Embankment, and that wonderful, passionate, fateful night of lovemaking. And although tears would dampen her pillow, she desperately needed those memories, was determined to remember their time together. Rebecca wasn't ready to let Ian go, not yet.

But as her due date drew near, she also began to lie awake worrying about the ordeal that faced her. Millions of women have had babies, she would try to reassure herself. If they could go through it, then so could she. But although she tried to push such thoughts away, she couldn't help recalling horror stories of women having long exhausting labours and suffering terrible agonies. And everyone knew that childbirth carried life-threatening dangers. What if something happened to her? What if her baby was left an orphan? And Rebecca had the added anxiety that the gin episode, which she now bitterly regretted, might in some way have harmed her unborn child. Rebecca knew that if, God forbid, her baby was affected, she would never be able to forgive herself.

15

Rebecca's daughter was born after a short but intensive labour in the early hours of a foggy November morning. Although Lizzie Fowler, the local woman who acted as midwife, disapproved of the unmarried status of her patient, even she softened as she washed and warmly dressed the tiny infant. And she had to concede that the girl in the bed had behaved well, biting on a piece of rag during the contractions, and obediently gripping the iron bedposts. There had been no screaming and cursing, no hysterics. Lizzie had seen it all. Although she had no formal nursing training, she'd brought many East End children into the world.

Unfortunately, a few were merely greeted with listless resignation, being just another mouth to feed. Other labours, mercifully rare, ended in heartbreak when, despite all her efforts and sometimes those of a doctor, they ended in tragedy. To lose a mother or baby was an affront to Lizzie, to lose both was devastating. Occasionally, a baby was born so badly deformed that Lizzie would turn her back on the mother and silently smother it. Such decisions would lie on her conscience for days, although in her opinion it was the kindest thing to do. But then to compensate, there was the longed-for child with the mother luminous with happiness, all pain forgotten. Lizzie, for all her stern exterior, never failed to be moved by such a scene. And this girl at the pub, unmarried or not, wanted this baby, there was no doubt of that.

Meanwhile Rebecca lay wearily among the crumpled sheets, feeling ashamed of the weak tears beginning to trickle down her cheeks. She turned to gaze unseeingly at the curtained window. Never had she imagined that giving birth would be as harrowing as this. Pain she'd been prepared for, although its intensity had both overwhelmed and exhausted her. To be frightened too – that was only natural. But what had affected her most profoundly was the desolation she'd felt. The loneliness that had swept over her as she struggled to withstand the contractions, and then to strain and push out her child, had been devastating.

When the pain had receded, and she'd waited, dreading the next excruciating wave, the image of Ian's smiling face – his eyes alight with love – had seared into her. This was his child, his baby being born; and the sadness that he would never know of the legacy he'd left, even bitterness that he wasn't aware of her suffering, had been unbearable. He would have been so tender, so supportive. And her mother's love too, if she had lived, would have given her strength.

And Rebecca knew she needed that extra strength, because now her tears were no longer just weak and emotional, but ones of self-pity and apprehension.

How was she going to manage – she was only nineteen? She had neither money nor her own home to bring up a baby. At least she'd got Ron and Sal, and she could only thank God for it. Even if she found it difficult to believe in a God who had taken so much away from her.

Following on that thought was the sudden realisation that *she* had someone else to think about now, a defenceless child, and she struggled from her self-absorption, suddenly turning to look anxiously at the midwife. Lizzie seemed to be taking a long time. Surely everything was all right? After all, although she'd only glimpsed the baby before it was whisked away, she'd heard the tiny wail . . . but since then . . . Rebecca began to feel increasing panic as she saw Lizzie still bending over her child. But then she straightened up, turned and came over to the bed, smiling at Rebecca's relief as she put the tiny bundle into Rebecca's eagerly outstretched arms. "There you are, luv. She's a fine, healthy, seven-pound baby."

Entranced, she gazed down at the crumpled, red face of her daughter, totally unprepared for the surge of overwhelming and fiercely protective love. Tearfully, she whispered, "Thank you, Lizzie, for everything you've done."

"Just doing me duty," Lizzie replied, now anxious to be away. She moved busily around the room, her capable arms tidying and organising, and once satisfied, she left the bedroom and went downstairs. Sal, weary and relieved, was waiting with the usual fee, plus a bit extra, and pushed a bottle of port into Lizzie's hands. "Thank God it's over!"

"She'll make a good mother, I'll say that for her," was Lizzie's parting remark, as she passed Ron coming in through the back door. He'd been given the task of disposing of the soiled brown paper that had protected the mattress, an old patched sheet, and the afterbirth wrapped in a threadbare towel. All were now securely parcelled up and dumped in the dustbin. "Everything okay?" he said, jerking his head in the direction of the bedroom.

"Everything's fine," Sal said. "Come on, we can go up now."

When they opened the bedroom door and went tentatively in, it was to see Rebecca propped up by pillows smiling happily at them. She drew the intricate shawl, a gift from Flossie, gently away from her baby's face. Sal came over to the bed and peered down, astounded as unfocused blue eyes stared up into her own. She'd never seen a baby so soon after its birth before. "Come and look, Ron," she said, "she's beautiful." Sheepishly, Ron came forward and put his forefinger into the baby's palm, his face creasing in a grin as her hand curled tightly around it.

"She's got a grip on 'er, no mistake."

"Have you finally decided on the name?" Sal wanted to know.

Rebecca nodded. "It might sound daft, but I'm going to call her Anna after *Anna of the Five Towns* – it's a book by Arnold Bennett, based in the Potteries. I thought it would give her a sort of link with Ian." She looked away for a moment, fighting weak tears, but then looked back at Sal. "And I've decided on Sally for her second name."

150

Sal stared wide-eyed at her. "You mean you've named her after me? Oh, Rebecca!"

"And a very good choice," Ron said gruffly.

"I'll never forget how good you've both been," Rebecca said. It was true, whatever would she have done without them?

Sal, almost overcome by emotion, muttered, "Well, you're family, aren't you? And," she said, pulling herself together, "so is this little one." She held out her arms. "Can I have a hold of my namesake, then?" Rebecca smiled as she watched Sal gingerly take the baby and cradle her in her arms for a few precious minutes, then turned to Ron and offered the small bundle to him.

He drew back in alarm. "No fear. I might drop 'er!"

Sal laughed, and with great care lowered Anna inside the warmly lined drawer at the side of the bed. "I'll just put a light blanket over her. Now let's all try and get some sleep – particularly you, Rebecca."

But although she was unutterably tired, Rebecca only slept fitfully, constantly waking up to check anxiously that her daughter was still breathing. Then, true to her word, Lizzie was there before breakfast, showing Rebecca how to breast-feed, checking the baby's umbilical cord, and giving detailed instructions on her care.

"Any problems, you know where I am," she said, and Rebecca watched her go with alarm.

Katie, though, dismissed her worries about the responsibility. "Sure, and aren't I one of seven? I've been changing nappies since I was eight years old. With you, Sal and meself to look after her, this baby will be spoilt rotten!"

But once Christmas was over, the New Year of 1947 heralded a bitter and harsh winter. From the middle of January until mid-March, there were constant heavy snowfalls, in some areas with drifts in excess of ten feet. Power cuts were common, and daily life became a constant battle against the elements. "You take your life in yer hands just walking along the pavement," Sal complained, as she came in from the butcher's. "Them blasted kids and their slides! Trouble is, they get covered with snow, and yer can't see where they are!"

Ron struggled with paraffin lamps in the outside lavatories, but to no avail; the pipes still froze over. Because of the extreme weather conditions, there was even a shortage of coal, and many people had to wear scarves and coats in the house, and even sleep in their clothes. Rebecca slept downstairs on the sofa, keeping Anna near the grate. Even with both bars of the electric fire on in her bedroom, the windows were still iced over in the mornings. And of course, having a baby in the house didn't make the hardship any easier.

Ron and Sal, already finding it difficult to adjust to the disruption a baby caused, occasionally relieved their feelings by grumbling to each other. "It's having that bloody clothes-horse everlasting round the fire, that gets to me," Ron grumbled to Sal. "I can never get near the bleedin' thing."

"I hate having that nappy bucket by the sink," Sal said, feeling a twinge of guilt at complaining. "But she's a lovely little thing, Ron, and this stage won't last long. At least she's sleeping through the night now." And then it began to rain, and with the thaw came the danger of flood damage, although everyone in the pub agreed that they were lucky compared with some areas of the country. But the winter was voted the worst anyone could remember.

"We'll need a damn good summer, after this lot," Sal grumbled, once it stopped raining. She was standing at the window, watching Ron sweep out the yard. "And look at the mess it all leaves."

"Never mind, Sal," Katie said, having arrived early for her shift. "It can only get better."

And it did, because the terrible winter was followed by a welcome warm summer, which brought people out. It wasn't uncommon to see a woman sitting on a chair outside her front door, enjoying the fresh air and a gossip with passers-by. It was at these times that, with Anna in mind, Rebecca thought wistfully of the garden at the Parrys' house in Wales, with its lawns, shady trees, and rose beds. But she was lucky in other ways. One of the customers had lent her an old pram, and Anna slept peacefully in a cot bought second-hand from Flossie's neighbour.

Rebecca had resumed her cleaning duties and still earned extra money from knitting, but she was beginning to feel increasingly restless. Although she loved caring for her baby, she chafed at the restrictions of the endless domestic routine, and found herself longing to return to the bar. She missed the banter and the company. Yet even the thought seemed disloyal, because that would mean Katie leaving. And Rebecca would miss her terribly. She'd had friends before, of course, both at school, and in Wales. But something always seemed to mean parting from them. First there was evacuation, and later the couple of girls she'd met in the Land Army had returned to their homes at opposite ends of the country.

But they all knew that Katie's time with them was limited, and Rebecca was hoping that even when she lived in the nurses' home, she'd still be coming to visit Conor and Maura and their new baby son, Michael. There was no reason to think that once she left the Unicorn, their friendship would end. Rebecca occasionally passed Gloria a couple of times in the street, but the other girl had merely given a nod, and looked haughtily away.

"Stupid cow," was Katie's apt comment, and Rebecca replied, "I won't lose any sleep over it."

And she didn't. Because Rebecca couldn't believe that anyone could possibly object to the existence of her beloved tiny daughter, who was a placid baby, with Ian's distinctive grey eyes. "He'd never be able to get out of *her*, even if he could," was Sal's often professed opinion; while Ron would nod, secretly pleased that Anna seemed fond of him, and would patiently jiggle her on his knee, and submit to her tiny exploring fingers.

Then one day in the autumn, Katie came in and told them she'd been accepted as a probationary nurse at St Bartholomew's Hospital. "And wasn't the Matron an auld dragon?" she told them. "She was worse than Sister Ignatius at the convent!" She picked up one of the antimacassars, draped it over her shoulders, and twirled around the room. "So, can you imagine me in a blue cape with red lining? Not to mention one of those darling little white caps."

"You'll look fantastic," Rebecca laughed.

"I just wish I had your figure," Katie said enviously. "You've been lucky, getting it back so quickly. While me – as Conor says, I'm 'comfortable'. Now what sort of word is that?"

"The wrong one," Rebecca said promptly. "I'd describe you as 'curvy', and men like that in a woman."

"Sure they do, don't they." Katie examined her reflection critically. "I suppose I'm not bad, and the uniform will help."

"You're supposed to be saving lives, not flirting with all and sundry," Sal commented, looked up from where she was nursing Anna.

"Oh, I will. I'll be Florence Nightingale the second, you'll see." She glanced sheepishly at Sal. "But this will mean I'll be leaving."

"Yes, I know. But we've been expecting it." Sal felt awkward; she wasn't normally one for giving praise. "It's bin a pleasure to have you working for us, Katie. We'll all miss you, Rebecca 'specially."

"Oh, I'll still come round, if that's all right?"

"Yer'll always be welcome." Sal got up and passed Anna over to Rebecca. "I think she needs changing, and from the pong I'd rather you did it!" Rebecca laughed, picked up her child, and went upstairs.

"Between you and me," Katie muttered to Sal.

"I'm hoping I can get Rebecca out a bit more once I start at the hospital. There's bound to be parties and things."

Once word got around that there was a vacancy for a cleaner, there was no shortage of applicants. Sal chose a quiet woman called Janet, whose husband had died at Dunkirk. She had two young lads, and, as she told them all, "they ate her out of house and home". She already took in ironing, and the extra money she'd earn at the pub would make all the difference.

And so life began as before, with Rebecca chatting with the customers in the bar, and glad to be back "in the swing" of things. And as the weeks turned into months, Anna began crawling and even tottering around holding on to the furniture. But it was all working out well, with Janet helping to keep an eye on her at lunchtimes, and in the evenings Anna would sleep in her pram in the sitting-room where she was within earshot, and rarely stirred when carried up to bed once the pub closed.

Then in November, there was the Royal Wedding to look forward to, with Sal, Ruby and Flossie going to join the crowds outside Westminster Abbey, hoping for a glimpse of Princess Elizabeth and her handsome Prince. Ron, of course, grumbled at being left with the extra work, but as Sal told him, "The day hasn't yet come when a Londoner can't cheer royalty."

True to her promise, Katie often came over to visit. She loved her nursing training, apart, she told them, from the sour old biddies of Sisters. "Talk about strict," she said, "it's worse than being at school."

"I bet they're good nurses, though," Sal said, and Katie had to agree.

"They run the wards like clockwork," she admitted. "I just wish they'd smile more. Anyway, haven't I got news! Some of the junior doctors are having a Christmas party, and you, Rebecca Lawson, are invited as me guest." Katie stared in triumph at them both.

Taken aback, Rebecca's first reaction was one of doubt. "Oh, I don't know, Katie . . ."

"I do," Sal said sharply. "It'll do you the world of good to go out among young people again. When is it, Katie?"

"Next Friday night."

"Right. We can ask Flossie to babysit." Sal got up briskly. "I'll pop along now and ask. Anna will be perfectly all right with her. She's done it before, when you two have gone to the pictures."

"But . . ." Rebecca looked at her astounded. "I haven't said I'm going, yet!"

"Of course you are – when Katie's been good enough to ask you!" Before Rebecca could protest, Sal was gone.

With a sense of panic, Rebecca realised she'd been manipulated.

"What's the matter?" Katie said. "Don't you want to come?"

"Of course I do . . . in a way, it's just that . . ." In any case, Rebecca thought wildly, what on earth would I wear?

"You'll enjoy it, trust me!" Katie said. "You've got to break out of this safe cocoon sooner or later, you know. You're nineteen, for heaven's sake, nearly twenty. There's a new life out there, Rebecca!" Rebecca could only stare at her in silence. Maybe there was, but was she ready for it?

16

The evening of the party was bitterly cold, but the crisp air only served to heighten Rebecca's sense of freedom. Closing the yard gate behind her, she made her way through the quiet streets, and on reaching the Tube Station, joined the crowd queuing for the next train. It was exhilarating to be out among people again; her world had become so narrow, so confined to the small back room and the bar of the Unicorn. Her only distraction was when taking Anna for an airing, or to do the shopping. Even visits to the pictures were rare. When she reached her destination, it was with increasing excitement that Rebecca emerged into the busy streets and bright lights of central London.

Walking briskly along the pavements, Rebecca drew the cream scarf she'd knitted closer to her throat, and tried to imagine what the evening ahead would be like. She'd never even been inside a hospital before, and it was with relief that she saw Katie hovering expectantly just inside the main entrance.

When the two girls arrived, the staff room, festively decorated with coloured paper chains, streamers and balloons, was already fairly crowded. At one end of the room was a long table covered with a white cloth, which looked suspiciously like a hospital sheet. One end served as an improvised bar, and the rest displayed plates of sandwiches, sausage rolls and mince pies.

At least I chose the right thing to wear, Rebecca thought, glancing at the other girls there. It was the dress Ian had liked so much, green with small white spots and a crossover bodice. Sal had lent her a pair of her favourite drop earrings, the ones she joked looked like real emeralds; and as she stood in a corner in her high-heeled shoes and sole pair of silk stockings, Rebecca began to feel her self-confidence returning. Katie looked fantastic, having invested both her savings and clothing coupons in a pink "New Look" dress, which, with its longer length and full skirt, was the height of fashion.

"It's all very dignified," Rebecca whispered, looking at the small groups of people, talking quietly.

"You watch it liven up once the consultants leave," Katie promised. "Apparently it's always the same at the beginning. Only a few come anyway – most are much too high and mighty for this sort of thing!"

Rebecca glanced around, trying to spot who they were. The silver-haired man in a pinstripe suit must be one, so must that tall academic-looking one in a dark suit and waistcoat. On the other side of the room, a portly man in a dinner jacket and bow tie stood in isolation, drink in hand, surveying the room. "He's probably going on somewhere else," Katie said. "Just slumming a bit first."

"Right, you two!" A stocky young man in a sports

jacket came up to them. "We can't have you standing there without a drink. What'll it be?"

"What have you got?" Katie said, grinning at him.

"Beer, sherry, Martini . . ."

"Sweet Martini for me," Katie said promptly. "How about you, Rebecca?"

"A lemonade, please."

"Yes, fine." After he'd gone, she whispered, "Who's he?"

"Dr Brian, one of the housemen – he's engaged to a third-year nurse. There – see that girl with long hair in the red dress? That's her."

Rebecca stared at the young nurse, and couldn't help feeling a pang of envy. It must be wonderful to have such a happy, secure future ahead of you. Once they had their drinks, Katie waved at a couple of fellow nurses across the room, and with Rebecca trailing behind, went over to join them.

"I see Dr Mason's turning on his charm," one, a dark-haired girl, laughed. "If he asks either of you to dance, just watch his bedside manner – it's lethal!"

"As if you'd know," joked Katie. All three girls stared at the tall, brown-haired young man smiling down at a blonde girl nearby, and just then he turned and winked. Rebecca suppressed a giggle, liking his expressive face, and the way his eyes crinkled at the corners. But then she looked away. She'd hoped not to feel like this – guilty if she felt attracted to anyone. Sal must have guessed it would happen. "It'll soon be two years since Ian died," she'd said, just before Rebecca left. "You've got to get on with your life. No amount of moping will bring him back."

But I'm not moping, Rebecca told herself, I'm loving being here. She met people all the time, of course, but how many doctors and professional people drank in the Unicorn? Katie must have sensed her thoughts, because she murmured, "Glad you came?"

Rebecca nodded, looking around the room again. There were about forty people there, and Katie began to point them out. Besides nurses and junior doctors, there were radiographers, physiotherapists and medical secretaries. "No Matron or Ward Sisters?" Rebecca asked.

Katie spluttered. "You're not serious! That would kill the party dead!" She paused, then her face split in a wide grin. "Look out, the gods are going."

They both watched as the consultants gradually drifted out, and instantly the whole atmosphere changed. As shoulders visibly relaxed, and ties were loosened, there began an undignified rush to the bar. Someone quickly went to the gramophone, changed the sedate music, and within minutes, several couples had taken to the floor and were jiving to Glenn Miller. Katie was whisked off, and seconds later Rebecca was being whirled around to "In the Mood" by an exuberant, chubby young man.

"What do you do?" she gasped when the music stopped.

"I'm in gynaecology," he said, clutching her hand and smiling down at her.

Rebecca felt the colour rush into her cheeks. That meant he spent his time looking at . . . To her dismay, she couldn't get the image out of her mind and as soon as he went to change the record, she hurried back to Katie. "Poor bloke!"

Katie couldn't stop laughing. "You are a ninny. It's just a job to them, you know."

Rebecca looked around the room, and then saw the young doctor she'd been fleetingly attracted to, dancing with the same blonde girl. "Pretty, isn't she?" Katie followed her gaze. "And she's top-drawer. The rest of us don't stand a chance."

However, both girls were soon in great demand as dancing partners, although eventually, as the amount of booze being consumed escalated, Rebecca decided she'd had enough of fending off wandering hands and having her toes trodden on by slightly drunk young men, doctors or not. After looking around, she spotted a spare seat on a small brown leather sofa in a corner, and threading her way through the noisy room, went to sit down. A tall, rather untidy-looking young man was already there, a little older than the others, who smiled slightly but didn't speak. Rebecca had noticed him earlier, mainly because he seemed so serious. Then she relaxed, enjoying the music, watching young couples grow ever more amorous, some just "smooching", but one or two in such passionate clinches that she began to feel embarrassed. And then she scolded herself for being a prude. Nobody else seemed to mind. You've led far too sheltered a life, she told herself, and then had to suppress wry mirth at the thought. An unmarried mother – sheltered was hardly how other people would describe her!

Without really being aware of it, Rebecca gave a

sigh, and the man next to her turned. "That was a deep one!"

Embarrassed, Rebecca said, "Oh, sorry."

He gazed intently at her and she suddenly felt flustered. Trying to think of something to say, she could only think to ask, "And what do you do at the hospital?"

"I'm hoping to specialise in psychiatry. What do you do? I can't recall seeing you around."

He was a doctor then, she thought. But as to his question, it was one she'd been asked several times that evening. And she'd given the answer that had led to heated discussion with Sal and Katie.

"There's no need to say anything about Anna," was Sal's firmly expressed opinion. "At least not immediately."

"I'm not ashamed of her," Rebecca said stubbornly.

"Of course you're not, who could be?" Sal jiggled the toddler fondly on her knee. "But be realistic, girl. If you go around telling every young man you meet that you've had an illegitimate baby, you're asking for trouble."

"Just because—"

"*I* know that," Sal said. "But they won't – not until they get to know you! I'm right, aren't I, Katie?"

The Irish girl nodded. "I'm afraid so."

"I'm not lying," Rebecca insisted. "It'll only be harder to tell someone later."

"Not if you wait until after your first date," Katie advised. "And only tell them then, if you're keen."

And so, when she'd been asked during the evening

164

what she "did", Rebecca had merely said that she helped her uncle run his pub. But now, there was something in the young doctor's voice and the keen intelligence in his eyes that made her hesitate. He glanced sharply at her, and said, "I'm David, by the way."

"Rebecca."

"Hello, Rebecca. You seem a bit reluctant to tell me how you spend your time." He grinned, "You're not a spy or something are you. You know, like Mata Hari?"

Rebecca laughed. "No, nothing like that." She looked away, as the colour rising in her cheeks, she told him, "I just help my uncle to run his pub." David looked appraisingly at the flame-haired girl by his side. With her light, easy voice with its hint of a Welsh lilt, she was, as far as he was concerned, the most attractive girl in the room. In fact, he'd been tempted to ask her to dance. But David had disciplined himself to resist such temptations. When he'd first begun studying medicine, he'd vowed to avoid emotional entanglements, and his determination was even stronger at this crucial stage in his career. But it was obvious, at least to a doctor with his experience, that Rebecca was concealing something. And then there had been that sigh, so deep for such a young girl. He was intrigued. "Who have you come with?"

"Katie O'Brien – she's a probationer nurse." At that moment Katie, entwined in a slightly amorous waltz, gave a little wave.

David looked at Rebecca again, aware of the slight

tension in her body, recalling the troubled look he'd seen in those unusual green eyes. He'd watched her earlier, when she'd been dancing, and seen her reserve, the way she'd slightly distanced herself. David decided to probe.

Rebecca was looking down at her hands, now bare of the hated Woolworth's brass curtain ring. She'd taken it off after Anna was born, deciding it was no longer necessary. Anyone seeing her pushing a pram would just assume she was the baby's auntie, or elder sister. But lately she'd begun wearing it again, knowing that now Anna was beginning to talk, her constant childish treble of "Mummy" was bound to provoke scornful glances. Tonight she'd bowed to pressure to leave it off.

"Nobody's going to take an interest in you, if they think you're married," Sal said briskly.

"I could be a widow," Rebecca pointed out.

Ron had surprised them both by joining in. "Nah, that's a bit unlikely, at your age. You take it off, and 'ave a good time."

And so Rebecca had. And was she having a good time? Certainly she was enjoying the atmosphere, the music, and the heady feeling of being among so many young people. But no matter how she tried to be light-hearted and flirtatious like the other young girls, the memory of Ian and his tragic death was always below the surface. But not only did she know that she needed to move on, she longed to.

David watched the fleeting expressions on her face, saw the wistful look in her eyes and said softly, "Rebecca, forgive me if I'm wrong, but I feel there's

166

something troubling you. I'm a very good listener, if you think it would help to talk about it. In complete confidence, of course. And sometimes it's easier with a stranger."

Startled, Rebecca glanced at him, was reassured by the gentle concern in his eyes and felt tempted. Where they were sitting at the far end of the room was quiet, and among all the noise, their low voices were unlikely to be overheard. "You don't come to a party to listen to other people's problems," she said tentatively.

"Oh, I'm a bit different from other people," he smiled.

She hesitated, "It's just . . . I don't know where to begin."

"Try the beginning." David changed his position on the sofa, turning to lean slightly towards her. "Tell me about your family, you know, where you grew up."

Rebecca looked at him and seeing that he was genuinely interested, haltingly began to relate all that had happened to her since the age of twelve. She paused, and waited a moment, but David remained silent. "And then," she said, twisting her hands nervously on her lap, "then, I met Ian . . ."

As he listened to the sad tale, David felt no emotion other than sadness for the girl at his side. He was too used to human frailty to be shocked by the news that she had an illegitimate child.

"And your little girl is – how old?"

"She's just had her first birthday."

They sat in silence for several minutes, then

eventually David said, "I've been wondering about the time you went up to the Potteries. I know you found out that Ian had been killed, but did you by any chance go to the local cemetery?"

Rebecca's eyes widened in surprise. "No," she said slowly, "I was in such a state, the thought never occurred to me."

"Seeing where someone is buried, tending their grave," David tried to explain, "can be a great comfort. With some people, until they've done that, they can't seem to come to terms with their loss."

Rebecca thought for a moment. "So you mean that might be what is stopping me, you know – from being able to get on with my life?"

"Is that what you feel is happening?"

Rebecca nodded. "It's difficult to explain, but it's as though something is holding me back. I just can't seem to feel part of things, not in the way I should."

"It's not unusual," David said. "We see it quite a lot, particularly with people who've lost someone during the war. Even when they've been reported 'killed in action', without the finality of a grave, they can't—"

"Come to terms with their loss." Rebecca quietly finished the sentence for him. David's words sounded so logical, so obvious. She suddenly found it unbelievable that not once since Ian had died, had it ever occurred to her to return to Stoke. She'd sometimes wondered how his mother was, of course, but it was as though her mind had drawn down a curtain. Ian had been killed, he was gone from her life, and all she'd been able to think about was her pregnancy, and since then, caring for his daughter. Why hadn't she wondered which cemetery he was buried in? Where his grave was, tried to visualise a headstone?

She turned to David with dismay. "Can you believe I never once thought of it?"

He smiled. "The mind is a strange thing, Rebecca. Maybe you needed time."

"I could take Anna with me," she suggested eagerly. She had a vision of how she would take flowers, how she could show Ian his tiny daughter. But crucially, she would be able, at last, to say goodbye. Suddenly Rebecca knew this was something she desperately wanted to do.

But then David saw doubt cloud her expression. "What's the matter?"

She looked at him ruefully. "I've just thought. It's too far to go just for a day – for a toddler, I mean. And I'd never be able to manage on the Tube and train, not carrying her, with a pushchair and everything we'd need to stay overnight." She paused and said with regret, "I'll just have to go on my own, and come back the same day." Even then, she thought, it might be difficult to arrange for someone to look after Anna.

David looked at her reflectively. "I've got an idea – don't go away!" He got up and Rebecca watched as he crossed the room to bend down to talk to Dr Mason, who was sitting with his arm around the same blonde. There was a short, earnest conversation, then the good-looking young doctor looked across at Rebecca, and nodded.

David returned with a triumphant expression.

"Problem solved," he said. "Guy comes from just outside Crewe, and he says any time he's going home for the weekend, he'll give you a lift."

Rebecca stared at him in protest. "But—"

David held up a hand. "No buts – honestly, it'll hardly be out of his way. He says Katie can let him know when." He looked down at her intently. "But firstly, you are sure this is something you want to do?"

"Oh yes," Rebecca didn't hesitate. "I just feel an idiot I didn't think of it before."

"Good." David leaned back in contentment. This had been a very satisfactory evening after all. He stifled a yawn. "Sorry," he said, "it's been a long day."

"And you could have done without my problems," Rebecca said, with a pang of guilt. She glanced at him with increasing interest. Dark, with slightly curly hair worn longer than was currently fashionable, she suddenly realised that in his own subtle way, David was very attractive. "You know," she said slowly, "I think you'll make a wonderful psychiatrist."

"Thank you," he smiled at her. "I hope so."

"Well, you've certainly helped me."

"I'll just send you the bill," he gave an infectious grin, and Rebecca began to laugh.

Katie, on her way over to them, thought how good it was to see her friend so light-hearted. "Come on, Cinders," she said. "Our carriage has already turned into a pumpkin, or should I say a Tube train!"

Rebecca stood up. David gazed up at her. "Good luck," he said quietly.

170

"Bye," she said, "and once again – thanks."

"Sure, you're a dark horse," Katie turned to whisper, as they made their way out of the crowded room. "Talk about aiming high!"

"How do you mean?"

"Monopolising the mighty Dr Knight. We nurses can't get a look-in."

"Then you don't have my charm, do you?" Rebecca laughed, and for some reason felt quite pleased that David wasn't a flirt. But then, she suddenly thought, the only thing he found interesting about you, Rebecca Lawson, was your problem. Charm didn't come into it!

17

Katie stared wide-eyed at Rebecca. "I still can't believe that from that one visit to the hospital you've got the chance to spend hours alone with Dr Mason? You do realise you'll have every nurse under thirty hating you?"

"I can't help that," Rebecca said. "But I don't think he'll be interested in me – he hardly gave me a second glance."

"I think our Dr Mason is the ambitious type," Katie said. "At least that's what everyone says."

"Well, he'd hardly further his career by consorting with the likes of me!" Rebecca picked up Anna and, putting her in the highchair, gave her a rusk. "In any case, I shan't take him up on it until the weather gets better. I don't fancy trailing around in the cold and wet."

"When do you think you'll go, then?"

"Probably in May, if that fits in." Rebecca tickled her baby's tummy, laughing at her delighted response. With a sunny disposition, and pretty dark-chestnut hair Anna was a favourite with everyone.

"Come to your Auntie Flossie, my little flower-pot," was a familiar refrain, and Sal and Rebecca would exchange smiles, amused by the various reasons the barmaid gave for her frequent social visits to the Unicorn.

"I just popped in to say they've got some oranges along at Brown's," she'd say, or, "Is there anything I can bring you from Spitalfields?"

Ruby, too, would sometimes ask to come "through to the back", and would spend half an hour nursing or playing with Rebecca's little daughter. "A little ray of sunshine, that's what she is," she often said.

But it was Ron's reaction that had surprised everyone. Nothing pleased him more than playing rough and tumble with the toddler. At first, Rebecca had been horrified to see him toss her in the air, but the baby's squeals of delight and the surety of his huge arms, eventually reassured her. Sal would just smile, her expression wistful, as she couldn't help thinking what a wonderful father he would have made.

Rebecca turned to Katie. "And what about you and that chap you were canoodling with?"

Katie blushed. "Oh, that was one of the housemen. He's taking me to the flicks on Saturday."

"What's that?" Sal said, coming in. "Don't tell me our Katie's got herself a boyfriend?"

"Not before time," Katie said. "Mind you, it's only a first date."

"Well, watch your step!" Sal said sharply, and then could have bitten her tongue off, as she saw Katie glance quickly at Rebecca. "I didn't mean—"

"It's okay, Sal," Rebecca said quietly.

"Sure, nobody needs worry about me." Katie hurriedly tried to make a joke of it. "It's the Catholic guilt, you see. Stops you having any fun!"

Sal bristled. "It's not only your lot who have morals, yer know. There's lots of good girls who've never bin to church."

"Of course," Katie began to flounder. "I didn't mean—"

"I don't think either of you meant anything!" Rebecca lifted an eager Anna out of the chair. "I'll just get this one ready, and then we can be off."

Thankful it wasn't raining, the two girls walked briskly along the narrow pavements, making their way through the streets to Shadwell. "It's going to take ages," Rebecca said, looking sadly at the ruined buildings and general air of depression. "To get things back to normal, I mean."

"I doubt if they'll ever be that," Katie said. "Although of course I didn't know what it was like before the war."

"Different to this! Never mind, we'll see a few trees and some grass when we get to the park." As she spoke, Rebecca had a fleeting memory of the gates into Hanley Park, just opposite Ian's home. How lovely it would be, she thought, to have somewhere like that on your doorstep. Most days – determined that Anna would get her daily ration of fresh air – she would strap her in the huge pram, and park it in the backyard as far away from the public lavatories as possible. "She's going to grow up with her earliest memories being beer crates, and a peculiar pong," she would joke to Ron and Sal, but at heart, Rebecca knew that the environment was far from ideal.

"How are Conor and Maura?" she asked.

"They're fine. Excited about the baby. Ah," Katie exclaimed as eventually they reached their destination, "here we are. God's fresh air!" Rebecca took deep breaths, almost gasping as the chill hit her lungs.

"I love open spaces," she said suddenly. "I think this one does too." They both looked down and laughed at Anna's shining eyes and button nose already red with cold. "It'll do her good," Rebecca said, but her smile concealed a pang of guilt, knowing how rarely she made such an effort. There just never seemed to be enough time. "Come on," she said. "Let's run." And they did, careering along the paths while Anna laughed and the two girls felt exhilarated and free.

Christmas passed, and the long, grey winter months gave way to gentler weather and blue skies. And now, all of Rebecca's thoughts were channelled into planning her trip to Stoke.

At the beginning of May, she wrote to Dr Mason. "He'll probably wonder what on earth I'm on about," she said, giving the envelope to Katie. "What do you bet he's forgotten all about it? After all, it was ages ago."

"Maybe." Katie frowned. "Best to be prepared for it."

But Rebecca knew she'd be bitterly disappointed if the offer of a lift fell through. She'd still go of course, alone and just for the day, but in her mind the trip had become almost a pilgrimage, and she desperately wanted to take Anna. But to try and carry a child, a heavy pushchair, and a large suit-case would be stupid. So, Rebecca could only wait anxiously until Katie's next visit.

Ron had his doubts about the whole project. "What's she got to go up there for, opening up a can of worms?" he complained to Sal. "Seems a daft thing to do, if you ask me."

"Oh, I don't know," Sal, fag in hand, inhaled deeply. "I think I can understand it in a way. And if she thinks it'll help her to put Ian behind 'er, I'm all for it."

"Do yer ever wonder what happened to Ian's mother?"

Sal looked sadly at him. "Have done at times. But you know as well as me – once people are taken into them asylums, they hardly ever come out."

When Katie came with the triumphant message that Dr Mason could take her the following weekend, Rebecca went into flurries of preparation. "The amount of stuff I need for her, just for one night, is ridiculous," she exclaimed the following day, looking up from a list she was writing.

"Are you taking her potty?" Sal glanced up from her newspaper.

"I think I'll have to."

"And what will you do with the soiled nappies if she has an accident?"

"I'll cope as best I can. I'll have no choice."

"Good of this doctor chap though," Sal commented, "coming all the way out here to pick you up."

Rebecca nodded and then grinned. "Katie says

he wants to come and see the real East End. That'll be a shock to him!"

"There's nothing wrong with the East End," Sal snapped. "We're real people down here, not like some of them toffs." She sniffed, "Most of 'em are no better than they should be!"

Dr Mason was late. Rebecca had been up since six, making sure she was organised, eating the cooked breakfast that Sal, hauling herself out of bed, had insisted on cooking. Now, Sal, still in her plaid dressing gown with her hair in steel curlers, sat hunched in her armchair with a fag in her hand, and wondered. Now that the time had actually arrived, she was beginning to have her doubts about the whole trip. All that way just to look at a grave? Morbid, some people would call it. And she wasn't sure she trusted these psychiatrists. What got most people by in this world was plain common sense. All this delving into minds – it wasn't natural!

Rebecca got up and went into the bar to peer out of the front window. "He probably won't come round the side," she fretted. "What do you think?"

"I think if he said nine o'clock, he should be here at nine o'clock," Sal told her. "Anyway, you've never said how much he knows – about you, I mean?"

"I've got no idea," Rebecca said. "But I'm wearing a ring, anyway. I don't want any 'tutting' from old ladies when Anna starts chattering." They both turned to smile fondly at the toddler, who, balanced on sturdy legs, was fiddling with the clasp on the large brown suitcase.

177

"Yer have got her reins?" Sal looked anxiously at her niece.

"I've got everything."

A loud, persistent knock at the front door startled them both, and then it was all panic, as Rebecca hurriedly hugged Sal, took the case and pushchair into the bar, came back for Anna, and went to open the door. Sal hurried up the stairs to the front bedroom, and standing at one side of the window, drew aside a corner of the net curtain and peered down.

"Flamin' Nora – just look at that!"

"Watcher doin'?" Ron turned over sleepily. He relished his weekend lie-in. "Come back ter bed!"

But Sal was far too interested in the scene below. "She never said he looked like bleedin' Cary Grant!" She watched as the young doctor laughed down at her niece, and saw the colour rise in Rebecca's cheeks. Suspicion flared. Could there be an ulterior motive in this offer of a lift? Nah, she dismissed the thought as she turned away – not with a kiddie along. Doctors were almost like gods to most people, but not to Sal. She'd been to see one once, who'd prescribed a bottle of tonic that tasted so foul she'd tipped it down the sink. But one thing she did know – they lived in another world from East End girls. I hope Rebecca remembers that, she thought grimly, climbing in beside her slumbering husband – we don't want any more trouble!

But such worries were far from Rebecca's mind. She'd almost forgotten how handsome Guy – as he'd immediately told her to call him – was. She glanced at his profile, and smiled, thinking that a sports car would have suited his debonair image far more than the staid Morris Eight. He struggled to fit the pushchair – still cumbersome even when folded – into the small boot, but by moving his own case on to the back seat, Guy eventually managed. Then almost as if he'd read her thoughts, he said, "Don't think this is my choice of vehicle. It's on loan from my mother. But as soon as I can, I'm going to buy an MG!"

"Red!" she said promptly.

"Now how did you guess that?" He turned and grinned, and Rebecca noticed again how his eyes crinkled at the corners. Somehow it made his whole face light up.

"Female intuition," she told him. Later, she stared out of the car window thinking with alarm – how can I feel like this? How can I be attracted to another man, when I'm on my way to see Ian's grave! It doesn't seem right! She didn't know whether Guy had seen her confusion, but he drove for the next half an hour in silence. With Anna on her knee and fascinated by the passing scenery, Rebecca tried to relax and enjoy the novelty of the journey. The Parrys – living a mile outside the village – had always driven to chapel, but Rebecca hadn't ridden in a car since she left Wales. Eventually, still unsure exactly how much Guy knew about her trip, and trying to think of something to say, Rebecca said, "Did David tell you why I'm going up to the Potteries?"

"He said you needed to go. Something about visiting a grave?"

Rebecca twisted the ring on her finger. She'd always remember David's gentle perception, and felt a sense of regret that she'd never see him again. Only the other day, Katie had told her that he'd left London, having been offered a more senior post at a hospital in Warwickshire. Then, aware that Guy was waiting for her to elaborate, Rebecca turned back to him. "Yes," she said. "Anna's father's." She told him about the Bolton football disaster, and how both Ian and his father had been killed.

"I remember that," Guy said. "It was terrible. I'm a bit of a football fan myself. In fact I came up to watch Stoke City beat Chelsea 2–1 a few weeks ago."

Rebecca sighed – men and their football! And she could just imagine the comments of the customers in the pub, who regarded Chelsea as the toffs' club. Well, he is a doctor, she thought wryly. She wondered what sort of background he came from. Different from her own, that was obvious. For one thing, even his mother had a motor car. And you only had to look at his clothes. The camel polo-necked sweater was of a quality far beyond her income.

"I am sorry. You're so young to be a widow," Guy said, and Rebecca froze. She glanced down in panic at the plain gold band on the third finger of her left hand. She could so easily just agree, and surely it wouldn't be the same as telling a blatant lie. At that moment, Anna began to squirm, and Rebecca reached down into the shopping bag at her feet, and took out a feeding cup of diluted juice. Each week she religiously wheeled Anna to the welfare clinic to collect the jar of cod liver oil and malt, and concentrated orange juice the government provided to supplement children's rations. It wasn't an enjoyable experience, as the two women behind the counter knew she wasn't married, but Rebecca had learned to ignore their tightened lips and contemptuous glances.

Then suddenly she heard the almost forgotten sound of her mother's voice, saying "*tell the truth and shame the devil*". It was so unexpected that Rebecca felt shaken, remembering how often she'd heard that phrase during her childhood. Almost without conscious decision, she found herself taking a deep breath.

"Actually, I'm not a widow." She was surprised just how even her voice was. "Ian and I were going to get married, but unfortunately he died too soon."

There was a silence. "I talked to David about what had happened, and how I felt," she said quietly, "and he advised me that going to see where Ian is buried might help me to move on."

To her surprise, after a moment, Guy reached over and lightly touched her hand. "Good," he said. "I'm glad I've been able to help."

The unexpected gesture touched her, and with enormous relief, Rebecca said simply, "Thank you." She glanced at him. "You can guess why I wear a ring."

"I like kids," Guy said suddenly. "But don't tell anyone – it doesn't go with my image!" Rebecca laughed.

"That's better," he said. "I don't bite, you know." He grinned at her, and Rebecca smiled back. "I've obviously got an image, then," he said. "Go on – tell me what the nurses say about me?"

"My lips are sealed," she teased. "In any case, you're only fishing for compliments."

"Of course I am. All handsome young doctors are conceited – I thought you'd know that!"

She smiled. "I don't know any. Just the ones I met at the party."

"Oh, you can't count old David. He's a misogynist."

"A what?"

"A woman-hater. He must be, to pass a lovely girl like you on to the likes of me." He glanced across at her, his eyes full of merriment, and Rebecca, now fully at ease with him, laughed. The rest of the journey, broken only by a brief stop at a transport cafe, was spent in easy conversation and with Rebecca trying to entertain a restless Anna, who eventually fell asleep.

And then they were approaching Stoke-on-Trent, and as Rebecca looked at the increasingly industrial landscape, with its distinctive bottle kilns, her mind went back to that other fateful Saturday. Again, she saw herself standing outside the empty house, knocking in vain, recalling how nauseous she'd been – how she couldn't even face a cup of tea. She could see the corner shop clearly, and the shopkeeper – what was her name? Oh, yes, Maggie. Again Rebecca remembered the shock, disbelief and devastating grief she'd felt when Maggie told her that Ian had been killed. Yet since then so much had happened.

Rebecca looked down at the child on her lap, and held her closer. And you, my darling, she thought, are the very best of all!

18

On that same Saturday, as Rebecca was approaching Stoke-on-Trent, Grace Beresford stood before the grey marble headstone inscribed with the names of her husband and only son. Bending down, she removed the dying flowers from the urn and emptied out the stagnant water. "These haven't lasted long, have they?" she murmured. "It's the weather, Jim. We're having a very warm spell. Never mind, we've got a lovely show of pinks in the garden – I'll bring some tomorrow." Grace leaned over and gently touched the top of the headstone, before turning to leave. A neatly dressed figure in a blue fitted costume, her dark but greying hair lifting gently in the breeze, she began to walk slowly out of the leafy cemetery.

Grace had always taken pride in her appearance, and made the most of her staff discount at the Marks & Spencer store in Hanley, where she still had a part-time job. When, after six distressing months, she'd eventually been discharged from the mental hospital, Grace had grimly resolved never to return. Despite protestations from the doctors, she saw her nervous breakdown as a weakness in her character, and still felt bitterly ashamed, feeling that she'd let herself down. I should have been stronger, she often told herself, only too aware of the traumas that countless other women had suffered during the last two World Wars. Friends said she was too hard on herself, that in peacetime you didn't expect to lose your whole family in a matter of days, but Grace couldn't help the way she felt. However, there was no room in her life now for listlessness or that most destructive of emotions, self-pity. Grace knew that it would only be with rigid self-discipline that she was going to be able to salvage something from the wreckage of her life. She was still on medication, but slowly it was being reduced, and she had hopes that soon she would be able to manage without it.

The main road was busy with Saturday morning traffic, and Grace had to wait at the kerb for several minutes before crossing over to make her way to the familiar corner shop to fetch a packet of tea. She was getting low, and she couldn't risk running out on a Sunday, when all the shops were closed.

Maggie had fretted for months before plucking up the courage to tell Grace about the young girl who had travelled up from London.

"What am I going to do?" she said to her sister, when Grace had eventually been discharged. "I feel I've got to tell her about it. Every time she comes into the shop I feel guilty for keeping it to meself!"

"Yer've got to give her time," Enid counselled. "It's a big thing, our Maggie, a nervous breakdown. Even though they've let her out, she'll still have some recovering to do. If you go opening up old wounds too soon, it'll only put her back."

And so Maggie had listened to her sister's advice and, although it hadn't been easy, she'd waited. And then, seeing the quiet woman gradually begin to smile again and able to chat to other customers, both women had decided that perhaps the time had come. "After all," Enid said, "she has been home for four months."

For Grace, it had been just a normal day when, the bell over the door tinkling as she entered the shop, she said, "Good morning, Maggie," and put her weekly order on the counter. She saw the shop-keeper glance furtively out of the window, and wondered why the small, wiry woman seemed so agitated.

"Mornin', Mrs Beresford. How are you? In general, I mean?"

Seeing the anxiety in Maggie's tired eyes, Grace sighed. People were very kind, but she wished they wouldn't lower their voices when asking how she was. Surely after two World Wars, everyone knew that mental health problems were nothing to be ashamed of? In that case, a tiny voice in her head said, why can't you apply that reasoning to your-self? She hurriedly shrugged the thought away, and smiled at Maggie. "I'm fine, thank you."

"Only, there's something I've been meaning to tell you." Nervously, Maggie began to tidy up the blue sugar bags on the counter. Curious, Grace waited.

"It's about when you were in . . ."

186

"St Edward's?"

"Yes, that's right. Now I would have told you this before, but Enid and me – well, we decided to wait until you were a bit stronger. I hope you'll understand."

"I'm sure I will, Maggie." Grace smiled reassuringly at her.

"There was this girl," Maggie said suddenly. "She came to the shop one Saturday afternoon. Lovely red hair she had, I've never forgotten it. She said she'd been knocking on your door and couldn't get an answer and did I know if you were away." Seeing Grace's puzzled frown, Maggie added, "She'd come up from London special like, had a suitcase with her."

Grace could only stare at her in shock and consternation. London! Her hand went to clutch at her throat – a girl with "lovely red hair"? That could only mean one person! No, surely not – but it must have been – who else could it be? Rebecca! In panic, she tried to follow what Maggie was now saying. "She knew nothing about it, the football disaster, I mean. And I guessed who she was, because I'd heard you saying that Ian'd got himself a girlfriend – someone he'd met in London."

And then Grace answered the question that had plagued both Maggie and Enid. "I never let her know," she whispered, her eyes wide with guilt and dismay. "I hadn't got an address or even a phone number. I searched the whole house for his diary, but Ian must have had it with him. There wasn't any way I could get in touch." Even now, Grace could

187

remember how frustrated she'd felt, how conscience-stricken.

Maggie, her lined face sorrowful at the memory, said, "I suppose it must have gone missing in all the chaos – not surprising, really. I don't know how I found the words to tell her, but I did. Eeh, that poor girl! You could see the shock in her, and I'll never forget watching her walk back along that street. Weeping, she was – it was the saddest sight I ever saw in my life."

Worried to see how her words were upsetting the woman before her, Maggie said with concern, "Now don't you fret yourself, Mrs Beresford. As I said, it was a long time ago. Only me and Enid didn't want to worry you, not at first."

"You're very kind." It was a struggle, but Grace managed to regain her composure. "And thank you, Maggie. I'm just sorry you had the job of telling her."

"That's all right, Mrs Beresford." Maggie straightened her shoulders, as another customer came into the shop. "Now, what can I get you?"

As Grace was leaving the churchyard, Rebecca, having waved goodbye to Guy, entered the vestibule of the Commercial Hotel; this time, it was a younger man, thin and intense looking, who was on the reception desk. She hesitated, and with some embarrassment signed the register as Mrs Rebecca Lawson.

"Do you want to leave the pushchair under the stairs?" he suggested. "It'll be quite safe." Rebecca nodded, and then as he picked up her suitcase, she carried Anna upstairs behind him, dreading that she'd be given the same bedroom, the one where, overwhelmed with grief, she'd spent that terrible night. But to her relief she was ushered into a larger one. Simply furnished, it had a double bed and even a rather shabby cot in one corner. "As you said you'd got a kiddie with you, we thought we'd give you a bit of space," the young man said.

"Thanks, that's really good of you." Rebecca flashed a grateful smile at him, and as soon as he'd gone, tore open the packet of cheese sandwiches she'd brought with her. She gave one to Anna and bit thankfully into another herself. She was absolutely starving. It was hours since she'd eaten, and she blessed Sal for making her have a proper cooked breakfast, and for the flask she'd insisted on packing. After Anna had demolished her sandwich, a Farley's rusk, and a square of chocolate, Rebecca sat her on the potty and unpacked their few belongings. Later, with Rebecca carrying Anna's "offering", they made their way along the corridor to the lavatory, and eventually, after a quick wash in the bathroom, and a tidy-up in the bedroom, they were ready to leave.

Yet now that the long-awaited moment had arrived, Rebecca found herself with mixed emotions. Part of her yearned to see where Ian was buried, she was hoping . . . she didn't really know what she was hoping. She had no experience of visiting an actual grave where someone was buried, as her parents had both been cremated. Another part of her felt troubled, worried that this visit might make it even more difficult for her to – not forget him, she would never do that – but to feel free to love again. In a way, she thought, I suppose I'm seeking a form of release. Now, as Rebecca gazed down into the trusting eyes of her daughter, she could only gather up her courage. "Okay, sweetheart," she said, "let's go and see your daddy."

With Anna strapped into her pushchair, Rebecca left the hotel and walked slowly by the side of the main road, down the hill to the cemetery she'd noticed on her previous visit. Of course, she couldn't be sure that this was where Ian was actually buried, but it seemed the logical place to visit first. It was a lovely summer afternoon, with just a hint of a slight breeze, and once inside the gates and away from traffic, Rebecca let Anna walk. Delighted by the freedom, the toddler was entranced by the squirrels and tried to chase them as they scurried among the borders and ran up the trees. Rebecca was anxiously searching the inscriptions. She walked along the paths, ignoring ancient graves, concentrating on newer ones, and scanning headstones further back. And then suddenly, she saw it. The grave, slightly apart from the others, was in front of a row of poplar trees, just a simple grey marble headstone with an empty urn beneath.

I should have brought flowers! Rebecca would always remember her first guilty reaction. What was she thinking of – to come all this way without even a posy from Anna? But that distracting thought was merely fleeting, as Rebecca, almost with a sense of dread, read the simple inscription.

IN LOVING MEMORY

James Frederick Beresford
1895–1946
also
Ian Donald Beresford
1918–1946
Both killed in a tragic accident
A dearly loved husband and a beloved son

R.I.P

Profoundly moved, Rebecca stood and gazed at Ian's name, knowing the image of those three carved words would remain in her memory forever. After a few silent moments, she said softly, "Hello, my darling. I'm sorry I didn't come before." Rebecca had often wondered whether, in some afterlife, Ian knew they had a child, and here in these peaceful surroundings, such a thought seemed almost believable. "And this little one," she said, her eyes now misting with tears, "is your daughter, Anna." Rebecca gently guided her forward, and bent down. "This is where your daddy is asleep," she said softly. "Do you want to say hello?"

Anna looked first at her mummy and then at the grey stone. "Hello, Daddy," she said uncertainly.

"Shall we go and buy him some pretty flowers?" Rebecca said.

Anna nodded, and then tugged at Rebecca's hand. "Go now?"

"In a minute." Rebecca stood before the grave.

It hadn't occurred to her that father and son would be buried together, but she supposed it made sense. There's probably room in there for his mother too, she thought sadly.

"All right," she turned to the restless toddler. "We'll go and find a flower shop. We can't have Daddy thinking nobody loves him, now can we?" Anna regarded her gravely, gave a little nod, and then suddenly began to run back along the path. "Wait!" Rebecca called, and chased after her with the pushchair, lifting the laughing child and buckling her safely in. But Rebecca had never felt less like laughing. There was only one word in her mind, one burning question. Why? And then, as she went out of the entrance, she thought with misery, I'll never know the answer, no one will.

Back at the hotel, she found out that there was a florist's shop "just up the road". Once there, Rebecca could only look with dismay at the prices on the buckets of cut flowers. The charges at the hotel, although moderate, had still made a hole in her meagre savings. But to her relief the cheerful, overall-clad assistant said they were closing soon and offered her a choice of carnations or roses at half-price. Rebecca didn't hesitate. "I'll take a dozen of the red roses, please!"

Half an hour later, she was back in the cemetery, and standing before the grave. Rebecca bent down and taking out the empty container from the urn, stood looking around for a tap.

"It's over there," a passer-by told her. "See – just on that corner." Without another word, she walked away – a small dumpy figure, carrying a shopping bag with a trowel on top.

A few minutes later, with Anna trying to help, Rebecca carefully arranged the flowers before the headstone, and stood back with pride. "There," she said, wiping her hands on a handkerchief. "That's better."

"Mummy, want drink," Anna whimpered, and with a lingering backward glance, Rebecca whispered, "Goodbye, see you tomorrow." As they made their way slowly back to the hotel again, Rebecca could only think that Mrs Beresford must be still in the mental hospital. Otherwise, surely, as she lived so near to the cemetery, she would have looked after the grave?

On Sunday mornings, Grace always allowed herself an extra lie-in. She'd never been particularly religious, and rarely attended church, but Sundays were still special. With the sound of church bells in the distance and the Morning Service on the wireless, it was a day for quiet reflection. She still kept up the tradition of a Sunday roast, although with only one ration book, the size of the joint was tiny. But she managed, and there was usually enough meat for a sandwich later. She knew that some people found Sundays boring, with all the shops closed and not a lot to do, and many women chafed that it was frowned upon to hang out washing or clean windows. "A wasted day," was the view of her house-proud neighbour, but Grace didn't agree. She wouldn't want Sunday to be just the same as every other day.

She enjoyed listening to "Two-way Family Favourites" with Jean Metcalfe, sometimes singing along with the requests. And Grace did sing, and more frequently now she laughed, and the fact that she could do so was still a source of wonder. I'm getting stronger, she thought. And after all, she was only just fifty. It had been a long, dark tunnel to travel through, and she knew she would never get over the tragedy; but, unlike her late husband and son, she'd been granted these extra years of life, and Grace was determined not to waste them. After breakfast, she went into the garden and, snipping a selection of Jim's favourite flowers, went back indoors and rolled them into a sheet of newspaper. Then Grace prepared her vegetables, put them in a basin of cold water and made a small rice pudding. Half an hour later, with the small joint on the middle shelf of the oven and the enamel dish on the bottom, she let herself out of the front door.

"Mornin', Mrs Beresford," a man on a bicycle called as he rode past. He was whistling "Don't Sit Under the Apple Tree", and she called after him, "Morning, Fred!" Carrying the flowers, she walked slowly along the road, feeling no need to hurry. It was a fine day, and Grace believed in making the most of England's changeable climate. After crossing over the now almost empty main road, she made her way to the cemetery, and walking along the familiar paths, paused now and then to look up at the trees. Ash, lime and rowan were in full leaf, the spreading branches and welcome shade adding so much to the peaceful scene. You'd never think there was a main road just outside, she thought. Then, as Grace turned the corner and the grave of her husband and son came into view, her step suddenly faltered. She stopped, staring in astonishment at the sight of the fresh flowers before the headstone, and then slowly walking forward, bent down to see if there was a card or message. There was nothing.

Grace drew back, gazing in bafflement at the long-stemmed red roses. Who on earth . . . ? Not once, in all the time she'd been out of hospital, had anyone else ever brought flowers. And why would they? The Beresfords were a family bereft of relatives. She had been an only child, and Jim's brother, of course, had died after the same accident. Both of their parents had been only children, so they didn't have cousins, and certainly neighbours or friends wouldn't bring flowers, knowing how often Grace went to the cemetery.

"Well, I'm mystified!" she muttered, and stood in utter perplexity for a few moments, then began to walk home in bewilderment, still carrying her own flowers. It was certainly no use leaving them, she thought. Lying on the ground and without water they'd be wilted by teatime.

Rebecca had spent a restless night. She'd hoped that Anna would be tired out from the journey the day before, but the toddler still awoke at half-past six. Sleepily, Rebecca took her into her own bed, and with cuddles and nursery rhymes, tried to keep her entertained until it was time to go down to the small dining-room for breakfast. When the waitress, a thin young girl with slightly protruding eyes, brought in her cooked breakfast, Rebecca looked down in puzzlement. At the side of one rasher of bacon and an egg, were two folded brown pancake-looking things. "Pancakes?"

The waitress giggled. "You're not from round 'ere, are you? They're oatcakes!"

Oatcakes! Suddenly, Rebecca remembered Ian enthusing about them, saying they were a regional speciality, unique to Staffordshire. "You tuck in, duck," the waitress said. "It'll set you up for the day."

I hope so, Rebecca thought, as she picked up her knife and fork. Unless they'll do me a packed lunch, I don't know what we'll be able to get at lunchtime – not on a Sunday. The hotel only provided bed, breakfast and an evening meal. Interspersed with feeding Anna her cereal and toast, Rebecca enjoyed the unusual breakfast, and tearing off a small corner of the oatcake, dipped it into her yolk and handed to Anna. The toddler regarded it with suspicion, and then ate it with relish. Smiling, Rebecca picked up the brown earthenware teapot and, pouring out her tea, cradled the cup in both hands. What was her plan for the day? She glanced out of the window. There was an inviting blue sky so Hanley Park was definitely on the agenda. Hopefully they could have a picnic, and maybe there would be ducks for Anna to feed – she'd love that.

But there was something else she was determined to do. And that was to walk once again along Redwood Avenue, and past the Beresfords' house. Rebecca was curious to see what had happened to it after all this time. If Mrs Beresford *was* still in that mental hospital, then would the house have been sold? Or maybe Ian's parents had only been tenants. Of course she could have gone to the corner shop the day before and found out all of these things, but she'd decided against it. One disadvantage of having striking red hair was that people always remembered you. And this time she would have a child with her, and despite the ring on her finger that really would start tongues wagging! Because increasingly, with every month that passed – Anna, with her unusual grey eyes, was beginning to look remarkably like her father.

However, her main priority was another visit to the cemetery. After all, how could she be sure whether she'd ever be able to come again? And so, an hour later, Rebecca, with Anna strapped in her pushchair, stood once again before the headstone, the roses she'd so lovingly arranged gently unfolding in the sunshine. And Rebecca began to understand exactly what David had meant. He was so right, she thought suddenly, because now I'll always have the memory of Ian's grave in this peaceful tree-lined setting. I'll be able to think of him lying here, with his father, close to where he was born. Somehow it gives the whole tragedy a sort of finality.

Standing alone in the quiet cemetery, Rebecca was also conscious not only of the headstone before her, but of the many ancient stone slabs, and also the military graves from two World Wars. All these people, she thought in wonderment. So many lives; all with their joys, their grief, their secrets.

She gazed again at Ian's inscription. "There's something I need to say to you, my darling," she murmured. "Now, while there are no other people near. I feel so close to you this morning." And shutting her eyes against the bright sunlight, Rebecca stood motionless for several minutes, letting her mind drift back to that first day when she'd threaded her way through a throng of sightseers in Trafalgar Square. How Ian had waited, tall and handsome, his dark hair lifting in the breeze, how on their very first date they had fallen in love. And then, with the image of his narrow, sensitive face clearly before her, Rebecca was at last able to whisper, "Goodbye, and God bless, Ian. I promise that I'll always love and take care of our daughter." Almost blinded by tears, with Anna growing restless, she turned and began to make her way slowly out of the cemetery. She had to pause at the gate to dab at her eyes with a handkerchief, and then, straightening her shoulders, with determination she wheeled the pushchair over to the other side of the main road.

"Life is for the living" was a phrase she had often heard, but it was only now that Rebecca fully understood exactly what it meant. "Come on, sweetheart," she said, bending down to Anna. "Let's go and find Hanley Park. Then you can go on the swings."

Grace, having finished her Sunday roast beef and washed the dishes, wiped down the mottled grey enamel of her stove, and hung the now damp tea towel over a rail to dry. On Sunday afternoons, she liked to read her library book, and going into the front room, she opened one of the windows ready to settle down in an armchair. She used this "special" room more often now that she lived on her own, one reason being that she no longer had to worry about it getting messy. Why did men always make a house untidy, she wondered, yet knew she would willingly change her sterile, tidy home for the busy warmth of a family one. She put her copy of *Gone with the Wind* on a side table, and wandered over to twitch the net curtain and look out on to the street. Everywhere was quiet, and she was about to turn away when she saw a young woman with a pushchair emerge from the entrance to the park, and glance over to the house. Grace hurriedly let the net curtain fall back into place – she would hate anyone to think she was nosy. Drawing back slightly, she watched the young mother pause on the pavement opposite and turn to stare directly at Grace's home. Then, to her surprise, as sunlight glinted on rich auburn hair, she saw the girl – for she was little more – cross over and lift the latch on her gate.

Rebecca could see that the house was definitely occupied. All the front windows were open, and the doorstep, unlike the time before, was fresh with red Cardinal polish. She glanced down at Anna, who, tired after their outing in the park, had fallen asleep, and then, still unsure of exactly what she was going to say, rapped gently.

With puzzlement, Grace went slowly into the narrow hall. Through the stained-glass window, she could see the outline of the girl's head and, yet again, the reddish tints of her hair. Suddenly, Grace had a vision of the freshly placed flowers on the grave, and thought in panic – it can't be! She was imagining things. Hesitantly she opened the door, and suddenly knew with absolute certainty that she was looking at the girl her son had wanted to marry. *"Eyes like deep pools of green water."* They had been the words of a poem Ian had written just before he died.

Rebecca, unnerved by the intense gaze of the small woman, her dark hair streaked with grey, stammered, "I'm sorry to bother you—"

But she never finished her explanation, never had time to ask her questions, because she was interrupted by one tensely spoken query. "Rebecca?"

Astounded, Rebecca could only whisper with incredulity, "Mrs Beresford?"

Grace nodded, then said quietly, "Come in."

Rebecca, flustered, glanced down at the pushchair, its wheels dusty from their last couple of hours in the park. "Leave her outside," Grace said, surprised how calm she sounded. "It's a pity to waste the fresh air, and she'll be quite safe."

Rebecca put the pushchair in a patch of shade, and stepping over the threshold of Ian's home for the first time, followed his mother into the front room. She was relieved to see that Anna's pink sunbonnet was clearly visible outside the bay window.

"Would you like a cup of tea?"

"Thank you, I'd love one."

Grace glanced quickly at the wedding ring on Rebecca's finger, and escaped to the kitchen, her thoughts and emotions in chaos. She didn't waste much time finding someone else, she thought with sudden bitterness. I wonder what her husband thinks of her traipsing all the way up here to visit Ian's grave? While she stood waiting for the kettle to boil, her mind raced with questions. Why had the girl come – now, after all this time? And then Grace had another thought – surely she couldn't be living in the Potteries? Disturbed and puzzled, with a shaking hand Grace put some biscuits on a china plate, and tried to calm her jangled nerves. Rebecca, who had taken a seat sat opposite the window, was gazing around the room, trying to imagine Ian as a child, a young boy, and later the man she'd loved, growing up in these surroundings. Against one wall there was a china cabinet displaying ornaments: ladies in crinoline dresses, horses with their foals, and small baskets of flowers – all of fine china. But it was the small oak sideboard that immediately drew Rebecca's attention. On it stood two framed photographs. One was of the wedding of Mr and Mrs Beresford, but Rebecca hardly glanced at that. She was gazing at the image of Ian on his graduation day. He stared out her, proud and smiling in his cap and gown. It was the first time since that fateful weekend when they'd made love, that Rebecca had been able to see an image of the handsome face she'd loved so much. The memories came flooding back and she was still trying to control her emotions when Mrs Beresford came back into the room, carrying a tray. She placed it on a small coffee table, then sat in the armchair opposite Rebecca.

"Milk and sugar?"

"One, please." Rebecca took the fluted cup and saucer offered to her, but refused a biscuit. "Thank you." There was an awkward silence, then Rebecca said, "How did you know it was me?"

Grace smiled quietly. "I had my ways."

"I wasn't sure whether you—"

"Were still in St Edwards?"

Rebecca nodded.

"I was only in there for six months," Grace said.

Rebecca stared at her. All this time, and she hadn't known. But then, it had been just the same when Ian had died. Not a soul had bothered to contact her then. Well, I'm damn well going to ask her why, she thought. Now, while Anna's asleep and it's just the two of us.

"I didn't know that," Rebecca said. She looked away for a moment, and then said in a tight voice, "and if I hadn't come up here looking for him, I might never have found out that Ian had died."

The accusation hung in the air between them, and Grace inwardly flinched. How many times had she felt guilty for failing to contact this girl? Ian had not only loved her – he'd been full of their plans to get engaged. It wasn't my fault, she thought with sudden despair. In spite of all the terrible shock and grief when the accident happened, I tried – I really did. She looked at Rebecca, saw the resentment on her face, and knew the girl deserved an explanation.

"I'm so sorry about that," she said, and her hands twisted nervously on her lap. "My only excuse is that I didn't know how to get in touch with you." At the disbelief on Rebecca's face, Grace said desperately, "I went through all Ian's pockets and his bedroom drawers, but although I found a few of your letters, I couldn't find any address, and there was no sign of his diary." Rebecca stared at her. She tried to remember how she had begun her letters to Ian, and realised that Mrs Beresford was right. All

Rebecca had written at the top was *"The East End pub"*. It had been a sort of joke between them, a reminder of where they had met.

And then Grace said, "I didn't even know the name of the pub where you lived. Ian may have told me once, when he first met you, but I couldn't remember it or exactly where it was. I only knew that it was in the East End."

"Didn't he ever leave a phone number when he came down?" Rebecca persisted, still not convinced.

Grace shook her head. "Not with me. He knew I'd never used a phone in my life. Maybe he did with his father."

She looked in appeal at Rebecca, who said in a tight voice, "We'll never know will we?"

Grace clenched her hands on her lap. She was finding this whole scene – the sudden appearance of Rebecca, the questions about that terrible time – almost unbearable.

"And how are you?"

At the question, Grace looked again at the lovely young woman Ian had been going to marry. She'd have been my daughter-in-law, she thought suddenly. I can't believe she's actually here, sitting in this room. She saw the genuine concern in Rebecca's eyes, and found herself warming to the girl. And then, as yet again her glance fell to the plain gold band, her voice was stiff as she answered, "I'm fine, thank you."

Rebecca sensed the coolness, the restraint, and suddenly realised why. I've got to tell her that I'm not married, she thought quickly, and then was filled with panic. Because she had to tell Ian's mother, not only that her only son had shamefully got a girl "into trouble", but that the child sleeping peacefully outside was her granddaughter.

20

With the clock ticking loudly on the mantelpiece, both women sat in taut silence. Rebecca was desperately casting around in her mind for the right words, while Grace, consumed with curiosity, was wondering where to begin. Eventually, it was the older woman who spoke first.

"I take it that those were your flowers on the grave?"

"You saw them, then?"

Grace nodded. "I went along first thing this morning. I'd cleared out the dead ones yesterday."

Rebecca stared at her. So the grave was cared for after all. She found the knowledge strangely comforting.

"Did you travel up by train?" Grace said, wondering whether Rebecca's husband had brought her.

"No, I had a lift. I came up yesterday and stayed overnight at the Commercial Hotel, just across the road."

Grace surveyed her. So, she had come up from London, after all. And on her own. Or had her husband dropped his wife and child off, then continued on a business trip, perhaps? But Grace hadn't worked at Marks & Spencer for years without developing a keen eye for quality clothes. This girl wasn't married to a professional man. Not unless he was mean.

"And how long are you staying for?" Grace was conscious that her voice, although polite, was cold, but her heart felt like ice. It was difficult to judge from one glimpse just how old that little girl outside in her pushchair was, but she must be over twelve months. Not much grieving there, she thought with bitterness. But then why, after all this time, was Rebecca visiting Ian's grave?

"I'm going back later this afternoon." Rebecca swiftly turned as she heard a fretful wail from outside the window. "Is it all right to bring her in?"

"Of course," Grace said, and the fact that Rebecca had felt the need to ask made Grace feel rather ashamed of her lack of warmth. She watched the slim figure of the young woman as she went out of the front door and then saw her bend over the pushchair. Grace had been disappointed when Ian had told her he wanted to marry a girl who was, in Grace's eyes, uneducated. It wasn't that she had anything against barmaids: why, her next-door neighbour had worked at a local pub for years, and a more genuine woman you couldn't hope to meet. But after the struggle to send and then keep Ian at university, Grace had hoped that he would find someone of his own intellectual level, marry someone with culture. But he'd really loved this girl, it had been apparent in the way his eyes had lit up as he'd talked about her, how he'd looked forward to her coming up to meet them.

Grace's eyes misted with tears. So much that might have been. So much that now would never happen. Hurriedly she brushed a hand across her eyes, and stood up as Rebecca returned, carrying the child, flushed with sleep, in her arms.

Grace moved forward with a smile – she loved children. "Hello, what's your . . ." But her voice, now gentle and welcoming, suddenly faltered as Grace stared speechlessly at the little girl who gazed solemnly back at her with the eyes of her dead son.

Rebecca's voice was quiet, shaky. "This is Anna."

In utter bewilderment Grace began to back away, her stunned gaze riveted on the baby, one hand reaching behind her for support. Almost trembling with shock and disbelief, she slowly lowered herself into the armchair. Rebecca had seen the shocked recognition, and as Ian's mother raised her searching, questioning eyes from child to mother, Rebecca steadily held her gaze. She went to sit opposite the other woman, holding Anna closely on her lap. Then with slow deliberation, Rebecca took off the plain gold band from the third finger of her left hand, and placed it on a small oak coffee table. "Woolworth's."

"You're not married?" Grace's voice came out in a whisper.

Rebecca shook her head. "Ian was the man I was going to marry." There was such pathos in those words, such heartache. "I don't suppose I need to tell you . . ."

Grace shook her head. She didn't need any words to confirm that the pretty little toddler looking shyly at her was Ian's daughter. She just couldn't belong to anyone else! That the son she'd thought so moral, so upstanding had got this girl pregnant outside marriage, was something she pushed to the back of her mind to deal with later. For now, she just couldn't take her eyes off Anna.

"He never knew," Rebecca said. Desperate that there should be no misunderstanding, she said with embarrassment. "It only happened the once – and that's when we decided to get married." Her voice dropped to a whisper. "I never saw him again."

At the misery in the softly spoken words Grace could only stare at her in growing horror. She could visualise only too well what the tragedy must have meant to this young girl. Not only losing the man she loved, but having to cope with discovering she was pregnant! Then Grace suddenly realised that Rebecca would have already known of her condition when she travelled up to the Potteries to try and find Ian. She must have been so bewildered, so desperate. I should have been here, Grace thought with despair. "Oh my dear, I'm so sorry."

Rebecca's anxiety and unease began to evaporate as she saw the warmth and genuine sympathy in the other woman's eyes. Then seeing her longing, Rebecca lifted Anna off her lap and gave her a gentle push towards Ian's mother.

Grace, her heart full of emotion, smiled encouragingly and held out inviting arms. After a moment's hesitation, Anna took the vital few steps needed, and then Grace was picking her up, holding her gently, smiling into those heartbreaking grey eyes. For the first time in the last two years, the tears welling in her eyes were not of grief and bitterness, but of disbelief, wonder and sheer joy. "She's beautiful. I can't tell you what this means to me," she managed to say, her arms now enfolding Anna more closely. "Having thought I had nothing, to find out I have a grandchild, a family again . . ." her voice broke, and Rebecca, now close to tears herself, said, "Oh, Mrs Beresford—"

"Please – don't be formal. My name's Grace."

Rebecca looked at her, at the loving way she was holding Anna, at her gentle smile, and thought how much the name suited her. I'm so glad I came, she thought suddenly. Somehow I feel more complete. It was as though there was a missing piece of jigsaw somewhere in my life.

"Are you going to tell her who you are?"

Grace looked down at her granddaughter, who, thumb in mouth was looking with interest around the room. She pointed at the china horse and foal in the display cabinet, looked up at Grace and said, "Gee gees."

"That's right, sweetheart," Grace said. "And do you know who I am? I'm your granny."

Anna looked across at her mother, and then repeated the new word. "Granny."

The sound of the childish treble uttering that emotive word made Grace fish in her cardigan pocket for a handkerchief. "I'm sorry," she said, dabbing at her eyes. "It's all been such a shock. However did you manage? When she was born and everything."

"My aunt and uncle, the ones who keep the pub, they were very good to me."

"I'm glad you had someone," Grace said, knowing that Rebecca had lost her parents in the bombing. And again she berated herself for being so weak as to have a nervous breakdown. "I feel awful. I should have been here, should have been able to give you some support."

Rebecca stared at her in astonishment. "It wouldn't have bothered you?" she said slowly. "The shame – all the neighbours knowing?"

Grace gave a deep sigh. "It might have done at one time – but after what I've been through, I'm a bit older and wiser now."

As Anna began to squirm, Grace lifted her down, while Rebecca suddenly glanced at the clock and realised that she needed to be getting back to the hotel. "I'll have to go," she said. "I'm being picked up at four o'clock."

Grace stared at her in dismay and sudden panic. "Please – will you leave me your address and tele-phone number?"

"Of course."

Grace gave Rebecca an old envelope and a pencil, and waited while she scribbled down the informa-tion. "Look, I'll have to go." Rebecca moved towards the hall and said, "Could I possibly use your—"

"Of course. It's through the kitchen, just outside the back door. Is there anything you need for the journey? A drink, biscuits perhaps."

Rebecca hesitated. "Biscuits would be useful, and if you could refill Anna's cup for me? Water will be fine."

While Rebecca took Anna off to change her, Grace

211

rinsed the feeding cup, noticing a new one was needed. "I wonder if I can help out?" she murmured, and with sudden pleasure realised that once again she would have someone to buy presents for. And then she realised that she still didn't know why, after all this time, Rebecca had decided to return to the Potteries. But the girl's reasons were personal, too private for her to ask this first time. And it was only the hope of seeing them both again that buoyed her spirits as minutes later she watched Rebecca wheel Anna back along Redwood Avenue, and gradually disappear.

Then turning away, Grace sat back in her armchair and closed her eyes. Her library book forgotten, she relived every moment of that wonderful, yet traumatic afternoon. And then she realised that beneath all the shock and the joy – and she still had to come to terms with Ian's part in all this – there was one emotion she'd thought she'd never experience again. She could now look forward to the future with hope and excitement, a future that promised that most precious gift of all – a child to love.

21

Guy was half an hour late but eventually drew up outside the hotel. Rebecca was ready and waiting in the vestibule, and he came in, carried out the pushchair and suitcase and loaded them into the boot. Rebecca settled herself in the passenger seat, with Anna on her knee.

"Good weekend?" he said, glancing at her.

"Yes, it was. How about you?"

"Not bad. Good to see the parents." But Guy didn't seem to be in the mood to talk, and long stretches of the journey were spent in silence, leaving Rebecca free to examine all her conflicting emotions after the astonishing events of the afternoon. They drove with the windows open, stopped briefly at the same transport café, and then when they got back into the car, Guy apologised. "Sorry to have been a grump."

"Not at all," Rebecca told him. "I'd got lots to think about."

"That makes two of us!"

She remained quiet for a moment, then said, "I actually met Ian's mother – she's out of the mental hospital, she was only there for six months."

"That's wonderful." He glanced sharply at her. "Or is it?"

Rebecca nodded. "Definitely."

"It must have been quite a shock, discovering she had a grandchild." He grinned. "I wish I'd been a fly on the wall!"

But Rebecca didn't smile back at him. The scene had been too full of emotion to joke about. And it could all have gone so differently. Grace could have treated her with contempt, like those women at the Welfare Clinic, and several others in the neighbourhood. It wasn't unusual for people to refuse even to acknowledge a child born on "the wrong side of the blanket". Looking down at the innocent, trusting face of her small daughter, Rebecca wondered how people could have such closed minds, how they could be so cruel. Although Grace hadn't seemed to judge her, Rebecca was realistic enough to know that Ian's mother would have been disappointed to discover that her fine educated son had got a girl pregnant. But as a result, you were born, she thought, kissing the top of Anna's head, and somehow the wonder of your existence seemed to overshadow it all.

Guy didn't speak again, apart from cursing a driver who gave a wrong hand signal. "Bloody idiot!" He obviously wanted to concentrate on the journey. It's a long way to drive she thought, and wondered how often he did the return journey.

"I expect your parents were glad to see you," she said, when they reached a quiet stretch of the road. "Do you have any brothers or sisters?"

"Oh yes," his expression suddenly became dark. "I have a brother, the saintly Charles."

214

Rebecca turned to look at him. "I take it you don't get on?"

"You could say that. Sanctimonious prig – saying he doesn't approve of the company I keep!"

Horrified, Rebecca turned and glared at him. "I hope you're not referring to me?"

Guy winced. "That wasn't very tactful of me, was it?"

No, Rebecca thought, it damn well wasn't.

"Okay, so I like a pretty girl! What's wrong with that?" Guy complained. He grinned at her. "I mean, do you think I'd have offered you a lift if you'd had a face like the back of a bus?"

"It's a good job I haven't then, isn't it?" she snapped.

"Hey, don't take offence. I've told you – he's a sanctimonious prig."

Maybe he is, she thought, turning away to stare out of the window. But he won't be the only one to think like that. She hated the thought of people discussing her. "Come on, Rebecca," Guy coaxed. "Don't go all huffy on me."

She glanced at him, and he gave a confident easy smile. He's a real charmer, she thought with reluctance, and he knows it. "Forgiven?" he said, and she nodded and smiled back, but with Anna clamouring for attention, there was little chance for further conversation, and Rebecca spent the rest of the journey trying to pacify her increasingly fretful child. Then at last they were approaching Stepney, and it was only minutes before Guy drew up outside the front entrance of the Unicorn.

Without switching off the engine, he got out of the car and opening the boot, put her belongings on the pavement. "Do you need a hand?"

"No, I'll be fine. Do you want to come in for a drink?"

He shook his head. "I'd better not. Look, if you want to go up again, just send a message through Katie."

"I will. And I can't thank you enough."

"It was a pleasure." He stood gazing at her for a moment as though he was going to ask her something, but then gave his now familiar grin and got back into the driving seat. With Anna in her arms, Rebecca watched him drive out of the street, then pushed open the door into the pub. As she went into the public bar, Ron, who had just finished serving a customer, saw her and came out to carry her things through to the back, and Sal came hurrying. She looked flushed and Rebecca noticed that her mascara was smudged. Suddenly she realised that her aunt, despite her peroxide hair, was beginning to look her age. "Bedlam in there, it is," she grumbled. "Good job Flossie could make it." She scooped up a tearful Anna in her arms. "And how's my little poppet, then? Tired, I can see that! Did you miss your Auntie Sal?" She glanced over at Rebecca. "Went well, did it?"

Rebecca, suddenly feeling utterly exhausted, nodded. "I'm shattered. I'll tell you all about it in the morning. I think I'll be asleep before closing time."

"Okay, ducks. I won't bother you with questions

now." Sal looked at her with concern. "Do you need anything to eat?"

Rebecca suddenly realised that apart from the biscuits Grace had provided, she'd had nothing to eat since lunchtime. "It's okay, Sal. I'll get myself a bowl of cereal and see if Anna will have some. That'll do."

There was a sudden raucous shout from the bar, and Sal said, "Gawd, just listen at 'em. It's Charlie Parker's sixtieth, and if he isn't careful he won't make his sixty-first, the amount of ale he's putting away!"

Rebecca laughed. She liked the affable Charlie, who often gave her his sweet ration for Anna. "You'd better get back and keep him under control."

Sal turned at the door. "Tell me all about it in the morning?"

"I promise."

It was just two weeks later that the parcel arrived. Sal brought it in, peering at the postmark. "Stoke-on-Trent!" She looked over to the table where Rebecca was sitting, coping with feeding a reluctant Anna. "I think we can guess who it's from. Here, give me the spoon. I'll play aeroplanes with her."

Rebecca took the parcel eagerly and tore off the wrapping. Inside there was an envelope and a pretty lemon-and-white child's dress. She held it out to Sal with pleasure. "How lovely. And just the right size." Sal examined the label. "Marks & Spencer – makes a change from the market!" She held it against Anna. "It suits her."

Rebecca was reading the note. It was just a few lines.

Dear Rebecca,

I can't tell you how I felt after you left that afternoon. It was all such a shock, as you could see, but I want you to know that I very much hope that both you and little Anna will always be part of my life. It will give me great pleasure to be able to send her a little gift now and then, so I hope you won't mind. I liked this dress as soon as I saw it.

With all best wishes,
Grace

And after a few weeks yet another parcel arrived. This time, carefully wrapped, there were two cardigans: one pink, one lemon. Both bore the 'St Michael' label and were in a slightly larger size. "At least we know they'll wash well," was Sal's comment. And this generosity continued over the next few months until, as Sal declared sharply, "This kiddie'll soon be the best dressed in the house."

"I don't suppose the poor woman's got anything else to spend her money on," Ron said gruffly. He was feeling a bit tired after spending the morning in the cellar. Those bleeding stone steps, he thought. They get steeper every week.

"That's what worries me," Rebecca said. "Her spending all her money, I mean. After all, as far as we know, she's only got her widow's pension."

"She might have got a bit of insurance, you know when . . ." Sal suggested.

Rebecca nodded. "Yes, I suppose so."

"Have you noticed how everything comes from M & S?" Sal said with a frown. "Haven't they got any other shops up there?"

Rebecca laughed. "I've no idea. Maybe it's because she knows I can change them if they don't fit."

"There is that, I suppose."

When Katie came round, she was more interested in talking about gossip at the hospital. And in bemoaning the fact that she was once again "without a fella". "I think I'll give up on doctors," she said morosely. But Rebecca knew exactly how Katie felt. Of course she wanted "a fella". She longed for love, for romance, like any girl did. But convention demanded commitment and marriage. The trouble with morals, Rebecca thought, is that they're all to do with the mind, and that bit is easy. It's the heart with its emotions and the treacherous body with its longings that make life difficult. Ever since Katie had told her that his romance with the blonde nurse was over, Rebecca had hoped that maybe Guy would get in touch. But so far she'd heard nothing. And she'd known he was attracted to her. Still, what did she expect? People liked peaches but they didn't want the stone inside. And that's what she was like – tempting on the outside, but with a bitter kernel. No man in a public position was going to get involved with a girl with a past like hers. And she wasn't even well educated. Rebecca had always been one of the brighter pupils at her school in London, but the bewilderment of evacuation at the difficult age of twelve, with its loneliness and constant fear for her parents' safety, had sabotaged her enthusiasm for learning. Mr and Mrs Parry had sent her to the nearest secondary school, but took little interest in her progress or lack of it. Yet again, they had done what they saw as their "duty", but no more. Rebecca had never felt that she fitted in, and had been too unhappy to take full advantage of the lessons.

Now Rebecca glanced at her friend. "Any gossip?"

"Not really, although Dr Mason stopped me in the corridor the other day. He was asking whether you were thinking of going up to Stoke again."

Rebecca shot a quick glance at Sal, who was darning one of Ron's socks, but she didn't make any comment. "I'm not sure," she said, "I'd like to and Grace has invited me to. She says I can stay with her, that I can have Ian's room."

Sal gave an audible sniff. "Not a good idea, in my opinion!"

"Why is that then, Sal?" Katie said.

"This girl needs to move on, not be dragged back into the past. How's she going to feel, sleeping in Ian's bedroom? I bet you what you like that his mother's kept all his things!"

Rebecca felt a surge of irritation. Sal had expressed this opinion before, and forcibly. "I've told you," she said, "considering that I've got a living reminder of him in Anna, I'm sure I can cope with a few books and aeroplane models, or whatever it is boys keep in their rooms."

"Maybe," Sal said stubbornly. "But I still think it would be a mistake."

Katie looked at them both. It was obvious what the problem was. Sal, understandably, was beginning to feel jealous of this unknown woman's intrusion into their cosy lives. Maybe she felt threatened, was worried that Grace would somehow usurp her in little Anna's affections. After all, being a great-aunt couldn't compare with the close relationship of a grandmother, and Sal must be acutely aware of it. I'll have a word with Rebecca later on, Katie thought – I bet that side of it has never occurred to her.

But Grace was aware. Not of Sal's feelings of course, but she was beginning to realise how insensitive it was to expect Rebecca to sleep in a room full of memories of Ian. Because his bedroom was exactly as he'd left it. A little tidier – she hadn't been able to bear the sight of his blue-and-white striped pyjamas flung carelessly on the unmade bed – but his slippers still lay beside it and his plaid dressing gown hung on a hook behind the door. The bed was now pristine beneath its maroon eiderdown, and she dusted and vacuumed the room once a fortnight, and regularly cleaned the small window and washed the net curtain. All his clothes still hung in the wardrobe, and during those first few months after she returned home, Grace would open the doors and bury her face in his best suit and favourite sports jacket, desperately trying to breathe in the remembered scent of her beloved son. Still displayed was a clockwork railway engine on the windowsill, and there were shelves of books, including all his Rupert Annuals, and his collection of biographies of famous painters. His own watercolour of Rudyard Lake hung on one wall, and a framed print of Turner's *The Fighting Temeraire* on the other. Even his briefcase lay propped against a cupboard, while the drawers were full of his personal belongings, including Rebecca's letters.

Now Grace gazed at it all with increasing consternation. She longed to have Anna a part of her life, and wanted to get to know Rebecca, hoping to learn to love her as the daughter-in-law she would have been. But what sort of incentive had she given the young mother? Just an invitation to come and stay in the room that was a shrine to the man she'd loved and lost. Not that Rebecca could know that, but perhaps if Grace could reassure her . . . Could she bear to let all this go? Grace was in an agony of indecision. Then her basic common sense prevailed. It had been selfish of her to keep the clothes and even his shoes. There was some poor soul out there who would be glad of them. She had managed to give Jim's good things away – realising that seeing them hanging there every time she opened their double wardrobe wasn't helping her recovery: now she must do the same with Ian's. I'll clear out all the drawers as well, she thought, and just keep essential personal mementoes. They can go with his father's in the ottoman. All his books and boyhood treasures could be stored in the box-room, safely out of sight.

After all, when she was older, Anna might like to see them.

And so it was that a month later, Rebecca received another letter.

Dear Rebecca,

It seems so long since I saw my little grand-daughter, and yet again I've been wondering whether you would like to come and stay one weekend before the summer ends. The box-room is full of junk and in any case would be far too small, so a neighbour of mine has redecorated Ian's room for me. It looks really pretty, with new wallpaper, new lino, and new curtains. I decided, you see, that it was time to move on. And I have you to thank for the strength to do it. I do hope you can come, although I know it will depend on whether you can get a lift.

I'm enclosing a picture book for Anna, and send my best wishes to your aunt and uncle,

Warmest regards,

Grace

Silently, Rebecca handed the letter over to Sal. She read it slowly and then looked across at her niece. "You'd better arrange to go," she said curtly.

Rebecca, mindful of Katie's warning, looked at her aunt, and struggled to find the right words. "I don't want you to feel . . ."

"What?" Sal's tone was sharp, defensive.

"That this takes away from how I feel about you and Ron. You've been a lifesaver to me. What's

223

more, you're my family, the only one I've got. You know what they say about blood being thicker than water."

Sal looked down at Anna who was playing with a spinning-top at her feet, and gave a deep sigh. "Yer both mean a lot to me, you know that."

"Of course I do, and you do to me. As for Anna, *you're* her grandmother as far as she's concerned."

"Do yer reckon?" Sal's face lit up with pleasure.

"Of course." Rebecca hesitated. "And kids usually do have two grannies, you know." I can remember both of mine, she thought, although she had no memory of either of her grandfathers. One had been killed in the Boer wars, and the other had died young of consumption. "So," she coaxed, "would it be all right for me to go? I mean, Flossie can have my wages for the hours she works, and this time it won't cost me anything for the hotel." Sal looked down. She'd been a selfish cow. The girl was right – Grace Beresford had every right to want to be involved. You'd soon be grumbling if she *didn't* take any interest, she thought with a twinge of shame. She gave the letter back to Rebecca. "Yer'll have to take your ration books, and remind me to send her a bottle of sherry or something."

Rebecca smiled with relief. "Thanks, Sal, that's really good of you. I'll give Katie a note for Guy the next time she comes."

Sal regarded her. It hadn't been only jealousy that had been bothering her. The girl liked this doctor – anyone could see that. She also knew that

Rebecca, like everyone else, would have to make her own mistakes. And if anything does develop, she thought with a wry glance at Anna, Sal could only hope that after the last one, her niece had learned her lesson!

22

When Katie gave Rebecca's note to Guy, he gave her his usual charming smile, before turning away to speak to a patient. Katie knew perfectly well that Rebecca found the young doctor attractive. But although he could coax a smile out of the most miserable patient, Guy was too flirtatious for Katie's taste. She liked her men more – what was the word? Solid, that was it. Her brother always teased her that she craved security, and it was true. Katie had seen enough abject poverty in Dublin not to want it happening to her. Also growing up, and then serving behind the bar in a city pub, had given Katie a certain degree of cynicism. She thought it unlikely that the ambitious young doctor would complicate his life by getting involved with an unmarried mother!

But she had a problem of her own. And that was trying to talk some sense into her stubborn sister-in-law. "I just don't understand you," Katie complained. It was a very hot day, so all the windows were open, and with irritation, she wafted away a bluebottle that was buzzing around. "Where's your Christian charity?"

"I'm as good a Christian as the next," Maura retorted. "Not like some I could mention." Her voice was, as always, quiet, but she didn't fool Katie for an instant. I should never have told her that sometimes after a night shift, I feel too tired to go to Sunday Mass, she thought crossly. Anyone would think she was my mother! Katie cast an exasperated glance at Conor, but he just rolled his eyes and grinned. "And what do you think?" she said sharply. "You've seen Rebecca? *Is* she the devil incarnate?"

He laughed. "I've told Maura, she's perfectly respectable."

"No she isn't, not quite," Maura said. "Even if there were tragic circumstances."

Katie lost her temper. "Oh, come on, Maura. Are you telling me there are no skeletons in your family cupboard?"

"Are you serious?" Maura looked affronted. "And me with a brother a priest?"

Katie compressed her lips and glanced at little Michael, who was busily trying to crayon in a colouring book. "Think about it," she said. "Here you are with a child only a few months younger than Anna, and not a playmate in sight. And there's that little girl, stuck in the back room of a pub. I don't think she's ever had the chance to make a friend. That can't be right, can it? It's not her fault her mother isn't married!"

Maura looked sheepish. "I know it would make sense to get them together. But," she glanced sideways at Conor, "I don't suppose he's told you about the notice that's gone up three doors away? You know – the house where she takes in lodgers. And we've tried so hard to be accepted."

Katie looked at Conor, and with tightened lips he said, "It's there in the front window for everyone to see. In large red letters – NO BLACKS, NO IRISH, NO DOGS."

Katie stared at them in horror. "Don't people know what that sort of thing can lead to? Haven't they learned anything? Look what happened to the Jews in Germany!"

"Prejudice is ingrained," Conor told her. "Passed down from father to son. You've seen it yourself in the auld country."

"And as for we Irish," Katie protested, "who are the priests in their churches? Not to mention the nurses in their hospitals!"

Maura gave a despairing shrug. "So you see, Katie, I just feel that for us to have an illegitimate child coming here – and we're only a couple of streets away so people will know who she is . . ."

Katie stared at them, seeing the genuine distress in Maura's eyes, and the awkward embarrassment in Conor's. "What is it that people have got against us?" she said quietly.

Conor shrugged. "The intelligent ones haven't got anything. But it's lack of education, Katie. It'll all change one day, you'll see."

"Well, I've never encountered any prejudice at the hospital!"

"As I've said, it's all to do with education. You're mixing with a different class of people there. But you do understand Maura's point of view," Conor said, "about Anna, I mean."

Katie gazed steadily at her brother. "In a way, yes.

But I think you're both making a mistake. You should be fighting such ignorance, not pandering to it. I can tell you now, Conor O'Brien, that your da wouldn't let some stupid neighbour rule *his* life!"

Two weeks later, Rebecca saw Guy's car turn the corner of the street, and hurriedly bade farewell to Sal, to stand outside the Unicorn, Anna in her arms, her suitcase and the pushchair by her side on the pavement. Once again, Sal, from the bedroom window, watched Guy, tanned and wearing an open-collared shirt, get out of the car, and smile down at Rebecca, who laughed at something he said. And suddenly Sal realised that this was the sort of life a girl like Rebecca *should* be leading – fun and laughter and mixing with younger people than herself and Ron. Katie had been a godsend, but she had other friends at the hospital to go out with, and only a limited amount of free time. Sal turned away, deciding not to go back to bed for a lie-in. Instead she went into the bathroom and turning on the taps, unwrapped a lavender bath cube she'd been saving, and crumbled it into the water. Several minutes later, she lay enjoying "a good soak", and couldn't help thinking that for an attractive girl and a good-looking young man to be in such close proximity for several hours, was tempting fate.

Rebecca, as they sped away, was certainly hoping it would. Seeing the warmth of Guy's greeting, and the way his gaze had flicked over her appearance, she knew he still found her attractive. And at least this time, she didn't have a rival – at least not as far as she knew. With Anna content on her lap with a small packet of dolly mixtures, Rebecca relaxed in the passenger seat, full of anticipation.

Guy, as he'd peered into his shaving mirror that morning, knew that this journey was going to be a difficult one. At least for him. He knew only too well his weakness for a pretty girl, and gained a lot of pleasure by indulging it. But although he'd wanted to see Rebecca again, he was beginning to have second thoughts. No matter how intriguing the girl by his side was, common sense told him that it would be tantamount to social suicide to get involved with her. Not only were Guy's own expectations high, so were those of his family. For an excellent doctor, with a good bedside manner, and family connections, to practise in Harley Street was not an unrealistic ambition. Therefore an impeccable marriage to someone of his own class was essential. Strong hints had already been made by his father that it was time he settled down. A suitable match had already been suggested, and it was only a matter of time before he proposed to the girl concerned. A merger, his father called it, of two main county families. And he *was* very fond of Caroline. Guy knew that he'd reached a stage in his life when it would be madness to begin a pleasurable affair with someone not only with an illegitimate child, but who lived and worked in an East End pub. The thought of the horror on his mother's normally serene face, was not a pleasant image.

Such a pity, he thought, glancing at Rebecca's slim yet curvaceous body. Rebecca, of course, had no idea of the thoughts racing through Guy's mind. She was well aware that he was, as Sal would put it, "way out of her league", but she didn't care. She was beginning to have such longings for "normal" things, such as fun, freedom, and yes – a little romance. Even if it didn't lead anywhere, surely there was nothing wrong with that? And so, to Rebecca's disappointment, the journey passed uneventfully, with just normal conversation and a little joking. Despite her encouragement, Guy's tendency to flirt – which she'd enjoyed so much on the previous trip – was absent. Again they stopped at the same transport café, where Guy ordered a bacon cob as well as a mug of tea for himself and a cold drink for Rebecca. "You could stand a spoon up in that," she teased, as he put plenty of sugar into the brown liquid. "Why is it that men always like it so strong?"

"We like a bit of body in it," he said, resisting the urge to let his gaze linger on the swell of Rebecca's breasts. She really was a peach – lousy luck about the kid. It's an unjust world, he thought, comfortable with the knowledge that his life had been one of privilege. Still, at least he was able to help Rebecca out by giving her a lift. But he'd have to be stern with himself, the temptation to respond to her obvious attraction to him, was almost irresistible.

Then an hour and a half later, they were approaching the Potteries again, and Rebecca found herself becoming nervous, as, not for the first time, she wondered what Grace had decided to do about Anna. It was going to be impossible to conceal her

231

identity. Poor Grace, she thought. This isn't going to be easy for her, and when they turned into Redwood Avenue and drew up outside number fifteen, she glanced at the bay window to see whether Ian's mother was hovering. But the net curtains showed no sign of movement.

Grace, once she'd received Rebecca's letter saying they were coming, had been in a frenzy of preparation. She'd hoarded her ration coupons until the long-awaited weekend, and only that morning, had baked little fairy cakes and iced them for Anna. A larger than usual joint of beef stood proudly behind the gauze of the meat safe in the pantry, and for today she'd prepared a ham salad, using lettuce and radishes from the garden, and home-grown tomatoes from Jim's small greenhouse. A red jelly was ready, and on the pantry shelf stood a tin of salmon, and a can of peaches.

But it hadn't only been her hands that had been busy – Grace had forced herself to grapple with a problem that could no longer be avoided. Theirs was a small quiet street, and most people had lived there for many years. They had seen each other's children born, learn to walk and go to school. Some had watched their sons leave to fight for their country. The visit of Rebecca for a whole weekend, with a child strongly resembling Ian, was bound to stir avid curiosity. I can't get away from it, Grace thought, as she walked down the garden path, trying to make the most of the September sunshine. I'm just going to have to tell people the truth. And she was well aware there would be one or two smug expressions. Ian had been the shining example, the local lad who'd gone to university. In her mind, Grace could already hear the voice of one neighbour in particular. "My lad may not have been bookish," she'd say, "but at least he didn't bring shame on his family."

The alternative would be to deny little Anna, and Grace could never do that. But first, she must talk to Rebecca about it. Grace was only too aware of how delicate their new relationship was, and her hope was that by the end of this first weekend together, she and Rebecca would have become – not close – it was too soon for that, but at least comfortable with each other.

Although from midday Grace had constantly gone to peer out of the front window, she was, to her disappointment, visiting the lavatory in the back porch when Guy drew up outside the house. He hauled Rebecca's belongings out of the boot and after she opened the gate, carried them up to the front door. She hesitated, wondering if she should offer him a cup of tea before he drove on to Crewe. But it wasn't her place to invite a stranger into Grace's house, and so she watched him pull away, and then turning, reached out to lift the knocker. "Me, Mummy?" Anna reached out her hand and tried to lift it, and smiling, Rebecca helped her to give a slight tap. Grace, coming through the kitchen heard it immediately and hurried to open the front door.

"I missed you," she said. "Would you believe I've been looking out for ages!" She held out her arms

233

to Anna, who drew back and buried her head in Rebecca's shoulder.

Seeing the disappointment on Grace's face, Rebecca said, "She's probably tired from the journey."

"Of course. What am I thinking of! Come on in, both of you, and I'll put the kettle on." Grace stood aside for Rebecca to pass, then picked up the suitcase, and stored the pushchair inside the hall. "I'm so glad you've come. I can't tell you how much."

Rebecca smiled at her, and put Anna down on the narrow Axminster runner. "Come through to the back," Grace said. "I've got a nice ham salad all ready and waiting."

"Oh, lovely." Rebecca followed her, where the square table in the centre of the small back room looked very inviting. Anna, of course, immediately saw the plate of fairy cakes, and was already trying to climb up on to a dining-chair. "Wee-wee first," Rebecca said firmly. "And then clean hands."

Grace watched with approval as her granddaughter was taken out to the back porch. Rebecca was a good mother – anyone could see that. She was hoping – so fervently – that the weekend would go well. Anna's existence had given such meaning to her life, such hope for the future. But her fear was that Rebecca might eventually find it easier to cut all ties with the past. After all, she was a young, attractive girl – it was only a matter of time before she met someone she wanted to marry. I'd understand that, Grace thought, I'd be glad for her, just as long as I can watch my granddaughter grow up.

Rebecca, too, was hoping that the visit would go well. It was vital that Anna should develop a loving relationship with her grandmother. After all, Rebecca thought as she came back through the small but spotlessly clean kitchen, how else is she to learn about her father?

23

Maggie was in the back room when she heard the jangle of the bell over the shop door. She glanced with irritation at the cuckoo clock on the wall. "Only ten minutes to closing time – some people always wait 'til the last minute."

"Do you want me to go?"

Maggie shook her head. "No, it's all right," she said, struggling to her feet. Her reluctance to ask too much of her younger sister was ingrained. Enid had suffered from tuberculosis in her early twenties, and had never recovered her original strength. "I've got a nice kipper for tea," Enid called after her and Maggie felt cheered, her mouth watering at the thought of the tasty fish with a nice bit of bread-and-butter. Thank goodness it's Sunday tomorrow, she thought. If the law allowed it, some of the customers would expect me to work seven days a week!

So it was not in the best of moods that she pushed open the beaded curtain that divided their living quarters from the shop. Then her eyes widened in surprise. It wasn't like Mrs Beresford to come in at this late hour. But as Maggie moved to stand behind the counter, she saw that Grace – of course she would never call her that – was holding open the shop door for a pushchair, and behind the pushchair was a young woman with flame-coloured hair. Maggie's hand went to her mouth. Oh, my God, she thought, it is . . . it's her!

Rebecca was standing still, seeing again the cards hanging on the wall with their combs, hairnets and hair slides, the shelves of cigarettes and tobacco behind the counter, and smelt the same odour of bread, bacon, cheese, Lifebuoy soap and fire lighters. Maggie was even wearing the same green overall. Nothing had changed. She said, "Hello, Maggie. Remember me?"

"I do that!" Maggie's gaze travelled down to Anna, who was regarding her with wide grey eyes. Heaven's above – the child was the very spit of—!

Stunned, Maggie glanced up at Grace who said quietly, "This is my granddaughter – Ian's little girl."

Maggie stared in utter astonishment at the woman whose family had been so well respected, while Rebecca said with embarrassment, "We would have been married if he hadn't been killed."

"Eeh," Maggie said, finding her voice at last. "So when you came up before you were already . . . ?"

Rebecca nodded. "Nearly three months."

Thank God I didn't know, was Maggie's swift reaction. But she was shocked, she really was – the girl had seemed such a decent sort.

"I only found out recently," Grace told her. "All this time Rebecca thought I was still in the hospital." She smiled fondly down at Anna, and seeing the toddler's beseeching gaze at a jar of lollipops on the

237

counter, laughed. "A nice red one?" As Anna's eyes lit up, Maggie took one out of the jar.

"Rebecca's come up to stay for the weekend," Grace told her, passing the lollipop into Anna's eagerly outstretched hand.

Maggie couldn't help staring in fascination at the child's mother. Who'd have believed it, she thought. Ian Beresford! And after all that fuss about him going to university, as well. "You're still living in London, then?"

"Yes, I am." Then after Grace asked for a tin of corned beef, and paid, Rebecca smiled at Maggie, and turned the pushchair around. "Nice to have met you again."

"And you, lass." Maggie watched them leave, then hurriedly began to wipe down the bacon slicer. Just wait until Enid hears this, she thought with excitement. She was tempted to hurry through now, but the titbit of scandal was too good to rush. And as she turned over the sign on the door to "Closed", and began to cash up, Maggie remembered the first time Rebecca had come into her shop – the trauma of telling her the terrible news, the never-forgotten image of her stricken face. Maggie never wanted to have an experience like that again. And now there was a child! It made the Beresford tragedy seem even more pointless.

Grace was smiling as they walked back along Redwood Avenue. "She's a good soul is Maggie. Do you know she and her sister Enid were born in the room above that shop – they've never lived anywhere else! But she does love a gossip. I sometimes think she lives her life through other people. It'll be all round the place by the middle of next week!"

"You must mind a bit, though," Rebecca said, feeling awkward. "About everyone knowing, I mean."

Grace glanced at her, and decided that if they were to have any sort of relationship, there had to be truth between them. "Of course I mind," she said. "But as I see it, I don't have a choice. And after all, Ian isn't with us any more, but his daughter is. She's the important one, now." She bent down to smile into Anna's eyes. "And you need your granny, don't you, my little one?" And I need you, she thought sadly, more than you'll ever know.

On Sunday morning at the Unicorn, Ron was relishing the rare chance to read his newspaper without interruption. It was like the old days, he reflected, before Rebecca came to live with them, and certainly there had been little peace for any of them since Anna was born. She was a smashing kid, but it was good to have a break from her constant chatter and demands. Ron couldn't understand why he felt so tired lately, and this particular morning, it had been a real effort even to get out of bed. Now, he slumped heavily in his armchair, grateful that for once he could relax for a bit before the pub opened.

It was during their busiest lunchtime period that Flossie sidled up to Sal. "What's up with Ron?"

"Nothing, why?" Sal glanced sharply along the bar, but her husband had his back to her.

"Dunno. Just a feeling I've got. He doesn't seem himself, that's all. A bit slow, like."

"We're none of us getting any younger, Flossie," Sal said sharply.

"You're telling me! And it can't help having a little 'un around, not when you're in business."

"Janet's a godsend, I can tell yer. She's a good cleaner, as well."

"Are you two wimmen serving, or what?" Ron bellowed.

"Cor, listen at him," Sal said, and Flossie hurriedly moved away to take an order. "Half of mild, is it?" Sal, irritated by Ron's interruption, flounced along the bar. "Right," she snapped. "Where's this stampede?"

Ron passed over some change, and ignoring the jibe turned to her. "Can yer manage if I go for a bit of a sit down?"

Sal looked at him in surprise. "Feeling a bit dicky?"

"Just tired."

"Better go and 'ave a rest then," she said looking at him with concern. "Me and Flossie'll manage all right." She watched him lumber off, then turned as the pub door opened and more customers began to trickle in.

Trade continued to be brisk for the next hour, but as soon as a lull came, Sal went over to Flossie and muttered, "Shan't be a minute – I'll just go and put the joint in the oven."

She went through to the back hall and gingerly opening the sitting-room door, half expected to find Ron asleep in his armchair, but instead saw her husband, his face grey and haggard, slumped awkwardly on the sofa. He was clutching his left upper arm and struggling in desperation for breath. "Pain . . . in my chest," he gasped. Stunned, Sal stared at him in growing horror, and then with overwhelming panic, she rushed out to the telephone, fumbled with the receiver, and dialled 999.

On that same Sunday morning, Grace and Rebecca, with Anna in her pushchair walked along to cross the main road, and went through the entrance to the cemetery. With Anna now running free, they walked slowly along the paths beneath the shady trees, with Rebecca listening while Grace told her about the funeral of her husband and son.

"There were lots of people in the church," she said, "teachers and pupils from Ian's school, and folk from the potbank where Jim worked. Stoke City Football Club sent a lovely wreath." They paused before the headstone, and Grace replaced the flowers in the urn with some pink-tipped rosebuds. "They should last a bit," she said.

Rebecca stood next to her with Anna clutching her hand, and could only think how poignant the scene was. Grace also felt the significance of the three of them being there together, and murmured, "I like to think they're looking down on us. After all, how do we know they're not?"

"We don't, do we?" Rebecca said quietly.

When they went back to Redwood Avenue, Rebecca took Anna to the children's playground in the park, while Grace went into the house and prepared the Sunday roast. It was then that Rebecca discovered what an excellent cook Ian's mother was.

She puts Sal to shame she thought, looking at the fluffy golden Yorkshire pudding. Her own cooking was improving, but that couldn't compare either. "Ian didn't get dinners like this when he came down to us," she said, enjoying the fresh peas from the garden.

"I think he'd have had other things on his mind," Grace said, smiling at Anna who, propped up on cushions heaped on to a dining-chair, was staunchly trying to feed herself. With splotches of vegetables and gravy around her mouth she looked messy, but happy.

"I'm so glad we came," Rebecca said, checking with anxiety whether any food had been dropped on to the carpet.

"Don't worry – she's fine," Grace reassured her, and couldn't help feeling a glow of satisfaction. I'm lucky, she thought, because we do seem to get on well together. The weekend had, to her immense relief, definitely been a success.

And when Guy came to pick them up, that's what Rebecca told him. "It went well," she said, as they drew away with Grace waving goodbye from the gate.

"Good." Guy was admiring the faint glow to her complexion. "Been sunbathing?"

She laughed. "Not exactly. I wouldn't dare with my fair skin. But we did sit in deckchairs in the garden, and then there was the park, of course."

"It seems to have done Anna good." And it was true, the toddler did look better for the weekend.

"It was all the fresh air," Rebecca said, with a guilty pang. "I'm afraid normally she's indoors far too much. How did your weekend go?"

"Fine." Guy hesitated for a moment, and then glanced at her. "In fact, can you keep a secret?"

Rebecca was intrigued. "Of course."

"Only I don't want it all round the hospital, not yet. The nurses are going to be devastated," he grinned. "Guess what? I'm engaged."

His words hit her like a stone. But what about all the hidden meaning in his glances, the warmth and flirtation in his eyes, particularly on their first trip. "Congratulations," she said, struggling to conceal her disappointment. "Who's the lucky girl?"

"Her name's Caroline. We've known each other since childhood."

Obviously very suitable then, Rebecca thought with a tinge of bitterness. "Your parents must be pleased."

"Delighted." Guy thought back to how, on Saturday morning, he'd been summoned into his father's study.

Rupert Mason, FRCS, was a feared figure in his local hospital, and an autocratic parent. "It has come to my attention," he said, sitting behind his large mahogany desk, "that you are consorting with a young woman with a bastard." He glared at his younger son through rimless spectacles, his normally pale face flushed with anger.

Guy winced at the blunt language. "The child's nothing to do with me!"

"I'm glad to hear it."

"I suppose Charles has been bad-mouthing me again!" Guy was furious, recalling his brother's sanctimonious reaction every time Rebecca's name had arisen. "All I've done is to give her a lift up to Stoke a couple of times."

"That's as maybe. It was still inadvisable. Anyway, your mother and I think now would be an appropriate time for you and Caroline to formalise your relationship."

Guy stared at him. "You mean you want us to get engaged?"

"Exactly. You're of an age, your tenure at the hospital will be ending shortly, and we have to look to the future."

Guy gazed at his father, wondering if the cold man before him ever thought or spoke in any other than a professional way. No concern as to what I want, Guy thought bitterly, forcing himself to remain silent as his father continued. "We only want the best for you, Guy. With Caroline at your side – and don't forget her excellent connections – your chances of advancement will be enhanced. Or," he barked, "do you want to end up as some country doctor?"

"Of course not."

"Caroline and her parents will be dining with us tonight," Rupert continued relentlessly. "Maybe it would be a good idea for you two young people to spend some time alone."

And, despite Guy's lingering thoughts of Rebecca's attractions compared to those of the eminently more suitable Caroline, that was exactly what happened. In the extensive garden of his childhood home, Guy made the proposal they'd both always known he would, and Caroline prettily and graciously accepted him. They'd kissed with genuine affection and gone back into the large detached house where, as they drank celebratory champagne, both sets of parents looked on with satisfaction, and Charles wore an expression of unbearable smugness. Now, seeing the flash of disappointment in Rebecca's eyes, Guy suppressed a sigh. This was one delightful girl he'd never enjoy, but he'd sown his wild oats, as they called it, and very pleasurable it had been too. It was just a pity it had to end. Then, glancing at Anna, he congratulated himself. *He* hadn't left behind any souvenirs, at least not as far as he knew.

The rest of the journey seemed flat, and Rebecca was glad when they were passing through the familiar bomb-damaged streets of Stepney. The area seemed even more devastated and dismal after the hours spent in the park and in Grace's lovely garden.

She turned to Guy, knowing she owed him a large debt of gratitude. "Thank you so much for the lifts. They've been a godsend."

He glanced at her in surprise. "Why the past tense? There's no reason I couldn't take you up again. Just send a note through Katie."

Rebecca, remembering what he'd previously told her about his brother's disapproval, looked doubtful. "I just thought . . ."

"I'm my own person," he told her, grimacing inwardly at his hypocrisy. "I don't let myself be influenced by other people." And when he drew up outside the Unicorn, and unloaded the car, Guy repeated yet again. "Don't forget – just let me know."

"I will." Rebecca waved goodbye, and then smiled down at a tired, crumpled Anna who was clutching her hand. "Let's go and see Uncle Ron and Auntie Sal. I bet they've missed us, don't you?"

24

Picking up Anna, Rebecca left the pushchair and suitcase outside the pub, and pushed open the heavy door. She went into the crowded public bar, then suddenly halted, staring with astonishment at the unusual sight of Ruby, red-faced and flustered, handing a pint glass to a customer who complained loudly, "What do yer call this, Rube, a pint of piss? Just look at the 'ead on it!"

Ruby flashed back, "Shut yer gob, Alf Baker, and count yerself lucky. If you can do any better, yer welcome to try!"

Flossie was at the other end of the bar, struggling to cope with a rush of orders, and then Ruby, suddenly glancing up, saw the young mother and child in the doorway, and called sharply, "Floss? She's 'ere!" A few of the men stood aside as Ruby hurriedly lifted the flap on the counter. "Come on through, ducks," she muttered, while Flossie hissed at a trusted customer. "Arnie, stand guard over the till for a few ticks." She turned, "As for the rest of you," she shouted, "yer'll just have to bide yer time!"

Once in the sitting-room, Ruby immediately held out her arms to take Anna. "Come on, poppet. You come and play with your toys and I'll get you a sweetie."

Flossie came in lugging the pushchair and suitcase then together, with grim yet sympathetic expressions, they confronted a now thoroughly alarmed Rebecca. "What's wrong?" she demanded, "what's happened? Where's Sal and Ron?"

Flossie and Ruby exchanged glances then Flossie said bluntly, "It's Ron, love. He's had a heart attack! Sal's at the hospital."

Rebecca stared at her in horror, and whispered, "How is he?"

Flossie shook her head. "He's bad, I'm afraid."

In panic, Rebecca went to push past them. "I must go there. She'll need me." But Ruby intervened, catching hold of her arm. "Yes, ducks, but can yer wait until closing? I'm as much use as a wet lettuce in there, and sod's law it's busier than usual! Ain't that right, Floss?"

Flossie nodded, her face flushed with exertion. "Been bedlam this last half-hour."

"Look," Ruby said. "Leave Anna in 'ere with me. I'll get her off to bed, and make us all a nice cuppa. You go in and sort that lot out!"

Rebecca, still stunned, could only nod, and then, trying to push aside her weariness after the long journey, automatically took charge in the bar. "Abaht time! What sort of pub do yer call this?" A burly man in a trilby hat blustered. Rebecca had never seen him before.

"A bloody good one, mate," a regular customer snapped. "'Ave a bit of respect, the landlord's bin taken ill."

"Well, I didn't know! I'll 'ave a pint, please miss."

"You'll wait your bleedin' turn," another man said. "My usual, please Rebecca, and any news on Ron?" Her stomach churning with anxiety, she shook her head. "No, I'll be going to the hospital when we close."

The evening, despite its brisk trade, dragged on unbearably, with Ruby lending a hand where she could, and then at last Rebecca, with overwhelming relief, was able to reach up for the bell and call for last orders. Half an hour later, she and Flossie were impatiently locking the doors, while Ruby had disappeared to fetch her son-in-law. "You get off as soon as you can," Flossie said. "I'll see to the glasses and everything."

"What about Anna? I can't just leave her."

"I'll stay over. I've already made up the bed in the spare room."

"Thanks, Flossie," Rebecca gave her a quick hug. "You're a good friend." Already she was picking up her warm cardigan, and then Ruby came back with a young, thickset man following. "Stan's got a van," she said, "he can take you straight to the hospital. And I've made yer some cheese sandwiches and a flask. I'll just fetch 'em from the kitchen."

Rebecca looked at them both. "Thanks," she said, her throat thick with anxiety and emotion, and then seconds later she was seated beside Stan, in a dilapidated van that smelt vaguely of decaying cabbage. As he chatted away on the short journey, he told her that he had a fruit-and-veg stall on the market. "Good luck," he said, as she scrambled out of the passenger seat; and as Rebecca went through the main entrance at the hospital, she thought how different this was from her visit on the night of the party. Then she'd been full of excited anticipation, now her only emotion was one of fear. After asking at the reception desk, she hurried along the endlessly long corridors. Eventually she turned a corner to see the abject figure of Sal, seated on a chair outside the double doors of Ward 19, her shoulders slumped, her attitude one of total weariness.

"Sal, how is he?" Sal looked up, and Rebecca was shocked at her haggard expression.

"He's holding his own, that's all they've told me." Her eyes filled with tears, and Rebecca sat beside her and took her aunt's hand in her own.

"Tell me what happened," she said quietly, and listened as Sal told her how she'd found Ron almost collapsed in the sitting-room.

"The ambulance came straightaway," she said. "I'm just thankful I went in when I did. I daren't think what would have happened otherwise." She dabbed at her eyes, and Rebecca reached down to the string shopping bag she'd brought.

"I've got a flask and some cheese sandwiches for us both. Do you think we could eat them out here?"

Sal shrugged wearily. "Shouldn't think so."

"Well, I'll stay, in case there's any news. You take the bag and find somewhere suitable, and then we'll change over."

Sal hauled herself up. "I could do with a stretch." She turned, "Did they manage at the pub?"

"Everything was fine," Rebecca said. "Flossie and Ruby have been bricks."

Sal nodded. "I won't be long." Rebecca watched her walk stiffly back along the corridor in her court shoes, her peroxide hair limp, her heavy make-up now blotched from tears, making her look somewhat incongruous in the hospital setting.

It was a long anxious night. A nurse came up to them, immaculate in her formal blue-and-white uniform and white frilled cap, and tried to persuade them to go home, but Sal flatly refused. Rebecca tried to keep up her aunt's spirits, and the two women talked in desultory whispers. "I think Katie's on night shift," Rebecca said. "I'm sure she's on the Children's Ward. Do you want me to go and find her – she might be able to tell us something."

Sal shook her head, and clutched at Rebecca's arm. "No, stay here with me." She glanced at her niece. "Sorry, I haven't asked how the weekend went."

"It was fine," Rebecca reassured her. "But never mind that, Ron's the important thing, now."

At last, after what seemed an eternity, a tired-looking doctor, with a stethoscope around his neck came out of the ward and walked towards them. Both women stood up, Rebecca slipping her arm supportively around Sal's shoulders.

"Mrs Bowler?" Sal made a gesture, and he indicated that they should sit down again, and sat beside them. "Your husband's heart attack was a serious one, I'm afraid, but he's now out of immediate danger. You can go in and see him for a few minutes, then I think you should go home and get some rest." He paused, then said, "He tells me he's a publican."

Sal, overwhelmed with relief and struggling with weak tears, could only nod.

The doctor frowned. "Not the ideal occupation for someone in his condition. You must understand that this attack will have weakened the valves in his heart. He's going to have to be very careful. We'll keep him in for a few days and monitor his progress. But in future, he must take things very easy. There must be no over-exertion, no worry. Do you understand what I'm saying?"

Rebecca said quickly, "Yes, we do, doctor."

He nodded. "Nurse will come out in a moment and take you through. Try to be quiet so that you don't disturb the other patients. Just you, Mrs Bowler, if you don't mind."

And so Rebecca waited while Sal went in to see her husband, and, utterly exhausted, leaned her head back against the wall. Whatever were they going to do? She and Sal couldn't run the pub on their own, not with little Anna running around. And Ron was going to need peace and quiet – a fat chance of that at the Unicorn. Stifling a yawn, she tried to push the worry from her mind. There would be time enough for problems later – for now it was enough that Ron had survived.

Several days later, an ambulance brought Ron home and, despite his protest, he was wheeled carefully into the pub. "What you do after is your own business, mate," one of the ambulance men told him, "but you're our responsibility until we leave."

Sal bustled around him, fussing, while Anna,

sitting on the floor with her favourite rag doll, watched wide-eyed.

Rebecca offered to put the kettle on. "Never mind that," Ron said. "I've done nothing *but* drink tea in that place. What I really fancy is a pint!"

"Did the doctors say you could drink?" Sal said sharply.

"They just said moderation in all things." Ron looked around the familiar room, which strangely seemed smaller than he remembered it. Must be after being in that huge ward he thought. Like a flaming barracks it was.

"Get him a half of bitter," Sal told Rebecca.

"Half? I've never drunk halves in me life!" Ron's face reddened with indignation.

"Well, you'll have to start," Sal snapped. "And look at you, red in the face already. You've got to calm down, Ron Bowler. No getting hot under the collar – not any more!"

Rebecca hurried into the bar, and minutes later brought Ron his foaming glass, saying, "I'll just go and open up."

"Who's seeing to the cellar?" Ron tried to get up.

"Stay where you are," Sal ordered. "Ruby's nephew's been coming in – he's a strong lad and between jobs. There's nothing for you to worry about. Just concentrate on getting your strength back."

Ron took an appreciative sip of his beer, and then after draining the glass with relish, wiped the froth from his upper lip. "I suppose you're 'aving to pay Flossie, as well?"

"So?" Sal said sharply. "We can manage it."

"That's two extra wages. We can't keep that up for long, Sal."

"Time enough to think about that when you've got over this lot!" Sal knew he was right. All the time he'd been in the hospital, with the doctor's warning imprinted indelibly on her mind, Sal had known there was only one solution. She'd often woken in the early hours, her mind wrestling to find an alternative, but it was useless. And during the following few weeks, seeing Ron struggling in vain to regain his usual vigour, Sal became even more resolved. She and Ron were going to have to give up the Unicorn. And she was dreading having to raise the matter. Late one evening, sick of worrying about it, she took Rebecca into her confidence. "It's the only solution," Sal told her. "We can't go on like this."

Rebecca nodded. "To be honest, I've been expecting it. But what will you do? Where will you go?"

"I've bin thinking about that. Cousin Ida's just moved down to Southend, and Ron's cousin Eric's there as well." She looked earnestly at Rebecca, "I thought maybe we could find a little flat, something on the ground floor – no stairs, if you see what I mean – it'd be a bit cheaper there. And there's lots of pubs and hotels with it being the seaside an' all."

"You mean to work in?"

"Yes, I'm all right, I could get a bar job, and Ron could get the sea air." She looked appealingly at Rebecca. "What do yer think? I haven't said anything to him, yet. I wanted to have it all clear in my head first."

254

"I think it's an excellent idea." Rebecca looked down at her hands. Sal wasn't the only one who'd been spending sleepless nights, worrying about the situation. Rebecca was only too aware of the difference in her uncle. How often had she seen Anna wearying Ron, seeking rough-and-tumble play, or had to scold the toddler for trying to clamber all over him. Now approaching her third birthday, Anna was becoming ever more wilful. How on earth was Ron to get the peace and quiet he so desperately needed?

"There's something else," Rebecca said after a moment.

"What's that, love?"

"When you do move, I don't think you should feel you have to provide a home for me and Anna. Not any more."

The bald words, spoken very quietly, lay between them. They both knew what the inference was. Ron needed to be able to relax, free from stress, and if Rebecca and Anna were living with them, then this would be impossible. And as Anna got older, it could only get worse. Sal had been struggling with the same agonising problem. Rebecca and little Anna were family, the only family she had. How could she even think of leaving them behind? Rebecca had only put into words both their fears.

Sal gazed with despair at her niece. "But what would you do? Even if you came down and got a little place near us, you'd never be able to afford it, not and pay someone to look after Anna. And I'm afraid, love, I've got to make Ron my priority now."

"Of course you have, and I wouldn't want to leave her with a stranger, anyway," Rebecca said.

The two women looked at each other in silence. Then with some reluctance, Sal said, "Is it a case of great minds thinking alike?"

Rebecca nodded. "Probably. The sensible thing would be to approach Grace. I mean, she's up there on her own and I know she only works part-time. I'm sure I'd be able to get a job, and we could share looking after Anna." She looked doubtfully at her aunt. "Or do you think it would be a bit cheeky to ask?"

Sal shook her head. "I think she'd jump at the chance." Her tone, however, was one of bitterness as she struggled against a sudden wave of jealousy. Stoke-on-Trent, as far as she was concerned, might as well be a foreign country. It was all so unjust. She and Ron had stood by Rebecca through all the bad times, had come to love little Anna as their own. They had both been looking forward to seeing her begin school, to watching her grow up. It had always been Sal's fervent hope that Rebecca would eventually marry a Londoner, and settle nearby. Rebecca, seeing the distress in her aunt's eyes, suggested tentatively, "If I did move up there, what's to stop you and Ron coming too? They have pubs in the Potteries as well, you know."

But Sal could only shake her head sadly. Southend was one thing – Ron might just about agree to that. After all, he'd always liked it, they'd gone there for their three-day honeymoon. And they both had a cousin there. But he'd never consider moving "up North", as he always, with some disparagement, referred to it.

256

"No, ducks," she said. "We're Londoners. It'd never work, not at our age."

Rebecca stared at her helplessly, knowing that her aunt was right. "I'd come down to visit you," she said earnestly. "No matter how small the flat was, we could manage on a camp-bed or something. And there would be the summer holidays, and Christmas."

"You're a good girl," Sal said. "I know you'd do yer best, but there'd be the train fares and everything."

"I might get a better-paid job," Rebecca pointed out. "And I might even meet someone who could give me a lift, like Guy did."

"It was good of him to stop by the ward and 'ave a word with Ron, when he was ill in hospital," Sal said. "Cheered him up no end that did."

Rebecca gave a quiet smile, recalling the moment she'd met Guy while walking along the hospital corridor on her way to visit Ron. Surprised to see her, Guy could only think how lovely she looked with the light from an adjacent window highlighting the brilliant auburn of her shoulder-length hair. Rebecca, thinking him more attractive than ever in his white coat, with a stethoscope dangling around his neck, told him about Ron's heart attack.

"Which ward is he on?"

"Nineteen."

"I'll try to drop by," he promised. "What's his full name?"

"Ron Bowler," she said, and then smiled. "Just look for the patient who looks like a boxer!"

He laughed. "I'd better watch my step, then."

With a warm smile, he'd continued on his way, and Rebecca gazed after him. So far, Katie hadn't mentioned his engagement, so she guessed it was still a secret.

Now, Rebecca just said, "I told you, he's a nice person." Sal glanced sharply at her, but Rebecca's expression gave nothing away. "So," she continued with some anxiety. "When are you going to talk to Ron?"

"First thing after breakfast. I thought maybe you could take Anna out for a couple of hours, give us a bit of time on our own?" Rebecca nodded, then turned away, a lump of emotion forming in her throat. She was going to miss the shabby old pub; it had become a home, a refuge to her. And of course, she couldn't be sure that Grace would wish to share her home with a girl she had only recently met.

Half an hour later, when she went up to bed, Rebecca gazed down at the sleeping form of her child. Anna looked so sweet and angelic, one chubby arm flung above her head, her dark eyelashes lying like tiny fans on her cheeks. "I'm afraid everything rests on you, sweetheart," Rebecca whispered, sadly. "Because if your granny says 'no', then I don't know what we'll do."

25

The following morning, once Rebecca and Anna had left, Sal turned to where Ron was sitting despondently in his armchair. He looked up at her. "Where've they gone, then? It's a bit early."

"Rebecca just fancied a bit of fresh air," Sal lied. She went to the door to check that Janet was busy upstairs, and then sat opposite. "I'm glad we're on our own, 'cos I wanted to talk to you." She waited until she had his full attention, then added, "Only I've bin thinking . . ."

"Good job you're sitting down, then."

Sal was relieved to hear him joking again. There had been too little of that lately. She drew a deep breath. "It's about the pub."

Ron tensed. "What about it?"

With trepidation, watching his face intently, Sal explained her plan. When he didn't speak, she pleaded, "We've got to accept it, Ron. We can't carry on any more – *you* can't carry on!"

Warily, she waited for her husband to bluster, to shout. But Ron did neither. He just gazed down at his huge hands resting limply on his knees, then muttered, "Whatever you think is best, Sal."

She stared at him, more disconcerted by his apathy

than if he had blustered and argued. And in that instant, any remaining doubts about the wisdom of her decision dissolved. "I'll write to Ida and your Eric, then. See if they know of anywhere going."

Ron nodded, then glanced up at her and said, shamefaced, "I'm sorry, Sal."

"Yer daft bugger. It's not your fault, and don't you ever go thinking it!" she snapped, but her eyes were soft and with a catch in his throat, Ron saw tears in her eyes.

"Don't worry, love, we'll be all right," he said, trying to reassure her.

Sal smiled with more confidence than she felt. "Of course we will. But there is one thing." She hesitated and then told him of the conversation she'd had with their niece the previous night. "So, Rebecca and Anna probably won't be coming with us. Yer have to admit it, Ron," Sal said. "You've been finding the little 'un a bit of a strain."

"Maybe," he said, "but I won't 'alf miss her."

"I'll miss both of them!" And I don't think anyone realises how much, Sal thought. But what other choice did they have?

She looked across at him, sadness etched on her face. "It'll be hard, at least at first, but we'll have each other and that's the main thing."

Ron nodded, forcing a smile, and couldn't help thinking – but for how long? Only he knew how his strength seemed to be draining away. Then he straightened his beefy shoulders. He was a fighter, wasn't he? And Sal was right – a quieter life and a breath of sea air might work wonders. And he'd known they would have to give up the Unicorn, but he just hadn't wanted to accept it. "Go on, then," he said heavily. "I suppose we might as well get it over with. Pass me a writing pad – I'll write to the Brewery."

A few days later, Grace, after reading Rebecca's carefully written lines, put down the flimsy letter, leaned back in her armchair, and closed her eyes as euphoria swept over her. She had never thought of herself as particularly religious, but hadn't she prayed for this very thing to happen – to have little Anna near her? It was a pity it had come as a result of Ron's heart attack, but these things happened, and she was determined not to let it spoil her joy. Grace tidied the kitchen, and then sat down to write back immediately to Stepney. Her mind was already racing with plans of what would have to be done, but she forced herself to concentrate, to compose a letter that would make Rebecca realise just how welcome her suggestion was. The girl had been so hesitant, so anxious in the way she'd worded her request, that Grace felt a rush of sympathy. It mustn't have been easy for her to confess that she needed somewhere else to live.

Rebecca found her hands trembling when the envelope marked Stoke-on-Trent arrived by return of post. Grace hadn't taken much time to consider – was that a good sign or bad?

"Go on, open it," Sal said. She and Ron exchanged anxious glances, while Rebecca tore open the envelope and took out the single sheet.

Dear Rebecca,

Of course you and Anna must come and live with me – my dear, you will both be so very welcome. I'm sorry that Ron's health is forcing your aunt and uncle to give up the Unicorn, but I'm sure they're doing the right thing. I'll do all I can to help you to settle up here, and please don't feel that you are imposing in the slightest, as I'm absolutely delighted at the prospect of this house being a home again, and already my head is full of plans.

Will write again later,
With kindest regards,
Grace

Rebecca, who had read the letter aloud, looked at them both, and suddenly found her eyes filling with tears. The relief was overwhelming, but the swift and positive reply had also given substance to what had previously been an idea, a hope. Now it was actually going to happen. As soon as Ron and Sal had found a flat in Southend, and a new licensee had been approved, then all their lives would change. And only now, with the letter lying limply on her lap, did Rebecca realise just how much she was going to miss the solid, family support of Ron and Sal. She saw too the same distress in their own eyes, and managed to say, "I'm going to miss you both – so much."

"Same here," Ron grunted, and bent to play "horsey" with Anna, to hide the sudden moisture in his eyes. Yer daft sod, he told himself. You're getting soft! And in his heart Ron knew he would never be the man he used to be.

Sal held out her hand for the letter and read it again. "You'll be all right with Grace," she said, with a pang of jealousy at the other woman's good fortune.

"She's not you, though, Sal," Rebecca said and dabbed at her eyes. "Not that I don't know how lucky I am."

"You feel like that now," Sal told her, "but you'll get used to it all, you'll see. And," she said reassuringly, "it's going to be a new life for you. Yer never know what the future might hold."

"I know." But that didn't stop Rebecca feeling apprehensive at the prospect of not only moving up to a strange area, but also being dependent for a home on someone she'd only known a few months. She and Grace had got on really well during a weekend, but that wasn't the same as living together on a daily basis. What if it didn't work out? But it was no use worrying Sal with her fears, and Rebecca got up as she heard Flossie's light tap on the back door. "Have you told Floss what's happening, yet?"

Sal shook her head. "No, I'll tell her today, and Janet as well. And I'll nip along and put Ruby in the picture. I wouldn't want her to hear from somebody else."

"Katie will be surprised," Rebecca said. "But I suppose she might have been moving on somewhere anyway, once she qualifies."

"That's true. She might even go back to Ireland,"

263

Sal said. "Nothing ever stays the same, love. I've found that out in life."

The leaving arrangements went smoothly, with Sal, having spent a day in Southend, returning with the breathless news that with the help of her cousin, she'd found a suitable flat. "On the ground floor, and furnished," she told them, "and there's even a bus stop right outside which will take us straight to the seafront."

"How many bedrooms?" Ron said, with a quick glance at Rebecca.

"One decent-sized one, and a little box-room. It'll just about take a single bed, so when Rebecca comes, either she or Anna will have to sleep on the sofa."

"Sounds fine to me," Rebecca said, a little unnerved about how quickly everything seemed to be happening.

Katie, although dismayed that Rebecca was leaving, took the news with equanimity. "It's the best thing that could happen, as far as Rebecca's concerned," she told Conor. "Stuck in that back-street pub all the time – it was no life at all."

"I'm sure she was glad of it at the time," Maura said tartly.

Katie gazed at her in exasperation. "Of course she was, and Ron and Sal are the salt of the earth. But you haven't met Rebecca. If you could have got off your high horse and lowered yourself, you'd have realised what I'm talking about!"

"Now then, girls," Conor said softly, his eyes narrowing.

Maura stared at her sister-in-law. "Oh, I'm the devil of the piece, am I?"

"I just think every case should be judged on its merits," Katie said stubbornly. "Rebecca had awful luck, that's all."

"Well," Conor said, looking sharply at his belligerent sister. "I just hope you don't have the same 'luck' as you call it. I'm standing in Da's place, while you're over here, you know."

Maura turned on him. "Conor O'Brien!! What a thing to say. You apologise to Katie for that slur on her character, this very minute."

Conor stared at his wife in bewilderment. A minute ago hadn't she been at it hammer and tongs with Katie, herself? Women, he thought, they never make any sense at all! After the sheepish apology had been given and accepted, Maura said in a milder tone, "You'll miss her though, won't you?"

"Yes," Katie said curtly, "even though I know you'll be relieved that I won't be 'infected' by her bad reputation. But we won't be losing touch, I'll make sure of it." And that, she thought, as she walked back to the hospital, is a promise.

Flossie had shed tears at the news of the forthcoming changes at the Unicorn. "Stupid, I know," she sniffed, "but it's the end of an era, Sal, yer can't get away from it." Ruby had merely turned away to hide her emotion. They both knew there was no alternative.

The Brewery soon found a new licensee, an ex-sergeant-major, with a black handlebar moustache and a blustering manner, and they were all relieved when, after meeting Janet, he said that he'd be keeping her on. The Unicorn was crowded to overflowing on Ron and Sal's last night, with many of the regulars calling out requests to "toothless Billy". Seated at the piano, supported by a constant supply of frothing pints, he played such tunes as "The White Cliffs of Dover", "The Lambeth Walk", and "Maybe it's Because I'm a Londoner". When finally, after Ron had announced to guffaws of pleasure "drinks on the house", and everyone had been served, Billy struck up "For He's a Jolly Good fellow!" Raucous voices bellowed the chorus with such emotion that, to his shame, Ron had to blink away tears. He and Sal were a popular couple, and there was much handshaking, many parting words, and the embarrassed presentation of an inscribed tankard. Then at last it was "chucking-out" time, and the bar was empty and suddenly seemed eerily silent.

For the last time, Ron shot the bolt on the main door of the pub he'd always been so proud of, and Sal draped the damp towels over the pumps. Rebecca looked at their faces, then quietly left.

Ron and Sal stood gazing at the public bar that had been such a huge part of their lives, and then Ron looked sadly at his wife. "That's it then, old girl."

"They've been good years, Ron." Sal, seeing the despondency in his eyes, went over to him and held him close. "We had a life before the Unicorn, and we will again. You'll see."

26

Ron and Sal left early on Saturday morning, and within an hour, Rebecca was carrying out her suitcase, three cardboard boxes and Anna's pushchair, to where Guy was waiting with the car. He loaded most of them into the boot – those that wouldn't fit he put on to the back seat where Rebecca also flung a couple of coats and a string bag. Then, as he got into the driving seat, she went back into the sitting-room to collect Anna from the arms of Flossie. "Thanks, Floss, hope you get on all right with the sergeant-major . . ."

Flossie, who had at last decided to "call time" on her days as a barmaid, shrugged. "It's only for a few weeks while he settles in." Over the past two years, the young mother and daughter had become almost like family to her, and both she and Ruby had tears in their eyes as Rebecca hugged them before turning to leave. With a lump in her throat, she cast one last lingering look at the shabby room, at the table where she'd shared so many meals with Ron and Sal, at the sofa with its poignant memories of the night that Anna had been conceived. Then, struggling to control her emotions, Rebecca carried her daughter away from her birthplace.

"All set?" Guy said, once she was settled in the car.

Rebecca drew Anna's inquisitive fingers away from the door-handle. "All set," she said, and holding the toddler's hand up, encouraged her to wave goodbye to Flossie and Ruby who were standing on the pavement outside the Unicorn.

The two women stood watching until the car disappeared, and then Flossie said, "Are you thinking what I'm thinking?"

Ruby nodded. "Out of our league, old girl, and what about that cravat!"

"He reminded me of David Niven." Flossie smiled wistfully.

Ruby grinned. "Spot on! But what do yer reckon, Floss? I've never known a man do somethin' for nothin'."

"Same thought crossed my mind," Flossie said, "although Rebecca says he's engaged."

"Our Fred was married, but it didn't stop him chasing after every bit of skirt he saw!"

"Well," Flossie said, as they went back inside the pub. "There's nothing we can do about it now. But I reckon Rebecca's got her head screwed on after what happened last time."

Ruby glanced around the pub. "Seeing as Janet's got the flu, we'd better get this place shipshape. After all, Ron did pay us for it."

"I know," Flossie said with reluctance, "but me heart isn't in it, not any more."

When Katie had told Guy what was happening, he immediately said that he'd been planning to go home that weekend anyway. He hadn't, but the chance of seeing Rebecca again had been too tempting to miss. Now, glancing at her, he admired yet again her classical bone structure, her finely-arched chestnut eyebrows, and of course, that glorious hair. He couldn't help comparing the girl sitting next to him to the one he'd be holding in his arms that evening. Caroline was what was termed in the county 'handsome'. A strong tennis player, with a good seat on a horse, she was not unattractive and her vigour and forthright manner appealed to him, but she didn't stir him in the way that Rebecca did.

"I'm hoping she'll sleep most of the way," Rebecca told him, as Anna squirmed on her lap. "You're going to sleep in a big bed when you live with your granny, aren't you, sweetheart?" Anna nodded, put her thumb in her mouth, and cuddled the tiny teddy bear that Janet had given her. Guy wasn't really interested. Children were, to him, only amusing for short periods, and he preferred them when they were older.

But Rebecca was a different matter. The fact that she would now be living reasonably near his home, and yet far enough away to be discreet, had opened up all sorts of enticing opportunities. Not, he assured himself, that he'd do anything to harm his career prospects, but maybe his days of having a bit of a "fling" weren't quite over after all, and what Caroline didn't know couldn't hurt her. Who, down in London, would know or even care what went on up in the Midlands, except Katie? And if he handled things with his usual finesse, then with any luck Katie wouldn't find out either. After all, Guy reassured himself, Rebecca couldn't be such a pillar of virtue or she wouldn't have got herself pregnant in the first place. I bet she's a real "goer", he thought, with red hair like that. He liked a girl with a bit of spirit. She wasn't the least bit common, either. What a pity that she didn't come from the right background!

Rebecca was delighted to find Guy once again the teasing, flirtatious companion of their first journey. Not that she read anything into it, knowing of his engagement to Caroline. It's just his way, she told herself. Hadn't Katie told her he was the darling of all the nurses? It was only a bit of fun. And she enjoyed his flattering attention, although there were moments when she felt uncomfortable, knowing that she would have hated Ian to behave like this with another girl.

Again they stopped at the same transport café, then with Anna sleeping most of the way, were soon approaching the Potteries, and at last drawing up outside 15, Redwood Avenue. Guy mentally made a note of the house number, began unloading the boot and carried Rebecca's belongings up to the front door. This time, it opened immediately.

Grace smiled with delight at Anna and held out her arms, gratified when the toddler went immediately into them. "This is Dr Mason," Rebecca said.

Grace held out her hand. "I'm pleased to meet you. Would you like a cup of tea before you go on?"

Guy hesitated, then said, "Thanks, that's very kind of you."

And so, amid the hustle and bustle of Guy bringing in Rebecca's belongings, Grace added an extra cup and saucer to the tray she'd already prepared, and carried it in. Seated in the small front room, Guy noticed the framed photograph on the sideboard of Ian in his cap and gown, and stared at it with both interest and sympathy, profoundly thankful that he hadn't gone to that fateful football match at Bolton too. Because although most of his friends supported Crewe Alexandra, Guy had always been a Stoke City fan. Handsome chap, he thought, no wonder Rebecca had fallen for him. He glanced around, surprised to see how neat and tidy everywhere was. But then these houses were so cramped, compared to what he was used to, that he supposed life would be unbearable otherwise.

But Rebecca found it impossible to relax. It didn't seem right somehow, for someone she found so attractive to be sitting in Ian's home, and she was relieved when twenty minutes later, Guy stood up to leave. She walked down the short path with him to the car. "Thank you again, for all the lifts," she said, then suddenly realised with disappointment that she would probably never see him again.

But Guy gazed at her intently for a few seconds, then said quietly, "I'll be in touch." As he drove along the street, he saw Rebecca raise a hand in an uncertain wave before going indoors, and could only berate himself for being an idiot. Because, despite all his previous good intentions, Guy knew he'd meant those parting words.

Over the next couple of weeks, Grace and Rebecca tried to settle into living together, each wanting to accommodate the other. It was strange for both of them, and at first there were many awkward silences. Grace tried her best to make both mother and child feel comfortable and at home, while Rebecca tried to keep Anna's inevitable disruption to a minimum and helped out with the housework. Neither found it easy. Grace had become used to living alone, to having a peaceful tidy house, while Rebecca had to adapt to a vastly different household to the chaotic one at the Unicorn. She missed the noise and bustle of the pub and once Anna was in bed, at first the evenings seemed long and empty.

However, to the relief of them both, Anna adapted quickly to her new surroundings, and well wrapped up against the increasingly cold weather, spent much of her time outdoors, wandering up and down the garden path, fascinated by the shrubs, and particularly the vegetable patch. Her first discovery of a "wriggly worm" caused endless delight as she set about collecting them in a small tin bucket. Both Grace and Rebecca smiled at her beaming face and rosy cheeks, while a visit to the children's playground in the park across the road, became a daily highlight. And sharing the care of the child they loved gradually drew the two women, so different in age, increasingly closer. It's going to be all right, Grace thought with relief one evening, as they both sat quietly reading their library books in the soft glow of a standard lamp. Rebecca caught her anxious glance and smiled reassuringly at her. As soon as she and Anna had arrived, Rebecca had immediately offered to pay an amount towards expenses, but wasn't surprised when Ian's mother gently refused. After all, Rebecca thought with embarrassment, she knows I haven't got any income. But that situation certainly couldn't continue, and every evening she scoured the Situations Vacant columns in the *Evening Sentinel*, trying to find a part-time job to fit in with Grace's hours at the Marks & Spencer store in Hanley.

"Maybe I'd better go down to the Labour Exchange," she said a few days later. "I could always do bar work again."

"But you said you wanted to try something different." Grace protested.

"I do," Rebecca said. "If only to see what I'm capable of." And it was true, all she'd ever done since returning to London was to serve behind the bar in the Unicorn, and, she thought with a shudder at the memory, be the pub's cleaner. Rebecca was desperate to try something new, and recalling how she'd once told Katie that she was interested in fashion, said tentatively, "I don't suppose there would be anything going at M & S?"

Grace gazed at her reflectively. She'd been thinking the same thing herself but . . . "I had thought of it," she said slowly.

"Are you worried about people finding out? About Anna, and me and Ian, I mean?" Rebecca said anxiously. "I wouldn't want to cause you any embarrassment."

Grace shook her head and smiled. "No, love, it's not that. I've told you, I'm not making any secret of Anna – my word, no! And what anyone says about

Ian can't hurt him now. I just wondered if we might not be asking too much of ourselves, not only living together but working in the same store as well." She looked with concern at the girl she couldn't help thinking of as her "daughter-in-law". Rebecca frowned. What Grace said made sense, but after all, apart from minor irritations – on both sides, she admitted to herself – everything was going so well, it would be a pity to spoil it.

"We'd never be there at the same time," she pointed out.

"That's true," Grace said, although she still felt some reluctance. But it would be wonderful to have sole care of her granddaughter. "I tell you what," she said, "I'll have a word with the supervisor tomorrow. It's coming up to Christmas, and they always need extra staff then. At least we could try it."

And so Grace did just that, and her supervisor mentioned it to the staff manageress. A few days later, Rebecca presented herself at the store.

She walked through the shop, liking the bustle and efficiency, the way the assistants in their smart blue nylon overalls kept the counters so well displayed. With slight nervousness, she knocked on the office door. Emily Dawson, a prim middle-aged woman with dark hair scraped back into a bun, looked up as she entered, and after inviting her to sit down, asked her to fill in a form. Then, after reading it, she said doubtfully, "You've had no shop experience at all?"

Rebecca shook her head. "Only bar work in my

uncle's pub. But I'm used to dealing with the general public and handling money. And I've always loved clothes and nice things."

Emily looked at the eager young woman before her. Normally she wouldn't have hesitated to offer a girl like this a job. However Marks & Spencer's staff were known to be of a high calibre, and it was difficult to ignore the disgraceful fact that Rebecca was an unmarried mother. But knowing the tragic story and the fact that Grace Beresford had vouched for her, Emily decided to use her discretion. Grace was a loyal and popular member of staff, and this was the first time she'd ever asked a favour. "All right, we'll take you on." She consulted a chart. "You'll need to alternate with Grace because of your child. So that means you'll be working on Mondays, Wednesdays and Saturdays. Yes, that will fit in quite well," she said with a smile that softened her stern expression. "Initially it will be just over the Christmas period and you'll be a filler-in, that means you won't be attached to any particular section."

The wage offered – which Grace had told Rebecca was higher than the one paid by any other store in the area – was more than Rebecca had earned at the Unicorn, even with tips. She left the store in high spirits, and then took the opportunity to wander around. Although Stoke was the seat of the city, Hanley was the main shopping centre, and she found there were three large department stores, several small fashion shops, British Home Stores and Woolworth's, and an indoor market hall. Rebecca smiled to herself at the thought of how Sal had

275

worried that she'd be "buried alive" in a provincial town.

Then, as she walked home past the Commercial Hotel, with its sad memories, Rebecca suddenly realised that as Christmas Eve fell on Saturday this year, she wouldn't be able to go down to Southend at Christmas. Maybe the store would allow her to change days with Grace, she thought in panic. But surely she couldn't ask for special treatment so soon – it might jeopardise her chances of a permanent job. It was a blow, as she missed Ron and Sal terribly, and she knew they'd be bitterly disappointed. Hopefully, I'll be able to go at Easter, she decided – they'll be more settled in by then, anyway.

And as time went on, Grace revelled in having sole charge of Anna, although, as she said ruefully to Rebecca, "I haven't got the energy I used to have." So a routine became established. Rebecca liked her job, enjoying both the work and the company of the other "girls", and in the evenings the two women would sit comfortably together, often knitting as they listened to the wireless.

But Grace knew that this was no way for a vibrant young woman to live and when Guy's letter arrived, she felt almost relieved.

"He wants to take me to the Victoria Hall," Rebecca said with surprise. "To an orchestral concert. Apparently he was supposed to be going with Caroline, but she's got the flu."

"Yes, people do come from a long way," Grace told her. "The acoustics are supposed to be among the best in the country. When is it?"

"Saturday night. Could you—"

"Of course." Grace smiled down at Anna who was playing with her doll. "She's a good little girl for going to bed, aren't you, sweetheart?"

Rebecca, hurrying to go to work, smiled and then happily spent the whole journey deciding what to wear. But she was also, with some discomfort, aware that her excitement was not only about going for the first time in her life to a concert, but also at the prospect of seeing Guy again. And that was stupid, she told herself. Remember that you're only the stand-in. He belongs to somebody else, and don't you forget it!

27

On Saturday night, wearing a green-and-gold blouse she'd bought specially for the occasion, Rebecca took her seat beside Guy on the front row of the balcony at the Victoria Hall. She leaned forward, looking with excitement at the audience in the stalls below, and in the tiered seats around the large ornate hall. It was such a rare treat to come out in the evening, and she had never been to anywhere as thrilling as this.

While the orchestra was tuning up, she opened the programme, and was relieved to see that she knew at least two of the items on it. The "Warsaw" Concerto – she remembered that from the film, *Dangerous Moonlight*. And *The Dream of Olwen* had been one of her mother's favourites. And then at last, the first violinist came out, took his place to polite applause, which rose to a crescendo as the conductor, who Guy told her was quite famous, strode out to bow and then take his place on the podium. When the performance began she became transfixed, not only by the soaring music but in watching the formally dressed orchestra, so beauti-fully controlled by the dignified conductor. And somehow, it seemed natural and in keeping with the pleasure of the evening, when the first item finished and Guy held her hand, whispering, "So glad you're enjoying it." Rebecca, not wanting to miss a second of what was happening on stage, flashed him a smile, leaving her hand in his.

Guy quietly congratulated himself on achieving exactly what he'd set out to do, when he'd made a note of the house number, and booked the concert tickets. Caroline, of course, knew nothing about it. As far as she was concerned, he'd had to go to a stag party for a friend. In the interval, he left Rebecca standing in a corner of the bar while he went off to buy their drinks; and threading his way back through the crowd, he noticed several admiring glances in Rebecca's direction. And she wasn't unaware of them, he thought with a grin, noticing her heightened colour and sparkling eyes. It was obvious that she was thoroughly enjoying herself, and he found that refreshing. It's a pity, he thought, that people get blasé about things. Caroline, for instance, would have been criticising the orchestra's performance and comparing it with others she'd seen, while Rebecca was just thrilled to be here.

"I don't think you could be happier if you were at a ball," he teased, as she sipped her lemonade.

"Cinderella, you mean," she laughed.

"Does that make me Prince Charming?" He smiled down at her with easy charm.

"That depends," she said lightly.

"Oh yes – on what?" Guy gently pushed back a stray tendril of hair from Rebecca's forehead, letting his finger linger on her skin, and gently trace the

279

outline of her cheek. Suddenly the warning bell went, and Rebecca, slightly disturbed by the intimacy, drained her glass and turned with relief to go back to their seats. Although acutely conscious of the warmth of Guy's hand once again holding her own, she pushed aside any misgivings, and was soon enraptured again by the brilliance of the performance. When the conductor turned to take the final bow, she applauded until her hands were sore, and turned to face Guy.

"I wanted it to go on forever," she said, and Guy laughed.

"There'll be another time."

His words echoed in Rebecca's mind as they queued to leave the Hall. I don't understand what's going on, she thought frantically. For instance, we should never have been holding hands nor should there be this attraction between us – it was obviously not only on her side, Guy's eyes and body language told her that. And when, as they began walking back to Redwood Avenue, he slipped his arm lightly around her waist, Rebecca became even more bewildered. He was engaged, for heaven's sake! She felt she should pull away, could almost hear Katie's voice in her head saying, "*ask him what he's playing at*", but she didn't want to appear some naïve girl, making a fuss about nothing. And yet Rebecca knew that one reason why she felt hesitant and inhibited, was because Guy was a doctor, someone from a totally different class. If it had been one of the blokes in the pub, she would have had no hesitation in slapping him down. Also, this evening with Guy had been so magical, that Rebecca didn't want to spoil things.

It's just Guy being Guy, she told herself, but when they turned into Redwood Avenue, he paused at the beginning of the road, drawing her to him beneath a large oak tree. For one long moment Guy gazed down into her widening eyes, and then he was kissing her, holding her close, and Rebecca despite herself, found herself responding. They kissed again, urgently deeply, and Guy swiftly opened the buttons on her coat and slipped in his hand to cup her breast. It was then, feeling the warmth of his skin through the silky fabric of her blouse that Rebecca, in panic and confusion struggled to push him away. "Sorry, sweetheart," Guy whispered, still lightly kissing her face, "you're just so beautiful, I couldn't help myself."

"But Caroline . . ."

Guy looked down at her, his expression troubled. "I'm not sure about Caroline any more," he said quietly.

Rebecca stared up at him. What did he mean? Was he saying that he was having doubts about his engagement because of her? But Guy didn't explain, he just released her, and then hand-in-hand they walked slowly along until they reached his car, parked outside the house. "Thank you for a lovely evening," he said, and shook his head at her invitation to come in. "No, I'd better be getting back." He smiled down at her. "Bye, poppet. See you soon."

Baffled, still reeling from what had just taken place, Rebecca watched him drive away and then, seeing Grace twitch the curtain, slid her key into the front door. She was longing to reach the privacy of her bedroom, where she could try and sort out her chaotic thoughts. Just what exactly had Guy meant by those astonishing words? But as Grace was obviously still up, that would have to wait. Rebecca took off her coat, and with a smile, handed Ian's mother the programme saying, "It was absolutely wonderful."

Guy, driving swiftly along the dark, almost deserted roads, was feeling quietly satisfied with the way the evening had gone. He'd always known that it would need a subtle approach with Rebecca, and now he'd sown a seed of doubt in her mind about Caroline, the next time would be that much easier. Because from the way Rebecca had responded to his kiss, Guy knew that he'd been right. There were hidden passions behind that lovely face, and he had every intention of enjoying them. Did he feel a stab of conscience? A little, but Guy had always been able to justify his behaviour where women were concerned. Nothing deep, no commitment. He had no illusions about himself – he was a damn fine doctor with a weakness for a pretty face. It wasn't his fault that women found him attractive. In any case he shrugged as he drew up at a set of traffic lights, it wasn't as though he intended to seduce a girl whose reputation could be ruined.

As the weeks passed, and she heard no more from Guy, Rebecca tried to push the incident firmly from her mind. You should know better than to read anything into it, she told herself. Haven't you learned anything about men? You heard enough of their talk when working behind a bar to know they're no angels! Guy probably hadn't been able to resist kissing a girl who was obviously attracted to him. But that was all it was, attraction, at least she thought it was. Certainly what she felt for Guy was a pale shadow of how she'd felt about Ian. Yet she'd enjoyed the physical intimacy of being held in Guy's arms and knew it had only been guilt about Caroline that had caused her to push him away. One thing I don't want to do, Rebecca thought guiltily, is to steal someone else's boyfriend.

Anna's second birthday passed, and Christmas arrived, with Grace and Rebecca enjoying the little girl's delight at the tiny Christmas tree, and her presents. Toys were still scarce, but Grace had managed to buy a second-hand doll with hardly any crazing to its composition head and pretty face. Anna was delighted that the doll's china-blue eyes opened and closed, and to complement its long dress, Rebecca had knitted a little white bonnet and bootees. Grace ruefully showed her the stamp on the back of the doll's neck stating it was made in Germany, but Rebecca just shrugged. "The war's over, Grace. Not all of the German people could have been Nazis. In any case, I should think this dates before 1939."

"What's her name going to be?" Grace smiled down at Anna's glowing face.

"Gloria!"

Rebecca laughed. "Where's she had that from?"

"The Christmas carols on the wireless. My, but she's quick!"

"I had a friend called Gloria once," Rebecca told her. "She dumped me as soon as she found out I was pregnant."

"Some friend!" Grace said in outrage.

But, as she prepared the festive dinner – Rebecca had offered to set the table and wash up afterwards – Grace couldn't help thinking of other Christmases. Her loss always seemed even more poignant on this special day. Jim had always insisted on peeling the potatoes and scraping the carrots. She'd trimmed the Brussels sprouts herself, not trusting him to do it properly! But it had been good to work together, with a morning service on the wireless, and often snowflakes fluttering against the windows. He'd loved Christmas had Jim, often getting a bit tipsy, enjoying his sherry trifle and mince pies. She remembered Ian's excitement as a child, and her anxiety on the Christmases he'd been away fighting in the war. But he'd come safely home only to . . . Her eyes filled with tears, and she brushed them away, turning with a determined smile as Anna wandered into the kitchen, clutching her new doll.

To Rebecca, it all seemed too quiet. By now, at the Unicorn, the bar, festooned with streamers would have been busy and noisy and she missed Sal's sharp humour, and Ron's solid, reassuring presence. But most of all, as always, Rebecca missed her mother. Milly had gone to great lengths, despite her husband's drinking, to make Christmas a happy one for them all. She'd made her cake and puddings in October, with Rebecca helping; had stayed up late on Christmas Eve baking mince pies. But those days had gone forever, and Rebecca forced a smile as she poured out a small glass of sherry for Grace. They had to help each other now.

On Boxing Day, Rebecca wrote to Ron and Sal, describing Anna's delight with their presents, and enclosing a crayoned drawing the little girl had done for them. "*Christmas seemed so strange without you both*," she ended, "*but I'll try and come down in the spring. Anna will be older and walking well by then, so I should be able to manage on the journey without a pushchair.*"

Then in January, Rebecca, to her delight was offered a permanent job at the store. But one morning in early February, she made a mistake. Having taken Anna to Hanley to buy new shoes, Rebecca gave in to her daughter's demands and wheeled her into the store to "see her granny". Grace, re-stocking the ladies' knitwear on her counter, looked up with surprise. She glanced quickly around, then leaning over the counter, whispered to her granddaughter, "Hello, sweetheart!"

"She wants to show you her new shoes," Rebecca said, and smiling, leaned down to retrieve them from the bag.

"Me, Mummy?" Anna begged, and clutching one, held it up to show Grace. Her childish treble was shrill, and Rebecca, with a jolt, saw Sylvia, a middle-aged woman on the next counter – men's knitwear – turn to look first at her and then at the child in the pushchair. She glanced swiftly at Rebecca's bare left hand, then glared at her.

Rebecca, who had already found Sylvia cold and

285

unfriendly, hissed, "Old fish-face looks as though she's going to have a heart attack!"

"Nobody likes her," Grace muttered. "She hasn't been here long, and she rubs everyone up the wrong way."

"She obviously didn't know about me!"

"A lot of the staff don't," Grace said with tight lips.

"I hope that woman doesn't go spreading it about," Rebecca said that evening as she helped Grace to wash the dishes. "I'm sorry, I should never have brought Anna in to see you!"

"No good crying over spilt milk," Grace said. "It's done now." But she *was* annoyed about what she considered to be a thoughtless and needless action. She'd been very careful about who she'd told about Rebecca and Anna, and Sylvia was just the type to go causing trouble.

"Perhaps I should have worn the ring, after all," Rebecca said.

"Didn't you feel it would stop you making friends, at least with the single girls?" Grace said, putting the lid back on the enamel bread bin.

"I haven't made any yet, not really. But yes, I'm sure it would," Rebecca said. "Still, maybe it would be better than being known as a scarlet woman!"

Grace laughed and turned to face her. "You're hardly that!"

"I am to some people," Rebecca said grimly.

But their fears were justified, because a few days later, when Rebecca walked into the staff canteen, there were a few averted glances and she could definitely sense an atmosphere. With flushed cheeks, she collected her rabbit stew from the serving counter, and after looking around for an empty seat, sat next to a dark-haired girl who worked on the children's wear section. The other women sitting at the table were all members of staff who Rebecca had worked with and they gave her friendly and supportive smiles. Hilda, a grey-haired woman nearing retiring age, leaned over. "I suppose you've noticed that Sylvia's been spreading rumours," she whispered. "Take no notice, it'll be someone else's turn next week."

Rebecca glanced across to a table by the wall, where Sylvia was sitting. Aged about forty, she had a thin discontented face, accentuated by her lank brown hair being scraped back from her forehead and pinned to one side with a hair grip. Her pale face was devoid of make-up. She was staring into space, one hand holding her cup, the other a cigarette.

Rebecca turned to Hilda, who was one of Grace's friends. "The problem is," she said, "that it's not just a rumour. As you know, it's true."

"Yes, well I know the full story," another woman said. "It wasn't your fault Ian was killed. He was a lovely lad an' all. He used to come in to see Grace, remember Hilda?"

She nodded. "I remember."

The dark-haired girl nudged Rebecca. "What are they talking about?" she said in a low voice.

"Oh, I made the mistake of bringing my kiddie in last week, and eagle-eye over there's making a meal of it." She nodded in the direction of Sylvia. "Only I'm not married."

The dark-haired girl gave a sharp intake of breath, then turning to face her asked, "Did I just hear the father was killed?"

Rebecca nodded. "Yes, in the Bolton football disaster. Both him and his dad."

"Oh, that's awful!" She looked with sympathy at Rebecca. "Really bad luck. My name's Betty, by the way."

"I'm Rebecca – that's if you're not ashamed to speak to me," she said with bitterness.

"We want none of that talk," Hilda said sharply. "We might have the odd difference, but we all get on well together, don't we girls?" The other women on the table nodded vigorously. "And whatever the reason, you've done Grace the world of good coming to live with her. We can do without upstarts like that Sylvia, with her nasty tongue. You take no notice, love." Hilda heaved herself up. "Don't forget to ask Grace if she'd like to go to the whist drive at St Mary's this week."

"Is she a Catholic, then?" Betty asked Rebecca.

She shook her head. "No, and neither am I. But that doesn't stop Grace going to their whist drives."

"You don't go, do you?"

"Not me," Rebecca laughed. "I'm too young for that!"

"Same here. I am a Catholic, though." Gradually, over the next couple of weeks, the two girls became friendly, and usually ate their midday meal together.

"M & S certainly look after their staff, don't

they?" Rebecca said one day, looking down at her shepherd's pie and fresh vegetables, knowing there was syrup sponge and custard to follow.

"I'm glad to hear you appreciate it!" She turned to look up at the assistant manager, who paused at their table and smiled down at them. He was a fresh-faced young man who, although only recently posted to the Hanley branch, was already popular with the staff.

"Oh, we do," Betty said, glancing up at him from beneath her dark, curling lashes. He smiled down at her, his eyes holding her gaze, while Rebecca watched with amusement.

"He fancies you," she whispered, once he'd left, and saw a blush rise in Betty's face.

"Go on with you!" The two girls laughed, and Rebecca realised how much she missed the teasing banter she used to share with Katie.

I need a social life, she thought with desperation, and soon, or my young life will be passing me by. And as she walked home that same evening, an umbrella shielding her from a heavy shower of rain, Rebecca mulled over the fact that she hadn't heard anything from Guy since that night when he'd kissed her. But then, what had she expected? That he was going to break off his engagement? And if he hadn't, no matter how much she liked him, did she really want him to get in touch?

28

The following Saturday evening, hearing a knock at the front door Rebecca, thinking it was a neighbour, called upstairs, "I'll get it!" Smiling at the sound of Anna's laughter in the bath, when she opened the door, the last person Rebecca expected to see was Guy!

"Don't look so surprised," he grinned. "I did say I'd see you soon."

Rebecca nearly said, "That was weeks ago," but thought better of it. She smiled and stood to one side, saying, "Come in."

Guy stepped into the narrow hall, and ran his hand ruefully through his hair. "Sorry it's been so long, it's just been life getting in the way. We had a flu epidemic at the hospital, for one thing."

"Oh. Is Katie all right? Have you seen her?"

"I've noticed her about, so I'm sure she's fine." He rubbed his hands together. "It's a bit chilly out."

"Do you want a cup of tea?"

"Yes, please, and would there possibly be a biscuit?" he said hopefully.

"Typical man!" Laughing, she went into the kitchen, and after a quick glance around, Guy followed her. "Where is everyone?"

"Upstairs – it's Anna's bed time."

He leaned casually against the kitchen wall. "I suppose you're wondering why I'm here?"

"I am, rather." Rebecca's mind was racing with possibilities.

"I've been to a medical conference at a hotel a few miles away. It was fascinating, but," he grinned, "not for a young lady's ears – all gynaecological stuff."

"Well, that's a daft thing to say," she retorted as she poured boiling water into the teapot. "Anyway, I didn't know you were going to specialise in women's problems."

"I'm considering it," he said, taking a ginger biscuit from the barrel she offered him. "After all, I'm told I have a way with them." His teasing eyes challenged her to rise to the bait, and Rebecca couldn't help laughing.

"Go on with you! I know from Katie what a good doctor you are."

She carried the tray into the front room, and he sat opposite her. "Before Grace comes down," he said urgently. "Do you think she would babysit while I take you out for dinner? Like several of the delegates, I'm booked into the hotel for tonight. Take pity on me, Rebecca, I can't face an evening of more medical discussion, and it's either that or eat alone."

"Dinner?" she repeated, and felt a flicker of excitement – have dinner in a hotel? She'd always wanted to do that. But then she hesitated, wondering whether she was fooling herself. After all she knew Guy was a flirt, knew that he was attracted to her, as she was to him. Or was she flattering herself? Then she suddenly decided that she was silly. How could having a meal with Guy possibly hurt Caroline, and to refuse would seem ungrateful after he'd been so helpful in giving her lifts. She'd be stupid not to go.

"I'd love to come," she told him, "and I'm sure Grace won't mind. I'll just pop up and ask her, and then get changed. But you'll have to give me at least half an hour!"

"Take as long as you like." He looked around the room. "Is there anything I can read while I'm waiting?"

With adrenaline surging through her, dispelling any weariness after a busy day at the store, Rebecca handed him the *Evening Sentinel*. Then, thankful she and Grace had decided to eat late, she hurried upstairs and peeped around the door of the box-room – now Anna's bedroom, where Grace was reading the last page of *Goldilocks and the Three Bears* to her already drowsy granddaughter.

"It's Guy!" Rebecca whispered.

Grace tucked the blanket around Anna, and tiptoed out. "That's a surprise," she said, raising enquiring eyebrows. Rebecca told her of Guy's invitation, and Grace frowned. It had been different the last time. After all, it would have been a pity to waste a concert ticket. But Guy wanting to take Rebecca out again? A flicker of suspicion rose in Grace's mind – he might be a doctor, but he was still a man, an engaged one at that! But then she looked at Rebecca's glowing face, and hadn't the heart to dampen her spirits. "Of course you must go. Had I better go down and make conversation? It seems a bit rude to leave him on his own."

"I wouldn't bother for a while," Rebecca said. "I've made him a cup of tea and he'll be glad of a bit of peace and quiet if he's been at a conference all day." She went into her bedroom, with Grace following, and flung open the door to her wardrobe. "I just don't know what to wear! There's this green-and-gold blouse but I wore that last time!"

"Yes, but that black skirt is just the thing," Grace said thoughtfully, "and you'll need to look smart. Just a minute, I might have something . . ."

Rebecca watched her hurry from the room without much hope. Grace always dressed smartly but she wore the sort of clothes suitable for her own age, not for Rebecca's! But she gasped when Grace came in carrying an elegant black lace evening blouse. The neckline was low, the sleeves long and fluted, and Rebecca loved it immediately. "That's gorgeous!"

"I had it for a special occasion, years ago. I was slimmer then. Try it on," Grace urged.

Quickly, Rebecca tried the blouse over her white opera top slip and fumbled to fasten the tiny velvet-covered buttons on the bodice. Then she turned to look in the mirror, and caught her breath. It was the most glamorous thing she'd ever worn. "What do you think?"

Grace surveyed her, seeing her sparkling eyes, yet feeling concern when she saw how the flimsy material clung to Rebecca's breasts, with the low-cut neckline revealing more than a hint of cleavage. But the girl was young and beautiful, surely she deserved to feel and look like this? No wonder Ian had fallen in love with her. And not for the first time, Grace wished she'd had the chance of seeing them together, that the young couple had been able to marry before the accident. Then Rebecca would have been her daughter-in-law, and truly part of her family.

But Grace just said, "It's perfect! I only wish I'd looked as good in it. But you'll need to borrow the black silk slip." She went to fetch it and also brought a string of pearls with matching earrings. "I feel as if half of me is going with you," she smiled, and felt a pang of envy touched with sadness. How long was it since she'd gone out for the evening dressed up like this, full of anticipation? And now, with Jim gone, Grace doubted whether she ever would again.

Rebecca spent ten minutes in the bathroom, then later, freshly made up, the glowing waves of her hair resting on her shoulders, she fastened the pearls around her neck and looked into the mirror with quiet satisfaction, and not a little pride. As she moved away the black georgette skirt with its silk lining and hundreds of knife pleats swished around her legs, making her feel ultra-feminine. She'd bought it from Ruby, and Rebecca smiled as she remembered Sal muttering, "That definitely came off the back of a lorry!" With a fleeting glance at the print of *The Fighting Temeraire* which still hung on the wall of the bedroom, she wished Ian had been waiting for her downstairs; but Rebecca knew that he would have wanted her to build a new life for herself. Then, going down to the sitting-room, she hesitated, and slipped on her warm winter coat before going in to tell Guy she was ready.

A few minutes later, Grace stood at the window, and lifting the curtain slightly, couldn't help some misgivings as she watched the car pull away. Then she chided herself and returned to her chair, to her library book. Rebecca was a sensible young woman – she was more than capable of looking after herself.

The hotel was about ten miles away – an impressive converted manor house in its own grounds. Rebecca looked around in awe as they walked through the wide oak-panelled hall, with a crimson-carpeted staircase rising from each side. Through one door, she glimpsed a bar, and then Guy was taking her coat, handing it to the receptionist, and guiding her through two double glass-paned doors into a large lounge. "Just give me a few minutes," he said.

Rebecca chose a high-backed chair on one side of the room and sat with a straight back, crossing her legs and feeling exquisitely elegant in such luxurious surroundings. The furniture was all antique; the thick-piled carpet, although its muted colours were fading, was still beautiful; while she could only gaze with admiration at the gold brocade drapes with festoons and tie-backs which framed the tall windows. There were a few other people sitting and chatting, and after comparing other women's clothes with her own, Rebecca was reassured that she was suitably dressed. When eventually Guy returned, he was wearing a dinner jacket and black tie. "Aren't we the handsome couple," she said, as he took her hand.

"With you looking like that, I'll be the envy of every man in the room," he smiled, and ushered her into a large dining-room hung with glittering chandeliers. Rebecca caught her breath at the impressive scene, at the tables with their white crisp tablecloths and pink napkins folded into fans, at the silver cutlery and crystal glasses. There were even slim vases of fresh flowers on the tables, while several uniformed waiters stood at intervals around the room. A formally dressed silver-haired man came forward to greet them and then led them to a table for two in the centre of the room.

Rebecca took care to sit gracefully on the chair the head waiter pulled out for her, and then once he'd left, smiled across at Guy, saying, "I feel as if I've died and gone to heaven!" He laughed, and then a waiter was handing her a leather-bound menu. To Guy's amusement, she spent ages in deciding what to choose, but eventually their order was taken, and she began to gaze around the room, taking in every detail of her surroundings, fascinated by the sophisticated scene.

"Hey," Guy said softly. "I'm here."

She turned back to him. "Sorry! I suppose those people over there are other doctors who've been at the conference?" She nodded towards two long tables at one end of the room occupied by earnestly talking men, although she noticed two middle-aged women among them.

"Well spotted. Now you can see why I'd rather be sitting here with you! It's a much more attractive view." He reached out a hand and covered her own.

296

"You really do look fantastic, you know, and as for that stunning blouse . . ." His gaze swept down to the swell of her breasts, and then he glanced away quickly as a superior-looking waiter approached. Guy, who had already studied the wine list, indicated his choice, and afterwards said, "I've ordered a Chablis for you, as you're having fish."

Rebecca said quickly, "Oh, I didn't realise you were ordering for me. I'm sorry, Guy, I don't drink."

"Sweetheart, you can't have a meal like this, and not have a glass of wine!"

"I always get a headache," she complained.

"Have you ever tried a really decent wine?"

When she shook her head, Guy said, "Well, don't you think this is a good chance to try? After all, you don't want to go through life depriving yourself of one of its greatest pleasures. It might not be necessary."

That did make sense, Rebecca thought doubtfully. "All right, then," she said. I might as well make the most of all this, she thought, it might never happen again! Then all her attention was on the delicious aroma of the oxtail soup placed before her.

Guy proved to be an amusing companion, and as Rebecca began to eat her fish, she took sips of the chilled white wine, discovering how much it complemented the food; and she began to relax and enjoy both her surroundings and the rare experience of being waited on.

"How's the wine?" Guy asked.

"Lovely." Rebecca sipped it again, and looked at Guy's beef with distaste. "I don't know how you can eat it looking pink like that, I like my meat well done."

"The chef would have a fit," Guy laughed, and a few minutes later a waiter paused by their table, lifted the Chablis out of its ice bucket and before she could protest re-filled Rebecca's glass. Then she thought, why not? If she *was* going to get a headache, surely the damage was already done.

The meal passed in enjoyable light banter, but, with her senses heightened by the wine, Rebecca was becoming intensely aware of the sensual over-tones. It was there, in Guy's eyes, every time he looked at her, in the warm caressing way he spoke to her, and, as they finished their coffee and he stubbed out his cigarette, she felt almost shy at the blatant desire in his eyes. "Are you sure you don't want a liqueur?"

She shook her head. "Positive. I've already had more to drink than I've ever had in my life." And I feel fine, she thought. In fact I feel absolutely wonderful. And she longed to be in Guy's arms again, to feel the heady sensation of his kisses. *What does it matter that it will never lead to anything,* a voice in her head said, *surely you deserve some happiness, some fun, after all you've been through.* But then her conscience reminded her. Caroline!

Rebecca looked down at the table, where Guy had reached out and turned over her hand, his thumb gently caressing her palm. "What's happening with Caroline?" she said quietly.

Guy's thumb became very still. "I can't answer that, sweetheart." He gave a helpless shrug. "There's all this family pressure, and I feel trapped in a way. I know I've got to sort out what I really want. And so," Guy pleaded, "I think we should keep all this to ourselves, at least for now, if you don't mind. I mean, I'm sure you write to Katie . . ."

"Now and again," Rebecca said. "But I haven't mentioned that we've been out together, because I know what a gossipy place the hospital is."

Relieved, Guy smiled, "That's what I like about you, sweetheart. You're not only beautiful, but intelligent too."

Rebecca felt a warm glow of pleasure. She was so lucky to have met someone like Guy, to have the experience of eating in this expensive hotel. But as he paid the bill, she wondered just what her feelings were for him. He was everything a girl could dream of – a doctor, handsome, unbelievably charming. Surely, she thought, I'm not going to compare every man with Ian for the rest of my life! But such thoughts were fleeting. For now, all she wanted was for this evening never to end. Guy must have read her thoughts, because he leaned over and said, "I've enjoyed being with you so much that I don't want to take you home yet. Shall we go into the lounge?"

Rebecca nodded, and then as he pulled out the chair for her to get up from the table, she staggered slightly. Steadying herself, she picked up her bag, and with Guy behind her, began to walk slowly out of the restaurant. Guy, noticing the incident, smiled to himself. As he'd hoped, when they reached the lounge, it was full and rather noisy, and he slipped an arm around Rebecca's shoulders. "Not for us,

I think," he said. "By the way did I tell you, that I've got this amazing room, with a genuine antique four-poster bed! The receptionist told me that Elizabeth I once slept in it."

"Gosh, you lucky thing!"

"Come on, I'll show it to you. It won't take a minute."

Rebecca hesitated. "I need to . . ."

"Okay. I think it's down there, past the reception desk. Probably best if you follow me up anyway, we don't want people getting the wrong idea! Honestly, it's worth seeing – you almost need a ladder to climb into it. Room number sixty-two, on the first floor."

A little dizzily, Rebecca made her way to the ladies' cloakroom, where she marvelled at the red plush velvet stools before the make-up mirrors. The rich know how to live, she thought with envy, and then a few minutes later sat on one to re-apply her coral lipstick. Just then the two women she'd seen sitting at the conference tables came in out of the cubicles and joined her before the mirrors.

"If they don't stop talking shop soon, I'll scream," one said.

"I know." The other woman, whose black hair was screwed tightly back into a chignon, dabbed at her nose with a powder puff. "Do you get the feeling they look down on us? We may not be industrial chemists, but we are qualified secretaries, for heaven's sake!"

"I know what you mean. And who else would send out notes of the conference!"

Rebecca paused, her lipstick still in her hand – industrial chemists? Frowning, she turned. "Excuse me, but could you tell me what conference you're attending?"

The black-haired woman looked at her in surprise. "The Institute of Vitreous Enamellers. Why?"

Rebecca tried to force her fuddled mind to concentrate. "There isn't another conference being held here – a medical one?"

"I'm sure there isn't – the hotel only has one conference room!" With curious backward glances, they both got up and left, leaving Rebecca feeling totally confused. A few minutes later, she stood up and began to walk on slightly unsteady legs into the reception hall, and then began to climb slowly up the stairs. Guy had been lying to her. Why? But even as she wondered, the obvious answer leapt into her mind. She could see it all now – the beautiful hotel, the seductive surroundings of the restaurant, the expensive bottle of wine. What had he said – an antique four-poster bed that Elizabeth I had slept in? And she'd fallen for it!

Fuzzily, Rebecca thought she should be flattered that he'd gone to so much trouble. But her eyes were already pricking with tears of bitter disillusionment. She'd been feeling so happy, so excited, and now all she felt was naïve and foolish. Room 62 was at the far end of a short corridor and the door was slightly ajar. Rebecca tapped and pushed it open. Guy was sitting in an armchair, one leg crossed languidly over the other, and smiled affectionately at her. "There you are!" He got up and waved at the massive bed in the centre of the room. "Have you ever seen anything like it?"

She'd been wrong – Guy had been telling the truth! Rebecca stared with admiration at the massive carved bedposts, with their faded tapestry canopy and drapes and drew in a shaky breath. Had she misjudged him? But he *had* lied about the conference! But before she could question him, Guy was behind her, his arms around her waist, his lips nuzzling at her bare neck and shoulder. "I've been longing to do this all night, you're driving me mad." His breath was warm on her skin, and almost against her will, Rebecca nestled close against him, as a delicious feeling of relaxation swept over. When he turned her to face him, she raised her mouth eager for his kiss, her blood hot in her veins, swift desire rising at the feel of his hands on her. They kissed long and deeply, again and again, Guy's tongue teasing hers, and when eventually he drew away Rebecca was trembling. But despite the emotions threatening to overwhelm her, she had to know! In a strained voice, she said, "Why did you tell me you'd come for a medical conference?"

Guy said sharply, "What do you mean?"

"I've just found out that there isn't one. All those people have come for one to do with ceramics."

Guy swore under his breath. He came towards her and taking her hand led her to sit on the edge of the bed. "You've rumbled me," he said ruefully. "I bow my head with shame."

"But I don't understand . . ."

"I wanted to be with you, alone, I've been desperate for you, and I didn't want it to be in the back of a car. I wanted us to spend time together, to have a wonderfully memorable evening." With one finger, he traced the outline of her low-cut bodice, lifting the lace slightly and stroking the soft swell of her breast. "You're so special, Rebecca." He gently coaxed her back until they were lying on the bed. "I think," he whispered, kissing her eyelids, cheeks, and finally hovering over her lips, "I think you want me as much as I want you. You're a very sexy young woman, did you know that?" Now his hand was moving beneath her skirt, caressing the warm flesh at the top of her stockings, but when his fingers crept further, Rebecca began to panic. "No, Guy!"

"You don't mean that, sweetheart," he said persuasively, already unbuttoning her bodice. He drew down the lacy material and bent his mouth to her breast, but now she was struggling against him, pushing hard at his chest. With a curse, Guy drew away, furious when Rebecca, hot, and flustered, stood up.

"Sorry, Guy, but no!"

"Come on, Rebecca, you're going to tell me next that you're not that sort of girl!"

Mortified, she slapped him hard across the face. "You've been planning this all along, haven't you? Well, let me tell you, *Dr* Guy Mason, that it will take more than a few lifts and a decent meal to get *me* into bed!"

"You were enjoying it so far!" Guy, frustrated and still aroused, was seething with anger. He wasn't used to being thwarted, and certainly not by a girl from the East End.

"You flatter yourself!" Rebecca straightened her clothing, and picked up her bag. "I'd like you to take me home, please – now!"

Guy glared at her and then flung open the bedroom door. "There's your escape," he said with sarcasm. They left the room and he waited with ill-concealed impatience while Rebecca collected her coat from Reception. As they walked to the car park, she felt the first sign of a headache, and neither spoke on the journey home; the icy silence was broken only when, as they approached Redwood Avenue, Rebecca said curtly, "I think it's better if we don't see each other again!"

"Don't worry, there's no chance!" Then Guy said curtly, "You're not going to be telling tales to Katie, I hope? Because two can play at that game, and I don't think you want your reputation to be any worse than it already is!"

Rebecca was fighting tears of humiliation. Her head was now beginning to hurt unbearably, and all she wanted to do was to get home and lie down in a dark room. "I wouldn't stoop to your level!" she said in a tight voice, and when the car drew up, she opened the door, slammed it and stalked into the house without a backward glance.

29

After a wretched Sunday with a pounding headache, Rebecca could only vow with vehemence never to drink again! It wasn't only the wretched after-effects – to her shame and embarrassment, she knew that if she hadn't overheard those two women talking in the ladies' powder room, then the previous night could have had a very different outcome. Even now she could remember the desire she'd felt, her initial passionate and abandoned response to Guy's kisses. It had only been her suspicions, her questioning, that had sobered her up slightly. And thank God it had been enough! With a jolt she remembered that she'd also been drinking on the night that Anna was conceived! But what had happened in that dimly lit sitting-room had been special, beautiful, the tender and passionate outcome of the love she and Ian felt for each other. It bore no resemblance to Guy's carefully planned seduction. Maybe she was one of those women people joked about – who was "anybody's" after a few drinks! Being practically teetotal, I've never given myself the chance to find out, she thought with bitterness. Rebecca knew that to some people she was "no better than she should be", a girl of easy virtue.

Surely that couldn't be true? In any case, she thought with despair as she scoured the meat tin after the Sunday roast, she couldn't just blame it on the alcohol – after one unplanned pregnancy, she should have had more sense!

Grace, after one look at Rebecca's stony expression when she'd come down for breakfast, had asked politely, "Did you have a good time?" and after Rebecca's curt, "Fine, thanks," had remained silent. As the hours passed, it became obvious that something had happened last night, and from the way Rebecca was clattering those dishes in the kitchen, she was upset about it. But Grace knew she had no right to question her. After all, the girl wasn't her daughter, and unfortunately never would be. But Grace could hazard a guess. Her instincts had been right – education or no education, men always kept their brains in their trousers; even, she thought sadly, glancing at Anna, her own son. But then, she could never regret having her little granddaughter. Anyway, she sighed, no matter how well we get on, if Rebecca chooses not to tell me, I don't suppose I'll ever know.

And so it was with diminished self-respect that Rebecca began her working week, and she was certainly in no mood to tolerate Sylvia's contemptuous glances. "If you've got something to say, why don't you say it to my face?" Rebecca hissed as she passed Sylvia's counter. "Or are you only good at whispering behind people's backs?"

"Hark at Lady Muck," Sylvia snapped. "I can't

see what someone like you has got to be high and mighty about!"

"Oh shut your spiteful face!" Even as the words burst out of her mouth, Rebecca was horrified. She glanced around in alarm, hoping there weren't any customers within earshot. But luckily, as it was early in the morning, the store was quiet.

But the incident shook her, because Rebecca prided herself on controlling her temper. When she'd first been evacuated, Mr Parry had taken one look at her and said in a loud tone to his wife, "Red hair and a bad temper to match, I've no doubt!" Twelve-year-old Rebecca, weary and hungry after two long and bewildering train journeys, had looked up at his cold, angular face, and miserably vowed to prove that she hadn't. And now, as she checked her float in the till, she was furious with herself. She'd let the scene with Guy affect her far too much. But Sylvia had seized her opportunity, and bristling with indignation had marched straight to the supervisor to complain. Half an hour later, Rebecca found herself facing a severe-looking Emily Dawson.

"Is this true? What I've been hearing from Sylvia?"

Rebecca gazed directly at her. "Yes, I'm afraid it is."

"You actually used those words – *shut your spiteful face?*"

Rebecca nodded, while her heart beat frantically. Why on earth hadn't she kept her stupid mouth shut! Surely Emily wouldn't sack her? And it was typical of Sylvia to come running to tell tales! "I can only apologise," she said to Emily. "I've put up with

307

a lot from Sylvia, and well, this morning, I just couldn't take it."

Emily looked at the proud girl standing before her. She liked Rebecca, had seen how quickly and efficiently she'd settled into the work. "It was the dirty look she gave me," Rebecca tried to explain. "You know, because I'm an unmarried mother. Usually I ignore her, but this time it just got to me. It's not very pleasant being on the receiving end of her malicious gossip all the time."

Emily, who made it her business to know everything that happened on her section, frowned. "Maybe, but that sort of talk isn't what Marks & Spencer's expects from its staff."

"I know. And I promise it won't happen again."

Emily considered. She was only too aware of Sylvia's nature and knew it had been a mistake to take her on – a customer had already complained about her attitude. But that was no excuse for Rebecca's outburst.

"I'll let it go this time," she said. "But do try to control your temper in future. Remember you're only a recent employee here . . ."

Acutely conscious of the implied warning, Rebecca said with relief, "I will, Mrs Dawson, thank you!"

Over the next few weeks, Rebecca recovered much of her confidence. Working with other girls helped. As she listened to them at break times, sometimes talking of their boyfriends and sly references to "being tempted", Rebecca began to realise that she'd been too hard on herself. After all, nothing had actually happened. My mistake was in being so naïve, she thought wryly. After working in a pub, I should have known better than to drink so much wine, particularly when I'm not used to it. Yet she'd loved that heady feeling of recklessness, the way she'd walked through the restaurant feeling desirable and excited. But she knew she'd also foolishly allowed herself to be swept away by the glamour of the evening. And, she thought, let's face it, what girl from my background wouldn't have found someone like Guy attractive? The best thing she could do was to learn from the experience and get on with her life.

On Thursday morning, on the fourth anniversary of the death of her husband and son, Grace wheeled Anna across to the cemetery.

"Put it there, beside mine," she said, and watched with pride and affection as her granddaughter carefully laid her small posy on the grave. "That's where your daddy and grandad are sleeping," Grace said gently.

"I know," Anna said. "Mummy says this is their special day."

Grace nodded. "Yes, she's coming to see them tonight, after work. You'll be in bed, then."

Anna nodded. She slipped her mittened hand inside that of her granny. "Are we going to the sweetie shop, now?" she said hopefully.

Grace smiled. "Yes, sweetheart." Anna loved to go to the corner shop to see "Auntie Maggie", where wide-eyed she would watch the whirring blade of the bacon slicer, and the ease with which the shop-keeper cut cheese with a long wire. Oblivious to the occasional cold glances from what Grace called *"po-faced customers"*, Anna would smile winningly up at Maggie, who, always a softie for a "little 'un", would sometimes give her a jelly baby. Grace though, noticed that Maggie never favoured Anna unless they were the only customers. But then, she was in busi-ness, after all.

With Grace encouraging her, Rebecca began to go out once a week. She got on well with Betty, and the two girls went to the cinema where they were first thrilled then shocked by *The Blue Lamp*, and enthralled by the western adventure and romance in *She Wore a Yellow Ribbon*. A couple of times they went dancing at the King's Hall in Stoke, when much to her frustration, Betty's father insisted on meeting them afterwards. "That's twice someone's wanted to take me home," she complained. "I felt like a kid, saying my dad would be waiting outside!"

Rebecca sympathised, but as they came out into the night air, she could only wish that her own father, for all his faults, could have been standing there. It was a continual source of sadness to her that neither of her parents would ever be able to see and love Anna – she was such a bright and sunny-natured child.

She and Katie still corresponded about once a month. Katie was busy studying for her final exams. *"I'm dying to come up and visit you,"* she wrote. *"I thought maybe in the summer – we could take Anna out for the day or something. And I don't mind in the least sleeping on the sofa – it's probably just as comfortable as my bed in the Nurses Home!"* There was little mention of Guy, although three weeks after "that evening", Katie had written to tell Rebecca that he was now engaged. *I bet all that talk of being unsure about Caroline was just another ploy,* Rebecca thought with bitterness. *How could someone be such a heel?*

But now Easter was approaching, together with a letter from Sal saying how much she and Ron were looking forward to seeing Anna again. Going down to the railway station to enquire about trains to Southend, Rebecca found that the fare was more than she'd anticipated; but having put money away every week in an old tea caddy, she could just about afford it. And at least, she wouldn't have to pay for Anna!

"How long will it take?" Grace asked.

"About four and a half hours, what with the Tube and everything."

Grace shuddered. "I can't stand the thought of those things. It doesn't seem natural, speeding along under the ground like that."

Rebecca laughed. "You get used to it."

"It'll be a long and tiring journey for Anna," Grace said doubtfully, "but you've no alternative really."

"No, I haven't. Ron and Sal are dying to see her."

"Of course they are," Grace said. "I bet they've missed her terribly. Are you all right for money?"

Rebecca nodded. "Yes, I've got enough saved, thanks."

Grace breathed a sigh of relief. Although with her widow's pension and the money she earned from her part-time job, she managed to stay out of debt, Grace still had to watch her pennies. There was the rent to budget for, a sum that had been no problem when Jim was bringing home a regular wage. But now, with her limited income, Grace had to be very careful. Each week, she counted out her "overheads", estimating the cost of gas and electricity, and the amount left over seemed to get smaller. Rebecca paid her share of the grocery bill, and took responsibility for Anna's needs, but so far Grace hadn't asked her for any other contribution, reasoning that the girl was young, she needed a few luxuries, some entertainment. When you get to my age, Grace sighed, and left on your own, the only option is a whist drive at a local church. But then she shrugged, despising herself for being so maudlin. She could sometimes afford to go in the cheap seats at the pictures, and she had always loved reading. Rebecca had joined the local library soon after her arrival, and they often read the same books, the shared interest helping to strengthen the growing bond between them.

On Easter Saturday, Rebecca and Anna set out for Southend. Rebecca kept their luggage to a minimum, and with a suitcase in one hand, the other firmly clasped that of her three-year-old daughter. Anna was wildly excited about going on a train, but after an hour became sleepy and Rebecca had to wake her before they arrived at Euston, so that they could share cheese sandwiches and a flask of weak tea. When they descended to the Underground however, Anna became terrified as the train came roaring out of the tunnel, and clung to her mummy, hiding her face in her skirts. Picking up her screaming child, Rebecca struggled on to the Tube, where luckily she spotted two empty seats, and with the suitcase on her knee, eventually managed to console Anna with a small bar of chocolate. Once they arrived at Liverpool Street Station and boarded the steam train to Southend, Anna was all smiles again, and settled down with a crayoning book.

Relieved, Rebecca began to relax, gazing out of the window at the unfamiliar passing scenery. She was beginning to feel impatient, excited even, as they finally approached their destination. Surely it couldn't be six months since she'd seen the two people who had given her refuge and supported her through the bad times? Sal and Ron were her link with her childhood, and Rebecca, despite having made a new life for herself in the Potteries, suddenly couldn't wait to see them again.

30

W hen Rebecca descended from the train, it took only one glance to spot Ron's burly figure standing on the platform among a small crowd of people. Anna let out a squeal of delight, and ran towards him where, his heavy features creasing in a wide grin, he swept her up into his arms.

"Hello, sweetheart. You 'aven't forgotten your Uncle Ron, then?" Anna flung her arms around his neck and pressed her cheek against his, as he turned to greet Rebecca, "Journey all right?"

"Yes, fine, although she didn't like the Tube much."

Ron put out a hand for the suitcase, but Rebecca shook her head. "No, you've got enough with Anna. In any case it's not heavy." This wasn't true, but she knew from Sal's letters that she was still concerned about Ron's health.

"Sal wanted to be here," Ron said, "but they were short-staffed this lunchtime – you know how it is."

"I certainly do!" Rebecca smiled up at him. It was good to see Ron's familiar ugly face again. He was a rock, she thought, as they walked towards the ticket barrier. All that first year after I came back to

London, he never asked questions, never probed, but I knew he was there if I needed him.

"We can get a bus outside the station," Ron told her, "it'll drop us off just outside the flat."

As they waited with impatience in the bus shelter, Anna began to fidget with excitement. "Can I go upstairs?"

"Oh, I don't know—" Rebecca began.

"Of course she can," Ron interrupted. "Don't go getting like Sal, making an invalid of me. I can climb a few stairs on a bus for heaven's sake. You can stay down with the case. It's not far. Here it comes, Anna. Quick, put yer hand out!"

Eagerly, Anna waved at the bus to stop, and fifteen minutes later they were entering Ron and Sal's new home. The flat was comfortable if small. The familiar three-piece suite crowded the square sitting-room and the oak dining-table was folded down against one wall. A new standard lamp with a red-patterned shade fringed with cream dominated one corner of the room, and turning to the other, Ron proudly showed Rebecca his pride and joy.

"A television set! Ron, what luxury!"

"Well," he said awkwardly. "It's rented, of course. But I spend a lot of time 'ere, what with Sal working and that. So we treated ourselves."

"And why not? You deserve it."

"Anna will love Muffin the Mule," Ron grinned, and then the door opened and Sal was breezing in, her face wreathed in a welcoming smile.

She held her arms out to Anna who rushed into them, reaching up to kiss Sal's pursed lips. "Just look

315

how tall you are, my darlin'! And prettier than ever."
She moved towards Rebecca and the two women
hugged each other.

"Oh, it's good to see you, Sal," Rebecca exclaimed.

"And you, girl. You're looking well." Sal turned
to Ron. "Have you got the kettle on?"

"Give me a chance, we've only just got 'ere!" He
ambled off to the kitchen.

"Don't tell me you're getting him domesticated
at last," Rebecca laughed.

"Oh, he'll go so far as making a cuppa," Sal said.
"And he'll wash the pots. And why not – he's not
running a pub any more." She smiled, "I'm not
grumbling – Ron does as much as he can."

Rebecca lowered her voice. "How is he?"

"Tell you later." Sal bent down to Anna. "Hasn't
anyone taken your coat off yet, poppet? Here, let
Auntie Sal do it for you."

Rebecca unpacked, and the rest of the afternoon
passed in catching up on gossip and events.
Apparently Flossie had been down to visit for a day,
having recovered from her varicose veins operation.
Ruby was well, while Janet was still cleaning at the
Unicorn, although she found the ex-sergeant-major
a bit of a martinet.

"How do the punters like him?" Rebecca asked.

Ron grinned. "Not a lot! But he'll learn. What he
could do with is a wife – like my Sal. That'd soften
him up a bit."

"Keep him in order, you mean!" Sal said tartly,
and Rebecca smiled, realising how much she'd
missed their banter. Anna was quiet, totally absorbed

in setting up her welcome present of a brightly-coloured cardboard shop, with its little bottles of sweets and packets of groceries. Later, indulging her, they all pretended in turn to be customers until, drowsy and yawning, she was put to bed in the small box-room.

"Don't worry about my sleeping on the sofa," Rebecca said to Sal. "I can squeeze in with Anna."

"Are you sure?"

"We can try it for tonight, anyway."

Later, they all settled down to the novelty – for Rebecca anyway – of watching television, and then after the Epilogue, Ron went to bed, leaving the two women sitting cosily before the dying embers of the fire. The room was warm, relaxing, in the soft light from the standard lamp, and Rebecca said, "You were lucky to find a flat like this, Sal."

"I know," she said. "It was only because our Ida knew it was coming up. She used to be friendly with the people who lived here before."

"Are you happy? Settled in?"

Sal nodded. "I missed the Unicorn at first, but it's a friendly bar where I'm working. And when the summer comes, we'll be able to get out on the front more. I'm looking forward to that."

"And how's Ron? The truth now . . ."

Sal sighed. "He's not the man he was, love. He gets tired very easily, but I suppose we've got to expect that. It was certainly the right decision to move down here, that's for sure."

"What does he do all day?"

Sal shrugged. "Reads the paper, watches the television whenever there's a programme on – even the test card." She smiled. "Every time there's an intermission and they show that potter's wheel we think of you."

Rebecca laughed. "I've never even been inside a potbank – that's what they call the factories up there. I'd like to, though."

Sal gazed at her, thinking she was looking even lovelier than ever. "You'll never guess who it was I bumped into last week?" she said suddenly. "Johnny Fletcher! Do you remember him? He moved down here with his mum in 1945."

"Of course I do. He was with Ian during the war."

"That's right, in fact Ian was looking for him that first day in the pub."

Rebecca nodded. She recalled the scene vividly, with Ian constantly looking over his shoulder each time the door opened.

"He didn't know – about Ian, I mean," Sal told her. "He seemed really upset when I told him."

"I don't suppose he knew about Anna, either?"

Sal shook her head. "He was shocked, I could tell that." She glanced uneasily at her niece. "He's insisting on coming to see you – I didn't know what to say."

Rebecca smiled at her. "Don't look so worried – that's okay with me."

"Good," Sal yawned, relieved, "because I said he could come tomorrow morning! I don't know about you, but I'm ready for bed."

★

On Easter Sunday, Anna was thrilled with her small chocolate Easter egg, and a hard-boiled real one, cooled ready for her to paint with a small box of watercolours that Flossie had brought. With guilt, Rebecca realised that she hadn't written to either Flossie or Ruby and decided that as soon as she got back, she'd send them a postcard of the Potteries' bottle kilns. And maybe Janet, too.

She helped Sal to prepare the vegetables, while Sal, who had intended to make a rice pudding, looked doubtfully at a bottle of milk. "Smell this – what do you think?"

Rebecca sniffed at the top. "It's all right, especially if it's going in the oven."

"That's what I thought." Sal turned at a loud knock. "That'll be Johnny. Can you let him in?"

Rebecca went into the sitting-room where Ron was reading a story to Anna, and through to the tiny hall, to open the door with a welcoming smile. The young man facing her, his fair hair slightly ruffled, seemed taller than she remembered him. "Hello, Johnny. How good to see you – come in."

"Hello, Rebecca. It's been a long time."

"It certainly has. Here, let me take your coat." She hung the slightly damp garment on a hook and led the way into the sitting-room, where Ron got up and held out his hand. "Good to see you, lad. How's your mother?"

"She's fine, thanks Ron, keeping busy." But Johnny was staring at Anna, who in turn was gazing shyly at him.

"Say hello," Rebecca coaxed without success.

Johnny sat in an armchair opposite, so that he was at the little girl's level. "It's uncanny," he muttered. "Her eyes, they're just like—"

"Her father's," Rebecca said quietly. Just then Sal came bustling in from the kitchen. "Yer found it, then?"

Johnny stood up. "No problem."

"Right, how about a glass of sherry? I think we've got a bottle somewhere."

"Yer can't offer an East End lad sherry, Sal!" Ron blustered. "'Aven't yer got any beer?"

"I don't keep any in the flat, as you well know," Sal snapped, "and that's because someone I know would be drinking it when he shouldn't. A cuppa then, Johnny?"

"That's fine, Sal."

"She keeps me on a tight rein," Ron grinned. "One pint a day, and I have to walk to the pub for it."

Johnny smiled, and then turned to Rebecca. "I was very sorry to hear about Ian."

"Thank you, Johnny." Rebecca gazed at him, thinking how much he'd changed. "What are you doing now?"

"I'm a salesman, selling office supplies. It's a good job, I even get a car with it, a Ford Anglia." He bent down again to Anna. "Let me guess how old you are. I know – you're ten?"

She giggled. "I'm not ten, am I, Mummy. I'm three!"

Johnny laughed, while Rebecca, gazing at him, felt bemused. He was much better-looking than she

320

recalled. But then she'd only seen him briefly across the bar, and, in the early days of serving in the pub, he'd just been one of many new faces. Also, she thought wryly, it was surprising how much difference smart clothes made.

Sal brought in a tray, and later after an exchange of small talk, Johnny got up to go. "Well, I mustn't keep you." But he lingered for a moment then said to Rebecca, "If you're not doing anything later, I could drive you round Southend, let you see the place."

"That's a good idea!" Sal intervened before Rebecca had a chance to answer. "We did have plans, but it's not much fun trailing round in the rain."

"I *would* like Anna to see the sea," Rebecca said, "and the forecast's not good for tomorrow, either."

"You'll come then?"

"Thank you, Johnny. We'd love to."

While Rebecca showed their visitor out, Sal hurried back into the kitchen. Damn, she thought, poking at the potatoes – the dratted things have gone in the water.

"Shall I make the gravy?" Rebecca offered as she joined her.

"If you would." Sal turned to her. "I suppose Grace is a smashing cook," she said with despair.

"She is," Rebecca said, and then leaned over to kiss her aunt's cheek, "and I'm very fond of her. But she isn't you, Sal, and don't you ever forget it."

★

321

As arranged, Johnny was there promptly at three o'clock, and with Anna on her knee clutching Gloria, Rebecca looked forward to seeing the town where her aunt and uncle had made their home. Johnny drove them straight to the seafront, and almost on cue there came a break in the clouds, and briefly, the scene shone in the weak sunlight. "Look Anna, there's the sea!" Rebecca told her. "The next time we come, it might be warm and sunny, and you could go and paddle in it. And make sandcastles, just like in your picture book. You'd like that, wouldn't you?" Anna nodded, beaming, and then the rain came again, just a fine drizzle but enough to make them get back into the car. Johnny drove slowly along the seafront, pointing out a funfair before drawing up to show them the pier.

"It's the longest one in the world – a mile and a half."

Impressed, Rebecca said, "Can we go on? I've brought our macs."

They got out of the car, and with Anna skipping between them, began walking along the pier. But almost immediately the drizzle changed to a downpour, and holding the macs over their heads, they ran to board the recently installed electric train. "I can't believe it," Rebecca laughed. "Riding on a train along a pier!" She turned towards Johnny, thinking how easy she felt in his company, and surprised an expression on his face she couldn't fathom. "You look very serious."

His face closed. "Do I? Sorry about that." He began to tickle Anna, who became helpless with laughter.

"Hey, stop that, the pair of you," Rebecca began, but the laughter became infectious, and they were a merry group by the time they alighted from the train. Fortunately the rain had ceased, and they stood by the pier rails, firmly holding Anna's hands and gazing back towards the shoreline. With the wind whipping the damp sea air against her face, Rebecca felt slightly nervous as she saw the huge expanse of grey water between them. Hastily, she peered over the rail to reassure herself that the pier was well supported, causing Johnny to laugh and reassure her that they were quite safe.

Later, he drove them through the town so that Rebecca could see the shops, and pointed out the pub where Sal worked. "Is she in there tonight?" he said a few seconds later.

Rebecca shook her head, "No, she's not working today."

"And when do you go back?"

"Tuesday morning."

"Then how would you feel about going there for a drink tomorrow night?" Johnny was drawing up outside the flat and turned to face her. "It would be nice for you to see where she works."

Rebecca hesitated, then said. "I'd love to. That's really thoughtful of you, Johnny. I'm sure Ron won't mind listening out for Anna."

Johnny gazed at her, and again she couldn't read his expression. "It's the least I can do," he said quietly. He refused her invitation to come in, and as Rebecca watched him drive away, she decided that Johnny Fletcher was a bit of an enigma. But, she had to admit as she tapped on the door of the flat, she rather liked him – in fact she liked him very much indeed.

31

The pub was larger than the Unicorn, but the lounge was already filling up when Rebecca and Johnny arrived. Sal, seeing them, waved, and when Rebecca went over, introduced her to the rest of the staff. "She's a smashing barmaid – I trained her meself!" she announced with pride, and then served Johnny with their drinks. He carried his frothing glass of beer and Rebecca's lemonade over to a quiet table in one corner.

For a moment they sat in silence, then he said, "Thanks for coming."

"It's me who should be thanking you."

He shook his head. "No. I needed to talk to you." He looked at her, his eyes full of concern. "I couldn't believe it when Sal told me all that had happened. First about Ian being killed, and then the predicament you were left in. It can't have been easy."

"It wasn't." In a quiet tone, Rebecca told Johnny of those nightmare weeks, of her bewilderment when, alone and secretly pregnant, she heard nothing from Ian. "We'd just got engaged, and I couldn't believe he'd just dump me," she said, "although I know other people did. Eventually, I decided to go up to the Potteries to look for him." She paused and then told him what had happened.

Johnny's gaze was full of sympathy. "So you ended up finding out from a stranger!"

She nodded. "It was the worst moment of my life." Her voice bleak, she added, "And I've had others."

"Yes, I heard you lost your parents in the bombing."

Rebecca went on to tell him how Grace had suffered a breakdown, and Johnny said with sadness, "What a tragedy – they were such a close family." He took a sip of his beer. "Having to come back and face everyone, to tell them you were pregnant – that must have taken a lot of courage."

Rebecca looked down. She could never admit to anyone how she'd tried to bring on a miscarriage. Even the thought of that harrowing scene in the steamy bathroom made her feel sick. And the guilt would always be with her. She said with a forced smile, "Well, I've got used to being thought of as that girl who's no better than she should be!"

"Don't make light of it, Rebecca," he said angrily. "The mother of Ian's child deserves better."

Surprised by his vehemence, she glanced up at him, and he said, "I knew Ian as well as one man can ever know another. We were together in that prisoner-of-war camp for two years. He was slightly older and better educated than me, but we became good friends. I learned a lot from him. I just can't believe he survived the war and then lost his life by going to watch football! It doesn't make any sense."

"I know."

They finished their drinks in silence, each with their own sad thoughts, and then Johnny said, "Do you want another drink?" He glanced round at the now crowded and noisy room. "Or if you like, we could go for a walk along the front – it's not too cold."

Rebecca hesitated, and then deciding it was a chance to make the most of the sea air, nodded. "I'll just pop and say goodbye to Sal." Putting on their coats, they left the pub, and getting into the car, drove the short distance to the seafront. Then they began to walk slowly along, glad to find that after the day's unsettled weather, and despite the Bank Holiday weekend, the promenade was fairly quiet.

"Have you thought," Johnny said after a few moments, "what it's going to be like for Anna when she goes to school?"

"In what way?"

"Kids pick things up from their parents. Believe me, it won't be long before someone starts calling her names." He glanced sideways at her, then said in a grim tone, "Bastard, for example."

Rebecca's temper flared, incensed at his use of the ugly word with regard to her small daughter, but before she could speak, Johnny was taking hold of her shoulders, roughly turning her to face him. "Like it or not, it's true," he insisted, "that's what the world is like, Rebecca. It won't matter that she's a smashing kid – it'll happen, believe me!"

She stared at him in consternation mixed with horror. Rebecca hadn't thought that far ahead. But with sudden despair, she knew that Johnny was absolutely right. Anna *would* suffer at school. And while Rebecca had learned to live with scorn, was still doing so, the thought of her child being subjected to such playground abuse appalled her.

Johnny, still gripping her shoulders, gazed down at her for a few seconds in silence, then said abruptly, "There is one way you could stop all of it. One way you could raise your head high, and Anna wouldn't have to suffer. I want you to marry me, Rebecca. Let me take care of both of you."

Rebecca stared up at him, speechless with shock. Marry him? Johnny was asking her to marry him? After floundering for an answer, she stammered, "But we hardly know each other!"

"We've made a start," he said. "Look, I know I haven't chosen the best of times or places to ask you, but I hadn't any choice. You'll be gone tomorrow, and then you'll be hundreds of miles away."

Confused, Rebecca tore her gaze from his and turned away to stare out to sea, where the lights from the promenade were reflecting on the grey expanse of water. She didn't turn, didn't even look at him as she asked, "Why, Johnny? Why would you want to do such a thing?"

"You're a beautiful girl, Rebecca. Any man would be proud to have you as his wife."

She twisted round to face him. "You're evading my question. I'll ask you again, Johnny. Why would a young, good-looking man ask someone he hardly knows to marry him?"

His jaw tightened, and suddenly Rebecca recalled

his angry words in the pub, "*the mother of Ian's child deserves better*"; how intense his gaze had been when he'd warned her about the problems Anna would face, the bitterness in his voice as he'd said the word "bastard".

She said softly, "It's something to do with Ian, isn't it?"

This time it was Johnny who went to stand at the rail, and for a moment the only sound was the sound of the steadily encroaching waves. His next words were simple and powerful. "Ian saved my life."

She drew a sharp intake of breath. "He never told me," she said, "but then he never talked about the war at all."

"Not many of us did. When we got home, we just wanted to put the whole wretched business behind us. Normality was what we needed." He turned to her. "Come on, I've kept you out here long enough. I know a place where we can get a cup of tea – even if it is late on a Sunday night." Rebecca, still reeling from the shock of his shattering proposal, nodded and tucked her hand into the crook of his arm as they left the seafront and walked a short way down a side street to a small café.

"It's not what you'd call posh, I'm afraid," Johnny whispered as he opened the net-curtained door. The large front window was misted with condensation, and a few men looked round from oilcloth-topped tables in an atmosphere thick with pipe and tobacco smoke. Johnny led the way to a vacant table and went up to the counter, soon to return with two thick breakfast cups of strong, steaming tea. Rebecca watched as he spooned sugar into his, liking his quick movements, noting his clean, manicured nails. Johnny Fletcher had certainly come a long way from his roots. And almost as though he'd read her mind, he said, "I won't be a salesman all my life, you know. You're looking at a man with ambition."

Rebecca believed him. There was something about Johnny, a suppressed energy. And again she thought how much she liked him. Taking a sip of her scalding hot drink, she said, "Will you tell me about it? What happened with Ian, I mean."

For a few seconds he was silent, then he slowly replaced the spoon in his saucer. "Being a prisoner of war in Germany isn't the best of experiences, Rebecca, but we were in one of the better camps, compared to some. There was harshness and deprivation, but when I got back and found out what our lads went through in Burma, I realised just how lucky I'd been." His lips twisted. "Never let anyone tell you there isn't evil in this world. If there's one thing this war has taught us, it's the depths to which human beings can sink." Rebecca remained silent, wondering what dark memories were surfacing within his mind.

"It was the boredom that was the worst," Johnny said suddenly. "The sheer, bloody boredom. And of course, we all felt it our duty to try and escape." He took out a packet of cigarettes, lit one, and she watched him slide the used match back into its box. "There was a tunnel," he said quietly. "It was well organised and safe, or so we thought. We worked for months in teams of three." He looked at her, his expression one of pain and resignation. "We really thought we were going to do it, that lots of us would get out. And then one day, the three of us, myself, Ian, and a chap called Archie were doing our shift. I was at the front digging, Ian was shoring, and Archie was keeping watch." He paused, and tensely Rebecca waited. "It collapsed," he said grimly. "Caved in, right on top of us. Being in front, I got the worst. Ian saw it coming and had a split second to duck back. I was, well, buried alive." His hand trembled slightly as he lifted the cigarette to his lips and inhaled. "Fags, eh," he said. "What would we do without them?"

Rebecca, her gaze fixed on his, didn't speak. She was imagining the terrible scene, hearing the noise of the soil cascading down, its crushing weight, and the terror of the trapped man beneath. "But he wouldn't leave me," Johnny said quietly. "He risked his own life, knowing that any second there could be a further fall, and he tore the flesh off his bare hands as he scrabbled at the earth to give me some air." His eyes darkened at the memory, and she could only guess at the anguish and fear he must have felt as the soil threatened to choke him.

"Do you still have nightmares about it?" she said softly. He nodded.

"How did you get out?"

"Ian knew that if he shouted back for help, the vibration could cause another fall," Johnny told her, "but it seemed a bloody eternity until Archie realised something was wrong. He raised the alarm and first Ian was dragged back on the trolley – a sort of wooden plank on wheels that we used – and then I was dug out." He stubbed out his cigarette and looked steadily at her. "A lesser man than Ian would have left me and saved himself."

Rebecca was profoundly moved, not just by the account of Ian's bravery, but by the respect and affection with which Johnny spoke of him. She leaned over and touched his hand. "But Johnny, you mustn't feel that you have to take on his responsibilities."

But Johnny just said, "I meant what I said, Rebecca." Suddenly he forced a lighter note into his voice, and he smiled at her. "It wouldn't be any hardship, you know, at least for me. Of course," he said with a wry smile, "you might feel differently."

Disconcerted, Rebecca looked away. She didn't know how she felt. The prospect of respectability, security, the joy of having her own home was fleetingly tempting. But surely liking someone wasn't a sufficient reason to marry them? Yet, she thought, how did she know she couldn't learn to love Johnny? After all, she'd only known him two days, perhaps when she got to know him better . . . And what about Anna, a voice whispered in her head. What would be best for her?

Johnny must have seen the indecision in her face, because he said gently, "I don't expect an answer immediately, you know."

She smiled at him with relief. "Thank you, Johnny. And thank you for the offer. I *will* think about it, honestly."

Later when, having driven her home, they stood outside the flat to say goodbye, Johnny hesitated, his eyes questioning. She smiled and moved towards him, willingly raising her face to his, curious to feel the touch of his lips. His mouth was warm despite the cold evening, his kiss gentle and fleeting, and then he gazed down at her, his eyes unfathomable.

"Don't forget what I said about Anna."

Seconds later she watched him drive away. Turning to knock on the door, her mind and emotions were in such turmoil that Rebecca knew she would find it almost impossible to sleep. And, unlike the previous night, she wouldn't be able to blame it on sharing a cramped single bed with a fidgety child!

32

After she returned to the Potteries, Rebecca waited a couple of days then one evening after Anna had gone to bed, she said quietly, "Grace, when I was in Southend, I met an old friend of Ian's called Johnny Fletcher."

Grace glanced up. "Isn't he the one Ian went down to London to look for?"

"Yes, that's right."

"I remember – of course, he'd moved to Southend. How is he?"

"Doing very well, he's working as a salesman." Rebecca hesitated. "We talked, Grace – about Ian, I mean."

Grace, looking at the girl opposite and seeing her serious, slightly tense expression immediately put aside her knitting. "What did he say?"

Rebecca slowly and carefully repeated what Johnny had told her about that harrowing scene in the tunnel. As the tale unfolded, Grace listened with growing horror, trying to imagine the claustrophobia, the desperation of the two young men, the fear of another and possibly fatal collapse. "And that's what he said? That Ian had saved his life?" As Rebecca nodded, Grace could only stare at her with both pride and distress. Why had her son never told them? Because to know of Ian's selflessness, his loyalty to his friend, would have meant so much to Jim – he would have been so proud. Moved to tears, she had to fumble for a hanky from her cardigan sleeve, while Rebecca watched with sympathy.

It was a little while before Grace was able to talk, but eventually she said, "What's he like? This Johnny?"

"He seems very nice," Rebecca said guardedly, and Grace, seeing the reticence in her eyes, picked up her knitting, began another row, and tried to control not only her curiosity, but also a flicker of anxiety. Was this young man the reason that Rebecca had been so quiet since she got back? The reason why she was supposedly listening to the wireless and knitting, and yet her hands were idle in her lap?

Rebecca couldn't settle to anything. Ever since Johnny's proposal, she'd been in an agony of indecision about whether to confide in Sal and Grace. After all, what he proposed was purely a practical way of solving the problems of Anna's illegitimacy. And this was a concern to all of them. But Rebecca also knew it would be impossible for Sal and Grace to be unbiased. Sal would be thrilled at the thought of her niece and great-niece moving to live nearby, and Grace would be distraught at the thought of losing her granddaughter. So rather than raise false hope for one and unnecessary stress for the other, Rebecca had decided to remain silent. As she stared thoughtfully into the flickering embers of the coal fire, she knew she couldn't make any decision yet.

Neither she nor Johnny had offered to write, but they had agreed that Rebecca would go down to Southend again in the summer, this time for a whole week. At least I'll get to know him better, she thought and suddenly realised how much she was looking forward to it.

Over the next few weeks, life carried on in the familiar routine, with both Grace and Rebecca enjoying working with the new season's fashions. And then at the beginning of May, Katie wrote that she'd like to come up to visit for a weekend: "*I can't wait to see you and Anna, and to meet Grace. I thought I'd catch a train late on Friday afternoon, and get one back on Sunday night. Would that be all right?*"

Grace agreed with enthusiasm. "I'll change days with you, then you can have Saturday off. I'm sure Mrs Dawson won't mind."

"You'll like Katie," Rebecca promised. "Sal used to say she was like a breath of fresh air."

Grace was already looking forward to meeting the young Irish nurse. The older Ian's mother became, the more she realised that being in the company of young people was invigorating. Despite the disruption of her tidy home, and the exhaustion of caring all day for a young child, her general health was improving all the time, and she was now, to her relief, able to manage without any medication.

And when Katie eventually arrived, with her dark hair, humorous blue eyes and easy smile, Grace liked her immediately. To Katie's delight, Anna ran to her, laughing as she was twirled round in young strong arms. "And aren't you getting a big girl?" Katie bent down and whispered, "There's a present for you in my bag. Shall we go and look?" Anna stretched out an eager hand, and seconds later was clutching a wooden toy. "It's a monkey on a stick. Look, watch me!" Katie showed her how to make it jump up and down, and fascinated, Anna crouched on the floor to experiment.

"Was the journey all right?" Rebecca took her friend upstairs so that she could leave her bag in the back bedroom. "Sorry, there's only my single bed. You could have it, and I'll sleep on the sofa."

Katie shook her head. "The journey was no problem, and I'll be fine downstairs. In any case, you need to be up here to listen out for Anna." She looked at the other girl. "You're looking great. The smoky air up here obviously suits you!"

"And how about you? A State Registered Nurse!" Rebecca looked at Katie with a pang of envy. "It must be wonderful to have achieved that."

"It's been damned hard work," Katie replied, "*and* having to cope with Sister and Matron. You wouldn't believe . . ." And then she was off, just as in the old days, making Rebecca double up with laughter.

"Oh, I've missed you," she gasped. "You always could crease me up!"

Downstairs, Grace, hurriedly putting the last touches to a shepherd's pie, smiled. It was good to hear laughter again, and not for the first time, she wished she'd been able to have more children. Maybe, she mused, they would have grown up to live nearby, popping in and ready with a helping hand. Grace had to admit that she missed a man's help about the house. She hated having to ask Fred next door for a hand sometimes. But she hadn't the confidence to cope with such things as leaking taps or frozen pipes. But then, she thought wryly, I never had to learn. Although Jim had taught Ian such practical jobs, they were considered a male preserve, just as cooking, cleaning and laundry were usually left to women.

There had been much discussion before her arrival as to how to entertain Katie, and Grace suggested a trip to Trentham Gardens. "The bus takes less than half an hour," she said.

"I went to the ballroom once with Betty," Rebecca said, "but it was dark, so I didn't see much of anything else. There was a lake, I remember that."

Grace smiled. "It's beautiful. It used to be the Duke of Sutherland's estate, but now it belongs to the people of Stoke-on-Trent. If the weather's good, you could have a picnic. Maybe take Anna to the outdoor swimming pool. Or go on a boat trip. And there's a little train, she'd love that."

Already Rebecca was full of excited anticipation. "I've never been to an open-air pool – oh," her hand went to her mouth, "Anna hasn't got a costume!"

"I'll buy her one," Grace promised.

So Rebecca had written to Katie telling her to bring her swimsuit, and with the forecast for the weekend being warm and sunny for both days, they decided to wait until Sunday for their day out. Saturday morning was reserved for gossiping, taking

Anna to the park, then shopping, and finally dancing at the King's Hall, to the big band sound of Ted Heath.

After their late night, both girls had a "lie-in" on Sunday morning until nine o'clock, with Grace quietly taking Anna downstairs at eight.

"She's wonderful," Katie whispered to Rebecca, as they washed and dried their breakfast dishes.

"I know," Rebecca said. "I'm very lucky." And the thought came into her mind that she'd be giving all this up if she married Johnny. The warm, comfortable relationship she and Grace now shared. And she couldn't help feeling that it had been such a huge step to move up to Stoke, to begin a new life. Was she prepared to leave it behind after what was, after all, only a few months?

"Penny for 'em," Katie said lightly.

"Tell you later," Rebecca whispered.

Grace came bustling in. "Now you're properly awake girls – did you have a good time?"

The girls glanced at each other and burst into laughter. "This one," Katie said, "behaved disgracefully!"

"I did not!"

"Do you know what she did, Grace? She only tipped a pint of beer over this poor chap's trousers!"

Rebecca grinned. "Well, knocked over, really. Served him right – flaming pest."

"Oh, one of those, was he? Had wandering hands!" The girls stared at her in astonishment, and Grace laughed. "I haven't always been this age, you know! I had my moments, though you might not think it now."

"And it's not too late for some more," Katie said cheekily, and Rebecca looked at Ian's mother in alarm, hoping she wouldn't be offended. But Grace just smiled, saying, "You never know what the future might hold." With a slight shock, Rebecca glanced at her in surprise, and realised that for her age, Grace was still an attractive woman. Of course she might meet someone else, she might even get married again. That would change everything. Rebecca suddenly realised that she could never take her present security for granted.

Later, Grace watched the three of them go to catch their bus, and with relief settled into an armchair with the Sunday newspaper. She'd been invited to go with them, but after yesterday, she was feeling too tired – the store was so busy on Saturdays. Now, with the prospect of a rare tranquil day stretching before her, she was determined to enjoy it.

The moment the two girls arrived at the imposing gates into Trentham, where Katie had insisted on paying the entrance fees, and saw the beautiful Italian Gardens stretching before them, their spirits rose even further. With Anna running free a short distance in front, Katie and Rebecca strolled along in the sunshine by the parapet overlooking the mile-long lake, in perfect contentment.

"Now then," Katie said curiously. "What were you going to tell me?"

Rebecca hesitated, and then told her of meeting

Johnny, and about his unexpected proposal of marriage.

Katie stared at her. "Heavens above, I bet you were flabbergasted! What's he like?"

"Taller than me, fair-haired and quite good-looking."

"Not someone who can't find himself a wife in the usual way, then?"

Rebecca shook her head. "Not at all. As I said to him, why on earth does he want to marry someone he hardly knows?"

"And?" But Rebecca was hurrying forward to pick Anna up as she stumbled and fell. "I told you to walk and not run," Rebecca scolded. But fortunately, there was no grazing on her knees, and after a half-hearted effort to cry, Anna trotted on again.

"So," Katie said impatiently, having caught up, "what did he say?" She listened with rapt attention as Rebecca related to her the incident in the tunnel, and how, because Ian had saved his life, Johnny felt it his duty to protect his dependants. "Now he's a man I'd like to meet," Katie declared. "You have to admire him, having principles like that!" Then she frowned, "What did he think you needed protection from?"

"Oh, prejudice, bigotry, you know – because I'm an unmarried mother." Rebecca paused, then said, "But his main concern was for Anna. He was quite intense about it, Katie. Said she'd be called names at school – 'bastard' for instance."

For a few moments they walked along in silence, then Katie said, "He's right, Rebecca. People can be so stupid." Her voice was grave as she watched the pretty child ahead, cute in her matching pink sundress and hat. "Tell me," she said, "does Anna have any playmates? Children who live in the same street?"

Rebecca flushed. "There's only one little girl her age. Her mother always tenses up when she sees us. I usually say 'good morning' or whatever, but she only ever nods. They live with the grandmother, and Grace says she probably takes her cue from her. She's very straight-laced apparently." Her eyes flashing with anger, she turned to Katie, "Honestly, do people think their kid will catch something if they play with Anna? It's not her fault she hasn't got a father!" Suddenly, unexpected tears of mortification pricked at her eyelids, but she blinked them quickly away, determined not to mar the beautiful day.

"Johnny's got a point, then!" was all Katie said, and the curtness of her tone made Rebecca glance sharply at her. But Katie, although tempted to confess the stiff-necked prejudice within her own family, out of loyalty to Conor and Maura remained silent.

A few minutes later, as they paused to gaze out over the beautiful scenery, with the trees in full leaf bending down to the water, Rebecca lifted up Anna to stand on the parapet, pointing out the motor launch full of passengers chugging gently around the lake. Then putting her down again, Rebecca turned to her friend. "So I should think seriously about it – marrying Johnny, I mean?"

"Yes," Katie said, after a slight hesitation. "For one thing I think it's true what he says about Anna, and for another," she glanced apprehensively at the other girl, then decided to take the plunge, "you've got to be realistic, Rebecca. Things won't get any easier as Anna gets older. I mean, you do like him, don't you?"

"Yes, I do, very much."

"There you are, then. As you say, wait until after the summer, but," she warned sharply, "don't waste your chance by dilly-dallying – I don't suppose he'll wait forever!"

Later, the atmosphere lightened, as Anna happily waved to passers-by from the miniature train that trundled around the gardens to the open-air pool. Once there, looking angelic in her flowered ruched swimsuit, she was slightly scared of the water at first, but soon she was shrieking with excitement as they splashed and played with her in the shallow end. "I feel awful," Rebecca shouted to Katie over the noise. "I should have taken her to the swimming baths – she loves it!" Katie laughed and then she was off, swimming with steady, even breaststrokes the length of the pool. After she'd done a couple of lengths, it was Rebecca's turn, but she could only manage a width, and even that was a struggle. "You've obviously had more practice," she complained, and when eventually they collapsed on to a grassy bank at the side, they were gasping for a drink.

Katie stood up and offered to go to the white Art Deco design café. "Lemon and lime?"

Rebecca nodded, calling after her, "And a Vimto for Anna – don't forget to bring a straw!"

She watched Katie walk away, who seemed

completely unselfconscious in her one-piece bathing costume. She'd long dismissed Conor's teasing that her figure was "comfortable", complaining it made her sound like a cushion. And why not, Rebecca thought. Because Katie, with her rounded perfectly proportioned figure, was never short of boyfriends.

After drying Anna, Rebecca wrapped a towel around her and putting on her sunbonnet gave her a picture-book to look at. Then, with her own hair now free from its confining bathing cap, she fluffed it with her fingers, and stretched out in the warmth and fresh air. Bliss, she thought, absolute bliss.

It was at least fifteen minutes later before Katie returned. Hearing her approach, Rebecca turned her head, shielding her eyes from the sun.

"You took your time," she began, and then as she saw the man standing behind her friend, Rebecca sat up, her heart pounding with shock.

"Look who I found!" Katie grinned, passing the drinks over.

"You make me sound like a stray dog!" He was smiling, his dark hair unruffled, his face tanned. It was the man Rebecca had last seen in a crowded staff room at a hospital Christmas party. The man she'd sat beside on a shabby leather sofa, the young doctor whose advice had changed her life.

33

"David!" Rebecca sat up in astonishment as he gazed smilingly down at her.

"Well done for remembering!" He lowered himself on to the grass to sit beside her. "It must be . . ."

"About two years," she said, flustered at seeing him again, and with embarrassment pulled up the front of her green swimming costume. "What on earth are you doing here?"

Katie flopped down in front of them both, one arm around her bent knees, and took a sip of her drink. "There he was," she said, "standing in front of me. I wasn't sure at first," she grinned, "having never seen him without any clothes on before – well, almost . . ." Katie hadn't worked with young doctors for three years without having a healthy disrespect for their dignity.

David laughed, his smile lightening his rather solemn features, and again Rebecca realised how attractive he was. "I'm visiting a hospital near Leek," he told her, "they've got a case I'm interested in."

Rebecca stared at him – surely that was where Grace had been. "You must mean St Edward's at Cheddleton?"

He nodded. "That's right. I decided this weather

was too good to waste, so I came to see the famous Trentham Gardens."

"He didn't recognise me, at first," Katie said. "But then, I was still a probationer when he was there. Of course I regarded all the doctors as gods then, so I knew *him* straightaway." She glanced over at him and said with a grin, "I soon found out the truth, though."

So did I, Rebecca thought with bitterness, as an image of Guy flashed into her mind.

David leaned over to look at Anna, who was regarding him with solemn eyes above her straw. "So, this is your little girl?"

Acutely conscious of his lean body so close to her own, Rebecca said, "Yes, this is Anna," and the little girl gave a shy smile.

"She's enchanting." He turned to Katie. "So, tell me all the news about St Bartholomew's."

Katie began to bring him up to date, causing David both to frown and at times to laugh aloud. Rebecca sat listening to them, so easy in their self-confidence, talking of professional matters, and hospital gossip, and she began to feel a sense of inadequacy. If only things had been different, she thought, if I hadn't been evacuated, I wonder what I could have achieved? She knew that her mother, at least, would have encouraged her. Maybe it isn't too late, she thought suddenly. What's that college called near us? Cauldon College – that was it. Perhaps she could go to an evening class and continue her education. English for instance – she'd always been good at that, and she knew she was fairly well read. "And all the nurses are heartbroken because Dr Mason's got engaged," Katie ended with a grin.

David smiled. "Yes, I knew that. Guy keeps in touch."

Rebecca glanced at him in alarm, then realised that Guy would hardly confide such a story – he was far too conscious of his image. That's if, she thought uneasily, he doesn't lie about what actually happened. Having served behind a bar, she had few illusions about how men liked to boast about their conquests, either real or imaginary!

"So," David said, turning to Rebecca. "As you're here, I take it that things went well when you came up to the Potteries that time."

Rebecca, flattered that he could remember so much about her, said, "Yes, they did. And I've got you to thank for suggesting something that actually changed my life. I'm living up here now, with Grace, that's Anna's grandmother."

"Good. I'm glad I was able to help."

"Hey," Katie said. "Why don't you ask David about that Sylvia woman?" She leaned forward, "Rebecca's got this awful woman at work, who looks down on her because of Anna. I mean, we all know how bigoted people can be, but . . ."

Rebecca felt uncomfortable, wishing Katie hadn't mentioned it, but told David, "It isn't so much what she does, or even says, but it's there in her attitude – almost as if she can't bear the sight of me. I mean, I can understand her disapproving, but it's more than that."

"What do you know about her?" he asked.

347

Rebecca looked at him in surprise. "Nothing really. She's very unpopular and tends to keep to herself."

"Maybe," David frowned, "it's the fact that you have a child that she resents, more than the fact you haven't got a husband. Is she married?"

"Well, she wears a ring."

"Find out if she has a family," he said. "It might be that she's either lost a child, or can't have one. Self-pity and envy can make people very bitter. It eats away at them, like a worm. She could be just a very unhappy woman. Try making the first move, Rebecca, offer her an olive branch."

"Or," Katie interjected with a grin, "she could just be a spiteful bitch!"

David glanced at his watch. "Right, I'm planning to drive back to Rugby at four, so I think I'll have another swim while the deep end isn't too crowded. I'll pop back and say goodbye once I've got changed." Both girls watched him dive cleanly into the water, and then swim with a powerful crawl. Katie glanced at Rebecca.

"Well, there's a turn-up for the book. I couldn't believe it when I saw him in the queue. I must admit," she said wistfully, "that he's really some-thing. It's just a pity he's a woman-hater!"

Startled, Rebecca said, "What makes you say that?"

Katie shrugged. "Just rumour. Certainly he never bothered with any of the nurses when he was at St Bartholomew's."

"Well, I don't suppose it goes with the job," Rebecca teased, "no matter how glamorous you all look in those uniforms." Then Anna began asking for the lavatory, and Rebecca hurried her away.

Several minutes later, Katie turned to see David, now dressed in an open-necked shirt and trousers, strolling up the bank. "Where's Rebecca?"

"Just coming." Katie nodded to where the young mother, with Anna clutching her hand, was walking towards them. The sun had dried her hair, which cascaded to her shoulders in a rich auburn cloud. Having given birth so young, Rebecca had easily regained her trim figure, although her breasts had never lost the extra fullness that motherhood had brought.

Conscious of David watching her, Rebecca smiled at him, then at his opening words, halted in shock. "Do you know, who you remind me of?" he said, "Aphrodite!"

"She was the goddess of love and beauty wasn't she?" Katie said, with a teasing grin in Rebecca's direction. But stunned at hearing David describe her in the same way that Ian had, Rebecca didn't answer. David looked a bit embarrassed, and hurriedly bent to give Anna a sixpence for sweets and an ice cream.

When he straightened up, he said, "I just wanted to say goodbye. Remember me to everyone at St Bartholomew's, Katie."

He turned to Rebecca, and paused a moment. "I'll say au revoir, then," he said quietly, and they both watched as he threaded his way through the sunbathers and out of sight.

"Now what do you suppose he meant by that?" Katie glanced curiously at her friend.

"I've no idea!" Rebecca evaded, "but I think we'd better make a move too, because of your train. It's time I got out of the sun anyway." But, she thought in confusion, as she began to pick up their belongings, what *did* he mean? Surely a man like David wouldn't be interested in a girl with a past like hers? Unless . . . but she dismissed the suspicion. She'd swear he was different from that treacherous Guy. But in any case, David couldn't have meant anything by that "au revoir", because for one thing, he didn't even know where she lived!

A week later, Grace, taking care of Anna while Rebecca was working, began the day in the usual way. First the little girl was lifted up on to a kitchen stool at the sink, where she played contentedly with the warm water, washing her red plastic tea set. Then, carrying a little duster, she followed Grace upstairs to "help" with the bedrooms. "Right," Grace said when they'd finished, and gone back to the kitchen. "I think we deserve a drink now, and then we'll go to the swings." Her face lighting up, Anna scampered off to the front room to find her sandals.

The doorbell rang when Grace was just about to put a couple of malted milk biscuits on a plate, and she went to open the door, hoping it wasn't gypsies. She was too superstitious to turn one away without buying anything, but she really didn't need any more clothes pegs! But it was only Lizzie, her next-door neighbour. "Can I borrow your wallpaper brush, love? Only Bert's got started on the decorating at long last, and I don't want to hold him up."

"Of course, Lizzie. Come on in." Grace led the way into the kitchen, and going into the larder, reached up to a shelf at the back where Jim had always stored his decorating tools. "There you are!"

But Lizzie seemed inclined to talk. "How's it going?" she said, her arms crossed over her flowered pinafore. "With the little 'un, I mean. Don't you find it a bit much?"

"Sometimes," Grace admitted. "But I do love having her here, and Rebecca."

"She seems a nice lass," Lizzie said, and Grace smiled, knowing that this middle-aged woman with her helmet of steel curlers, had, at first, been distinctly chilly in her attitude. But Anna's beaming smile was enough to soften even the most hardened heart.

"Do you still go to the whist drives at St Mary's?"

Grace nodded. "Yes, I go with a friend from work."

"They don't try and convert you, then?"

Grace laughed. "No, not at all. You should try it – it's a pleasant evening."

"Yes, I might do. Oh," she fished in her pinafore pocket, "this is for Anna." She held out a thin bar of Cadbury's milk chocolate.

"Lizzie, that is good of you. Here, you can give it to her yourself." Grace turned and led the way back into the tiny hall, then with a sudden lurch of her stomach, she saw to her horror that she'd left the front door open!

"Anna?" she called quickly and went swiftly into the front room expecting to see the child still struggling with her sandals. It was empty, and so was the back room where the silence seemed to mock them.

Grace shouted Anna's name again as she ran upstairs. But there was no answering giggle, no sound of footsteps.

"I'll look out the front," Lizzie called, while Grace frantically searched the bedrooms, constantly calling Anna's name in rising panic, looking inside the wardrobes, under the beds, in the bathroom – anywhere that a small child could have hidden. She almost stumbled as she hurried back down the staircase. "Can't see her anywhere," Lizzie said with alarm, "I've checked the back garden as well."

But Grace was already rushing out of the front door, calling back to Lizzie, "I'll check the swings, you go down the street!"

Surely Anna wouldn't have crossed the road on her own? She might have been warned enough not to, but Grace knew how impulsive small children could be. If she has, at least she hasn't been run over, she thought frantically, but she could easily have been knocked down by a swing, or fallen from the slide! However, when Grace reached the children's playground, it was totally deserted. "Anna?" she shrieked, hurrying along the paths. "Anna?" By now, Grace's breath was coming in painful gasps, and her legs were trembling. Eventually she gave up the search and turning, made her way as fast as she could back to the park gates hoping, praying that Lizzie would be waiting for her, holding Anna safely by the hand. But Lizzie was standing on the pavement shrugging helplessly. Grace was beginning to feel ill, her heart hammering with fear, her skin clammy and moist.

"I've been all along," Lizzie said. "There's not a sign of her. We'd better get some help!"

"Quickly," urged Grace, and the two women began to go from door to door, anxiously enquiring, and other neighbours surged out to help as soon as they knew a small child was involved.

"This won't do that woman a bit of good," muttered one. She didn't know Grace at all well, but everyone knew of her tragedy and that she'd had a nervous breakdown. "The kid can't have gone far, surely?"

"Yer never know," another woman said, "children can get pinched. And if she's got as far as the main road . . . Look in all the gardens, she might be hiding in a shed!"

The fruitless search went on for another half an hour, and Grace, becoming more and more distraught, knew she couldn't delay any longer in telling Rebecca. And, she thought with growing hysteria – there was the police – she should be ringing the police . . .

Then suddenly there came a shout of triumph. "She's here!"

Anna, bemused by all the attention, came out of a side gate, hand-in-hand with another little girl. The child's mother was behind them, her expression somewhat embarrassed.

"I had no idea," she tried to explain. "Jill was inside her tent on the back lawn, playing tea-parties. I never thought at first to check whether the kiddie was there. She must have followed us when we came back from shopping! Jill went straight into the garden through the side gate, but I went in to put the shopping down before I locked it. I'm ever so sorry."

Grace stared down at her granddaughter who looked up at her in bewilderment, confused by the crowd of people; and Grace, her voice so harsh it was almost unrecognisable, demanded, "What did you think you were doing, running off like that?"

Anna's bottom lip began to tremble and her eyes filled up with tears. "I wanted to play with the little girl," she sobbed, "I never played with nobody before."

There was a stunned silence, disturbed by a few audible intakes of breath, as the group of women and a lone man – who was on night shift – digested the pathos of the child's words. Jill's mother flushed and she said, "I hadn't realised—" She bent down to Anna. "If your granny says you can stay, you're very welcome."

Grace said simply, "Thank you." Then, gathering Anna into her arms, she hugged her tightly, almost overwhelmed with relief. "It's all right, sweetheart, you can play with Jill for a bit. Be a good girl now, and do what her mummy tells you."

The two children ran off while Grace thanked her neighbours, who filtered back home, one or two shaking their heads in concern. Lizzie walked slowly back with Grace, saying, "I'd better go and see what Bert's doing. He was stuck up a ladder, last time I saw him. I bet he thinks *I've* got lost, never mind Anna!" She looked at Grace's pale face. "Are you sure you're all right?"

"I'm okay – and thanks, Lizzie." Grace went

inside the still open door, and managed, despite her shaking hands, to make a cup of tea. Putting in extra sugar, she took it into the front room and collapsed wearily into an armchair. And now the crisis was over, her body, her nerves, reacted to the stress, and a sob rose in her throat as weak tears brimmed into her eyes and rolled unheeded down her cheeks. How could she have done such a thing, how could she have been so careless as to leave the front door open? She wasn't *fit* to look after her grandchild! The road outside might be fairly quiet, but cars were becoming more frequent, and there were often delivery vans. For the rest of the day, Grace was in a constant state of agitation. She was dreading Rebecca's reaction to what had happened – there was certainly no way it could be hidden from her. And that was illustrated within minutes of Rebecca arriving home from work.

"Hello, sweetheart," she said as Anna ran to greet her, "have you had a nice day?" Rebecca swung her into her arms and carried her into the kitchen, where Grace was cutting a loaf of bread.

Anna beamed at her mummy, "I been playing with Jill!"

"Jill?" Rebecca glanced enquiringly at Grace, but didn't wait for her to answer as she saw how drawn she looked. "Are you all right?"

Grace evaded Rebecca's gaze. "Jill's that little girl who lives along the street. You know, whose mother is about your age?"

"I know exactly who you mean," Rebecca said wryly. "And she let her precious child play with

Anna? That's a turn-up for the books. How did that come about?" Then she glanced again at Grace's weary face. "You come and sit down, Grace, you look all in. I can get the tea." Grace put down the bread knife and followed her into the front room. Rebecca plumped up one of the cushions and as Grace lowered herself weakly into an armchair, said, "What's the matter?"

Grace could hardly bear to look at her. "Anna got out this morning," she whispered.

"Got out? How do you mean?"

"Lizzie came round, wanting to borrow a wall-paper brush and," Grace could hardly get the words out, "I must have left the front door open . . ."

Rebecca swung round to Anna. "You didn't go out on your own? You know you shouldn't do that, not without me or Granny – you naughty girl!"

Anna began to cry. "I didn't cross the road, Mummy!" while Rebecca's stomach lurched at even the possibility. She turned to face Grace, who halt-ingly, began to relate the whole nerve-racking episode.

Rebecca listened in growing shock, and in a tight voice demanded, "And how long did it take to find her?"

"Nearly three-quarters of an hour. I'm so sorry, Rebecca," Grace's voice was now shaking, "I don't suppose you'll trust me with her any more."

Rebecca was struggling to control her anger. Even if Anna had been naughty to run off, she wasn't even three yet. It was Grace's responsibility to look after her! Then before the hot words of condemnation could burst from her, Rebecca looked at the older woman, saw the worry in her eyes, the pallor on her face, and felt a stab of anxiety. Grace had only recently begun to confide in her about those first dreadful months after her nervous breakdown, and Rebecca knew how long it had taken for her to become less fragile, more stable. Suddenly Rebecca realised that she must be very careful how she handled the situation. With a huge effort she tried to push aside her own feelings, as Grace insisted, her eyes filling with tears, "It shouldn't have happened. I should have been more careful."

"You must stop blaming yourself so much – it could happen to anyone," Rebecca told her gently. "Just one moment's inattention, that's all it takes. And I don't want to hear any more nonsense about my not letting you look after her any more. You're marvellous with Anna, you know you are."

For a few moments their positions were reversed, with the older woman seeking reassurance from the younger. "Do you really think so?"

"I know so," Rebecca said. "And at least something good came out of it. Anna's at last been able to play with another child." Although, she thought grimly, it took what could have been a tragedy to bring it about.

"That's true," Grace said, dabbing at her eyes.

Later, Rebecca worked through her anger as she stood in the kitchen and vigorously peeled and sliced potatoes. Everyone knew it was impossible to watch a child twenty-four hours every minute, but to leave the front door open . . .

But the incident had also highlighted Anna's isolation, a fact that Rebecca knew she really should try to do something about. Otherwise, how was the child to cope when she went to school? She needed to learn to share, to play with other children. And once again, Rebecca wondered how people could be so narrow-minded that they were willing to deprive a small child of friendship because of the shame of her mother. She also knew with absolute certainty that today's scare wouldn't have happened if she'd been looking after Anna herself. And after all, wasn't that what most mothers did? Cared for their children themselves? But for that you needed to be married with a home of your own! Rebecca was comfortable with Grace and deeply grateful for her support, but ever since she'd been twelve she'd lived in other people's houses. A vision flashed before her of a house she could decorate and furnish to her own taste – a kitchen of her own, a pretty bedroom, somewhere she could put down roots, where she could build a new life. She lowered the chipped potatoes into the spitting fat then suddenly paused, staring thoughtfully at the cream distempered wall. There *was* a solution to all of this, and the prospect of marrying Johnny was becoming more attractive with every day that passed.

34

Anna's disappearance had several repercussions, and to Grace's overwhelming relief, all of them positive, although her own self-confidence remained shaken. She found herself constantly checking on Anna's whereabouts, and kept the front door locked and bolted. But now, when she walked along the road, several people who had seemed to avoid her since her breakdown, would call out a cheery greeting as she went by, or even, if she had Anna with her, bend down and talk to the little girl. Grace, who previously had felt hurt when an acquaintance passed by with just a quick nod, now wondered if they'd merely felt awkward, and hadn't known what to say. Just as it was when someone had been bereaved. Which, of course she had – tragically, three times in one week. I should have been more charitable, she thought, and made allowances for human nature.

But of course, Anna had benefited the most. She'd been invited to go and play with the other little girl on several mornings since the incident. Usually, it was Grace who took her along, but on the odd occasion that Rebecca had, she'd sensed a shy friendliness from Clare, the other young mother. At least,

Rebecca thought, she doesn't look the other way when she sees me now. It was her hope that they could become friends, but apparently both Clare's husband and his mother who lived with them, were very religious, so Rebecca thought that was probably too much to hope for. Both she and Grace had issued a return invitation to Jill, but so far this hadn't been accepted, and both women guiltily attributed the reason to themselves. Grace assumed that Clare might not trust her to keep Jill safe, while Rebecca thought it was because of her own supposed "unsuitability".

At work, Rebecca was covertly watching Sylvia. Rebecca had discovered that Sylvia was, indeed, childless. She was also, according to one of the cooks who lived in a neighbouring street, married to a "right snotty sort of bloke". Not a lot of warmth and affection there, then, Rebecca decided. Could David be right? Was Sylvia so unhappy that it made her envious of others, bitter and resentful that she was barren? It was such a harsh word, Rebecca thought, almost as hurtful as bastard. "Rather you than me!" was Grace's comment, when Rebecca told her that she was going to offer an olive branch. "Still, I suppose it's possible that this doctor knows what he's talking about. But," she warned, "don't be surprised if she bites your head off."

And so, Rebecca, going into the canteen for her coffee break, with trepidation walked over to where Sylvia, as usual, was sitting alone. "Mind if I join you?" she said, conscious of heads turning to stare at her in amazement.

"Yes, I do, actually!" Sylvia exhaled a perfect ring of cigarette smoke. With an effort, Rebecca ignored her and sat at the table. "I just thought," she said, with what she hoped was a friendly smile, "that we might bury the hatchet, so to speak."

"I don't know what you're talking about!" Sylvia looked at her coldly. "If you mean that I don't want to associate with the likes of you, then that's my prerogative."

Stung, and despite all her good intentions, Rebecca snapped, "I only had a baby, you know, I'm not a prostitute!"

Sylvia simply gave a thin smile and raised her finely plucked eyebrows. The implication in her contemptuous glance was obvious, and Rebecca's temper flared up. Katie was right – the woman was just a spiteful bitch! Olive branch or not, she wasn't going to let *that* pass! Furiously, she snapped, "How dare you? Is it because you can't have children yourself? That you're jealous?" Sylvia recoiled as if she'd been struck, her neck becoming mottled with ugly red blotches of anger.

"Jealous," she flashed, "of someone like you? You flatter yourself. And as for kids, I wouldn't thank you for one of the noisy brats!" But her retaliation hadn't prevented her guard from slipping, and in that one instant Rebecca saw the misery in her eyes, and knew that David was right.

"I'm sorry," she said swiftly, "that was unforgivable of me."

Sylvia gazed at her for one long moment, then lowered her eyes, took a last draw on her cigarette, and slowly put the lipstick-stained stub into an ashtray. "I probably bring out the worst in you," she said, "I do most people."

"Well, you don't make much of an effort, do you?" Rebecca said bluntly, thinking she might as well make the most of her opportunity while she could. Sylvia didn't say anything, she just began to gather up her handbag.

"Sylvia . . ." Rebecca put out a hand across the table. Not touching the other woman of course, but just a gesture to delay her. "If that was true, about your not being able to have children, I mean – it's not my fault, you know, nor anyone else's. You could have friends here if you wanted to. And we've all had our problems. Look at Grace, for instance?"

"Grace?" Sylvia paused, "What about her?"

Rebecca stared at her, hardly able to believe that she didn't know of Grace's double tragedy. Then she remembered that Sylvia had only joined the store a few months ago, and rarely mixed with the other staff. Slowly, Rebecca told her sad story, ending with the words, "Finding out she had a granddaughter has made all the difference to her." As she talked Rebecca saw Sylvia's eyes dilate with shock and even sympathy, before her expression once again resumed its usual hard mask.

Neither spoke as they went back to their respective sections, and Rebecca thought – well, I've done my best, now only time will tell whether it makes any difference.

★

It was ten days later that the letter arrived. Grace brought it in, frowning at the postmark. "One for you – from Warwickshire."

Rebecca glanced up from the floor where she was kneeling to fasten Anna's sandals. Warwickshire? Then immediately there came the thought – David? But no, surely it can't be? With a racing pulse, she got up and took the envelope. "I'll take it with me," she said quickly. "Now, be a good girl, sweetheart." Bending, Rebecca kissed her daughter, grabbed a cardigan from the balustrade in the hall, and was gone before Grace could ask any questions.

Carefully locking the front door, Grace smiled down at Anna. "Now, we both know who that might be from, don't we?"

Acutely conscious of the letter inside her handbag, Rebecca walked quickly to work, in an effort to arrive at the store earlier than usual. And she did, in time to nip into one of the toilet cubicles, where she could sit and read David's letter in privacy.

Dear Rebecca,

I hope you don't mind, but I got your address from Katie. However, I asked her not to tell you, as I wanted this letter to be a surprise. I meant what I said when I bid you "au revoir". I would very much like to see you again, and was wondering whether, if I were to come up next weekend, you would care to go out for the day somewhere? The invitation does, of course, include Anna. I believe that Dovedale is quite beautiful, and is within a reasonable distance, or perhaps there is somewhere else you would like to visit.

Please don't hesitate to refuse if you'd prefer not to meet,

With kindest regards,
David.

Astonished, and yet with growing excitement, Rebecca read through the letter a second time, and then hearing voices outside, she pushed it into her bag, flushed the chain and went over to the sink to wash her hands.

"Good morning," Sylvia lifted her head from where she was checking the seams in her stockings.

"Good morning," Rebecca said, while one of the girls standing behind Sylvia rolled her eyes in astonishment.

"Hark at her, getting sociable all of a sudden," she said, when Sylvia left.

"Well, it's better than her usual sour face, so maybe we should give her a chance," Rebecca suggested.

The other girl shrugged. "It'll take more than a 'good morning', for that!"

During the day Rebecca found it almost impossible to concentrate on work, her mind was racing so much. She would have to reply to David of course, and straight away. And she knew exactly what she was going to say.

But later, it wasn't until after they'd eaten, and were in the kitchen washing up, that Rebecca satisfied Grace's curiosity. "The letter was from David," she said. "You know . . ."

"The young psychiatrist?"

"That's right." Rebecca hesitated, "He wants to come up and take me out for a day next weekend, and Anna as well."

"That's nice of him – to include Anna, I mean." Grace glanced at her. "Are you going to go?"

Rebecca nodded. "I think so. Although why he's interested in me, I can't think," she shrugged, "After all it's not as if I'm educated or anything."

Grace put down her tea towel and turned to face her. "Education isn't everything, you know. You're an intelligent girl – anyone can see that. If you'd been working full-time, I bet Mrs Dawson would have been thinking about recommending you for promotion. And remember that because of the war, lots of people missed out on their schooling, through no fault of their own."

"I'd thought of going to night school at Cauldon College," Rebecca admitted. "Would you mind?"

"Looking after Anna, while you go? Of course not, she's usually asleep anyway," Grace said. "I think that's a good idea." She glanced at Rebecca. "Does David say where he wants to take you?"

"Dovedale. Do you know it?"

"I do indeed, it's a beauty spot in the Peak District." Grace turned to fill the kettle. "It's lovely there, perfect for a day out. You could take a picnic, or there's the Izaak Walton Hotel. I've never been in – it was a bit pricey for us, although I don't suppose that will worry a doctor."

"Oh, I don't think they earn that much, not when they're young."

"Depends on their background," Grace said drily. "But I've never known a poor one. Nor a poor dentist or solicitor! By the way, how did you get on with Sylvia, today?"

"Okay. She said 'good morning', anyway."

"She actually smiled at me, yesterday," Grace said, as she wiped the cutlery.

"It looks as though David was right then, and my making the first move has paid off."

"Maybe. Although you know, lots of people have disappointments in their lives – it doesn't excuse having an attitude like hers!"

"Any improvement is welcome!" Later, Rebecca settled down with a calendar, crossing off the days until she planned to go down to Southend. She paused, pencil in hand. It's four years since Ian died, she thought, and in all that time, discounting Guy, I never met anybody I liked. Now, it's just like waiting for a bus – two have come at the same time! But was it fair to Johnny to go out with David? Yet when she'd left Southend, there was no understanding between them, just a hope of deepening their friendship. And the time for that, the last week in June, was approaching very soon. Also Rebecca knew that she owed it to Johnny to find out if she had feelings for someone else. David had so often been in her thoughts since that day by the pool. Although, she told herself, as she hardly knew him, it might just be an initial attraction. And spending a whole day together was bound to reveal if they had anything in common. I just hope he doesn't find me boring, she thought with sudden apprehension.

366

35

Down in Southend, Sal was also crossing off the weeks on her calendar. "Only three more to go," she told Ron, who was studying the racing pages.

"What is?"

"What do yer think? Until Rebecca comes!"

"How am I supposed to know what you're talking about? I'm not a bleedin' mind reader!"

Sal ignored him. "Then we'll know it, with the little 'un here for a whole week." She got up and picked up his used cup and saucer to take into the kitchen.

"Are yer sure Rebecca can manage?" Ron frowned, "In that little bed? It's not like a couple of nights, is it?"

"She'll say if she can't, and there's always the sofa."

Ron looked up at her. "How are yer, Sal? You've been a bit quiet lately."

"You should count yer blessings, then!"

He looked at her with sudden concern. Not that such a sharp retort was unusual, but there was something different about Sal lately. Ron put down his paper. "Come on love, what's bothering you?" He attempted humour, "You're not up the duff, we know that!"

"Gerrof, you daft haporth," but Sal did at least smile. She put the cup and saucer down again, and sat in the armchair opposite her husband. "I think it's just that I'm missing the Unicorn," she confessed. "Don't get me wrong, I like it 'ere, but I miss Floss and Ruby, and our regulars. It's okay at the pub where I am now, but it's not the same."

"I know what you mean. Yer can't replace old friends that easy!" Ron added with some guilt, "If it hadn't been for my dodgy ticker, we'd still be there."

"I wish I hadn't told you now," she said. "I knew you'd go on like that. I've told yer before, you didn't ask to have a heart attack." And that's something else that's getting me down, she thought – the constant worry about whether you'll have another!

"Yer'll feel better when Rebecca comes," Ron said hopefully.

"Johnny Fletcher seems to be looking forward to it as well," she said. "He came into the bar the other day, and was saying then that it wouldn't be long." And, Sal thought, that's what started me off in a way, because Johnny didn't come in on the off-chance. He was checking that Rebecca's actually coming. And he took the time to have a chat, too. He's a smashing young chap, and she could do a hell of a lot worse. All Sal's hopes were pinned on something coming of it. The only problem is that if it didn't happen, if Rebecca and Anna didn't move down to live near, she didn't think she'd be able to bear it!

Ron scratched his head as he looked thoughtfully at his wife. He knew exactly what was going through her mind, as it had his – ever since Johnny had shown up in their flat. Now for Rebecca to marry another East Ender, one who'd done well for himself, would be perfect as far as Ron was concerned. He'd have something in common with this one, not like Ian, whom Ron had never really felt comfortable with. He believed in each keeping to their own – it stood to reason that a marriage worked better that way.

"Yer know what?" Ron said. "You sit there, and we'll 'ave a piece of that fruit cake you made." He heaved himself out of his chair, and passing, placed a heavy hand on Sal's shoulder. "Time will tell. There's nothing we can do about it."

David had written back to say that it wasn't necessary for Rebecca to bring a picnic lunch, as there was a hotel nearby. Grace gave a wry smile; life was so much easier when you had money.

As the day grew nearer, Rebecca found herself becoming increasingly nervous. She kept wondering whether David was going to drive back that same day, or if he planned to stay somewhere overnight. In which case, she worried, should they have offered to put him up? But they could hardly expect someone in his position to sleep downstairs on the sofa as Katie had done.

Grace too had very mixed feelings. In one way, she was looking forward to meeting this young doctor. After all, his advice had led to the chain of events that had brought Anna into her life. But she couldn't help feeling apprehensive. Surely he wouldn't come all this way unless he was seriously interested? Grace had never been to Rugby, but she knew it was quite a distance from the Potteries. You're letting your imagination run away with you, she told herself. Marriage is probably the last thing on his mind, particularly to a girl in Rebecca's position. But that didn't stop Grace from worrying, even though common sense told her that Rebecca was bound to build a new life eventually. But when she did, it was Grace's fervent hope that it wouldn't mean her losing close contact with her beloved grand-daughter.

And so it was with some trepidation that, on the following Saturday morning, Grace got up to greet the man Rebecca ushered into her front room. "This is Dr Knight, Grace," Rebecca said.

"Oh, please call me David," he said holding out his hand.

Grace shook it and said, "And I'm Grace," then as Anna came shyly forward, bent to encourage her to talk to their visitor. Rebecca went to the kitchen to make David a cup of tea after his journey.

There was a short silence, then Grace said, "Have you been to Dovedale before?"

David shook his head. "No, although I'm originally from Lichfield, I don't know the Midlands terribly well."

"At least you're lucky with the weather." The fact that David was a psychiatrist was making Grace feel uncomfortable.

David, gazing at the quiet, neatly dressed woman before him, guessed what was going through her mind, and decided the best option was to bring the subject up himself. "I've been to the Leek area once, though," he said. "I went to Cheddleton, to visit St Edward's. Rebecca probably told you. I must say I was very impressed with the hospital, and its staff."

"Yes, I was a patient there a few years ago. I found them very good," Grace told him.

David gazed at her with sympathy, knowing what it must have cost her to admit having had some sort of mental illness. One day, he hoped to see attitudes change. After all, what difference was there between illness of the mind and illness of the body? But he just said, "That's nice to hear." He glanced across at the sideboard. "Is this your husband and son? Do you mind if I –?" As Grace nodded her consent, he got up and picked up the wedding photograph. "A fine-looking man," he said. "You must miss him." But the photograph that David was really interested in was of Anna's father. So, this was Ian. As he studied the likeness, seeing the keen intelligence in Ian's grey eyes – so uncannily reproduced in Anna, David said quietly, "You also have a fine son."

He returned to sit opposite Grace again, and she gazed at him. "Don't you mean 'had'," she said, and he heard the heartbreak in her voice.

"No, Grace, I don't," David said gently. "Not even losing Ian can take away his existence. You will always be able to find him in your memories."

Grace looked at him and felt her eyelids prick with tears. Anna, who was lying on the floor with her colouring book, suddenly glanced up and said, "Why are you sad, Granny?"

371

"I'm not, darling." Grace blinked away the tears, and looking once again at David, said, "You're a very unusual man. Did you know that?"

He grinned, and suddenly looked years younger. "I could take that in several ways!"

And then Rebecca came in, carrying a tray that she set on the coffee table. David's glance swept admiringly over her summer dress of white, patterned subtly with green, and with a sweetheart neckline and cap sleeves. Grace, silently observing, suppressed a sigh. The atmosphere was already charged with the obvious attraction between these two young people, but it was only too apparent that David came from a completely different background. Surely there wasn't going to be further heartbreak for Rebecca? What she needs, Grace thought, not realising how closely her views coincided with those of Sal and Ron, is to meet someone on her own level, of her own class. A man who can understand how much courage it had taken to bring up an illegitimate child. Not, Grace mused that Rebecca fitted the mould of a working-class girl. The years she'd spent in Wales, living in the home of a professional couple, had been formative ones, refining any rough edges that might have been there. Certainly she bore little resemblance to the East End people Grace saw portrayed in films. Then, as Rebecca got up to remove the tray, Grace also rose and bent to take Anna's hand. "Come on sweetheart. It's time to go. How about doing a wee-wee first?"

Minutes later, the car, a green saloon, sped away and Grace went back indoors. David was not only attractive, she thought but extremely likeable. Brains, looks, sensitivity, and the glamour of being a doctor – it would be a rare young woman who could resist a man like that. Well, Grace thought as she settled down with her knitting, one thing is for sure, nothing I can do or say can influence things.

Dovedale was breathtaking in its beauty, with steep wooded walls of rock rising high above the stream running through the ancient limestone gorge. Already there were many other visitors there; a lone walker striding out, a young couple sauntering hand in hand, a family with children running ahead, a group of keen hikers with their stout boots and knapsacks. In the warm sunshine, with just a hint of a breeze, it was with both anticipation and a sense of peace and enjoyment that Rebecca began to stroll beside David. She breathed in deeply, relishing the crisp clean air, which seemed so thin after the smoky, dust-laden atmosphere she'd become accustomed to. With Anna reluctantly clutching her hand – so far she was shy of holding David's – Rebecca felt little need to talk, she was just content to absorb the scenery, to stare up at the huge crags and rocks, partly covered with lichen. Anna was wriggling, wanting to be free, and Rebecca said, "No, I've told you, you've got to hold my hand because of the water!" She glanced at the flowing river at the side of the path they were walking along. They had decided to leave the pushchair in the car boot, and now she was wondering whether it had been a mistake.

David crouched down before the fretful child.

"Would you like to ride on my shoulders – you'll be like a giant then and can see everything?" Anna's face lit up, and she glanced for reassurance at Rebecca, who nodded and smiled. Seconds later, Anna was perched on David's broad shoulders, with his hands securely holding her ankles.

"She used to do that with Ron," Rebecca told him, "but Sal had to put a stop to it."

David glanced enquiringly at her, and she told him of Ron's heart attack. "So that's why you moved up here," he commented. "You must tell me the full story, how you met Grace, everything – once we have the chance of a quiet talk," he added with a grin, as Anna began to squeal with excitement. What she'd seen was a sable-and-white collie trying to cross the famous stepping-stones and suddenly losing its footing, thrashing around wildly before slipping from the wet rocks into the river. But within seconds it was struggling out and on to the bank, shaking its shaggy coat free of the water, and scampering to rejoin its owner. They both shared in Anna's laughter. It was now nearly lunchtime, so they decided to postpone a longer walk until later, and walked back to the entrance to the gorge, and then up to the picturesque hotel that Grace had mentioned. According to information in the oak-beamed reception hall, the hotel was named the Izaak Walton after the author of *The Compleat Angler*, who loved to fish in the River Dove. A converted seventeenth-century farmhouse set before the backdrop of the Derbyshire Peaks, it was full of character, and Rebecca was enchanted. They were both hungry, so despite the warm summer day, they chose a delicious steak-and-kidney pie with fresh vegetables, and ice cream to follow.

"Happy?" David smiled across the table at her.

"Absolutely." For one long moment they gazed into each other's eyes, and then, for the first time, David touched her. He reached over to cover her hand with his own, and Rebecca, feeling the warmth and sensitivity of his touch, curled her fingers around his, smiling back at him. David knew how he felt – was beginning to feel – about the girl sitting opposite, but until now he hadn't been sure of how Rebecca saw him. He knew that she was grateful to him for his advice. Knew too, that an outing such as this was a rare treat for her. But simple friendship wasn't what David needed. Rebecca stirred him as no other woman had, and it wasn't just sexually, he was intrigued by the courageous way she'd coped with her life. A life so marred by tragedy. I suppose, he thought, it's one of the benefits of the deprivations of the war years. Living with self-denial on a daily basis had strengthened the character of the whole nation. But, he mused, as he watched Rebecca gently wipe ice cream from Anna's mouth, not every girl would have kept an illegitimate baby. Most would have had the child adopted. Thank God, he thought with an inward shudder, that she hadn't been desperate enough to risk going to a back-street abortionist.

And so later they walked again along the paths of Dovedale, and crossed the stepping-stones themselves, with David gingerly balancing on the rocks and carrying Anna safely in his arms. Then when Anna tired, they found a quiet spot to relax on the grass. Although other people were passing nearby, the scene felt a peaceful one as they watched the rippling water. And now, David asked the questions, and Rebecca willingly gave her answers, so that eventually he knew all that had happened to her since their first meeting. And while she talked, he watched the shadows in her expressive eyes, saw the love there as she talked of her child, the quiet determination as she told him of her plan to improve her education. And while Anna slept peacefully in the shade of the overhanging branches above them, it was then his turn to talk. "I grew up in Lichfield," he said, and told her how he'd loved to try and sketch the three spires of its Cathedral. "Then I went to school in Rugby. That's one reason I was so pleased to get a post there." Glancing at her, he realised she hadn't made the connection with the famous public school, and went on to tell her how fascinating he found his work.

"So you're an only child just as I am," Rebecca said.

"Yes, but I'm a great deal luckier," he said. "I still have my parents."

"Was your father a doctor too?"

David shook his head. "No, he was a barrister. Dad always hoped I'd follow in his footsteps, but it wasn't for me."

"And the war?"

"I was in the Medical Corps. In fact it was my experience there that fostered my interest in psychiatry."

376

Then as Anna began to stir, the tranquil moment was lost, and David glanced at his watch. "I think we'd better be making tracks."

Rebecca glanced at him with slight anxiety. "It does seem a lot of driving for you to do. First you've got to take me back, and then drive all the way to Rugby."

David smiled at her. "It's a good job I've got a friend who lets me have his petrol ration. But it's been worth every mile. In any case, I've only got to drive as far as Lichfield. I'm staying over with my parents."

Reassured, Rebecca took Anna's hand and, with David holding the other one, they walked back along to the stepping-stones, to face crossing the river again. This time, much to Anna's excited fear, David pretended to wobble precariously in the middle, but eventually they reached the other side, with Rebecca carefully following.

As they drove home, David began to wonder if he was ever going to have the chance to be alone with Rebecca. Acutely conscious of her bare legs so near his own, of the scent of her, of her very presence, he was longing to hold her in his arms, to feel her mouth beneath his own. But having Anna with them, delightful though she was, hadn't entirely been conducive to any romantic overtures. It was a pity, he thought, that the child wasn't tired enough to sleep, then he could have found a secluded place to park. But Anna was full of energy, bouncing up and down on the back seat, wanting to play "I spy".

Rebecca, too, was acutely conscious of the sexual

tension between them, and was frantically wondering how they could be alone. And then suddenly, she thought – the park! When eventually, David took his hand off the steering wheel and briefly pressed her own, Rebecca said tentatively, "Would you have time to come and look at the park, before you leave? It's just across the road, and we could leave Anna with Grace."

David turned to her, and saw that her thoughts mirrored his own. "I have as much time as we need," he said.

When they arrived, Anna ran into the house full of her exciting day and eager to tell Grace about the dog that had fallen into the water. Rebecca came in behind her, carrying their things, and whispered, "I'm just going to show David the park, but don't let Anna know where we've gone." Rebecca added with some embarrassment, "We just need a few minutes on our own."

"And why not?" Grace said, and taking her granddaughter's hand, said, "Let's go into the garden and pick some raspberries for tea. I've got a jelly for you as well."

Rebecca returned to the car, where David was leaning against the bonnet, smoking a cigarette. "All set," she said, and together they crossed over the road and went through the gates into the park. Once inside, he took her hand and they strolled along the tree-lined paths, pausing for a moment to admire the scented roses in the flowerbeds. Then continuing through the lower park, they reached the Victorian bridge overlooking the canal.

And it was there, that they finally found themselves alone.

At last David felt able to draw Rebecca into his arms, and as his lips came down to hers, they tasted their first kiss, a gently questioning one, as they tried to explore their growing feelings for each other. Rebecca felt the reassuring warmth of his mouth upon her own, David the softness of hers, and then he was kissing her more deeply. Rebecca moulded her body against his, responding at first hesitantly, and then with a swift passion which delighted her. But all too quickly, their privacy was shattered by a couple of boys walking past, who grinned and nudged each other. Reluctantly David and Rebecca separated for a moment, and then once the boys had disappeared, they were kissing once more, but again had to reluctantly draw apart as an elderly couple approached, walking slowly and with arthritic difficulty. "I don't think we've chosen the ideal spot," David said with a wry smile.

"I suppose we could find somewhere more secluded, but," Rebecca hesitated, "it seems a bit—"

"Not quite the right place, is it?" David took her hand, and they began to walk slowly back to the park entrance. "When can I see you again?"

"The trouble is I normally work on Saturdays."

"Oh, I see. It would have to be on a Sunday then?"

"It seems such a long way to come for just one day. But I'm afraid we haven't the space to put you up."

"Is there somewhere nearby I could stay?"

"There's the Commercial Hotel – it's only a few minutes away and it's reasonable."

"That's what I like," he teased, "a woman who'll look after my money."

"Or," Rebecca said suddenly, remembering with embarrassment that David was probably used to better things, "there's the North Stafford Hotel. That's close and one of the best hotels in the area."

"Is it now?" David said thoughtfully. "Somewhere decent we could have a meal, then?"

Oh, help, not again, Rebecca thought! But then, she reminded herself, David wasn't Guy. And she was no longer the naïve girl she'd been a few months ago. She'd be a fool not to have learned from that experience!

"I'm on duty next weekend, I'm afraid," David told her, as they passed through the park gates. "But I could make the one after."

Rebecca swung round to face him. "Oh, I can't. I'll be in Southend then. It's been arranged for ages."

"When do you come back?"

"Not until Sunday night." Rebecca stared at him in consternation. That would mean another three weeks before she could see him!

David frowned. "Blast! I'm not sure whether I'm on duty then or not." There was a short silence, then he suggested, "Look, suppose I come down to see you in Southend?"

Rebecca felt a wave of panic sweep over her. Her conscience was already bothering her about Johnny, even though she knew no promises had been made. She desperately needed to see him again, to spend time with him, if only to sort out her feelings. Rebecca knew that before David appeared on the scene, she'd been seriously thinking that if the week went well, she might accept Johnny's proposal. For David to come down to Southend at this crucial time could only lead to all sorts of complications. And after all, despite the wonderful day they'd spent together, she had no idea whether their romance was going to lead anywhere. And once again, as it had done before at crucial times in her life, her mother's voice echoed softly in her head: *Don't throw the baby out with the bath water, love.*

36

D avid, having seen the panic on Rebecca's face, waited a moment, then seeing Rebecca floundering, said in a grim tone, "On second thoughts, perhaps that's not such a good idea. We'll just have to wait."

Rebecca glanced at him in consternation, but could read nothing from his taut features. Going through the park gates, they crossed the road in an uneasy silence, and David followed Rebecca into the house to say a brief goodbye to Grace and Anna.

When, a few minutes later, Rebecca, still feeling anxious, came out with him to the car, David opened the door immediately, and briefly kissing Rebecca on the cheek, said, "Have a good time. And thank you for a lovely day."

"Thank *you*," Rebecca said, and with her emotions in turmoil watched him drive away. It was obvious that David had taken offence about Southend. And she didn't blame him! Whatever must he think of her? One minute she was kissing him passionately, the next keeping him at a distance. But, she thought with dismay, what else could I have done? She turned to go in, suddenly feeling tired, and hoping that Grace would offer to put Anna to bed.

David was not only confused, he was angry, and as he drew up at a set of traffic lights, his fingers drummed tensely on the steering wheel. For some reason his suggestion that he went down to Southend had completely flustered Rebecca. And to his mind, that could mean only one thing. Yet she had been so delightful all day and David knew he was, for the first time in his life, very close to falling in love. There had been other girls of course, but he'd never felt about any of them the way he felt about Rebecca. And when he'd held her in his arms, when they'd kissed, he could have sworn that she was sincere in the way she was beginning to feel about him. Yet there was obviously someone else in her life – what other explanation could there be? For God's sake, keep your head, David told himself, as the lights changed to green and he pulled away. No matter how you feel about her. Getting involved with an unmarried mother was already fraught with problems – did he really need any more?

As the train drew in to the railway station at Southend, Sal, who had been frantically scanning the carriages, hurried past the porters on the platform to lift Anna down, while Rebecca followed with their cases. Over Sal's head she could see Ron waiting, his heavy features creasing in a huge grin of welcome. Rebecca felt her eyes prick with sudden tears. No matter how fond she was of Grace, these two dear people were her family, and always would be. And then Ron was moving forward, swinging Anna briefly into his arms before, catching Sal's warning glance, he reluctantly put her down again. Rebecca kissed them both, and in answer to Anna's clamour, took her to wave goodbye to the train driver who was leaning out of the hissing steam engine. Then they went out into the sunshine, quickly boarded a bus and within twenty minutes were at the flat. It wasn't until the unpacking was done, and Ron had been sent for fish-and-chips, that Sal mentioned Johnny. "He came into the pub," she told Rebecca, "wanting to know if you were definitely coming, and checking it was still the same date."

Rebecca felt the colour rise in her cheeks. "He said he was going to try and take his holidays the same week," she explained.

"Did he now?" Sal turned away, checking the plates warming in the oven, a smile of satisfaction on her face. Rebecca continued cutting a crusty loaf into thin slices, and spreading them with a scrape of butter. Then, much to her relief, Ron's arrival with his appetising parcel ended the conversation, and the women busily divided the food between four plates before it got cold.

Already, and worryingly to Rebecca, she was longing to see Johnny again. And yet it was only days since she'd been in David's arms, had responded so warmly, even passionately to his kisses. I'm so confused, she thought with despair as later she shared the narrow single bed with Anna. Gently Rebecca straightened her small daughter's limbs to give more space and turning over, stared blankly at the flow-ered cotton curtains. Maybe, she thought, now that David's in my life, when I do meet Johnny again,

I'll see him differently – *know* that marrying him would be the wrong thing to do. And then the decision would be made for me. Because to marry Johnny when she was attracted to someone else would be grossly unfair and a recipe for unhappiness for both of them. And yet Rebecca knew he was right. Anna did need the safety net of a normal family so that she could be shielded from scorn. However, remembering her own childhood, Rebecca was acutely aware that a family also needed to be a happy one. Duty is all very well, she thought, but hadn't she read somewhere that it was a cold bed-fellow? Rebecca thought wistfully of the passion and tenderness she'd experienced with Ian. And all week she hadn't been able to stop thinking about David, of those delicious moments in the park, of the joy of being held in his arms. The way his kisses had inflamed her senses made Rebecca realise yet again how much she needed the intimacy of lovemaking. Was it selfish of her to want happiness and fulfilment for herself? And Johnny too deserved a loving relationship – especially after all he'd been through in the war years. But, she thought, tossing and turning, she had to remember the huge advantages that marriage to Johnny would bring. Restless, Rebecca turned over to face her sleeping child, feeling Anna's sweet breath on her face. As for David, she thought, no matter how attracted he is to me, how likely is *he* to propose? Not very, with a past like mine. Whereas with Johnny . . . And so the thoughts went round and round in her mind until, despite the long journey, and the bustle of settling in, it wasn't until the early hours that she managed to drift off to sleep.

The following morning dawned bright and sunny, and Anna grew more and more excited as they all prepared to spend the day on the beach. Sal had taken a couple of days off, while Ron was looking forward to relaxing on a deckchair and taking Anna down to the water's edge. "Just paddling, mind," he warned her. "Yer can jump over the little waves, but that's all. No going any further."

"I won't, Uncle Ron."

"I might paddle meself," Sal announced. "Seawater's supposed to be good for yer feet."

"Don't you go down yourselves?" Rebecca stared at them in amazement. They both looked shame-faced. "Nah," Ron said. "We stroll along the front, and sometimes hire a deckchair for a bit, or sit in the Marine Gardens, but we don't often go on the beach, do we, Sal?"

She shook her head. "It's more for kids and fami-lies. There's not much reason when it's just the two of us. It's different now Anna's here, isn't it, my chicken?"

But Rebecca, although joining in their high spirits, was tense, constantly expecting the doorbell to ring. And when they eventually left at eleven o'clock to catch their bus, Sal said, with a feeling of disap-pointment, "I thought Johnny might have turned up."

Once at the seafront, and after waiting in a short queue to hire deckchairs, they stood for a moment searching the already crowded beach. Then Ron spotted a space fairly near to the sea and before Sal could object, he picked up Anna, who was tightly clutching her bucket and spade, and led the way across the soft sand. Sal carried their deckchairs, while Rebecca trailed behind with her own and two shopping-bags. One bulged with towels and swim-suits, the other with a flask of tea, a bottle of Tizer, a greaseproof packet of ham and cheese sandwiches, and Ron's newspaper. Once at their chosen spot, Rebecca changed Anna into her swimsuit, then frowned. "I should have put mine on underneath my clothes! I never thought!"

"Don't worry," Sal said. "I've got just the thing."

Johnny, annoyed with himself for arriving too late at the flat, had guessed that Rebecca would want to take Anna to the beach on their first morning. And it hadn't been difficult to work out that the spot they'd choose would be within a short distance of their bus-stop. Now, he mused, as he strolled along the promenade, it was just a matter of finding them. And several minutes later he did. Three deckchairs grouped to face the sea, and it would have been difficult to spot them among so many others, if it hadn't been for the sun glinting on Rebecca's hair. She was standing up, shielded by a huge gaudy towel that Sal was holding around her, and Johnny watched with amusement Rebecca's contortions, as she wrig-gled out of her clothes, until at last she emerged. Her skin was so white it was almost translucent against the green costume she was wearing. Whenever Johnny had thought about Rebecca during the past few months, and it had been often, the image in his mind had always been of a girl wrapped up warmly in a winter coat, and cream beret. It had been her eyes he'd remembered most, green and expressive, which had been so shadowed as she'd talked of her own past, and at first horrified and then full of compassion as she'd listened to his account of that terrible scene in the tunnel. Now, seeing what a fantastic figure she had, he realised that she was, as East Enders would say, "a right smasher". No wonder Ian had fallen for her.

Johnny collected a deckchair, went down the steps on to the beach, and with his feet sinking into the soft sand, began to weave his way through the crowd of holidaymakers. Anna looked up, and seeing his wave smiled uncertainly. Ron turned, grinned, and gave Sal a sharp nudge in the ribs. She opened her eyes with irritation. "What?" Then seeing Johnny smiling down, her face split into a grin. "How did yer find us?"

He decided not to say that he'd seen Rebecca getting changed. "They don't call me Sherlock Holmes for nothing!"

Rebecca, hearing his voice, immediately sat up. Johnny, in a short-sleeved blue shirt and trousers, was exactly as she remembered him, relaxed and friendly, his smile warm as he said quietly, "Hello, Rebecca."

"Hello, Johnny."

He began to unfold his deckchair, putting it up in a space next to hers. Sal turned to Ron, telling him to cover his head against the sun, and taking out his white handkerchief, he tied a knot in each corner and settled it on his balding scalp. His one concession to beachwear was to roll up his flannel trousers and the sleeves of his striped shirt. Still wearing braces and with socks turned down over his black shoes, he looked, Rebecca thought with a fond smile, exactly like a comic character on a seaside postcard. Sal, comfortable in her flowered cotton frock and white sandals, bent down to Anna. "Ready for a paddle? And you can come, yer lazy lummock," she told Ron. "Take yer shoes and socks off! It's bin years since yer let the fresh air get to those feet!"

Ron bristled, then seeing her eyes flash in the direction of Johnny and Rebecca, obeyed.

"I'll take her in properly later on," Rebecca said.

"And me," Johnny said. "I've already got my swimming trunks on, and I brought a towel."

"Proper boy scout, aren't you?" Rebecca laughed.

"I have my moments!"

Sal, encouraged to see them apparently so at ease with each other, smiled with satisfaction. Then she and Ron, with Anna between them full of excitement, began to make their way to the sea's edge.

Rebecca and Johnny watched them go, then Johnny said, "How have things been with you? Since Easter, I mean."

"Fine. And you?"

"Good. The job's going well." Johnny trailed his fingers in the soft sand at the side of his deckchair. "I took the week off, as I promised. Is it still okay with you if we spend most of it together?"

"You haven't changed your mind, then?" Rebecca knew she didn't need to specify what she meant.

Johnny shook his head. "No, I haven't."

"In that case I think we need to."

He turned to face her, his gaze holding hers. "And you? You're still considering it, then?"

37

To Rebecca's relief, although they spent much of the next few days together, Johnny, after that first question on the beach, didn't refer to his proposal again. And without that pressure, she was able to relax and enjoy getting to know him better. For all his easygoing nature, Johnny had depth to him, and as he talked to her of his ambitions, she realised that this was one East Ender who was determined to improve himself. Just as I am, she thought suddenly, one warm evening when they were strolling along the promenade. As he turned to take her hand, something he'd only recently begun to do, she said, "Do you know, Johnny Fletcher, there's one thing I don't understand about you?"

"My irresistible attraction to women?"

She laughed. "No, the fact that you've hardly got any Cockney twang."

"Neither have you."

"Yes, but that's because of all those years in Wales."

"And those years I spent in the Camp had an influence on me, as well. Most of the men in my hut were from very different backgrounds, and it doesn't take a genius to work out that people tend to judge you on the way you speak." He grinned at her. "Maybe I was aping my betters, but even my mates were amazed when I got home. 'Specially my mum – she thought she'd spawned a changeling!" Rebecca laughed.

"But you never lose it really," he said. "I can easily slip back into the apples and pears stuff. But then with my job, I wouldn't want everyone thinking I was a 'wide boy', now would I?"

"You're certainly not that! And neither are lots of people who live in the East End."

"I know," he said, "but that's the English for you. They do like stereotypes." He hesitated, then added, "Ian told me that."

"Did he? They do it with unmarried mothers too. We're all 'tarred with the same brush'."

Her tone was bitter, and Johnny glanced at her with sympathy. "I think a lot of these narrow attitudes will change," he told her. "This last war's made a big difference to everyone. But it won't happen overnight." He turned towards her. "Talking of mothers, mine has been asking to meet you."

"I'd love to meet her," Rebecca said, and felt a stab of anxiety. "You have told her about Anna?"

"I've told her."

"And?"

"Don't worry," he said, "it'll be all right, you'll see." Johnny paused as they came to a side stall. "Fancy some whelks?"

She shook her head. "I'd rather have chips."

"Done," he said promptly. "You can't say I don't know how to spoil a girl!"

She laughed, but then Rebecca was finding that

she laughed a lot when she was with Johnny. She arrived back at the flat just before Sal was due, and Ron got up from his armchair, yawning. "Seein' as you'll be up, I'll get beneath the sheets."

"Has Anna been all right?"

"Good as gold," Ron said.

Rebecca said goodnight, and went into the kitchen to make some cocoa. Later when she and Sal sat on opposite sides of the fireplace, she couldn't help being reminded of the Unicorn. "Just like the old days, isn't it?"

Sal sighed. "They were good times."

"Hard work, though."

"I didn't mind that. But," she shrugged, "needs must."

"Other doors open," Rebecca pointed out. "Who'd have thought you'd be living at the seaside, for instance?"

"I know, but that doesn't mean I don't miss the East End." She looked at her niece. "How about you?"

"Yes, of course I do. Particularly Flossie, Ruby and Janet. And the noise and humour in the bar. We had some smashing regulars didn't we? Right characters most of them." She grinned. "Do you remember Dewdrop? I wonder if anyone's bought him a handkerchief yet? Of course I miss it – after all, it's where my roots are. But the people in the Potteries aren't that different, you know. There's still a strong sense of community."

"And you say you get on well with Grace." It's like a scab, this jealousy, Sal thought, I will keep picking at it. She knew it was stupid. After all, the woman *was* Anna's grandmother. And her offer of a home to Rebecca had been a godsend.

"Fine. You'd like her, Sal. I was only thinking, maybe she could come down with me sometime and stay in a bed-and-breakfast or something. What do you think?"

What Sal thought was that her time with Rebecca and Anna was too precious to share! But all she said was, "Yes, why not."

There was a short silence as they both drank their cocoa, and then Sal, unable to restrain her curiosity any longer, said, "And how are you getting on with Johnny?"

Rebecca grinned at her aunt. "I bet you've been dying to ask!"

"Can you blame me?"

Rebecca didn't know what to answer. She only wished she knew exactly how she did feel about Johnny. She was becoming very fond of him, but that was all it was, affection. And she sensed it was the same with him, because so far, apart from holding her hand, he hadn't once touched her, or shown in any way that he wanted to. It might be only a matter of days since she'd arrived, but Johnny must know that this short time they had together, was absolutely crucial.

"Well," she began, "I do like him . . ."

"Only like?" Sal felt a stab of disappointment.

Rebecca was tempted to tell Sal about Johnny's proposal. But she knew that her aunt would immediately see such a marriage as the perfect solution.

As it was in so many ways. Yet if Rebecca explained what was holding her back, if she told Sal about how she'd met David, how attracted she was to him, she knew Sal would be scathing, would scoff at the possibility of such a romance becoming serious. Rebecca could almost hear her words: "*Stop reaching for the stars, girl. You'll only get hurt.*" And with despair, Rebecca knew that her aunt was probably right.

"Yes," she said, after reflection, "at the moment it is just like, perhaps even more than that—"

Sal immediately seized on the hesitation. "You mean it might lead to something else?" She beamed at her niece. "You could do a lot worse, girl. He's straight as a die, is Johnny."

"Ian saved his life," Rebecca said suddenly, and found herself telling Sal the whole story.

"Well, I never!" Sal stared at her. "Now, you tell Ron that in the morning, do you hear?"

"I will." Rebecca hesitated and then said, "What's Johnny's mother like?"

Sal shrugged. "Don't know really, because she never came into the pub. I know her by sight, of course. She looks a decent sort."

"Did you know his father?"

Sal shook her head. "She was a widow when she moved in, I believe. I think Johnny would have been about fourteen. Why?"

"I just wondered. He wants to take us to meet her."

"Really?" Sal said, and felt a flicker of excitement. Now this *was* significant. Don't say anything, she warned herself. Just keep your fingers firmly crossed!

Then glancing at the clock, she finished her cigarette and stubbed it out in the ashtray. "Well, I'll be off ter bed. Are you coming?"

"Shortly."

For a long time Rebecca sat gazing into the dying embers of the fire. In a way, she couldn't help wishing that she hadn't met David again. Everything would be so much simpler. But that would have meant she would never have spent that wonderful day with him at Dovedale, would never have known the exhilaration of being held in his arms. Even the image of his thin face, of the way his eyes lit up when he smiled, was enough to make her feel soft and warm inside. Everything is happening too quickly, she thought with increasing panic. I need more time – desperately. But would Johnny give it to her? And if he did, and she went back to Stoke without anything being decided between them, could that risk her losing him? And Rebecca was reminded yet again, as she eventually slid into bed beside her child, of the reason why Johnny had proposed in the first place.

It was not until one evening, two days before Rebecca was due to leave, that Johnny kissed her. Earlier, the day had followed its familiar pattern. A family grouping on the beach, with Sal joining them when her shifts allowed, and Ron, after their picnic lunch, trudging back across the sand, to catch a bus to the flat. "It's no use, I need me afternoon nap," he'd say, and although Johnny offered to drive him, Ron always refused. "I've told yer, I've not lost the use of me legs. I get enough mollycoddling from Sal."

They watched him go, and Rebecca commented, "I think he's looking much better than when they first moved down."

Johnny bent down to Anna, who was absorbed in putting little Union Jack flags on her sandcastle. "Do you want a ride on the donkeys?" Her face alight with eagerness, she scrambled up.

"Yes, please!"

Rebecca, watching them go, saw Johnny lift her up on to the patient animal's back, and Anna lean forward to pat the grey donkey's neck as, with its bells jingling, they moved forward. Johnny walked along beside them both, making sure she didn't fall off, and Rebecca couldn't help thinking what a wonderful father he'd make.

That same night, he took her to the Sun Deck Theatre on the pier to watch the colourful variety show, and afterwards as they walked hand-in-hand back along the promenade, Rebecca's lips were still curving with laughter. It was when they reached a quiet stretch, and paused to look over the rail at the softly surging sea, that Johnny turned to her and gently drew her into his arms. As his lips came down to hers, Rebecca closed her eyes, intensely curious to feel his mouth on her own. It was warm and firm, and she found herself responding with genuine affection. For one long moment they clung to each other, and then Johnny drew away and gazed down at her. "That wasn't too bad, was it?"

She shook her head and smiled up at him. "Not too bad at all."

"Then shall we try it again?" He bent down to

her upturned lips, and this time Rebecca found herself responding even more, and Johnny's kiss became harder, more searching. Eventually, he lifted a finger and brushed aside a stray tendril of her hair. "Have I ever told you what a good mother you are?" he said.

Slightly bewildered, Rebecca shook her head, wondering what had suddenly made him say it at that particular time. But it was nice to hear, and again she smiled up at him, but Johnny was already turning, this time tucking her arm into the crook of his elbow, as they continued walking along. Both were silent, each with their own thoughts, and it was much later, when they parted at the door of the flat, that Johnny again drew her into his arms. This time his kiss was gentle and considerate, and after he left, Rebecca found herself gazing after him in some confusion. Because she suddenly realised, that although she'd spent hours dwelling on her feelings for him, she still had no idea how Johnny felt about her. His shock proposal had been made out of decency, even impulsiveness. He had, she reminded herself, still been recovering from the shock of hearing about Ian's death. But he too must be facing the reality that not only would he be offering a home and respectability to his best friend's child, he was also committing himself to sharing his life with a woman he may not love. Good looks are one thing, Rebecca admitted, and if I'm honest we're both blessed with those. But was that attraction enough to sustain a life-long partnership?

She'd been longing for Johnny to kiss her, hoping

that her reaction would guide her decision. Because if she'd felt uncomfortable, had recoiled in any way, then that would have solved her problem. But now she felt more mixed up than ever. Because although his touch hadn't "melted her" in the way that David's did, being held in Johnny's arms hadn't been any hardship at all.

38

The following afternoon, Johnny drove to a back street situated some distance from the seafront. Rebecca, holding Anna by the hand, followed him up the red Cardinal polished steps of a bay-windowed villa, which, like several of its neighbours, displayed a "No Vacancies" sign in the front window. Despite Johnny's reassurance, she felt distinctly nervous, but as soon as they went in, Elsie Fletcher came forward to welcome them. Small and thin, her tired face was a map of a hard-working life, but her smile was welcoming, and after one searching glance at Rebecca, her first words were to Anna. "My, you're a pretty little thing. Are you 'aving a nice 'oliday?" Anna nodded, and clung shyly to Rebecca's hand as they went through the narrow, spotlessly clean hall, into a square kitchen which had a small sofa and armchair squashed into one corner. Elsie apologised. "Sorry about this, but we 'ave to make do during the season."

"You're obviously busy, then, judging by the sign outside," Rebecca said.

"Yes, booked up right through," she said proudly.

"And it's all because of Mum!" Johnny turned to Rebecca. "She does a smashing fry-up."

"I do me best. Anyway, it's good to meet you, Rebecca. Now sit yerselves down, and I'll put the kettle on. How's Ron and Sal?"

"They're fine," Rebecca said, and sat on the sofa with Anna perching beside her.

"Where's Queenie?" Johnny asked.

"Gone ter the pictures! Yer know what she is for Douglas Fairbanks!" Elsie turned to Rebecca. "That's me sister. This is her place really, at least since her hubby passed on." She went to a dresser and passed over a framed wedding photograph. "That's Queenie." As Rebecca gazed down at it, Elsie added, "She was glad of us coming to live with her, wasn't she, Johnny?"

He nodded. "It was the best thing for all of us."

"And how about you, Rebecca," Elsie said, "do you like Southend?"

"Very much." As Elsie busied herself with the teacups, Rebecca glanced around. The large dresser dominated the room, crammed with crockery and with a divided wooden box brimming with cutlery on its narrow shelf. Through a door she could see in the scullery a wooden airing-rack with a pulley, on which rested a selection of ironed sheets, pillow-cases, towels and tea towels. Rebecca wondered just how a young man fitted into this busy household. There wouldn't be much privacy, and as the largest bedrooms would be allocated to guests, she imagined Johnny wouldn't have much personal comfort either. And the thought struck her that perhaps he was just as anxious to have his own home as she was.

"Where did you live before you moved to Stepney?" she asked later, as she took a jam tart from the plate offered to her.

"Shoreditch," Elsie said curtly.

"Did you just fancy a change?"

But Johnny answered her question. "We got the chance of a better house, didn't we, Mum?"

"That's right."

Rebecca glanced from one to the other, sensing a sudden reserve. Just then Anna pulled on her arm and whispered into her ear. Rebecca turned to Johnny. "Where's the . . . ?"

They stayed for about an hour, and then as they were leaving, Elsie gave Anna a small bag of jelly babies. "Only 'ave one now, or you won't eat yer tea." To Rebecca, she simply said, "I'm glad he's brought you. Give me best to Ron and Sal."

"I'm sure they'd love to see you, some time," Rebecca said. "They'd enjoy a chat about Stepney."

Elsie looked pleased. "I'd like that."

It wasn't until later, after she and Anna were back at the flat, that Rebecca was able to examine what had been puzzling her throughout the afternoon. The obvious reluctance from both Elsie and Johnny to talk about Shoreditch had been marked. And there was another strange thing. Although displayed on the dresser there was a framed wedding photograph of Queenie and her husband, there was no matching one of Elsie's wedding day. Into Rebecca's mind flashed Johnny's vehement insistence that Anna would be taunted as a bastard when she went to school: *It will happen, believe me!* She remembered

402

the intensity of his gaze, the harshness of his voice. A suspicion flickered in her mind. It was a shocking thought – but could he have been speaking from his own experience?

On their last evening, Johnny took her dancing at the Kursaal Ballroom in the Marine Park, when to her delight Rebecca discovered that he was an excellent dancer. However, there were still moments, particularly when the vocalist sang "Love is the Sweetest Thing" when she couldn't help thinking wistfully of David, but she pushed the thoughts away. It wasn't fair on Johnny to make comparisons.

Later they strolled hand-in-hand by the sea in the still balmy night air. Although it was dark, the lights along the Esplanade reflected not only on them, but also on the incoming tide, and Rebecca thought how romantic the scene was. Eventually she said, "We've been so lucky with the weather. The forecast for the rest of the summer isn't too good at all."

Johnny turned to her. "I think we've got far more important things to talk about than the weather," he said quietly.

"Yes, I know." Rebecca's voice was equally quiet, and impulsively she stood on tiptoe and kissed him gently on the lips.

He gazed down at her. "What does that mean?"

Rebecca shrugged helplessly. "Oh, I don't know, Johnny, I really don't. Tell me, do you still feel the same – about marrying me, I mean? After all, this week has been a sort of testing time for both of us."

403

For one long moment, Johnny didn't answer. Then, he said, "Yes, I still feel the same."

Rebecca slowly turned away and as she began to walk along again, he fell into step beside her. For several minutes neither spoke, then Rebecca said, "I'm just not sure, Johnny, I wish I were. I've loved being with you, I really have. But to be honest I think I need more time. It's such a big decision. And don't you see? It can't just be about Anna. It's got to work between us, or in the end it will lead to us all being unhappy."

"And you don't think it could? Work between us, that is?"

"I'm not saying that at all. But we've known each other such a short time—"

Johnny took her arm, turning her round to face him. His expression was serious as he looked down into her upturned face, at her eyes – those pools of green – which were full of confusion, even turmoil. "Hey, stop panicking," he said. "There's no pressure, at least not yet." He gazed searchingly at her. "Is there something you're not telling me? For instance, have you met someone else? I'd rather you were straight with me."

And Rebecca found herself incapable of lying to him. "Only recently," she confessed, "and purely by chance. In a way I wish I hadn't, it would make things so much easier."

Johnny frowned, not sure whether he felt jealous or not. He gazed down at Rebecca, trying to imagine her being held in someone else's arms. "Do you think he's serious?"

She shook her head. "I doubt it. But it's too soon to say. I've only seen him a couple of times. But I can't imagine an ambitious doctor wanting to marry an unmarried mother, can you?"

Johnny whistled softly. "A doctor! Well, I can't compete with that!"

Her temper flared. "That's nonsense, Johnny! You're one of the most genuine people I've ever met. Any girl would be lucky to have you for a husband." And it was true, she thought. He was so easy to talk to, so open and friendly. Marriage to Johnny would be – *comfortable*, that was the word. "And how about you?" she said. "I can't believe the girls aren't chasing after you."

He laughed. "Well, maybe one or two have given me the eye."

"Exactly, and that's my biggest fear – that you might meet someone else."

"Hadn't you better make sure of me, then?" But he added swiftly, "I'm only joking. You've obviously got to sort out how you feel about this other bloke. What's his name, by the way?"

"David." She told Johnny how they'd first met at the hospital Christmas party and then again by the swimming pool at Trentham.

"Sounds a good chap."

"He is. You'd like him."

"Want to bet?" He grinned down at her, and she laughed.

"Oh, Johnny, why am I even hesitating?" Impulsively she leaned up to kiss his cheek, but he turned to capture her lips with his own, and their

405

kiss, so warm, even loving in a way, almost weakened Rebecca's resolve. She gazed up at him and sensing her uncertainty, he placed a finger gently on her mouth.

"No decisions," he said. "I think you were right in wanting to wait. But I do think we need to put a time limit on this, otherwise it's not fair to either of us. Will you be coming down at Christmas?"

"I hope so."

"Then let's make that our deadline. And before then, I think I should come up to Stoke. Shall we write this time?"

She nodded, and made him promise to tell her if he met someone else. "Let's have truth between us, Johnny."

Later, Rebecca watched his car disappear into the distance with mixed feelings. It had been such a wonderful week and she was not only going to miss him, but also Sal and Ron. Suddenly Stoke-on-Trent seemed a long way away, and Christmas an eternity, and it was only the prospect of seeing David again that lifted her spirits. And I can't even be sure of that, she thought, remembering the coolness between them when they'd parted.

39

With Rebecca and Anna away in Southend, the week had been a revealing one for Grace. At first she'd enjoyed having the house to herself again, being able to relax in the afternoons and to read without constant interruption and childish clamour. On the days she wasn't working, she took the opportunity to clear out drawers and cupboards, washing her net curtains, only making herself a snack meal. But after a few days, in the late afternoons and evenings, she found herself feeling aimless in the silent house, even standing at the front window looking out for some sign of life – something she'd seen other lonely people doing. And Grace didn't want to turn into one of those. Was this how she would feel once Anna and Rebecca were no longer sharing their lives with her?

And when Rebecca did return, with Anna brimming with excited chatter about the holiday, and "Uncle Johnny", Grace felt a huge surge of pleasure. How she'd grown to love them both. But although her mind was full of questions, she was hesitant to say anything. I don't have the right, she thought yet again. I'm in "no man's land" – neither her mother nor even her mother-in-law. But that didn't stop her wondering exactly what was going on! However, she remained silent, although it didn't escape her notice that Rebecca was always the first to rush into the hall when the post was delivered. Now who, Grace wondered, is she so anxious to hear from – is it this Johnny, or David?

And then a letter did arrive, with the postmark of Southend. But it was from Sal, enclosing a couple of snapshots. Rebecca glanced at them, smiled, and passed one over to Grace. "This is Johnny," she said. "You'll be able to put a face to the name, now."

Grace gazed at the photo, seeing not only a tall, earnest-looking young man, sitting on a low wall, smiling into the camera, but someone she instinctively knew she would like. For a moment she tried to imagine him with Ian, perhaps walking round the perimeter of the POW camp or playing cards in their hut. "Let me see?" Anna tried to take the photograph.

"Don't snatch," Rebecca scolded. "You'll tear it. Here, you look at this one – it's of you, sitting on a donkey."

She laughed at Anna's squeal of delight and then turned again to Grace, who said, "Johnny looks nice. Sort of dependable and easygoing."

"That's exactly what he is," Rebecca said, taking back the photo and studying it. "You'll like him, Grace."

"How do you mean?"

"He's thinking of coming up. I thought he could stay at the Commercial Hotel." She smiled, "They do a good breakfast with oatcakes. That's where I first had them."

"You've really taken to those, haven't you?"

"I certainly have, especially grilled with cheese on. Anna likes them too, don't you sweetheart?" Anna nodded. She'd already lost interest in the photos, and was busy undressing her doll. The two women watched as she dressed Gloria in a pink pram-suit and bonnet knitted from a pattern in *Woman's Weekly*.

But now, with the mention of Johnny coming up to Stoke, Grace could no longer contain her curiosity. "Do I take it that you and Johnny . . . ?"

Rebecca hesitated, then said, "It's a bit complicated, Grace. Not quite in the way that you mean, but I don't really know, not yet." Then she glanced at Ian's mother, and guessed correctly that behind her carefully composed expression, there was another question burning. "I suppose," Rebecca said, "you're wondering how David comes into all this?"

"I was rather."

Rebecca shrugged helplessly. "I've no idea, Grace. He hasn't been in touch since I got back, and it's two weeks now." She looked away, not wanting Grace to see how upset she was. Grace felt a pang of sympathy. When Rebecca had returned from her day at Dovedale, there had been a light in her eyes and vivacity in her manner that had told Grace all she needed to know. However, whether it would all lead anywhere was another matter.

"Did he say he'd get in touch?"

"Yes. But maybe I'm reading too much into just one day out, Grace. After all, I haven't had much experience of these things." Maybe not, Grace thought, and if it had been that Guy, nothing would have surprised me. Too charming by half, he was. But David was different – she'd felt he was a man you could trust.

The following Saturday was very busy at the store, and it was with relief that in the middle of the afternoon, Rebecca went into the canteen for her break. Betty was already there, dying to talk about her new boyfriend, Alan. She'd met him a couple of months ago at a dance at Longton Town Hall, since when they'd been inseparable. And now it seemed that Alan was already hinting at an engagement.

"Isn't it a bit soon?" Rebecca said with a frown, then added quickly, "I don't know why I said that! Ian and I were just the same, we both knew straight away."

"Of course we won't be able to afford to get married for ages," Betty confided. "Alan works on the pots, and as you know, they don't pay well."

Rebecca knew that the expression "on the pots" was the local saying for anyone who worked on a potbank. "What exactly does he do?"

"He's a caster. He pours slip – that's liquid clay – into moulds. He's been there since he left school, and hopes to get to foreman of the casting shop one day."

"Oh, good." Rebecca turned to give a friendly wave to Sylvia, who had gone to sit with another woman at an adjoining table. "The difference in that woman is unbelievable!" Betty whispered.

"I know." Rebecca glanced at her watch. "Well, back to the fray. I'll see you later!"

"Still no word from David?" Rebecca shook her head, not trusting herself to speak.

Right up to the moment that David had entered the swing doors of the Hanley branch of Marks & Spencer, his mood was one of uncertainty and confusion. As a man, a doctor, whose expertise was to see clearly not only the root of any problem but also the best way of dealing with it, he had found the past three weeks the most frustrating of his life. And, although he hated to admit it, he knew what had been clouding his judgement. An emotion he had never experienced before, and now knew deserved being called the ugliest of emotions, that of jealousy. His thinking with regard to Rebecca had become irrational – at least that was the conclusion he had, after much heart searching, eventually reached. And now that he was thinking more clearly, he felt ashamed of his overreaction. How arrogant it had been to resent so angrily – after only one day together – Rebecca's consternation when he'd suggested visiting her in Southend. No matter that for those hours he'd felt closer to her than to anyone else in his life, that holding her in his arms had been a revelation. He had no claims on her, none at all. And as the days passed, David realised that his instinctive assumption that there was someone else was just that – instinct. He had no basis for such a suspicion. There could be other perfectly legitimate reasons why Rebecca hadn't wanted him to join her. She may have felt she needed to know him better before she introduced him to Ron and Sal. She might, for instance, not have wanted to share her limited time with them, which was quite understandable. And could it be simply that he had assumed too much? That her urgency for meeting again hadn't matched his?

And this morning, unable to concentrate even on his morning paper, he'd decided that he'd been wrong not to write, flung it aside, and given in to an overwhelming compulsion to see her again. Now, standing just inside the doorway, David scanned the shop floor before him, searching among the neatly dressed assistants serving on the counters. But there was no sign of flame-coloured hair, and he began to stride quickly down the aisles and through the racks of clothes, only to arrive back at the entrance in frustration. He glanced at his watch. Could she be on her break? And so he waited, browsing impatiently around the menswear section, and then turning, David suddenly saw her. She was walking towards a women's knitwear counter a short distance from him, and even in her blue uniform, she was just as striking, just as lovely. Her expression was slightly strained and David felt a sudden stab of guilt. Was she thinking of him, upset and wondering why he hadn't been in touch? God, what a fool he'd been. David waited until Rebecca was back behind her counter, and then threaded his way through clusters of people until he was standing before her. Rebecca, who had bent down to retrieve stock, straightened, and David saw her eyes widen with recognition and delight and then their words collided. "David! What are you doing here?" and "I thought I'd surprise you!"

Rebecca, whose heart had somersaulted at the shock of seeing him, tore her gaze away to serve an impatient elderly woman, who wanted her to measure a particular jumper. Two other customers were now waiting, and David hovered for a while, then realised that his presence was causing awkwardness. When at last she was able to speak to him again, he leaned over the counter and whispered, "I've booked into that hotel you mentioned. Okay if I pick you up for dinner at seven-thirty?" Rebecca's nod and the glow in her eyes were all he needed, and with one last lingering glance, David threaded his way through the crowds and out of the store.

Rebecca, hardly able to believe that David had actually come into the store to find her, automatically did her job, but her mind was racing with questions. Why hadn't he written? Even more crucial – what should she wear? The same outfit she'd worn to go out with Guy? It was certainly the most "dressy" thing she could think of. And she'd loved the feel of the silky fabric against her skin. She also knew how seductive it was, and suddenly that became desperately important. Tonight she wanted him to see her purely as a woman, not as a young mother. But then, that outfit hadn't brought her much luck last time. Rebecca dismissed the thought as being silly and superstitious. Besides, she certainly couldn't afford to buy anything new, even if there had been time.

"You're looking pleased with yourself!" Sylvia said, when later they met in the ladies' cloakroom. Rebecca glanced sharply at her, but Sylvia was

413

actually smiling, something she was beginning to do more and more.

"I'm being taken out to dinner at the North Stafford, at least that's where I think it is," Rebecca said.

Sylvia shook her head. "Too posh for the likes of us." She glanced at Rebecca. "I shouldn't think you'd need to worry though – not with the way you speak."

"It's only because I was evacuated," Rebecca told her. "I'm an East Ender, don't forget."

"Did you ever see any of those Pearly Kings and Queens? I've seen them on the films."

"A few times, yes."

"I'd love to go to London," Sylvia said, her voice envious. It constantly amazed Rebecca how many people in the area had never visited their country's capital. It's so parochial up here, she thought, and yet that was part of its charm. The people, despite often leading quite non-adventurous lives, were so very warm and genuine. And, Rebecca thought suddenly, having lived through two World Wars, all most of them want is probably just to be able to lead a quiet, safe life.

"Why don't you?" she said. "You could have a holiday there. There are some quite cheap places to stay."

Sylvia looked doubtful, then said, "I suppose we could go for Wakes week. I mean there's nothing to say you've always got to go to Blackpool or Rhyl, is there?"

"Exactly." Rebecca finished drying her hands and turned to leave. Well, that was actually a normal

414

conversation, she thought to herself – clever David! And the thought of his name brought with it a warm glow at the thought of the evening ahead.

David, meanwhile, relaxing on the double bed in a spacious bedroom at the first class hotel Rebecca had recommended, was equally full of anticipation. Tonight was their first real date, and he was planning to make it a romantic one.

40

The imposing North Stafford Hotel was built in the Victorian style and, with a large statue of the famous Josiah Wedgwood dominating its frontage, was the first building anyone saw when arriving at the main railway station. Extensively used by prosperous local businessmen and factory owners, it had a well-deserved reputation for excellence. Visitors were also frequent from overseas, travelling to Stoke-on-Trent for meetings with the local china manufacturers, or for trade exhibitions. Rebecca had often wanted to go inside – even a glimpse of the reception area hinted at luxury – and so it was with a growing sense of excitement that she waited while David first locked his car, and then ushered her through its main doors, and into the Cocktail Bar.

"What would you like to drink?" he said, once they were seated.

"I'll have an orange juice, please."

David looked quizzically at her, and a few minutes later returned to their table with their drinks, then settled back in his chair to sip his gin and tonic. "I don't know about you, but I'm starving."

"Me too."

"We'll just have one drink then, and go through

to the restaurant. You're not feeling tired after your long day?"

She shook her head. "Coming here has given me a new lease of life!" David gazed thoughtfully at her. From what he knew of her background, Rebecca's experience of the finer things of life would have been distressingly limited. And suddenly he desperately wanted to be the one to show her such things, to share in her delight and appreciation. When they left to go into the restaurant, he took her hand – so cool and slender – into his own. How perfectly it seemed to fit and David, although familiar to such surroundings, found himself looking at the elegant restaurant and trying to imagine how impressive it would be to someone like Rebecca. It was opulent yet tasteful and already there was a buzz of conversation from the many occupied tables. The Head Waiter led their way to a quiet table in one corner, and again, as she had that time with Guy, Rebecca enjoyed having her chair pulled out and her starched napkin unfolded and placed on her lap.

"Right, let's get the serious stuff over then!" David said briskly, as they opened the menus, and after a few moments Rebecca asked, "What's pâté?"

"A sort of posh meat paste," David grinned. "Only usually rather good. They'll serve it with warm toast."

"Oh, I fancy that!" She smiled back at him. "What starter are you having?"

"The same," he said promptly. "What about your main course?"

"I don't know. I'd really like to try something I wouldn't have at home."

"Do you like fish?"

She nodded. "I've never had sole, though."

"It's nice and light," he told her, "but if you go for that, I'll ask them to fillet it for you. You don't fancy the beef?"

Rebecca shook her head. "Grace is cooking roast beef for dinner tomorrow." She glanced up at him. "You're invited by the way, and I promise you her Yorkshires are out of this world!"

"Sold!" He grinned, then hesitated. "You're talking about lunchtime, I suppose?" Rebecca felt the colour rise in her cheeks. Of course, people like David would call it lunch. "Yes," she said with some embarrassment.

Eventually, David decided to order the same as Rebecca, and then as soon as their order had been given, the wine waiter was at his elbow. David looked across at Rebecca. She may not have dined out at many, if any, restaurants like this, but having worked and lived in a pub, she might have definite preferences. "White, I think," he said. "Do you have a favourite?"

"I never touch alcohol," she told him, and there was such finality in her tone that David, slightly taken aback, didn't pursue the matter, merely ordering his own wine and a jug of water.

Vastly relieved that, unlike Guy, he hadn't tried to persuade her, Rebecca gazed around the room, admiring the rich texture of the curtains, the high ceilings with their deep and ornate cornices, the elegant lighting, the atmosphere of good food and comfortable living. She turned to face David, and

418

saw the amusement in his eyes. But his expression wasn't patronising – it was warm and gentle. For a moment, the breath caught in her throat, and when David reached out a hand, she eagerly slipped her fingers into his. "I haven't told you yet just how beautiful you look," he whispered. His gaze swept down her throat to the swell of her breasts, their alluring cleavage revealed by her black lace evening blouse. "Your skin is amazingly white," he said huskily, "I don't think I'll be able to concentrate on the meal at all!"

Rebecca smiled across at him, the touch of his skin on hers, the sensation she'd felt as their hands touched, his compliment all adding to her delight in the evening. He's wonderful, she thought suddenly, and there flashed into her mind an image of the sheer joy that had swept over her when earlier that afternoon, she'd first seen him standing before her in the store. But then their starter arrived, and as their meal progressed, they talked easily, each interested in finding out even more about the other. David told her of how much he liked the hospital where he was working, although it was quite possible in the future he might move elsewhere. "I mean to be a consultant by the time I'm forty," he told her. "I warn you, I'm fiercely ambitious."

"I would have liked the chance to be," she said in a wistful tone.

"But you tell me you're thinking of going to night school?"

"Yes. I've got an awful lot of catching up to do."

They became silent, as a waiter poured their

coffee. Although David offered, Rebecca had refused a liqueur, and David teased her, saying, "At least you're not an expensive date!" But Rebecca's answering smile had been forced, and as David sipped his brandy, he looked at her thoughtfully, his professional acumen detecting that there was an issue here. Some trauma with alcohol abuse in her childhood perhaps? Or maybe an unfortunate experience she'd had? However, when the waiter left, he simply returned to their topic of conversation.

"Rebecca, never make the mistake of confusing education with intelligence," he told her. "Believe me, I know a lot of boffins who are useless when it comes to daily living or relationships. And in my work I've come to realise that the most important thing is character." He leaned forward earnestly. "It's no mean feat you know, to decide to keep your child, to have to rely on your own reserves of strength. And it took initiative to first seek out what had happened to Ian, and then to come back up here to try and come to terms with your loss. What you have, my darling, is courage, and that is something to be very proud of."

"Thank you," Rebecca said softly, loving his endearment. And his words did make her feel better. Although they didn't alter the fact that there was a large gulf between them, both in education and background. But she pushed such doubts to the back of her mind. For now it was enough just to enjoy being with him in this lovely hotel.

However, later she found herself fighting dismay,

panic and disillusionment, because David said when they stood up to leave, "That was a smashing meal, and did I tell you I've got a double room? It's a lovely big one, well furnished too."

Walking before him out of the restaurant, Rebecca's whole body was tense, her throat closing with angry tears. She couldn't believe it was all happening again! But then she realised it had simply been a comment, because David, without any hesitation, led the way outside the hotel to where his car was parked. Overwhelmed with relief and euphoria, Rebecca managed to regain her composure, and caught at his arm. "Let's walk, it'll only take a few minutes, and it's a lovely night."

Holding hands they walked slowly along the quiet streets in the soft night air, and although once David kissed her, he said ruefully, "I think I'm a bit old for street corners!" She laughed, hoping that Grace would already have gone to bed, and was relieved when they drew near to the house to see a light in the front bedroom window. Quietly, she unlocked the door, and closed it behind them, then led the way into the front room, where almost before she could turn, David was drawing her to him, his mouth coming down to meet her own willing one with a rough urgency.

"You've driven me mad all evening," he said huskily, "I've been longing to do this," and before she could stop him, swiftly bent to touch his lips to the soft whiteness of her breasts. And suddenly she didn't want him to stop, and began stroking his dark hair, holding his head closer to her, exulting at his almost reverent kisses on her bare skin. As David's fingers began to move aside the lace of her blouse, his hand searching, probing, caressing, she arched her back until he was holding her full breast and then he was kissing her again, first on her exposed nipple, and then her mouth, his tongue searching hers. For several long moments, they remained entwined, kissing, loving, with David's hands moving disturbingly over her body. And then he suddenly pulled away, his breath ragged. Together they went to sit on the sofa, where Rebecca, in turmoil at the intensity of their passion, began in panic to re-fasten her blouse.

When she turned to him, he kissed her again, but this time David's lips were gentle. "I'm sorry, I don't know what got into me!" Then he gazed into her eyes, his expression intense. "Rebecca, I don't want you to think that because of what's happened in the past, that I have little or no respect for you. It's just that," he ran a hand through his hair, "you're so bloody beautiful, it's enough to drive a man wild." But even as he kissed her again, Rebecca's mind was frantically seizing on his earlier words. What did he mean – "*what's happened to you in the past?*" Was he talking about Ian, about her being an unmarried mother? Or had Guy, despite her threat, boasted about that night at the hotel? After all, he would never have dreamed that she'd become involved with David, or even see him again. Had Guy spread his poison, as he'd threatened to? She'd kept her part of the bargain, but had he kept his? I don't trust him an inch, she thought with bitterness!

David, seeing the anxiety flickering in her eyes, wondered why his words had upset her. "What's the matter?"

"Nothing . . . I . . ."

"Rebecca, what I meant was that despite what just happened, you can trust me. I've no wish to bring any more trouble into your life."

"Oh, I see." With a sigh of relief, she snuggled against him. But David, even as he held Rebecca close against him, felt puzzled. What else could she have thought he meant by mentioning her past, except that he'd never risk making her pregnant? Then the thought struck him, both unwelcome and bringing with it a stab of jealousy. Could it be that there had been someone else since Ian?

The following morning, the household was in a frenzy of activity as Grace bustled about and then, from the recesses of a drawer, brought out a white damask tablecloth and napkins. "A wedding present," she said, and proceeded to put up the ironing board.

"I'll do that," Rebecca said quickly, and added, "you don't need to go to all this trouble, Grace."

"Oh, yes I do! I've no qualms about my cooking, but we do know how to do things properly in the Potteries, you know. And if I'm entertaining a doctor, it's being done right!"

One glance at Grace's determined expression made Rebecca enter into the spirit of things, giving the cutlery an extra rub, and going into the garden to return with some roses for the table. Again, Grace bent down to one of the cupboards in the sideboard and emerged in triumph with a glass-and-chrome rose bowl. "Give it a quick wash," she said, "it hasn't been used for a bit."

And when David arrived, after a relaxing morning in the hotel lounge with the Sunday papers, it was to be greeted by an excited Anna, the appetising aroma of meat roasting, and a warm welcome. "Would you like a glass of sherry?" Grace asked almost immediately, having checked there was some remaining in the bottle from the previous Christmas.

"That would be very nice, Grace, thank you." After she'd gone, David leaned forward to Rebecca. "I hope I haven't put her out."

"She's loving it," Rebecca whispered. "But I warn you, I'll expect you to help me with the washing-up afterwards."

"Good chance to be alone," he grinned. "A kitchen can be a romantic place – close proximity and all that."

She laughed, and then Anna claimed his attention, wanting to show her attempts to write the alphabet. The day was an outstanding success, with David genuinely appreciative of the food. As he'd hoped, there were several intimate moments with Rebecca in the kitchen, and afterwards they took Anna to the swings, and then later wandered around the park alone, linking hands, stealing kisses in isolated spots, and just talking.

"Another time," he said, "we could go out for the day, perhaps to the pool at Trentham or something."

He paused and looked down at her. "You do want me to come again?"

"What do you think?"

Over the next couple of months, David came to see Rebecca whenever he could, sometimes staying overnight at the North Stafford, occasionally driving to spend just Sunday with her. And Grace, on the sidelines, watching their relationship blossom, saw Rebecca become more relaxed with him, happiness shining from her eyes. Anna too was happy to see "Uncle David", who listened with such interest to her chatter, and patiently taught her to play draughts.

But letters from Southend still continued to arrive. Grace noticed how reflective Rebecca was after reading them, often staring into space afterwards, her expression one of perplexity. "Johnny's doing really well," she said once. "Apparently, he's their best salesman."

"Good," Grace said, as her nimble fingers cast on for a new cardigan for Anna. "Does he see much of Ron and Sal?"

Rebecca nodded. "He says they're fine. Oh, and his mother went round to see them. She and Sal have started to go to the pictures together." She smiled. "Ron only likes westerns."

Grace laughed. "That was Jim all over. He used to like Randolph Scott." She glanced over at Rebecca. "Is he still talking of coming up?"

Rebecca nodded. "The third week in September."

Grace hesitated. Dare she say it? "How will David feel about that?" Her tone was gentle, but she put down her knitting, every nerve end taut as she waited for an answer.

And it didn't come immediately. For the simple reason that Rebecca didn't know what to say. Already it was almost the end of August, and she had never mentioned Johnny to David. So she just said, "I haven't worked that out yet."

Grace compressed her lips. She couldn't understand what Rebecca was up to. Surely she wasn't the sort of girl to two-time a man? Either of them for that matter! Grace had grown fond of David, and this Johnny looked thoroughly decent too. I only hope you know what you're doing, young lady, she thought grimly. Because I don't think David is a man who would stand for any shenanigans.

41

As the days and weeks passed, with Johnny's visit ever more imminent, Rebecca found herself in a constant state of anxiety and confusion. Although David was on duty that particular weekend, he was certain to find out about Johnny. Anna was bound to chatter about it, might even show David any present Johnny had brought. Rebecca felt that realistically she had only two choices. She could tell Johnny not to come – explaining that there was no future for them after all, that her relationship with David was serious. But then she didn't know that, did she? She knew how she felt – she was in love with him. Deeply, passionately in love. But even in their most intimate moments, he'd never once told her he loved her. Of course, they had only been together for a few months and in normal circumstances, that wouldn't have been a problem. Or, she could simply tell David the truth. But Rebecca was fearful of the consequences. Wouldn't any man, if his girlfriend told him that another man wanted to marry her and soon, feel that he was being given some sort of ultimatum? She could ruin everything.

Sometimes she was sorely tempted to confide in Grace, to ask her advice. Rebecca knew that the older woman was bewildered about the situation, it was obvious by her carefully closed expression whenever Johnny's name was mentioned. But to do that would be disloyal to Sal, and Rebecca wished now that she'd been open with both women.

Katie was the only one to know the full story, and it was to her that Rebecca poured out her worries, but Katie had no answer, either. "*I don't know what to advise you,*" she wrote. "*Johnny sounds a sweetie, and David, of course, is gorgeous. But you're right to worry that you could lose both, and it would be idiocy to turn Johnny down until you know David's intentions. You are a lucky devil having two men on the go. And here's me without a single one! To be honest, I've been feeling really homesick lately. It would have been different if I'd met someone, but although I'm lucky to have Conor and Maura nearby, I not only miss Mammy and Da, but also Dublin. The West End is all very well, but to me it can't compare with Grafton or O'Connell Street!*"

And so Rebecca continued to wrestle alone with her problem, and then David made a suggestion that both surprised and delighted her. "It's my mother's birthday next weekend," he told her. "Do you think Grace would look after Anna? Just for the Sunday?"

"I'm sure she would," Rebecca said, her spirits soaring. "You mean—"

"Yes, I've been thinking of taking you to Lichfield – this seems the ideal opportunity. I always go on her birthday, I think it would be a hanging offence if I didn't!" He grinned down at her as they sat on the back seat of the car. Over the summer, David had discovered a quiet spot at the side of a country road only a few miles out of the city. With the car pulled on to the grass verge and parked beneath overhanging branches it had become a sort of refuge for them, provided them with the privacy they desperately needed.

Now, with the rain pattering gently on the roof, Rebecca, thrilled at the prospect, said, "I'd love to come."

"She usually has a bit of a party – a few friends for lunch, that sort of thing," he explained.

"What do your parents know about me?"

David saw the apprehension in her eyes, and said reassuringly, "Absolutely nothing."

She gazed at him in bewilderment, "But—"

He placed a finger gently on her lips. "Shush now, sweetheart. There's no need to worry." He wound down the side window of the car slightly, and taking a silver case from his inside jacket pocket, extracted a Players cigarette, lit it with his matching lighter, and exhaled. "I've given this some deep thought," he said. "I've learned a lot about human nature these past few years – I've never believed that all knowledge is contained in textbooks. And the simple fact is that people often react instinctively to expectation. I haven't until now told my parents that I've even met you. And that's because I knew," he said, "that the questions would come." David flicked the ash from his cigarette out of the window. "And," he added, "I didn't want to have to answer them."

Astounded, Rebecca could only stare at him. Was he telling her that he was ashamed of her past, that he wanted to conceal it? Because if so, no matter how much she loved him, nothing in this world would make her tell lies, or make her deny Anna's existence. David, glancing at her, saw the flash of anger in her eyes and said quickly, "No, don't get me wrong. Hear me out – please?"

Tensely, Rebecca gave a slight nod, and he said, "When I phone my mother towards the end of next week, I shall simply tell her that I'd like to bring someone with me, and her name is Rebecca. Nothing else." Seeing her wary expression, and even slight alarm, he explained, "I want my parents to meet and welcome you in the same way they would anyone. No preconceived ideas, no anxieties. They can always learn about Anna later."

She continued staring at him, as she tried to sort out her feelings. She understood what he was trying to achieve, but . . . "I can't see how that would work," she said, "because I'm bound to be asked questions, either by your parents or even other people. For instance, how will I explain my living with Grace? Or why I moved up to the Potteries in the first place? I'd just get in a mess trying to avoid the truth, and I couldn't just blurt it all out, about Anna and everything, because that would be unfair on your parents."

He gazed at her ruefully. "You see what you do? You cloud even my reason, and that's my stock-in-trade!" He took her hand in his, gently stroking each finger in turn. "You're absolutely right, it was a stupid idea. It's just that I desperately want them to see you as the lovely girl you are, not to judge you before you even arrive."

Rebecca fell silent, already a worrying image building in her mind of these unknown people. One was a barrister who, David told her, was now a KC, while the other was a teacher, although apart from during the war, apparently she'd never worked since she married. I am what I am, she thought with bitterness. Soiled goods, a barmaid, an unmarried mother who's now working in a shop. Hardly the sort of girl they would have chosen for their only son. But didn't every mother view her son's girlfriend as a prospective daughter-in-law? And judge her accordingly? Suddenly, Rebecca desperately wanted, as David had suggested, for his parents to have an open mind when they met her. "I've changed my mind," she said suddenly. "I think we should do it your way. I'll just have to – what's that word Jane Austen uses? Try to dissemble, that's it! But," she turned to him, "will you promise me that you *will* tell them, and sooner rather than later?"

He gazed down at her, and laughed. "You never cease to surprise me. Jane Austen, indeed!"

"And why not?" she countered. "Public libraries have shone light into many working-class minds. Haven't you ever read *How Green was my Valley*?"

"Of course I have, touchy!" He put a finger under her chin, lifted it and gazed intently into her eyes. "Just you enrol for those evening classes, and as soon as possible."

"I will. In the meantime, you haven't answered my question. Will you promise to tell your parents – at the right time?"

"I promise." He drew her into his arms. "Enough

431

of talking, let's make the most of what time we have left."

The moment David departed for Rugby, Rebecca's thoughts became frantic. I'll have to buy a new frock, she thought, something smart. It was absolutely crucial that she made a good impression not only on David's parents but also their friends.

"Go to Exclusive Gowns," Grace advised. "I've never been in myself, but they have lovely things in the window. And at least clothes rationing has finished."

"I bet they're expensive, though."

"You've got a bit put by, haven't you?" Grace knew that Rebecca had opened a Penny Savings Account at the Post Office, and the girl was hardly a spendthrift.

"Yes, but—"

"Then use it," Grace said briskly. "You're only young once, and in any case, you'll need to hold your own among all those posh folk!" Rebecca grimaced inwardly. That was what was bothering her.

A few days later, with Anna clinging to her hand, Rebecca stood hesitantly before the exclusive fashion shop she'd often passed, and then pushed open the glass door. The interior, any sound muted by its red carpet, was brightly lit by two glass chandeliers. With a velvet-covered Queen Anne chair on one side, and the walls lined with racks of beautiful clothes, the atmosphere was redolent with luxury. Feeling some-what ill-at-ease, Rebecca stood just inside the entrance, and almost immediately a slim woman,

432

elegant in a black dress and pearls, appeared from the back of the shop, and walked towards her. "Good morning. Can I be of assistance?"

"Could you show me some dresses in my size, please? I'm a thirty-six." The woman's glance swept discerningly over Rebecca's figure, and she nodded. "Yes, of course. What sort of dress were you looking for?"

Rebecca hesitated. "Something simple, yet smart."

The owner of the shop – Rebecca had decided she was much too superior to be simply an employee – began flicking through some of the hangers. "Is it for a special occasion?"

"Yes, a birthday lunch."

"Town or country?"

Rebecca felt puzzled. What difference did it make? "It's in Lichfield."

"Ah, county, then." She took out a dress and draped it against her. "This is very classic, and would suit your colouring." As Rebecca gazed at it doubtfully, she hung it outside the polished fitment. "Or this one?" she took out another dress, and then as Rebecca shook her head, replaced it. "Have you got something definite in mind?"

"Not really, no." What Rebecca wanted to do was to browse through the selection of clothes herself but instinctively knew this would be frowned upon.

"Some things look better on than off! Why not take your little girl into the changing-room, and I'll bring you a selection?" Before Rebecca could protest she found herself whisked into a curtained cubicle, where Anna, overwhelmed by the whole experience, perched wide-eyed on an ivory-painted chair in one corner. Within seconds a number of hangers were passed in to her, and tentatively Rebecca glanced at the price of one. Her hand went up to her mouth in horror. She couldn't pay all that! Not just for a dress! No wonder they didn't put the prices in the window! I'd better leave, she thought, but then couldn't resist the temptation to at least try them – if only to see if expensive clothes did feel different. The first two didn't appeal at all, and almost relieved, she replaced them on their hangers.

And then she saw it. The dress was white, with a mandarin collar, nipped-in waist and cap sleeves. And threaded through the waist was a black patent belt. Almost with excitement she began to unfasten the buttons, then slipped it over her head. Seconds later, she was gazing into the full-length mirror. The image staring back at her was one more shapely and confident than she'd ever seen before, and suddenly Rebecca wanted that dress more than she had ever wanted anything. With fingers that trembled slightly, she turned over the price tag. It was exactly double the amount she'd been prepared to spend. But, she reasoned with a racing pulse, she already had a pair of patent court shoes, and Betty had a black patent handbag that was almost new! So not having to buy accessories would help. Could she possibly afford it? Rebecca turned again and again before the mirror, admiring the skirt's flare, and whispered, "Does Mummy look pretty in this?"

Anna nodded. "Like a princess." She swung her legs in boredom. "Can we go now?"

"Soon. You've been very good." Rebecca stood for one long moment struggling with her conscience, then took off the dress and replaced it on its hanger. Seconds later she was standing before a small walnut desk at the far end of the shop, where the owner, with a bored expression, was sitting. "I'd like this one," Rebecca said. "Could you put it on one side for me if I pay half now, and then bring the rest in about an hour?"

"Yes, of course." The woman's face brightened. "I was just going to come and see how you were getting on. But," she smiled with condescension, "I think you've chosen well."

I certainly hope so, Rebecca thought, because I feel as guilty as hell!

42

The three graceful spires of Lichfield Cathedral were visible long before they actually reached their destination. "It's the only cathedral in the country with three spires," David told Rebecca. "They're known as The Ladies of the Vale."

"Dr Samuel Johnson was born in Lichfield, wasn't he?" she said.

"He was." David smiled down at her. "And you're the one who's always saying that you're uneducated!"

"I only know because Grace told me!"

"You're too honest for your own good!" David swung the car into a long drive, and Rebecca caught her breath as she saw the gabled house, surrounded by well-tended lawns and flower borders. Fleetingly there came into her mind an image of her own childhood home, the mean terrace house in a narrow East End street, the often barefooted children playing hopscotch, the women standing with arms crossed over their pinafores gossiping. She came from a different world.

"Here we are!" David drew to a halt, and turned to look at her. "I'll say it again, sweetheart. You look absolutely wonderful. I don't know where you found that dress, but you'll outshine every other woman here."

Rebecca, her stomach churning with nerves, smiled gratefully at him, and then they were inside the wide oak-blocked hall, an old settle on one side, a gleaming side table on the other, on which a Wedgwood vase of peach roses gave off a delicate scent. There was the muted sound of voices and laughter coming from a partly open door on the right, and David gave her an encouraging smile. For a few seconds they stood unnoticed inside the room, and then from a small group of people, a slightly-built and exquisitely dressed woman came forward, her face alight with welcome.

"David darling!" She leaned up to accept his kiss on her cheek.

"Happy birthday, Mum!" He gazed down at her with affection and gave her a beribboned package. "New dress?"

"A present from your father." Celia Knight turned swiftly. "And you must be Rebecca." Hazel eyes looked keenly into green just long enough not to be impolite, then, "Welcome, my dear. You must come and meet Richard." As she swept away, David took Rebecca's hand, and they followed the small, but determined figure, until she touched the sleeve of a well-built man who had his back to them. He turned, saw David, and his face creased into a delighted grin.

"David. So glad you could make it."

"Now would I dare to miss?" The two men smiled at each other, their affection obvious. "May I introduce Rebecca?" David said, ushering her forward.

437

"An absolute pleasure." Richard Knight smiled down at her, but not before Rebecca had seen the appreciation in his eyes. One bonus point for the dress, she thought.

"It's Rebecca's first visit to Lichfield," David said.

"Really?" David's mother turned to her. "So, where are you from, Rebecca?"

"I live in Stoke-on-Trent."

"Ah, the Potteries – such a fascinating place. We have friends there, don't we, Richard?"

"We certainly do. But you haven't got a drink. What would you like, Rebecca?"

"A soft drink, please. Just a lemonade or something."

"An orange juice?"

She nodded, "That would be lovely."

"I'll come and get my own," David said, and followed his father to where an array of drinks was displayed on a mahogany sideboard.

"This is a lovely room, Mrs Knight." It was the most impressive sitting-room Rebecca had ever seen. Not only because of its length, but also its graceful proportions. With daylight streaming in from the leaded bay windows at the front, and the French windows leading on to a terrace at the back, the room, even with a sprinkling of guests, didn't seem crowded.

"Do you like it?" David's mother said, with a pleased smile, and Rebecca looked at the beamed ceiling and massive carved fireplace, and wondered how anyone could not.

"Oh yes," she said, "very much."

There was a short silence, then Celia said, "How long have you known David? Forgive me for asking, but he tells us absolutely nothing about his private life." She smiled to take out any sting from her words. "Typical of sons, I believe."

Rebecca smiled and said, "I met him a couple of years ago at a hospital party in London, and then we met by chance at Trentham Gardens a few months ago. Do you know it?"

"Of course. A lovely place." She turned as her husband and son joined them.

"Here we are." Richard Knight gave Rebecca her drink, and then with a guilty look over his shoulder, murmured to his wife, "We'd better circulate a bit. Everything organised in the kitchen?"

She nodded. "But you're right. Catch up with you later, Rebecca."

Left on their own, David grinned. "Had the third degree yet?"

"I think it was beginning."

"Don't take any notice of Mum, she's a good sort really. Just very protective of her only chick."

"I've never thought of you as a clucking chicken," she laughed.

"And thank goodness for that! Not exactly a manly, romantic image." Their eyes met, and he whispered, "I wish we could scoot out of here and be alone."

"Ssh," she said in alarm, "someone will hear you."

"I don't care if they do. They'd only be jealous." He leaned forward and kissed her lightly on the cheek. "I couldn't help that."

Rebecca, feeling embarrassed glanced quickly around, hoping no one had noticed, and stared straight into the eyes of David's mother, who smiled, but not before Rebecca had seen the thoughtful look in her eyes.

Lunch, in a rather formal dining-room, was a merry affair, its smooth efficiency achieved by the Knights' daily help, cheerfully carrying in steaming dishes, and unobtrusively whisking away used plates. Rebecca, to her relief, was sitting next to David, who was at his mother's right hand while Richard sat at the opposite end of the oblong table. The rest of the guests, obviously part of an established social circle, were middle-aged couples; the men chatting about golf, the women about holidays, clothes and the latest scandal. Much of the conversation had little relevance for Rebecca, as she knew nothing about golf, and didn't know any of the people whose names were mentioned. But she listened with a smile, her gaze flickering around the animated faces, and gradually she began to relax, enjoying the delicious food, and the novel experience of being in such a beautiful house. She also found it fascinating to see David in his home environment, noticing how socially at ease he was. It must be something that private education gives people she thought, now aware that David's school in Rugby was a famous public one.

"And what do you do, Rebecca?" Startled, she looked up from her roast lamb. A middle-aged man with a thin moustache, who was sitting on her other side, turned to her. "Are you also a member of the medical world?"

Rebecca hesitated and then gave the answer she'd mentally rehearsed. "No," she said brightly, "I'm interested in fashion – I'm with Marks & Spencer."

"Really!" he turned to a woman on his left. "Damn good company to work for, according to your Neville."

"That's right," she nodded, her mouth full of food, then a few seconds later, added, "you may know him, he's the Area Manager."

Rebecca smiled and shook her head. "No, I'm afraid our paths haven't crossed."

"Well, of course they wouldn't, Staffordshire isn't in his area. Honestly, Binkie, your knowledge of geography is abysmal!"

Not the least perturbed, she twinkled up at her husband. "Oh, silly me!"

"Are you long-standing friends of the Knights?" Rebecca hurriedly changed the subject.

"Oh Lord yes, we've known them for yonks. John was at school with Richard. They were both at Rugby, as David was."

"And *he's* a dark horse," a man sitting opposite Rebecca said. "Never a glimpse of his love life for years, and then he turns up with a stunner like you in tow."

"You make her sound like a filly," John remarked, and poured Binkie another glass of wine. "Everything's horses to Harry," she said. "Do you ride, Rebecca?"

"No, I never have."

Then, as conversation turned elsewhere, Rebecca felt David's foot nudge against hers. She turned to

441

meet his amused gaze. "Coping all right?" he whispered.

"Fine." Beneath the hum of conversation, she murmured, "Who's the blonde sitting near your father, she keeps looking daggers at me."

"Oops! I was hoping you wouldn't notice. She, my love, is the girl who's been trying to nab me for years."

"Really?" Rebecca turned and met hostile blue eyes. "I see what you mean."

"Not a chance – I only like redheads!" He grinned, then turned away as his mother claimed his attention.

Later, after the Knights had said goodbye to the last remaining guest, Rebecca offered to help in the kitchen, but Celia shook her head. "No, Mrs Dean and I can manage. Let David show you the garden, it's lovely at the moment." And it was. The lawn was velvet-smooth and the herbaceous borders a riot of colour. There was a graceful willow, and a cluster of fruit trees, one heavily laden with pears. How Grace would love this, Rebecca thought. Hand-in-hand, she and David walked slowly, pausing at times as he pointed out a particular bloom.

"You had a very privileged childhood," she said, "growing up in a place like this."

"I know."

"You do realise, don't you, just how different our backgrounds are?"

"I'll forgive you for yours, if you'll forgive me for mine?" David smiled down at her, and then said, "You're not worried about it, are you? You were perfect in there. Every man in the room envied me."

Rebecca smiled, and wished she could just enjoy the summer, being with David, loving him, without all this anxiety about the future. But with Johnny's ultimatum of Christmas hanging over her, she desperately needed to know if there was the slightest chance of David proposing to her. Was she expecting too much? Was it too soon? And yet all her instincts told her that he was as crazy about her as she was about him. And if he wasn't serious about her, then why had he treated her with such respect? Not once, despite their passion for each other, had David ever overstepped the boundaries.

But once they were back indoors, where tea was being served, the difficult questions, as Rebecca had known they would, began. They were relaxing in the sitting-room, Richard contentedly enjoying his pipe, Celia looking from her son to his girlfriend with undisguised curiosity.

"Tell us about yourself, Rebecca," she said. "This son of mine has told us nothing. For instance, you say you met in London?"

Rebecca, sitting by David on a chintz-covered sofa, felt him tense slightly. But Celia's gaze was friendly – interested and curious; there was warmth in her eyes, and encouraged, Rebecca said, "Yes. I was born there."

"Really? Richard knows London quite well, as it happens. In fact he's going down there this week. Which part?"

"Stepney."

Richard glanced at his wife. "It's in the East End."

"That suffered a lot in the Blitz, didn't it?" Celia said with a frown.

"That's right, Mum." David told her. "In fact Rebecca's parents were both killed in it. She lost her home as well."

Celia leaned forward, her eyes full of sympathy. "Oh, I'm so sorry, my dear."

"I was an evacuee at the time," Rebecca explained, even now finding it difficult to talk of the tragedy. "In Wales – I was there for five years."

"Was it all right? Were the people good to you?" Celia's voice was full of concern.

"They were fine," Rebecca said, and added honestly, "at least I think they did their duty as they saw it. Mr Parry was a solicitor, and a lay preacher at the local chapel. But they were good people in their way. After all, they didn't ask to have a strange girl foisted on them."

"And what brought you up to the Potteries?" Richard asked.

Rebecca glanced at David, and he saw the plea in her eyes. His gaze searched hers, and she nodded slightly. What was the point of avoiding it? The truth would come out sooner or later.

But David intervened before she could speak. "I think it's my place to answer that question," he said quietly. "Rebecca lives with Grace Beresford, whose son and husband were killed in the Bolton Football disaster. Rebecca was engaged to her son, Ian, who was a teacher."

Richard put down his pipe and leaned forward,

his face sombre. "That must have been such a blow. And so you moved up to be with his mother? But how did you meet someone from the Potteries?"

"When I came back to London after the war ended, my aunt and uncle offered me a home at their pub, the Unicorn," Rebecca explained. "I was serving behind the bar, and Ian came in looking for an old army pal."

There was a short silence, then Celia said, "It must have been terrible for you, and for his mother. Life doesn't seem to have treated you very well so far, Rebecca."

Richard was saying little, and Rebecca couldn't read his expression. But then David, to her surprise, suddenly stood up. "Time we were leaving, I think," he said and bending down, kissed his mother on the cheek. "Don't forget I have to take Rebecca home and then drive to Rugby. It was a lovely birthday lunch. Glad you liked the silk scarf."

"A perfect choice," Celia said, "and thank you, Rebecca, for the chocolates. It's been lovely to meet you."

"You too," Rebecca smiled. "I've had a lovely time."

Minutes later, they were leaving the house, going out into the late afternoon's sunlight, and within seconds had driven away. Both were quiet for the first couple of miles, then Rebecca said in a tight voice, "You obviously wanted to leave before I told them about Anna!"

"Dissemination, that's all. The human brain can process a series of shocks much better one at a time.

445

This way, by the time they find out, Mum and Dad will have become reconciled to—"

He stopped speaking suddenly, but Rebecca finished his sentence with bitterness, "The fact that I'm a girl from an East End pub?"

David swore under his breath and covered her hand with his own. "I didn't mean it like that."

"It's true, though, isn't it? In their world, your ideal girlfriend would be someone from the same background as themselves."

"I can't deny it. But life isn't always perfect, is it? And honestly, Rebecca, I'm handling this in the best possible way."

"Of course, I forgot. You know all about human nature!"

"Bloody hell!" David turned the steering wheel sharply and veered off the country road to pull on to a grass verge. He turned to face her, "What are we arguing about, for heaven's sake?"

"I'm not arguing."

"Well, you're upset about something." David ran his fingers through his hair in exasperation. "I thought the afternoon went really well."

"It did. It's just that . . ." She looked down. "I suppose putting it into words brought it all back, the bad times, I mean. And then when you so obviously wanted to escape before the truth about Anna came out . . ." she turned back to face him, "it just made me feel that I had something to be ashamed of. And do you know what, David? I'm not! Neither of loving Ian, nor of having Anna!"

He gazed at her in consternation. "I know that –

of course I do! Look," he switched on the ignition. "I've obviously made a mistake. Do you want to go back?"

Rebecca shook her head. "No, that would make the whole thing seem too dramatic. Let's just go home."

43

The Unicorn was, as usual, busy at lunchtime on the following Tuesday and the well-dressed man who came in, had to wait to be served. A few of the customers glanced curiously at him, but he spent his time observing closely his surroundings, and the three people serving behind the bar. Eventually, a military-looking man who was obviously the landlord said, "Yes, sir?"

Richard Knight asked for a gin and tonic. The pub was shabby, as was the area surrounding it, but they both had a vibrant character he could only admire. In his profession as a barrister, Richard had met people from all walks of life, and had learned many years ago not to make snap judgements based on lack of education or poverty. One of the most intelligent men he'd ever met had been a docker, a homegrown philosopher whose reasoning had been equal to many lawyers. And so, it was not with condescension that Richard had entered the Unicorn's doors, yet he had to admit that Celia's anxiety was well-founded. It seemed bizarre that the poised young woman who had charmed everyone at the party had emerged from a background like this. Her years in a better household in Wales would have helped, of course, but even so . . . Richard glanced with speculation at one of the barmaids, a blonde sour-faced girl he'd heard someone call Gloria. The other was a heavily made-up brunette at the other end of the bar. He leaned forward, "Excuse me, I wonder if you knew a girl who used to live here? Rebecca?"

Gloria's eyes narrowed as she took in the affluence of the man standing before her. That suit never came off the market! "Who wants ter know?"

Richard hesitated. "She's a friend of my son's," he said, "and was telling me about this place recently. Her aunt and uncle used to run it, didn't they?"

"Ron and Sal. Yes, they did." Gloria's eyes narrowed. Trust that jammy cow to come up with a rich boyfriend! Or was this gent lying? It was more than likely he was her "sugar daddy".

"They moved to Southend," she told him, "but Rebecca went up North somewhere to live with 'er kid's granny." That's wiped the smile off his face, she thought with glee. "Oh, didn't yer know about that? Mind you, I'm not surprised she kept it quiet, if yer know what I mean!"

"Gloria?" A man shouted, "Me tongue's hangin' out over 'ere!"

Richard, his expression grim, watched her flounce along the bar. Then with one swift movement he drained his glass, turned and walking past a stout red-faced woman sitting in one of the alcoves, left, needing to get outside, to breathe in some fresh air. As he strode along to find a taxi, his thoughts were of Celia and of her shock when he told her what

449

he'd discovered. And you, David, he thought angrily, have some explaining to do.

It was the following day, when the letter arrived. Rebecca picked up the cheap blue envelope from the mat in the hall, and recognising the ill-formed handwriting, frowned. Taking it into the front room, she sat and tore open the envelope. The letter contained only a few lines:

Dear Rebecca,

Just to say that this posh geezer came into the pub today. About 50 with grey hair and a tache. Gloria's behind the bar now – she won't last, miserable cow, we regulars will see to that!

Anyway, she was talking to him and someone sed they heard your name mentioned. Don't know what she told him, but he didn't look too happy when he left. I thought you ought to know.

Hoping this finds you as it leaves me,
Ruby

Rebecca slowly put down the letter, and stared into space. Richard! It couldn't possibly be anyone else! She had no illusions about what Gloria would have told him! She always did have a spiteful streak! But now David's parents were going to think she'd lied to them – or at least concealed the truth. This is all David's fault, she thought with bitterness. If he'd been straightforward instead of all this psychology he's so keen on, then I would have told them about Anna myself. What did he call it – dissemination of facts? Rebecca recalled her mother saying that "*some people are too clever for their own good!*"

I'm going to have to ring him, she thought wildly, try to warn him before his father phones. She glanced at the postmark on the envelope. Ruby, bless her, had posted it the same afternoon. Rebecca guessed that Richard would have returned home late that evening. Her stomach churning with anxiety, she hurried outside to the garden where Anna was digging with a toy trowel. "Look, Mummy, I found a dandelion."

"Oh yes! Come on in, sweetheart, Mummy needs to go and phone someone."

"Can we go to the swings, after?"

Ten minutes later, Rebecca, with her little girl squashed in beside her, was standing inside the nearest public telephone box. She dialled the operator and asked for the number of the hospital where David worked. Once through, Rebecca inserted her money, and as a voice answered, pressed button A. "Could I speak to Dr Knight, please?"

"Please hold the line."

Rebecca crossed her fingers in an agony of impatience. Then to her relief, she heard David's voice. "David? It's Rebecca."

"Rebecca! Are you all right? Is there something wrong?"

In a tense voice, she told him about Ruby's letter. "The man *has* to be your father, I'm sure of it! Have you heard from him?"

There was a short silence. Then David, in a voice tight with anger, said, "Not yet, but I've no doubt

451

I will. Look, Rebecca, I don't want you worrying about this. I'll deal with it."

There was an abrupt click as he replaced the receiver, and Rebecca stared down at the black mouthpiece in bewilderment. What did he mean – don't worry? How could she help it? But then Anna was tugging at her hand, uncomfortable in the confined space, and pushing open the heavy red door, Rebecca took her across to the children's playground.

In the early afternoon, Rebecca was just finishing the ironing, when a knock came at the front door. She opened it to find Jill's mother facing her. "She's driving me mad for Anna to come round," Clare said. "Would that be all right?"

Rebecca turned to her daughter, who was gazing up at her in delight. "Can I go, Mummy?"

"Yes, of course. I'll just get her coat," Rebecca said. She knew better than to ask Clare in. The contact between them was still minimal, if cordial. After arranging to fetch Anna in a couple of hours, Rebecca felt almost a sense of relief, as she watched the two children skip along the pavement. She desperately needed some time alone, time to think – to sort out in her mind the daunting implications of the last few days.

When Rebecca returned from Lichfield, Grace had been eager to know every detail of the house, the garden, the guests and the food. And in relating them, the enormity of the social divide she must cross if she was to have a future with David had become painfully clear to Rebecca. Yes, she'd coped with the lunch party – thanks to the expensive dress – but that had been only for a few hours. If she married David, then she would face all sorts of demanding adjustments. Haven't I had enough challenges and struggles in my life, she thought with despair! She was still seething that Richard had felt it necessary to check on her background! And yet in a way she couldn't blame him. She knew how protective she felt towards Anna, and presumably that carried on no matter how old your children were.

Suddenly Rebecca was too restless to sit. I need to get out, to walk, she thought, if only to stop these thoughts whirling round in my head. And half an hour later, Rebecca was still walking, worrying about what was happening with David and his father, afraid of David's reaction when he found out about Johnny, who was actually due to arrive in a matter of days. And the problem of what decision to make was beginning to make her feel ill. I've only got myself to blame, she thought in despair. She'd been stupid not to tell Sal when Johnny first proposed. And she could have told Grace too, instead of trying to shield them both from anxiety. At least then she would have had someone to confide in, to ask for advice.

Having come out of the top park gates, she began to make her way home and glancing up as she approached St Mary's Church, found her steps faltering as she remembered the Irish priest she'd met on the train. On that first fateful journey up to Stoke, she'd been too full of distress to want to talk to anyone, but she'd never forgotten him. Rebecca knew he was still at St Mary's, because Grace came to whist drives in the church hall. But then she gave a wry smile – she couldn't expect him to give up his time to someone who wasn't one of his parishioners. She wasn't even a Catholic for heaven's sake!

But surely it couldn't do any harm to go inside and sit for a few minutes? She pushed open the studded dark oak door and closed it silently behind her. The interior of the church was dim, apart from suffused light streaming in from an ornate stained-glass window. The central altar, covered by a green silken cloth embroidered with gold thread and some words in Latin, was adorned with brass candlesticks and two vases of flowers. There was no one else in the church, and Rebecca hovered, undecided where to sit, and then walked quietly to a small side altar, where a statue of the Virgin Mary gazed down at her, her expression one of calm compassion. Recalling scenes she'd seen on films, Rebecca put a coin into a stand with a few lighted candles on, and taking a new one from the box below, held it to an existing flame, and then placed it in a holder. Silently she stood, head bowed, and, for the first time in many years, she prayed earnestly for guidance. After a few moments, she turned and sat in a pew for a very long time, so deep in thought that she didn't hear someone approach behind her, then quietly depart. But then later, the soft footfall did disturb her and she turned to gaze into the kindly eyes of Father Flynn. He spoke softly. "Can I be of any help or—"

"I'm not a Catholic, Father."

He smiled. "None of God's children are when

they first come into this world." He gazed down at her. "You're welcome to a cup of tea in the Presbytery if you . . ."

A few minutes later, Rebecca was seated in a cluttered, book-lined study, where a thin, bustling housekeeper brought in a tray of tea. Her gaze flickered curiously over Rebecca, but she said nothing, simply departing and closing the door firmly behind her.

"Now," the priest said, once they had their tea, "why don't you begin at the beginning." And so Rebecca told him the whole story, of her young and tragic life, of the Unicorn, the loss of Ian, of Anna and Grace, and of the dilemma she now faced. "I don't know what to do for the best, Father," she said. "I have to think of Anna's future, too."

"This Johnny sounds a fine young man. Do you love him at all, now?" Rebecca shook her head. "Not in the way I love David, but there is affection between us."

"And you feel that affection could possibly grow into love?"

She hesitated, then gave a slight nod.

"And yet you're saying that you could stand before God and make your vows to Johnny, with another man in your heart? You know, child, you can't manipulate your life. And you certainly shouldn't try to manipulate someone else's."

Rebecca felt the colour rise in her cheeks. "You're saying that I should tell Johnny the truth?"

"At least then it would be his decision as well as yours."

"And David?" she whispered.

"Look into your soul, Rebecca. It's there you will find the answer."

44

Late on Saturday morning, Johnny drew up outside 15, Redwood Avenue, switched off the engine and looked at the neat bay-windowed semi-detached house. So, he thought with both interest and sadness, this was where Ian had been born, had grown up, and left to serve his country. But then, his reverie disturbed by the twitch of a net curtain and Anna's excited wave, Johnny got out of the car, lifted his weekend case out of the boot, and was already inside the gate when the front door opened.

"Johnny!" Rebecca, her eyes alight with welcome stood aside, while Anna beamed up at him.

"Granny's gone to work," she told him, "so Mummy could be here."

"That was very kind of her! Have you got a hug, young miss?" He swept Anna up into his arms and whispered, "I've got a surprise for you in my case." Immediately she wriggled to be put down and ran expectantly into the front room.

"What is it?"

"It wouldn't be a surprise if I told you. Now, close your eyes."

As the little girl obeyed, Johnny flipped the clasp on his case, and delved inside. He gave her a small flat parcel wrapped in brown paper and tied up with string. Anna managed to undo the loosely tied bow, and revealed a box of children's water-paints. "Ooh, thank you!"

"There's a painting book as well!" Johnny gave it to her, and she ran off to fetch a cup of water.

"Wait a minute," Rebecca called, "I'll put some newspaper on the table."

Johnny turned to her. "It's good to see you." He kissed her on the cheek.

"And you too! How was the journey?"

"Long!"

"I bet you're dying for a cup of tea. I'll put the kettle on."

Johnny glanced around the room, and seeing Ian's photograph on the sideboard picked it up. With a sigh, he studied the smiling face of the man who had been his closest friend, the man who had saved his life, and whose own had been cut short in such a senseless way. Then he carefully replaced the photograph, and wandered into the kitchen to chat to Rebecca.

It wasn't until much later, when Anna settled in the back room with her new paints, that Johnny was able to talk to Rebecca alone.

"So," he said, sitting in an armchair in the front room, "now we have a bit of time to ourselves, maybe we can stop catching up on things in Southend, and talk about what really matters. How are you?"

"Fine," Rebecca said hesitantly. "And you?"

"Fine. And before you ask, no, I haven't met

anyone else." Seeing her quizzical look, he laughed. "Okay, I've taken a couple of girls to the pictures, but there was nothing in it, honest!" He looked searchingly at her. "Are you still seeing that doctor chap?"

Rebecca nodded.

"And?" his question was soft.

Rebecca gazed at him, at his friendly, open face, at the young man she knew to be so very decent.

"I need to talk to you, Johnny."

That same afternoon, having managed to get some hours off, David drove from Rugby to Lichfield with grim determination. His father had telephoned just as Rebecca had warned he would, but only to say that he had something to discuss, and could David go over as soon as possible. Which was exactly what David had intended to do, ever since hearing the strain in Rebecca's voice as she'd told him of the letter.

Turning into the circular drive before the house, David locked up his car, and using own key, went through the front door and strode through the wide hall and into the sitting-room. His parents were expecting him. Richard was standing before the huge fireplace with its embroidered fire screen; Celia was perched anxiously on the chintz sofa.

"You made good time," Richard said.

"Would you like some tea?" Celia raised her cheek for her son's kiss.

David straightened up and looked at them both. "I think we can skip the pleasantries."

459

His parents both looked startled. David turned to his father. "What the hell did you mean by going to check up on Rebecca's background?"

Celia glanced frantically at her husband. "I'm afraid that was my idea. How did you know?"

"Rebecca," David told her, "received a letter." He turned to his father. "Did you really think your visit would go unnoticed?"

Richard stared at him, his expression like granite. "I have no apology to make. I think it's as well that I did!"

"And why is that?"

"Because of what I found out!" Richard wasn't sure whether to glare at his son, or to regard him with compassion. Was it possible that Rebecca had concealed the shocking truth? After a pause, he said, "I have to ask you this. Did you know that Rebecca has a child? One born out of wedlock?"

"For God's sake, of course I knew!"

Richard's tone was now icy. "And you didn't think fit to acquaint your mother and I with this fact?"

David sat in an armchair, his body tense. "I was going to tell you. We both were. In fact Rebecca was angry that we left before we did so."

"You didn't tell us anything at all about her," Celia said. "We had to question her ourselves. Why was that, David?"

Slowly, he explained, as he had to Rebecca, what his reasons had been. They both regarded him in silence, then Richard said with a frown, "You seem to attach a great deal of importance to our opinion of her. Am I to take it that this relationship is serious?"

"I think that would be a safe assumption, yes."

"But you've only known her a few months," Celia protested.

"I know. And that's why I've been holding back, to be absolutely sure." He looked at them both, regretting that what he had decided, what he must say, was going to cause them pain. "And now I am sure. I want to spend the rest of my life with Rebecca, and intend to ask her to marry me."

"Even if that involves taking on another man's child?" Richard said abruptly.

"Even if that involves taking on another man's child! Who, incidentally is called Anna, is three years old, and absolutely delightful."

Richard sat heavily on the sofa next to his wife. "I can't deny that Rebecca is a charming girl, and very attractive, but . . ."

"You don't fancy the idea of your daughter-in-law bringing an illegitimate child into the family?"

"Be fair, David. I think most people would feel like that," Celia said.

David gazed silently at her, seeing her anguish, knowing that his mother was only reflecting society's harsh attitude towards unmarried mothers. And yet, he thought with bitterness, all Rebecca had done was to honestly express her love. There was no cruelty, no crime involved. "I'm sorry," he said eventually. "I do understand how you both feel. But there is no room for negotiation on this."

Richard and Celia exchanged apprehensive glances. Then Richard, his reluctance obvious, said, "In that case, David, we'll have to accept it. And we

461

will support you whatever happens. But this won't be easy either for us, or for you."

David gave a tight smile. "You may have nothing to worry about. Have you considered that Rebecca might not want to be part of our family? After all, you haven't exactly made her feel welcome by going to the Unicorn. She could, in fact, quite easily turn me down."

On Sunday morning, Rebecca walked with Johnny to the cemetery, showed him Ian's grave, and then went for a stroll along the tree-lined paths, leaving him a few moments of privacy. Ten minutes later, they crossed the main road, and with silence between them, began to walk home. Then Johnny said, "It's a good spot."

"Yes, it is."

Johnny put his arm gently around her shoulders. "He was lucky to have you in his life, even though it was for such a short time."

"Thank you, Johnny." Rebecca smiled up at him, and he gazed down at her. "And I'm glad I met you, too," he said softly.

And it was this scene that David, having managed to change his duty at the hospital, saw as his car turned the corner into Redwood Avenue. Rebecca, her slim back to him, her auburn hair glinting in the sun, was strolling along the pavement, encircled in the arm of a tall young man. With shock and incredulity, David drew to a halt, watching as the couple, smiling at each other, turned into the gate and went into the house. David sat as though frozen, trying to control his jealousy, struggling to remain calm, to be rational. Because, despite what he'd just seen, even in his bewilderment David couldn't believe that Rebecca would deceive him like this. No, there had to be another explanation, there had to be! Slowly, he pressed the accelerator, and drew his car over to park in its usual place. There was, he thought grimly, only one way to find out!

It was Grace who opened the door. He saw the consternation on her face, the panic in her eyes and became even more apprehensive. What the hell was going on?

"David!"

"You sound rather shocked to see me," he said quietly.

"We didn't know—"

"I was coming? Is that a problem?" His tone was sharp.

Grace suddenly realised that, arriving as he had only seconds after Rebecca and Johnny, that he must have seen the couple together. She turned with relief as Rebecca came hurrying out of the front room.

"David!" But David's kiss was fleeting. He held her shoulders and gazed intently down at her, unable to restrain his impatience.

"Who was that man you were with?"

"That was—"

"That was me!" Johnny came into the hall. He held out his hand. "Johnny Fletcher. And you must be David."

"Johnny was in the German POW camp with

463

Ian," Rebecca, sensing David's anger, frantically tried to explain.

Johnny stared steadily at the man before him, knowing how things must have looked, knowing how he would have felt himself in a similar situation. Turning swiftly to Anna, who, clutching her doll, was watching them all, he said, "Shall we go over to the playground?" He held out his hand to the little girl, and seconds later, they were gone.

Rebecca, her insides churning, glanced with apprehension at David, and then led the way into the front room. "I've been anxious all week," she said, facing him, "wondering what happened with your parents."

But David refused to be side-tracked. "Why have you never mentioned Johnny before? You must have known he was coming?"

Dismayed, Rebecca bit her lip. "It's a long story, David, and a complicated one. Would you mind if I told you another time?" She looked up at him in appeal and seeing the honesty and anxiety in her lovely green eyes, David felt his misgivings suddenly disappear. Damn it, he loved this girl, trusted her, didn't he?

"Of course, you can." He added ruefully, "Sorry, sweetheart, I've discovered I've got a jealous streak, much as I hate to admit it." He drew her close and kissed her, murmuring at last the words Rebecca had so long wanted to hear. "It's just that I love you, so very much."

45

Rebecca and David were married the following June, at a picturesque church near the centre of Lichfield. In the months before the wedding, they bought and furnished their first home – a spacious semi-detached house in a small village near Rugby. "This is just a start," David told her. "As I've said, it's possible we may live elsewhere in a few years if I get a consultancy." But Rebecca hardly listened – she was much too excited at the prospect of moving in after their honeymoon. She loved it all, the sunny kitchen overlooking a private garden, the two cosy reception rooms, and to find that the third bedroom was large enough for Ron and Sal or Grace to come and stay had been the final deciding factor.

The wedding reception was held at a local hotel, where Rebecca, elegant in an ivory silk dress and jacket, and with a confection of tulle and fresh flowers on her hair, sat by her husband's side on the top table. Beside her was Ron, proud to have given her away in the church, stiff and uncomfortable in a slightly shiny navy-blue suit. Next to him was Sal, stiffly corseted, wearing a flowered suit and straw hat, then came Katie, and Betty, with Anna between them, all three bridesmaids in long pale pink satin.

"What do you think of the flowers?" David turned to smile at her. "They were my special choice, a secret between myself and Anna."

Rebecca looked with pleasure and admiration at the elaborate centrepiece of red roses. "They're beautiful."

"I asked her what your favourite flowers were, and do you know what she said? 'Mummy says red roses mean love.'"

Rebecca's eyes misted slightly, remembering how she used to show Anna Ian's single red rose pressed inside a book.

"And I do love you," he whispered.

"I love you, too."

Eventually, the formal meal over, the guests settled back in anticipation of the telegrams, speeches and champagne toasts. When the best man, a colleague of David's from the hospital, rose from his seat, Grace, sitting with Johnny in a prominent position adjacent to the top table, tensed. Best men's speeches were notorious for innuendo, telegrams could be embarrassing, and in Rebecca's case, that was the last thing the girl needed. But the doctor, slightly older than David, spoke with sensitivity interspersed with clever humour, and both she and Johnny glanced at each other with relief and relaxed. Grace wondered yet again why Guy hadn't been invited. After all, he and David had been close friends – but Rebecca had been adamant.

Afterwards, Rebecca and David happily mingled with their guests, chatting to people they knew, and to ones who had travelled some distance to be with

466

them. Then, when inevitably they became divided, Rebecca crossed over the room to where, seated in their own tight group, were Sal, Ron, Flossie and Ruby.

"Eeeh, love, you look a treat, don't she, Floss?" Ruby beamed.

Flossie was so moved she had to blink away tears. "I'm so glad for yer, love."

"She'll be one of the nobs, and no mistake," Ruby said, glancing around the room. Both women were dressed "up to the nines". Flossie in lilac and grey, Ruby in bright red, which, Rebecca thought fondly, didn't sit well with her florid complexion.

"How are your rooms?" she asked.

Flossie grinned at her. "Posh!"

Ruby, who had never stayed in a hotel before, said, "I could take to this life, ducks, being waited on all the time!"

Rebecca laughed. Sal just sat gazing at her niece, hardly able to reconcile this beautiful and poised young woman with the raw young girl who had come to live with her all those years ago. Grace, sitting with them, was quietly getting to know the people who had been, and would continue to be, important in Rebecca's life. "You won't forget," Rebecca reminded her, "to take home half of one of the tiers of the cake? There should be plenty for the girls at work, and could you take some across to the shop for Maggie and Enid?"

"Of course, I will." Grace smiled up at her, and Sal realised that she liked this woman, the one she'd so stupidly resented for so long. I hope she finds someone, Sal thought, maybe marries again. It'll be hard for her, going back to living alone.

"And you'll take a piece back for Janet?" Rebecca said to her aunt. "Tell her I hope she'll soon feel better. It was a pity she couldn't come."

Ron, who had been watching Johnny and Katie, said, "'Ave yer seen those two?" They all looked round, and Rebecca, seeing the way that Johnny was gazing down at her friend, smiled to herself. She exchanged delighted glances with Sal who raised her eyebrows and flamboyantly crossed her fingers, making them all laugh.

Surveying the merry group from a distance, were Richard and Celia. "I can't imagine we'd have much in common with any of them," murmured Celia.

"Maybe not," said Richard. "But they're Rebecca's only family, and from what David tells me, they're what we rather superior mortals call, 'the salt of the earth'."

Celia glanced sharply at him. "I hope you're not inferring that we're snobs!"

Richard shrugged. "We're a product of our background, Celia, just like everyone is."

For a moment Celia was silent, then said, "I have to admit that I've never seen David so happy. And she really is a lovely girl. As for little Anna . . ."

Richard smiled. "As David said, she's delightful."

They watched as Rebecca sought out her daughter who, in the charge of the two older bridesmaids had, as everyone commented, been a "little angel". She took Anna's hand, gave it a slight squeeze, and led her to the arrangement of red roses on the top table.

"I want you to choose one," Rebecca told her. "A very special one, and then we can save it to press in a book."

Gravely, Anna studied the mass of red roses, then reached out a hand and plucked a perfectly formed one from the centre. Turning, she held it up to Rebecca, then said, "I've got a new daddy now, haven't I?"

"Yes, my darling, you have."